Contents

Tales From The Land Of The Brave

Traditional tales, fables and sagas from Scotland

4th edition revised and updated

Compiled, adapted & edited by Clive Gilson

Tales from the World's Firesides

Cover image by Clive Gilson

Preface

For more than twenty years I have been collecting and telling stories, gathering words like driftwood from far shores, and then shaping them into new fires for others to sit beside. My own writing moves between the luminous borders of magical realism and science fiction, yet always with one foot in the older world of folktale and myth. Over the years I have assembled thousands of stories from across the globe, many long out of print or preserved only in the pages of nineteenth-century collections. My aim has been simple but stubborn - to keep these voices alive, to build a living library that reflects the shared imagination of humankind.

In working with early sources, I'm always mindful of the times that produced them. The collectors of the eighteenth and nineteenth centuries were devoted, but they also carried assumptions that we now recognise as narrow or unjust. Where I can, I adapt with care, reshaping without erasing, seeking to preserve the pulse of the story while freeing it from prejudice. Each tale carries full attribution to its original collector and source, along with notes on origin and culture, so that the thread of inheritance remains unbroken. These are not my tales. These tales belong to the peoples and places that first told them. My task is only to keep them in motion.

This volume, *Tales from the Land of the Brave*, draws its life from Scotland, a country whose stories are as wild and luminous as its weather. From the Atlantic-battered isles to the shadowed glens of the Borders, Scotland has always spoken in the language of the otherworldly. Its legends breathe sea mist, peat smoke, and the cry of curlews over empty moorland. The tales gathered here come from that fierce beauty, bringing us stories of courage and trickery, of kindness and uncanny retribution. They are filled with the light and darkness that mark all human dreaming.

The wider Fireside Tales project has now wandered far beyond these shores, to Ireland and to the forests of Europe, the islands of the Pacific, and beyond. Yet Scotland feels like the right place to honour the mystery of life as told in stories. Its landscapes hold a power and a beauty that almost listens to soul. Its people, past and present, have always understood that a story is both a shield and a mirror, a way of remembering what the wind and rain might otherwise wash away.

I have a personal bond with this land. Each year I spend many months in Galloway, a region of sandy coastal beaches, estuaries, forests and hills, where time moves at its own deliberate pace. It's there, in the hush between sea and sky, that I do most of my writing, during quiet hours when the world feels old again and the voices of these tales rise easily through the stillness.

From that solitude, these stories continue their long journey, carrying with them the wild heart of Scotland and the timeless pulse of storytelling itself.

Clive

Bath 2025

Assipattle and the Mester Stoorworm

Assipattle and the Mester Stoorworm is one of Scotland's great dragon-slaying tales, preserved in The Scottish Fairy Book (1910) by Elizabeth Wilson Grierson.

Grierson's retelling, drawn from traditional Orcadian and Shetland sources, reflects the northern strain of Scottish folklore, gritty, sea-salted, and heroic without ornament. In her introduction to the Fairy Book, Grierson distinguishes such tales from the Celtic romances of the Highlands, calling them "the homelier stories of spirits and goblins that the Lowlands knew." Assipattle and the Mester Stoorworm bridges these traditions: it is both mythic and domestic.

In far bygone days, in the North, there lived a well-to-do farmer, who had seven sons and one daughter. And the youngest of these seven sons bore a very curious name, for men called him Assipattle, which means, "He who grovels among the ashes."

Perhaps Assipattle deserved his name, for he was rather a lazy boy, who never did any work on the farm as his brothers did, but ran about the doors with ragged clothes and unkempt hair, and whose mind was ever filled with wondrous stories of Trolls and Giants, Elves and Goblins.

When the sun was hot in the long summer afternoons, when the bees droned drowsily and even the tiny insects seemed almost asleep, the boy was content to throw himself down on the ash-heap amongst the ashes, and lie there, lazily letting them run through his fingers, as one might play with sand on the sea-shore, basking in the sunshine and telling stories to himself.

And his brothers, working hard in the fields, would point to him with mocking fingers, and laugh, and say to each other how well the name suited him, and of how little use he was in the world.

And when they came home from their work, they would push him about and tease him, and even his mother would make him sweep the floor, and draw water from the well, and fetch peats from the peat-stack, and do all the little odd jobs that nobody else would do.

So poor Assipattle had rather a hard life of it, and he would often have been very miserable had it not been for his sister, who loved him dearly, and who would listen quite patiently to all the stories that he had to tell; who never laughed at him or told him that he was telling lies, as his brothers did.

But one day a very sad thing happened - at least, it was a sad thing for poor Assipattle. For it chanced that the King of these parts had one daughter, the Princess Gemdelovely, whom he loved dearly, and to whom he denied nothing. And Princess Gemdelovely was in want of a waiting-maid, and as she had seen Assipattle's sister standing by the garden gate as she was riding by one day, and had taken a fancy to her, she asked her father if she might ask her to come and live at the Castle and serve her.

Her father agreed at once, as he always did agree to any of her wishes, and sent a messenger in haste to the farmer's house to ask if his daughter would come to the Castle to be the Princess's waiting-maid.

And, of course, the farmer was very pleased at the piece of good fortune which had befallen the girl, and so was her mother, and so were her six brothers, all except poor Assipattle, who looked with wistful eyes after his sister as she rode away, proud of her new clothes and of the rivlins which her father had made her out of cowhide, which she was to wear in the Palace when she waited on the Princess, for at home she always ran barefoot.

Time passed, and one day a rider rode in hot haste through the country bearing the most terrible tidings. For the evening before, some fishermen, out in their boats, had caught sight of the Mester Stoorworm, which, as everyone knows, was the largest, and the first, and the greatest of all Sea-Serpents. It was that beast which, in the Good Book, is called the Leviathan, and if it had been measured in our day, its tail would have touched Iceland, while its snout rested on the North Cape.

And the fishermen had noticed that this fearsome Monster had its head turned towards the mainland, and that it opened its mouth and yawned horribly, as if to show that it was hungry, and that, if it were not fed, it would kill every living thing upon the land, both man and beast, bird and creeping thing.

For 'twas well known that its breath was so poisonous that it consumed as with a burning fire everything that it lighted on. So that, if it pleased the awful creature to lift its head and put forth its breath, like noxious vapour, over the country, in a few weeks the fair land would be turned into a region of desolation.

As you may imagine, everyone was almost paralysed with terror at this awful calamity which threatened them, and the King called a solemn meeting of all his Counsellors, and asked them if they could devise any way of warding off the danger.

And for three whole days they sat in Council, these grave, bearded men, and many were the suggestions which were made, and many the words of wisdom which were spoken, but alas! no one was wise enough to think of a way by which the Mester Stoorworm might be driven back.

At last, at the end of the third day, when everyone had given up hope of finding a remedy, the door of the Council Chamber opened and the Queen appeared.

Now the Queen was the King's second wife, and she was not a favourite in the Kingdom, for she was a proud, insolent woman, who did not behave kindly to her step-daughter, the Princess Gemdelovely, and who spent much more of her time in the company of a great Sorcerer, whom everyone feared and dreaded, than she did in that of the King, her husband.

So the sober Counsellors looked at her disapprovingly as she came boldly into the Council Chamber and stood up beside the King's Chair of State, and, speaking in a loud, clear voice, addressed them thus:

"You think that you are brave men and strong, oh, you Elders, and fit to be the Protectors of the People. And so it may be when it is mortals that you are called on to face. But you be no match for the foe that now threatens our land. Before him your weapons be but as straw. 'Tis not through strength of arm, but through sorcery, that he will be overcome. So listen to my words, even though they be but those of a woman, and take counsel with the great Sorcerer, from whom nothing is hid, but who knows all the mysteries of the earth, and of the air, and of the sea."

Now the King and his Counsellors liked not this advice, for they hated the Sorcerer, who had, as they thought, too much influence with the Queen, but they were at their wits' end, and knew not to whom to turn for help, so they were fain to do as she said and summon the Wizard before them.

And when he obeyed the summons and appeared in their midst, they liked him none the better for his looks. For he was long, and thin, and awesome, with a beard that came down to his knee, and hair that wrapped him about like a mantle, and his face was the colour of mortar, as if he had always lived in darkness, and had been afraid to look on the sun.

But there was no help to be found in any other man, so they laid the case before him, and asked him what they should do. And he answered coldly that he would think over the matter, and come again to the Assembly the following day and give them his advice.

And his advice, when they heard it, was like to turn their hair white with horror. For he said that the only way to satisfy the Monster, and to make it spare the land, was to feed it every Saturday with seven young maidens, who must be the fairest who could be found, and if, after this remedy had been tried once or twice, it did not succeed in mollifying the Stoorworm and inducing him to depart, there was but one other measure that he could suggest, but that was so horrible and dreadful that he would not rend their hearts by mentioning it in the meantime.

And as, although they hated him, they feared him also, the Council had even to abide by his words, and pronounced the awful doom.

And so it came about that, every Saturday, seven bonnie, innocent maidens were bound hand and foot and laid on a rock which ran into the sea, and the Monster stretched out his long, jagged tongue, and swept them into his mouth; while all the rest of the folk looked on from the top of a high hill - or, at least, the men looked - with cold, set faces, while the women hid theirs in their aprons and wept aloud.

"Is there no other way," they cried, "no other way than this, to save the land?"

But the men only groaned and shook their heads. "No other way," they answered, "no other way."

Then suddenly a boy's indignant voice rang out among the crowd. "Is there no grown man who would fight that Monster, and kill him, and save the lassies alive? I would do it; I am not feared for the Mester Stoorworm."

It was the boy Assipattle who spoke, and everyone looked at him in amazement as he stood staring at the great Sea-Serpent, his fingers twitching with rage, and his great blue eyes glowing with pity and indignation.

"The poor bairn's mad; the sight has turned his head," they whispered one to another, and they would have crowded round him to pet and comfort him, but his elder brother came and gave him a heavy clout on the side of his head.

"You fight the Stoorworm!" he cried contemptuously. "A likely story! Go home to your ash-pit, and stop speaking havers;" and, taking his arm, he drew him to the place where his other brothers were waiting, and they all went home together.

But all the time Assipattle kept on saying that he meant to kill the Stoorworm, and his brothers became so angry at what they thought was mere bragging, that they picked up stones and pelted him so hard with them that he took to his heels and ran away from them.

That evening the six brothers were threshing corn in the barn, and Assipattle, as usual, was lying among the ashes thinking his own thoughts, when his mother came out and bade him run and tell the others to come in for their supper.

The boy did as he was bid, for he was a willing enough little fellow, but when he entered the barn his brothers, in revenge for his having run away from them in the afternoon, set on him and pulled him down, and piled so much straw on top of him that, had his father not come from the house to see what they were all waiting for, he would, of a surety, have been smothered.

But when, at supper-time, his mother was quarrelling with the other lads for what they had done, and saying to them that it was only cowards who set on bairns littler and younger than themselves, Assipattle looked up from the bicker of porridge which he was supping.

"Vex not yourself, Mother," he said, "for I could have fought them all if I liked; ay, and beaten them, too."

"Why did you not essay it then?" cried everybody at once.

"Because I knew that I would need all my strength when I go to fight the Giant Stoorworm," replied Assipattle gravely.

And, as you may fancy, the others laughed louder than before.

Time passed, and every Saturday seven lassies were thrown to the Stoorworm, until it was felt that this state of things could not be allowed to go on any longer, for if it did, there would soon be no maidens at all left in the country.

So the Elders met once more, and, after long consultation, it was agreed that the Sorcerer should be summoned, and asked what his other remedy was. "For, by our troth," said they, "it cannot be worse than that which we are practising now."

But, had they known it, the new remedy was even more dreadful than the old. For the cruel Queen hated her step-daughter, Gemdelovely, and the wicked Sorcerer knew that she did, and that she would not be sorry to get rid of her, and things being as they were, he thought that he saw a way to please the Queen. So he stood up in the Council, and, pretending to be very sorry, said that the only other thing that could be done was to give the Princess Gemdelovely to the Stoorworm, then would it of a surety depart.

When they heard this sentence a terrible stillness fell upon the Council, and everyone covered his face with his hands, for no man dare look at the King.

But although his dear daughter was as the apple of his eye, he was a just and righteous Monarch, and he felt that it was not right that other fathers should have been forced to part with their daughters, in order to try and save the country, if his child was to be spared.

So, after he had had speech with the Princess, he stood up before the Elders, and declared, with trembling voice, that both he and she were ready to make the sacrifice.

"She is my only child," he said, "and the last of her race. Yet it seems good to both of us that she should lay down her life, if by so doing she may save the land that she loves so well."

Salt tears ran down the faces of the great bearded men as they heard their King's words, for they all knew how dear the Princess Gemdelovely was to him. But it was felt that what he said was wise and true, and that the thing was just and right, for 'twere better, surely, that one maiden should die, even though she were of Royal blood, than that bands of other maidens should go to their death week by week, and all to no purpose.

So, amid heavy sobs, the aged Lawman - he who was the chief man of the Council - rose up to pronounce the Princess's doom. But, before he did so, the King's Kemper - or Fighting-man - stepped forward.

"Nature teaches us that it is fitting that each beast has a tail," he said, "and this Doom, which our Lawman is about to pronounce, is in very sooth a venomous beast. And, if I had my way, the tail which it would bear after it is this, that if the Mester Stoorworm does not depart, and that right speedily, after he have devoured the Princess, the next thing that is offered to him be no tender young maiden, but that tough, lean old Sorcerer."

And at his words there was such a great shout of approval that the wicked Sorcerer seemed to shrink within himself, and his pale face grew paler than it was before.

Now, three weeks were allowed between the time that the Doom was pronounced upon the Princess and the time that it was carried out, so that the King might send Ambassadors to all the neighbouring Kingdoms to issue proclamations that, if any Champion would come forward who was able to drive away the Stoorworm and save the Princess, he should have her for his wife.

And with her he should have the Kingdom, as well as a very famous sword that was now in the King's possession, but which had belonged to the great god Odin, with which he had fought and vanquished all his foes. The sword bore the name of Sickersnapper, and no man had any power against it.

The news of all these things spread over the length and breadth of the land, and everyone mourned for the fate that was like to befall the Princess Gemdelovely. And the farmer, and his wife, and their six sons mourned also; all but Assipattle, who sat amongst the ashes and said nothing.

When the King's Proclamation was made known throughout the neighbouring Kingdoms, there was a fine stir among all the young Gallants, for it seemed but a little thing to slay a Sea-Monster, and a beautiful wife, a fertile Kingdom, and a trusty sword are not to be won every day.

So six-and-thirty Champions arrived at the King's Palace, each hoping to gain the prize.

But the King sent them all out to look at the Giant Stoorworm lying in the sea with its enormous mouth open, and when they saw it, twelve of them were seized with sudden illness, and twelve of them were so afraid that they took to their heels and ran, and never stopped till they reached their own countries, and so only twelve returned to the King's Palace, and as for them, they were so downcast at the thought of the task that they had undertaken that they had no spirit left in them at all.

And none of them dare try to kill the Stoorworm; so the three weeks passed slowly by, until the night before the day on which the Princess was to be sacrificed. On that night the King, feeling that he must do something to entertain his guests, made a great supper for them.

But, as you may think, it was a dreary feast, for everyone was thinking so much about the terrible thing that was to happen on the morrow, that no one could eat or drink.

And when it was all over, and everybody had retired to rest, save the King and his old Kemperman, the King returned to the great hall, and went slowly up to his Chair of State, high up on the dais. It was not like the Chairs of State that we know nowadays; it was nothing but a massive Kist, in which he kept all the things which he treasured most.

The old Monarch undid the iron bolts with trembling fingers, and lifted the lid, and took out the wondrous sword Sickersnapper, which had belonged to the great god Odin.

His trusty Kemperman, who had stood by him in a hundred fights, watched him with pitying eyes.

"Why lift you out the sword," he said softly, "when your fighting days are done? Right nobly have you fought your battles in the past, oh, my Lord! when your arm was strong and sure. But when folk's years number four score and sixteen, as your do, 'tis time to leave such work to other and younger men."

The old King turned on him angrily, with something of the old fire in his eyes. "Wheest," he cried, "else will I turn this sword on you. Do you think that I can see my only bairn devoured by a Monster, and not lift a finger to try and save her when no other man will? I tell you - and I will swear it with my two thumbs crossed on Sickersnapper - that both the sword and I will be destroyed before so much as one of her hairs be touched. So go, an' you love me, my old comrade, and order my boat to be ready, with the sail set and the prow pointed out to sea. I will go myself and fight the Stoorworm, and if I do not return, I will lay it on you to guard my cherished daughter. Perhaps, my life may redeem hers."

Now that night everybody at the farm went to bed betimes, for next morning the whole family was to set out early, to go to the top of the hill near the sea, to see the Princess eaten by the Stoorworm. All except Assipattle, who was to be left at home to herd the geese.

The lad was so vexed at this - for he had great schemes in his head - that he could not sleep. And as he lay tossing and tumbling about in his corner among the ashes, he heard his father and mother talking in the great box-bed. And, as he listened, he found that they were having an argument.

"Tis such a long way to the hill overlooking the sea, I fear me I shall never walk it," said his mother. "I think I had better bide at home."

"Nay," replied her husband, "that would be a bonny-like thing, when all the country-side is to be there. You shalt ride behind me on my good mare Go-Swift."

"I do not care to trouble you to take me behind you," said his wife, "for methinks you do not love me as you were used to do."

"The woman's havering," cried the Goodman of the house impatiently. "What makes you think that I have ceased to love you?"

"Because you will no longer tell me your secrets," answered his wife. "To go no further, think of this very horse, Go-Swift. For five long years I have been begging you to tell me how it is that, when you ride her, she flies faster than the wind, while if any other man mount her, she hirples along like a broken-down nag."

The Goodman laughed. "Twas not for lack of love, Goodwife," he said, "though it might be lack of trust. For women's tongues wag but loosely, and I did not want other folk to ken my secret. But since my silence has vexed your heart, I will even tell it you.

"When I want Go-Swift to stand, I give her one clap on the left shoulder. When I would have her go like any other horse, I give her two claps on the right. But when I want her to fly like the wind, I whistle through the windpipe of a goose. And, as I never ken when I want her to gallop like that, I aye keep the bird's thrapple in the left-hand pocket of my coat."

"So that is how you manage the beast," said the farmer's wife, in a satisfied tone, "and that is what becomes of all my goose thrapples. Oh! but you are a clever fellow, Goodman, and now that I ken the way of it I may go to sleep."

Assipattle was not tumbling about in the ashes now; he was sitting up in the darkness, with glowing cheeks and sparkling eyes.

His opportunity had come , and he knew it.

He waited patiently till their heavy breathing told him that his parents were asleep; then he crept over to where his father's clothes were, and took the goose's windpipe out of the pocket of his coat, and slipped noiselessly out of the house. Once he was out of it, he ran like lightning to the stable. He saddled and bridled Go-Swift, and threw a halter round her neck, and led her to the stable door.

The good mare, unaccustomed to her new groom, pranced, and reared, and plunged, but Assipattle, knowing his father's secret, clapped her once on the left shoulder, and she stood as still as a stone. Then he mounted her, and gave her two claps on the right shoulder, and the good horse trotted off briskly, giving a loud neigh as she did so.

The unwonted sound, ringing out in the stillness of the night, roused the household, and the Goodman and his six sons came tumbling down the wooden stairs, shouting to one another in confusion that someone was stealing Go-Swift.

The farmer was the first to reach the door, and when he saw, in the starlight, the vanishing form of his favourite steed, he cried at the top of his voice:

"Stop thief, ho!

Go-Swift, whoa!"

And when Go-Swift heard that she pulled up in a moment. All seemed lost, for the farmer and his sons could run very fast indeed, and it seemed to Assipattle, sitting motionless on Go-Swift's back, that they would very soon make up on him.

But, luckily, he remembered the goose's thrapple, and he pulled it out of his pocket and whistled through it. In an instant the good mare bounded forward, swift as the wind, and was over the hill and out of reach of its pursuers before they had taken ten steps more.

Day was dawning when the lad came within sight of the sea, and there, in front of him, in the water, lay the enormous Monster whom he had come so far to slay. Anyone would have said that he was mad even to dream of making such an attempt, for he was but a slim, unarmed youth, and the Mester Stoorworm was so big that men said it would reach the fourth part round the world. And its tongue was jagged at the end like a fork, and with this fork it could sweep whatever it chose into its mouth, and devour it at its leisure.

For all this, Assipattle was not afraid, for he had the heart of a hero underneath his tattered garments. "I must be cautious," he said to himself, "and do by my wits what I cannot do by my strength."

He climbed down from his seat on Go-Swift's back, and tethered the good steed to a tree, and walked on, looking well about him, till he came to a little cottage on the edge of a wood.

The door was not locked, so he entered, and found its occupant, an old woman, fast asleep in bed. He did not disturb her, but he took down an iron pot from the shelf, and examined it closely.

"This will serve my purpose," he said, "and surely the old dame would not grudge it if she knew 'twas to save the Princess's life."

Then he lifted a live peat from the smouldering fire, and went his way.

Down at the water's edge he found the King's boat lying, guarded by a single boatman, with its sails set and its prow turned in the direction of the Mester Stoorworm.

"It's a cold morning," said Assipattle. "Are you not well-nigh frozen sitting there? If you will come on shore, and run about, and warm yourself, I will get into the boat and guard it till you return."

"A likely story," replied the man. "And what would the King say if he were to come, as I expect every moment he will do, and find me playing myself on the sand, and his good boat left to a smatchet like you? 'Twould be as much as my head is worth."

"As you will," answered Assipattle carelessly, beginning to search among the rocks. "In the meantime, I must be looking for a wheen mussels to roast for my breakfast." And after he had gathered the mussels, he began to make a hole in the sand to put the live peat in. The boatman watched him curiously, for he, too, was beginning to feel hungry.

Presently the lad gave a wild shriek, and jumped high in the air. "Gold, gold!" he cried. "By the name of Thor, who would have looked to find gold here?"

This was too much for the boatman. Forgetting all about his head and the King, he jumped out of the boat, and, pushing Assipattle aside, began to scrape among the sand with all his might.

While he was doing so, Assipattle seized his pot, jumped into the boat, pushed her off, and was half a mile out to sea before the outwitted man, who, needless to say, could find no gold, noticed what he was about.

And, of course, he was very angry, and the old King was angrier still when he came down to the shore, attended by his Nobles and carrying the great sword Sickersnapper, in the vain hope that he, poor feeble old man that he was, might be able in some way to defeat the Monster and save his daughter.

But to make such an attempt was beyond his power now that his boat was gone. So he could only stand on the shore, along with the fast-assembling crowd of his subjects, and watch what would befall.

And this was what befell!

Assipattle, sailing slowly over the sea, and watching the Mester Stoorworm intently, noticed that the terrible Monster yawned occasionally, as if longing for his weekly feast. And as it yawned a great flood of sea-water went down its throat, and came out again at its huge gills.

So the brave lad took down his sail, and pointed the prow of his boat straight at the Monster's mouth, and the next time it yawned he and his boat were sucked right in, and, like Jonah, went straight down its throat into the dark regions inside its body. On and on the boat floated, but as it went the water grew less, pouring out of the Stoorworm's gills, till it stuck, as it were, on dry land. And Assipattle jumped out, his pot in his hand, and began to explore.

Presently he came to the huge creature's liver, and having heard that the liver of a fish is full of oil, he made a hole in it and put in the live peat.

Woe's me! but there was a conflagration! And Assipattle just got back to his boat in time, for the Mester Stoorworm, in its convulsions, threw the boat right out of its mouth again, and it was flung up, high and dry, on the bare land.

The commotion in the sea was so terrible that the King and his daughter - who by this time had come down to the shore dressed like a bride, in white, ready to be thrown to the Monster - and all his

Courtiers, and all the country-folk, were fain to take refuge on the hilltop, out of harm's way, and stand and see what happened next.

And this was what happened next.

The poor, distressed creature - for it was now to be pitied, even although it was a great, cruel, awful Mester Stoorworm - tossed itself to and fro, twisting and writhing.

And as it tossed its awful head out of the water its tongue fell out, and struck the earth with such force that it made a great dent in it, into which the sea rushed. And that dent formed the crooked Straits which now divide Denmark from Norway and Sweden.

Then some of its teeth fell out and rested in the sea, and became the Islands that we now call the Orkney Isles, and a little afterwards some more teeth dropped out, and they became what we now call the Shetland Isles.

After that the creature twisted itself into a great lump and died, and this lump became the Island of Iceland, and the fire which Assipattle had kindled with his live peat still burns on underneath it, and that is why there are mountains which throw out fire in that chilly land.

When it was plainly seen that the Mester Stoorworm was dead, the King could scarce contain himself with joy. He put his arms around Assipattle's neck, and kissed him, and called him his son. And he took off his own Royal Mantle and put it on the lad, and girded his good sword Sickersnapper round his waist. And he called his daughter, the Princess Gemdelovely, to him, and put her hand in his, and declared that when the right time came she should be his wife, and that he should be ruler over all the Kingdom.

Then the whole company mounted their horses again, and Assipattle rode on Go-Swift by the Princess's side, and so they returned, with great joy, to the King's Palace.

But as they were nearing the gate Assipattle's sister, she who was the Princess's maid, ran out to meet him, and signed to the Princess to lout down, and whispered something in her ear.

The Princess's face grew dark, and she turned her horse's head and rode back to where her father was, with his Nobles. She told him the words that the maiden had spoken, and when he heard them his face, too, grew as black as thunder.

For the matter was this: The cruel Queen, full of joy at the thought that she was to be rid, once for all, of her step-daughter, had been making love to the wicked Sorcerer all the morning in the old King's absence.

"He shall be killed at once," cried the Monarch. "Such behaviour cannot be overlooked."

"You will have much ado to find him, your Majesty," said the girl, "for 'tis more than an hour since he and the Queen fled together on the fleetest horses that they could find in the stables."

"But I can find him," cried Assipattle, and he went off like the wind on his good horse Go-Swift.

It was not long before he came within sight of the fugitives, and he drew his sword and shouted to them to stop.

They heard the shout, and turned round, and they both laughed aloud in derision when they saw that it was only the boy who grovelled in the ashes who pursued them.

"The insolent brat! I will cut off his head for him! I will teach him a lesson!" cried the Sorcerer, and he rode boldly back to meet

Assipattle. For although he was no fighter, he knew that no ordinary weapon could harm his enchanted body; therefore he was not afraid.

But he did not count on Assipattle having the Sword of the great god Odin, with which he had slain all his enemies, and before this magic weapon he was powerless. And, at one thrust, the young lad ran it through his body as easily as if he had been any ordinary man, and he fell from his horse, dead.

Then the Courtiers of the King, who had also set off in pursuit, but whose steeds were less fleet of foot than Go-Swift, came up, and seized the bridle of the Queen's horse, and led it and its rider back to the Palace.

She was brought before the Council, and judged, and condemned to be shut up in a high tower for the remainder of her life. Which thing surely came to pass.

As for Assipattle, when the proper time came he was married to the Princess Gemdelovely, with great feasting and rejoicing. And when the old King died they ruled the Kingdom for many a long year.

Black Colin of Loch Awe

The tale of Black Colin of Loch Awe, adapted by Maud Isabel Ebbutt in her Hero-Myths & Legends of the British Race (1910), draws from the heroic narrative traditions that link the Welsh Mabinogion with the wider Celtic and Scottish cycles of legend. In this version, Colin is cast as a warrior of unyielding courage, a chieftain bound to the rugged heart of Argyll.

Ebbutt's retelling, written in the Edwardian fascination with national myth, lends Colin's story the rhythm of epic poetry. Her prose heightens the elemental qualities of the tale, iron, fire, water, blood, while preserving the Celtic melancholy that runs beneath the hero's defiance. Within her collection, Black Colin of Loch Awe stands as both a regional legend and a symbol of the broader British mythic spirit: the conviction that identity and destiny are forged in struggle, and that the land remembers every oath, every fall, and every act of valour.

The Knight of Loch Awe

During the wars between England and Scotland in the reigns of Edward I and Edward II, one of the chief leaders in the cause of Scottish independence was Sir Nigel Campbell. The Knight of Loch Awe, as he was generally called, was a schoolfellow and comrade of Sir William Wallace, and a loyal and devoted adherent of Robert Bruce. In return for his services in the war of independence Bruce rewarded him with lands belonging to the rebellious MacGregors, including Glenurchy, the great glen at the head of Loch Awe through which flows the river Orchy. It was a wild and lonely district, and Sir Nigel Campbell had much conflict before he finally expelled the

MacGregors and settled down peaceably in Glenurchy. There his son was born, and named Colin, and as years passed he won the nickname of Black Colin, from his swarthy complexion, or possibly from his character, which showed tokens of unusual fierceness and determination.

Black Colin's Youth

Sir Nigel Campbell, as all Highland chiefs did, sent his son to a farmer's family for fosterage. The boy became a child of his foster-family in every way; he lived on the plain food of the clansmen, oatmeal porridge and oatcake, milk from the cows, and beef from the herds; he ran and wrestled and hunted with his foster-brothers, and learnt woodcraft and warlike skill, broadsword play and the use of dirk and buckler, from his foster-father. More than all, he won a devoted following in the clan, for a man's foster-parents were almost dearer to him than his own father and mother, and his foster-brethren were bound to fight and die for him, and to regard him more than their own blood-relations. The foster-parents of Black Colin were a farmer and his wife, Patterson by name, living at Socach, in Glenurchy, and well and truly they fulfilled their trust.

He Goes on Crusade

In course of time Sir Nigel Campbell died, and Black Colin, his son, became Knight of Loch Awe, and lord of all Glenurchy and the country round. He was already noted for his strength and his dark complexion, which added to his beauty in the eyes of the maidens, and he soon found a lovely and loving bride. They dwelt on the Islet in Loch Awe, and were very happy for a short time, but Colin was always restless, because he would fain do great deeds of arms, and there was peace just then in the land.

At last one day a messenger arrived at the castle on the Islet bearing tidings that another crusade was on foot. This messenger was a palmer who had been in the Holy Land, and had seen all the holy places in Jerusalem. He told Black Colin how the Saracens ruled the country, and hindered men from worshipping at the sacred shrines, and he told how he had come home by Rome, where the Pope had just proclaimed another Holy War. The Pope had declared that his blessing would rest on the man who should leave wife and home and kinsfolk, and go forth to fight for the Lord against the infidel. As the palmer spoke Black Colin became greatly moved by his words, and when the old man had made an end he raised the hilt of his dirk and swore by the cross thereon that he would obey the summons and go on crusade.

The Lady of Loch Awe

Now Black Colin's wife was greatly grieved, and wept sorely, for she was but young, and had been wedded no more than a year, and it seemed to her hard that she must be left alone. She asked her husband, "How far will you go on this errand?" "I will go as far as Jerusalem, if the Pope bids me, when I have come to Rome," he said. "Alas! and how long will you be away from me?" "That I know not, but it may be for years if the heathen Saracens will not surrender the Holy Land to the warriors of the Cross." "What shall I do during those long, weary years?" asked she. "Dear love, you shall dwell here on the Islet and be Lady of Glenurchy till I return again. The vassals and clansmen shall obey you in my stead, and the tenants shall pay you their rents and their dues, and in all things you shall hold my land for me."

The Token

The Lady of Loch Awe sighed as she asked, "But if you die away in that distant land how shall I know? What will become of me if such woeful tidings should be brought?"

"Wait for me seven years, dear wife," said Colin, "and if I do not return before the end of that time you may marry again and take a brave husband to guard your rights and rule the glen, for I shall be dead in the Holy Land."

"Wait for me seven years, dear wife"

"That I will never do. I will be the Lady of Glenurchy till I die, or I will become the bride of Heaven and find peace for my sorrowing soul in a nunnery. No second husband shall wed me and hold your land. But give me now some token that we may share it between us, and you shall swear that on your deathbed you will send it to me; so shall I know indeed that you are no longer alive."

"It shall be as you say," answered Black Colin, and he went to the smith of the clan and bade him make a massive gold ring, on which Colin's name was engraved, as well as that of the Lady of Loch Awe. Then, breaking the ring in two, Colin gave to his wife the piece with his name and kept the other piece, vowing to wear it near his heart and only to part with it when he should be dying. In like manner she with bitter weeping swore to keep her half of the ring, and hung it on a chain round her neck, and so, with much grief and great mourning from the whole clan, Black Colin and his sturdy following of Campbell clansmen set out for the Holy Land.

The Journey

Sadly at first the little band marched away from all their friends and their homes; bagpipes played their loudest marching tunes, and plaids fluttered in the breeze, and the men marched gallantly, but with heavy hearts, for they knew not when they would return, and they feared to find supplanters in their homes when they came back after many years. Their courage rose, however, as the miles lengthened behind them, and by the time they had reached Edinburgh and had taken ship at Leith all was forgotten but the joy of fighting and the eager desire to see Rome and the Pope, the Holy Land and the Holy Sepulchre. Journeying up the Rhine, the Highland clansmen made their way through Switzerland and over the passes of the Alps down into the pleasant land of Italy, where the splendour of the cities surpassed their wildest imaginations, and so they came , with many other bands of Crusaders, to Rome.

The Crusade

At Rome the Knight of Loch Awe was so fortunate as to have an audience of the Pope himself, who was touched by the devotion which brought these stern warriors so far from their home. Black Colin knelt in reverence before the aged pontiff, whom he held in truth to be the Vicar of Christ on earth, and received his blessing, and commands to continue his journey to Rhodes, where the Knights of St. John would give him opportunity to fight for the faith. The small band of Campbells went on to Rhodes, and there took service with the Knights, and won great praise from the Grand Master, but, though they fought the infidel, and exalted the standard of the Cross above the Crescent, Colin was still not at all satisfied. He left Rhodes after some years with a much-diminished band, and made his way as a pilgrim to Jerusalem. There he stayed until he had visited all the shrines in the Holy Land and prayed at every sacred spot. By this time the seven years of his proposed absence were ended, and he was still far from his home and the dear glen by Loch Awe.

The Lady's Suitor

While the seven years slowly passed away his sad and lonely wife dwelt in the castle on the Islet, ruling her lord's clan in all gentle ways, but fighting boldly when raiders came to plunder her clansmen. Yearly she claimed her husband's dues and watched that he was not defrauded of his rights. But though thus firm, she was the best help in trouble that her clan ever had, and all blessed the name of the Lady of Loch Awe.

So fair and gentle a lady, so beloved by her clan, was certain to have suitors if she were a widow, and even before the seven years had passed away there were men who would gladly have persuaded her that her husband was dead and that she was free. She, however, steadfastly refused to hear a word of another marriage, saying, "When Colin parted from me he gave me two promises, one to return, if possible, within seven years, and the other to send me, on his deathbed, if he died away from me, a sure token of his death. I have not yet waited seven years, nor have I had the token of his death. I am still the wife of Black Colin of Loch Awe."

This steadfastness gradually daunted her suitors and they left her alone, until but one remained, the Baron Niel MacCorquodale, whose lands bordered on Glenurchy, and who had long cast covetous eyes on the glen and its fair lady, and longed no less for the wealth she was reputed to possess than for the power this marriage would give him.

The Baron's Plot

When the seven years were over the Baron MacCorquodale sought the Lady of Loch Awe again, wooing her for his wife. Again she refused, saying, "Until I have the token of my husband's death I will be wife to no other man." "And what is this token, lady?" asked the

Baron, for he thought he could send a false one. "I will never tell that," replied the lady. "Do you dare to ask the most sacred secret between husband and wife? I shall know the token when it comes." The Baron was not a little enraged that he could not discover the secret, but he determined to wed the lady and her wealth notwithstanding; accordingly he wrote by a sure and secret messenger to a friend in Rome, bidding him send a letter with news that Black Colin was assuredly dead, and that certain words (which the Baron dictated) had come from him.

A Forged Letter

One day the Lady of Loch Awe, looking out from her castle, saw the Baron coming, and with him a palmer whose face was bronzed by Eastern suns. She felt that the palmer would bring tidings, and welcomed the Baron with his companion. "Lady, this palmer brings you sad news," said the Baron. "Let him tell it, then," replied she, sick with fear. "Alas! fair dame, if you were the wife of that gallant knight Colin of Loch Awe, you are now his widow," said the palmer sadly, as he handed her a letter. "What proof have you?" asked Black Colin's wife before she read the letter. "Lady, I talked with the soldier who brought the tidings," replied the stranger.

The letter was written from Rome to "The Right Noble Dame the Lady of Loch Awe," and told how news had come from Rhodes, brought by a man of Black Colin's band, that the Knight of Loch Awe had been mortally wounded in a fight against the Saracens. Dying, he had bidden his clansmen return to their lady, but they had all perished but one, fighting for vengeance against the infidels. This man, who had held the dying Knight tenderly upon his knee, said that Colin bade his wife farewell, bade her remember his injunction to wed again and find a protector, gasped out, "Take her the token I promised; it is here," and died, but the Saracens attacked the

Christians again, drove them back, and plundered the bodies of the slain, and when the one survivor returned to search for the precious token there was none! The body was stripped of everything of value, and the clansman wound it in the plaid and buried it on the battlefield.

The Lady's Stratagem

There seemed no reason for the lady to doubt this news, and her grief was very real and sincere. She clad herself in mourning robes and bewailed her lost husband, but yet she was not entirely satisfied, for she still wore the broken half of the engraved ring on the chain round her neck, and still the promised death-token had not come. The Baron now pressed his suit with greater ardour than before, and the Lady of Loch Awe was hard put to it to find reasons for refusing him. It was necessary to keep him on good terms with the clan, for his lands bordered on those of Glenurchy, and he could have made war on the people in the glen quite easily, while the knowledge that their chief was dead would have made them a broken clan. So the lady turned to guile, as did Penelope of old in similar distress. "I will wed you, now that my Colin is dead," she replied , "but it cannot be immediately; I must first build a castle that will command the head of Glenurchy and of Loch Awe. The MacGregors knew the best place for a house, there on Innis Eoalan; there, where the ruins of MacGregor's White House now stand, will I build my castle. When it is finished the time of my mourning will be over, and I will fix the bridal day." With this promise the Baron had perforce to be contented, and the castle began to rise slowly at the head of Loch Awe, but its progress was not rapid, because the lady secretly bade her men build feebly, and often the walls fell down, so that the new castle was very long in coming to completion.

Black Colin Hears the News

In the meantime all who loved Black Colin grieved to know that the Lady of Loch Awe would wed again, and his foster-mother sorrowed most of all, for she felt sure that her beloved Colin was not dead. The death-token had not been sent, and she sorely mistrusted the Baron MacCorquodale and doubted the truth of the palmer's message. At last, when the new castle was nearly finished and shone white in the rays of the sun, she called one of her sons and bade him journey to Rome to find the Knight of Loch Awe, if he were yet alive, and to bring sure tidings of his death if he were no longer living. The young Patterson set off secretly, and reached Rome in due course, and there he met Black Colin, just returned from Jerusalem. The Knight had realized that he had spent seven years away from his home, and that now, in spite of all his haste, he might reach Glenurchy too late to save his wife from a second marriage. He comforted himself, however, with the thought that the token was still safe with him, and that his wife would be loyal; great, therefore, was his horror when he met his foster-brother and heard how the news of his death had been brought to the glen. He heard also how his wife had reluctantly promised to marry the Baron MacCorquodale, and had delayed her wedding by stratagem, and he vowed that he would return to Glenurchy in time to spoil the plans of the wicked baron.

Black Colin's Return

Travelling day and night, Black Colin, with his faithful clansman, came near to Glenurchy, and sent his follower on in advance to bring back news. The youth returned with tidings that the wedding had been fixed for the next day, since the castle was finished and no further excuse for delay could be made. Then Colin's anger was greatly roused, and he vowed that the Baron MacCorquodale, who had stooped to deceit and forgery to gain his ends, should pay dearly for his baseness. Bidding his young clansman show no sign of recognition when he appeared, the Knight of Loch Awe sent him to the farm in the glen, where the anxious foster-mother eagerly awaited the return of the wanderer. When she saw her son appear alone she was plunged into despair, for she concluded, not that Black Colin was dead, but that he would return too late. When he, in the beggar's disguise which he assumed, came down the Glen he saw the smoke from the castle on the Islet, and said, "I see smoke from my house, and it is the smoke of a wedding feast in preparation, but I pray God who sent us light and love that I may reap the fruit of the love that is there."

The Foster-Mother's Recognition

The Knight then went to his foster-mother's house, knocked at the door, and humbly craved food and shelter, as a beggar. "Come in, good man," said the mistress of the house, "sit down in the chimney-corner, and you shall have your fill of oatcake and milk." Colin sat down heavily, as if he were overwearied, and the farmer's wife moved about slowly, putting before him what she had, and the Knight saw that she did not recognise him, and that she had been weeping quite recently. "You are sad, I can see," he said. "What is the cause of your grief?" "I am not minded to tell that to a wandering stranger," she replied. "Perhaps I can guess what it is," he continued, "you have lost some dear friend, I think." "My loss is great enough to give me grief," she answered, weeping. "I had a dear foster-son, who went oversea to fight the heathen. He was dearer to me than my own sons, and now news has come that he is dead in that foreign land. And the Lady of Loch Awe, who was his wife, is to wed another husband to-morrow. Long she waited for him, past the seven years he was to be away, and now she would not marry again, but that a letter has come to assure her of his death. Even yet she is fretting because she has not had the token he promised to send her, and she will only marry because she dare no longer delay."

"What is this token?" asked Colin. "That I know not: she has never told," replied the foster-mother, "but oh! if he were now here Glenurchy would never fall under the power of Baron MacCorquodale." "Would you know Black Colin if you were to see him?" the beggar asked meaningly, and she replied, "I think I should, for though he has been away for years, I nursed him, and he is my own dear fosterling." "Look well at me, then, good mother of mine, for I am Colin of Loch Awe."

The mistress of the farm seized the beggar-man by the arm, drew him out into the light, and looked earnestly into his face; then, with a scream of joy, she flung her arms around him, and cried, "O Colin! Colin! my dear son, home again ! Glad and glad I am to see you here in time! Weary have the years been since my nursling went away, but now you are home all will be well." And she embraced him and kissed him and stroked his hair, and exclaimed at his bronzed hue and his ragged attire.

The Foster-Mother's Plan

At last Colin stopped her raptures. "Tell me, mother, does my wife seem to wish for this marriage?" he asked, and his foster-mother answered, "Nay, my son, she would not wed now but that, thinking you are dead, she fears the Baron's anger if she continues to refuse him. But if you doubt her heart, follow my counsel, and you shall be assured of her will in this matter." "What do you advise?" asked he. She answered, "Stay this night with me here, and to-morrow go in your beggar's dress to the castle on the Islet. Stand with other beggars at the door, and refuse to go until the bride herself shall bring you food and drink. Then you can put your token in the cup the Lady of Loch Awe will hand you, and by her behaviour you shall learn if her heart is in this marriage or not." "Dear mother, your plan is good, and I will follow it," said Colin. "This night I will rest here, and on the morrow I will seek my wife."

The Beggar at the Wedding

Early next day Colin arose, clad himself in the disguise of a sturdy beggar, took a kindly farewell of his foster-mother, and made his way to the castle. Early as it was, all the servants were astir, and the whole place was in a bustle of preparation, while vagabonds of every description hung round the doors, begging for food and money in honour of the day. The new-comer acted much more boldly: he planted himself right in the open doorway and begged for food and drink in such a lordly tone that the servants were impressed by it, and one of them brought him what he asked - oatcake and buttermilk - and gave it to him, saying, "Take this and begone." Colin took the alms and drank the buttermilk, but put the cake into his wallet, and stood sturdily right in the doorway, so that the servants found it difficult to enter. Another servant came to him with more food and a horn of ale, saying, "Now take this second gift of food and begone, for you are in our way here, and hinder us in our work."

The Beggar's Demand

But he stood more firmly still, with his stout travelling-staff planted on the threshold, and said, "I will not go." Then a third servant approached, who said, "Go at once, or it will be the worse for you. We have given you quite enough for one beggar. Leave quickly now, or you will get us and yourself into trouble." The disguised Knight only replied, "I will not go until the bride herself comes out to give me a drink of wine," and he would not move, for all they could say. The servants grew so perplexed that they went to tell their mistress about this importunate beggar. She laughed as she said, "It is not much for me to do on my last day in the old house," and she bade a servant attend her to the door, bringing a large jug full of wine.

The Token

As the unhappy bride came out to the beggar-man he bent his head in greeting, and she noticed his travel-stained dress and said, "You have come from far, good man", and he replied, "Yes, lady, I have seen many distant lands." "Alas! others have gone to see distant lands and have not returned," she said. "If you would have a drink from the hands of the bride herself, I am she, and you may take your wine now", and, holding a bowl in her hands, she bade the servant fill it with wine, and then gave it to Colin. "I drink to your happiness," he said, and drained the bowl. As he gave it back to the lady he placed within it the token, the half of the engraved ring. "I return it richer than I took it, lady," he said, and his wife looked within and saw the token.

The Recognition

Trembling violently, she snatched the tiny bit of gold from the bottom of the bowl, which fell to the ground and broke at her feet, and then she saw her own name engraved upon it. She looked long and long at the token, and then, pulling a chain at her neck, drew out her half of the ring with Colin's name engraved on it. "O stranger, tell me, is my husband dead?" she asked, grasping the beggar's arm. "Dead?" he questioned, gazing tenderly at her, and at his tone she looked straight into his eyes and knew him. "My husband!" was all that she could say, but she flung her arms around his neck and was clasped close to his heart. The servants stood bewildered, but in a moment their mistress had turned to them, saying, "Run, summon all the household, bring them all, for this is my husband, Black Colin of Loch Awe, come home to me again." When all in the castle knew it there was great excitement and rejoicing, and they feasted bountifully, for the wedding banquet had been prepared.

The Baron's Flight

While the feast was in progress, and the happy wife sat by her long-lost husband and held his hand, as though she feared to let him leave her, a distant sound of bagpipes was heard, and the lady remembered that the Baron MacCorquodale would be coming for his wedding, which she had entirely forgotten in her joy. She laughed lightly to herself, and, beckoning a clansman, bade him go and tell the Baron that she would take no new husband, since her old one had come back to her, and that there would be questions to be answered when time served. The Baron MacCorquodale, in his wedding finery, with a great party of henchmen and vassals and pipers blowing a wedding march, had reached the mouth of the river which enters the side of Loch Awe; the party had crossed the river, and were ready to take boat across to the Islet, when they saw a solitary man rowing towards them with all speed. "It is some messenger from my lady," said the Baron, and he waited eagerly to hear the message. With dreadful consternation he listened to the unexpected words as the clansman delivered them, and then bade the pipers cease their music. "We must return; there will be no wedding to-day, since Black Colin is home again," he said, and the crestfallen party retraced their steps, quickening them more and more as they thought of the vengeance of the long-lost chieftain, but they reached their home in safety.

Castle Kilchurn

In the meantime Colin had much to tell his wife of his adventures, and to ask her of her life all these years. They told each other all, and Colin saw the false letter that had been sent to the Lady of Loch

Awe, and guessed who had plotted this deceit. His anger grew against the bad man who had wrought this wrong and had so nearly gained his end, and he vowed that he would make the Baron dearly abide it. His wife calmed his fury somewhat by telling him how she had waited even beyond the seven years, and what stratagem she had used, and he promised not to make war on the Baron, but to punish him in other ways.

"Tell me what you have done with the rents of Glenurchy these seven years," he said. Then the happy wife replied, "With part I have lived, with part I have guarded the glen, and with part have I made a cairn of stones at the head of Loch Awe. Will you come with me and see it?" And Colin went, deeply puzzled. When they came to the head of Loch Awe, there stood the new castle, on the site of the old house of the MacGregors, and the proud wife laughed as she said, "Do you like my cairn of stones? It has taken long to build." Black Colin was much pleased with the beautiful castle she had raised for him, and renamed it Kilchurn Castle, which title it still keeps. True to his vow, he took no bloody vengeance on the Baron MacCorquodale, but when a few years after he fell into his power the Knight of Loch Awe forced him to resign a great part of his lands to be united with those of Glenurchy.

Canonbie Dick and Thomas of Ercildoune

Canonbie Dick and Thomas of Ercildoune, as retold by Elizabeth Wilson Grierson in The Scottish Fairy Book (1910, J. B. Lippincott Company), draws upon the rich Border traditions that blend folklore with prophecy. The tale follows Canonbie Dick, a bold and somewhat reckless man who refuses to heed warnings about the uncanny.

Grierson's adaptation, like much of her work, softens older oral versions while keeping their eerie grandeur intact. The story reflects the Scottish fascination with liminal places, where the mortal world meets the supernatural, and the enduring presence of Thomas the Rhymer as a guardian of secret knowledge. In her telling, the moral is implicit: mortal arrogance falters in the face of powers older and stranger than reason. The tone is part cautionary, part elegiac, capturing that distinct Border mood where history, legend, and night air seem made of the same woven mist.

It chanced, long years ago, that a certain horse-dealer lived in the South of Scotland, near the Border, not very far from Longtown. He was known as Canonbie Dick, and as he went up and down the country, he almost always had a long string of horses behind him, which he bought at one fair and sold at another, generally managing to turn a good big penny by the transaction.

He was a very fearless man, not easily daunted, and the people who knew him used to say that if Canonbie Dick dare not attempt a thing, no one else need be asked to do it.

One evening, as he was returning from a fair at some distance from his home with a pair of horses which he had not succeeded in selling, he was riding over Bowden Moor, which lies to the west of the Eildon Hills. These hills are, as all men know, the scene of some of the most famous of Thomas the Rhymer's prophecies, and also, so men say, they are the sleeping-place of King Arthur and his Knights, who rest under the three high peaks, waiting for the mystic call that shall awake them.

But little recked the horse-dealer of Arthur and his Knights, nor yet of Thomas the Rhymer. He was riding along at a snail's pace, thinking over the bargains which he had made at the fair that day, and wondering when he was likely to dispose of his two remaining horses.

All at once he was startled by the approach of a venerable man, with white hair and an old-world dress, who seemed almost to start out of the ground, so suddenly did he make his appearance.

When they met, the stranger stopped, and, to Canonbie Dick's great amazement, asked him for how much he would be willing to part with his horses.

The wily horse-dealer thought that he saw a chance of driving a good bargain, for the stranger looked a man of some consequence; so he named a good round sum.

The old man tried to bargain with him, but when he found that he had not much chance of succeeding - for no one ever did succeed in inducing Canonbie Dick to sell a horse for a less sum than he named for it at first - he agreed to buy the animals, and, pulling a bag of gold from the pocket of his queerly cut breeches, he began to count out the price.

As he did so, Canonbie Dick got another shock of surprise, for the gold that the stranger gave him was not the gold that was in use at the time, but was fashioned into Unicorns, and Bonnet-pieces, and other ancient coins, which would be of no use to the horse-dealer in his everyday transactions. But it was good, pure gold, and he took it gladly, for he knew that he was selling his horses at about half as much again as they were worth. "So," thought he to himself, "surely I cannot be the loser in the long run."

Then the two parted, but not before the old man had commissioned Dick to get him other good horses at the same price, the only stipulation he made being that Dick should always bring them to the same spot, after dark, and that he should always come alone.

And, as time went on, the horse-dealer found that he had indeed met a good customer.

For, whenever he came across a suitable horse, he had only to lead it over Bowden Moor after dark, and he was sure to meet the mysterious, white-headed stranger, who always paid him for the animal in old-fashioned golden pieces.

And he might have been selling horses to him yet, for aught I know, had it not been for his one failing.

Canonbie Dick was apt to get very thirsty, and his ordinary customers, knowing this, took care always to provide him with something to drink. The old man never did so; he paid down his money and led away his horses, and there was an end of the matter.

But one night, Dick, being even more thirsty than usual, and feeling sure that his mysterious friend must live somewhere in the neighbourhood, seeing that he was always wandering about the hillside when everyone else was asleep, hinted that he would be very glad to go home with him and have a little refreshment.

"He would need to be a brave man who asks to go home with me," returned the stranger, "but, if you will, you can follow me. Only, remember this - if your courage fail you at that which you will behold, you will rue it all your life."

Canonbie Dick laughed long and loud. "My courage has never failed me yet," he cried. "Beshrew me if I will let it fail now. So lead on, old man, and I will follow."

Without a word the stranger turned and began to ascend a narrow path which led to a curious hillock, which from its shape, was called by the country-folk the "Lucken Hare."

It was supposed to be a great haunt of Witches, and, as a rule, nobody passed that way after dark, if they could possibly help it.

Canonbie Dick was not afraid of Witches, however, so he followed his guide with a bold step up the hillside, but it must be confessed that he felt a little startled when he saw him turn down what seemed to be an entrance to a cavern, especially as he never remembered having seen any opening in the hillside there before.

He paused for a moment, looking round him in perplexity, wondering where he was being taken, and his conductor glanced at him scornfully.

"You can go back if you will," he said. "I warned you that you were going on a journey that would try your courage to the uttermost." There was a jeering note in his voice that touched Dick's pride.

"Who said that I was afraid?" he retorted. "I was just taking note of where this passage stands on the hillside, so as to know it another time."

The stranger shrugged his shoulders. "Time enough to look for it when you would visit it again," he said. And then he pursued his way, with Dick following closely at his heels.

After the first yard or two they were enveloped in thick darkness, and the horse-dealer would have been sore put to it to keep near his guide had not the latter held out his hand for him to grasp. But after a little space a faint glimmering of light began to appear, which grew clearer and clearer, until they found themselves in an enormous cavern lit by flaming torches, which were stuck here and there in sconces in the rocky walls, and which, although they served to give light enough to see by, yet threw such ghostly shadows on the floor that they only seemed to intensify the gloom that hung over the vast apartment.

And the curious thing about this mysterious cave was that, along one side of it, ran a long row of horse stalls, just like what one would find in a stable, and in each stall stood a coal-black charger, saddled and bridled, as if ready for the fray, and on the straw, by every horse's side, lay the gallant figure of a knight, clad from head to foot in coal-black armour, with a drawn sword in his mailed hand.

But not a horse moved, not a chain rattled. Knights and steeds alike were silent and motionless, looking exactly as if some strange enchantment had been thrown over them, and they had been suddenly turned into black marble.

There was something so awesome in the still, cold figures and in the unearthly silence that brooded over everything that Canonbie Dick, reckless and daring though he was, felt his courage waning and his knees beginning to shake under him.

In spite of these feelings, however, he followed the old man up the hall to the far end of it, where there was a table of ancient workmanship, on which was placed a glittering sword and a curiously wrought hunting-horn.

When they reached this table the stranger turned to him, and said, with great dignity, "You have heard, good man, of Thomas of Ercildoune - Thomas the Rhymer, as men call him - he who went to dwell for a time with the Queen of Fairy-land, and from her received the Gifts of Truth and Prophecy?"

Canonbie Dick nodded, for as the wonderful Soothsayer's name fell on his ears, his heart sank within him and his tongue seemed to cleave to the roof of his mouth. If he had been brought there to parley with Thomas the Rhymer, then had he laid himself open to all the eldritch Powers of Darkness.

"I that speak to you am he," went on the white-haired stranger. "And I have permitted you thus to have your desire and follow me hither in order that I may try of what stuff you are made. Before you lies a Horn and a Sword. He that will sound the one, or draw the other, shall, if his courage fail not, be King over the whole of Britain. I, Thomas the Rhymer, have spoken it, and, as you knowest, my tongue cannot lie. But list ye, the outcome of it all depends on your bravery, and it will be a light task, or a heavy, according as you lay hand on Sword or Horn first."

Now Dick was more versed in giving blows than in making music, and his first impulse was to seize the Sword, then, come what might, he had something in his hand to defend himself with. But just as he was about to lift it the thought struck him that, if the place were full of spirits, as he felt sure that it must be, this action of him might be taken to mean defiance, and might cause them to band themselves together against him.

So, changing his mind, he picked up the Horn with a trembling hand, and blew a blast upon it, which, however, was so weak and feeble that it could scarce be heard at the other end of the hall.

The result that followed was enough to appal the stoutest heart. Thunder rolled in crashing peals through the immense hall. The charmed Knights and their horses woke in an instant from their enchanted sleep. The Knights sprang to their feet and seized their swords, brandishing them round their heads, while their great black chargers stamped, and snorted, and ground their bits, as if eager to escape from their stalls. And where a moment before all had been stillness and silence, there was now a scene of wild din and excitement.

Now was the time for Canonbie Dick to play the man. If he had done so all the rest of his life might have been different.

But his courage failed him, and he lost his chance. Terrified at seeing so many threatening faces turned towards him, he dropped the Horn and made one weak, undecided effort to pick up the Sword.

But, before he could do so, a mysterious voice sounded from somewhere in the hall, and these were the words that it uttered:

"Woe to the coward, that ever he was born,

Who did not draw the Sword before he blew the Horn."

And, before Dick knew what he was about, a perfect whirlwind of cold, raw air tore through the cavern, carrying the luckless horse-dealer along with it, and, hurrying him along the narrow passage through which he had entered, dashed him down outside on a bank of loose stones and shale. He fell right to the bottom, and was found, with little life left in him, next morning, by some shepherds, to whom he had just strength enough left to whisper the story of his weird and fearful adventure.

42

As he was one day at work in the hill casting (digging) peats, he heard a voice which seemed to call to him out of the air. It commanded him to dig under a little green knoll which was near, and to gather up the small white stones which he would discover beneath the turf. The voice informed him, at the same time, that while he kept these stones in his possession, he should be endued with the power of supernatural foreknowledge.

Kenneth, though greatly alarmed at this aerial conversation, followed the directions of his invisible instructor, and turning up the turf on the hillock, in a little time discovered the talismans. From that day forward, the mind of Kenneth was illuminated by gleams of unearthly light, and he made many predictions, of which the credulity of the people, and the coincidence of accident, often supplied confirmation, and he certainly became the most notable of the Highland prophets.

The most remarkable and well known of his predictions is the following: "Whenever a McLean with long hands, a Fraser with a black spot on his face, a McGregor with a black knee, and a club-footed McLeod of Raga, shall have existed; whenever there shall have been successively three McDonalds of the name of John, and three McKinnons of the same Christian name, - oppressors will appear in the country, and the people will change their own land for a strange one." All these personages have appeared since, and it is the common opinion of the peasantry, that the consummation of the prophecy was fulfilled, when the exaction of the exorbitant rents reduced the Highlanders to poverty, and the introduction of the sheep banished the people to America.

Whatever might have been the gift of Kenneth Oer, he does not appear to have used it with an extraordinary degree of discretion, and the last time he exercised it, he very nearly paid a heavy price for his divination.

On this occasion he happened to be at some high festival of the McKenzies at Castle Braan. One of the guests was so exhilarated by the scene of gaiety, that he could not forbear a eulogium on the gallantry of the feast, and the nobleness of the guests. Kenneth, it appears, had no regard for the McKenzies, and was so provoked by this sally in their praise, that he not only broke out into a severe satire against their whole race, but gave vent to the prophetic denunciation of wrath and confusion upon their posterity. The guests being informed (or having overheard a part) of this rhapsody, instantly rose up with one accord to punish the contumely of the prophet. Kenneth, though he foretold the fate of others, did not in any manner look into that of himself, for this reason, being doubtful of debating the propriety of his prediction upon such unequal terms, he fled with the greatest precipitation. The McKenzies followed with infinite zeal, and more than one ball had whistled over the head of the seer before he reached Loch Ousie. The consequences of this prediction so disgusted Kenneth with any further exercise of his prophetic calling, that, in the anguish of his flight, he solemnly renounced all communication with its power, and, as he ran along the margin of Loch Ousie, he took out the wonderful pebbles, and cast them in a fury into the water. Whether his evil genius had now forsaken him, or his condition was better than that of his pursuers, is unknown, but certain it is, Kenneth, after the sacrifice of the pebbles, outstripped his enraged enemies, and never, so far as I have heard, made any attempt at prophecy from the hour of his escape.

Kenneth Oer had a son, who was called Iain Dubh Mac Coinnach (Black John, the son of Kenneth), and lived in the village of Miltoun, near Dingwall. His chief occupation was brewing whisky, and he was killed in a fray at Miltoun, early in the present century. His exit would not have formed the catastrophe of an epic poem, and appears to have been one of those events of which his father had no intelligence, for it happened in the following manner:

Having fallen into a dispute with a man with whom he had previously been on friendly terms, they proceeded to blows; in the scuffle, the boy, the son of Iain's adversary, observing the two combatants locked in a close and firm gripe of eager contention, and being doubtful of the event, ran into the house and brought out the iron pot-crook, with which he saluted the head of the unfortunate Iain so severely, that he not only relinquished his combat, but departed this life on the ensuing morning.

Ewen of the Little Head

Ewen of the Little Head is a grim and haunting Highland legend, adapted from an anonymous source and included in Folk-lore and Legends: Scotland (W. W. Gibbings, London, 1889). Set on the Isle of Mull, it tells the story of Ewen, son of the powerful chief of Clan Maclean, whose tragic fate became the source of a local curse.

The story reflects the fatal mixture of pride, loyalty, and vengeance that marks much Highland folklore. Its language and rhythm evoke the harsh landscape and the darker side of clan honour, where family feuds spill into the supernatural.

About three hundred years ago, Ewen Maclaine of Lochbuy, in the island of Mull, having been engaged in a quarrel with a neighbouring chief, a day was fixed for determining the affair by the sword. Lochbuy, before the day arrived, consulted a celebrated witch as to the result of the feud. The witch declared that if Lochbuy's wife should on the morning of that day give him and his men food unasked, he would be victorious, but if not, the result would be the reverse. This was a disheartening response for the unhappy votary, his wife being a noted shrew.

The fatal morning arrived, and the hour for meeting the enemy approached, but there appeared no symptoms of refreshment for Lochbuy and his men. At length the unfortunate man was compelled to ask his wife to supply them with food. She set down before them curds, but without spoons. When the husband inquired how they were to eat them, she replied they should assume the bills of hens. The men ate the curds, as well as they could, with their hands, but Lochbuy himself ate none. After behaving with the greatest bravery in the bloody conflict which ensued, he fell covered with wounds, leaving his wife to the execration of the people. She is still known in that district under the appellation of Corr-dhu, or the Black Crane.

But the miseries brought on the luckless Lochbuy by his wife did not end with his life, for he died fasting, and his ghost is frequently seen to this day riding the very horse on which he was mounted when he was killed. It was a small, but very neat and active pony, dun or mouse-coloured, to which the Laird was much attached, and on which he had ridden for many years before his death. Its appearance is as accurately described in the island of Mull as any steed is at Newmarket. The prints of its shoes are discerned by connoisseurs, and the rattling of its curb is recognised in the darkest night. It is not particular with regard to roads, for it goes up hill and down dale with equal velocity. It's hard-fated rider still wears the same green cloak which covered him in his last battle, and he is particularly distinguished by the small size of his head, a peculiarity which, we suspect, the learned disciples of Spurzheim have never yet had the sagacity to discover as indicative of an extraordinary talent and incomparable perseverance in horsemanship.

It is now above three hundred years since Ewen-a-chin-vig (Anglicised as Hugh of the Little Head) fell in the field of honour, but neither the vigour of the horse nor of the rider is yet diminished. His mournful duty has always been to attend the dying moments of every member of his own tribe, and to escort the departed spirit on its long and arduous journey. He has been seen in the remotest of the Hebrides, and he has found his way to Ireland on these occasions long before steam navigation was invented. About a century ago he took a fancy for a young man of his own race, and frequently did him the honour of placing him behind himself on horseback. He entered into conversation with him, and foretold many circumstances connected with the fate of his successors, which have undoubtedly since come to pass.

Many a long winter night have I listened to the feats of Ewen-a-chin-vig, the faithful and indefatigable guardian of his ancient family, in the hour of their last and greatest trial, affording an example worthy the imitation of every chief, perhaps not beneath the notice of Glengarry himself.

About a dozen years since some symptoms of Ewen's decay gave very general alarm to his friends. He accosted one of his own people (indeed he never has been known to notice any other), and, shaking him cordially by the hand, he attempted to place him on the saddle behind him, but the uncourteous dog declined the honour. Ewen struggled hard, but the clown was a great, strong, clumsy fellow, and stuck to the earth with all his might. He candidly acknowledged, however, that his chief would have prevailed, had it not been for a birch-tree which stood by, and which he got within the fold of his left arm. The contest became very warm indeed, and the tree was certainly twisted like an osier, as thousands can testify who saw it as well as myself. At length, however, Ewen lost his seat for the first time, and the instant the pony found he was his own master, he set off with the fleetness of lightning. Ewen immediately pursued his steed, and the wearied rustic sped his way homeward. It was the general opinion that Ewen found considerable difficulty in catching the horse, but I am happy to learn that he has been lately seen riding the old mouse-coloured pony without the least change in either the horse or the rider. Long may he continue to do so!

Those who from motives of piety or curiosity have visited the sacred island of Iona, must remember to have seen the guide point out the tomb of Ewen, with his figure on horseback, very elegantly sculptured in alto-relievo, and many of the above facts are on such occasions related.

Farquhar MacNeil

Farquhar MacNeil is one of the more haunting tales from Elizabeth Wilson Grierson's The Scottish Fairy Book (1910), a collection that sought to preserve the strange, moral, and often melancholy folk traditions of Scotland. The story tells of Farquhar, a proud and restless fisherman living on the Isle of Barra, whose greed and defiance of warning lead him into supernatural peril.

Like many of Grierson's adaptations, the story is both a moral fable and an evocation of landscape. The Atlantic is not simply a setting but a living power, darkly conscious of human pride. Grierson's retelling, drawn from oral Gaelic sources, emphasises the tension between courage and folly, faith and defiance, in a community steeped in both Christianity and older sea-spirits.

Once upon a time there was a young man named Farquhar MacNeill. He had just gone to a new situation, and the very first night after he went to it his mistress asked him if he would go over the hill to the house of a neighbour and borrow a sieve, for her own was all in holes, and she wanted to sift some meal.

Farquhar agreed to do so, for he was a willing lad, and he set out at once upon his errand, after the farmer's wife had pointed out to him the path that he was to follow, and told him that he would have no difficulty in finding the house, even though it was strange to him, for he would be sure to see the light in the window.

He had not gone very far, however, before he saw what he took to be the light from a cottage window on his left hand, some distance from the path, and, forgetting his Mistress's instructions that he was to follow the path right over the hill, he left it, and walked towards the light.

It seemed to him that he had almost reached it when his foot tripped, and he fell down, down, down, into a Fairy Parlour, far under the ground. It was full of Fairies, who were engaged in different occupations.

Close by the door, or rather the hole down which he had so unceremoniously tumbled, two little elderly women, in black aprons and white mutches, were busily engaged in grinding corn between two flat millstones. Two other Fairies, younger women, in blue coloured print gowns and white kerchiefs, were gathering up the freshly ground meal, and baking it into bannocks, which they were toasting on a girdle over a peat fire, which was burning slowly in a corner.

In the centre of the large apartment a great troop of Fairies, Elves, and Sprites were dancing reels as hard as they could to the music of a tiny set of bagpipes which were being played by a brown-faced Gnome, who sat on a ledge of rock far above their heads.

They all stopped their various employments when Farquhar came suddenly down in their midst, and looked at him in alarm, but when they saw that he was not hurt, they bowed gravely and bade him be seated. Then they went on with their work and with their play as if nothing had happened.

But Farquhar, being very fond of dancing, and being in no wise anxious to be seated, thought that he would like to have a reel first, so he asked the Fairies if he might join them. And they, although they looked surprised at his request, allowed him to do so, and in a few minutes the young man was dancing away as gaily as any of them.

And as he danced a strange change came over him. He forgot his errand, he forgot his home, he forgot everything that had ever happened to him, he only knew that he wanted to remain with the Fairies all the rest of his life.

And he did remain with them - for a magic spell had been cast over him, and he became like one of themselves, and could come and go at nights without being seen, and could sip the dew from the grass and honey from the flowers as daintily and noiselessly as if he had been a Fairy born.

Time passed by, and one night he and a band of merry companions set out for a long journey through the air. They started early, for they intended to pay a visit to the Man in the Moon and be back again before cock-crow.

All would have gone well if Farquhar had only looked where he was going, but he did not, being deeply engaged in making love to a young Fairy Maiden by his side, so he never saw a cottage that was standing right in his way, till he struck against the chimney and stuck fast in the thatch.

His companions sped merrily on, not noticing what had befallen him, and he was left to disentangle himself as best he could.

As he was doing so he chanced to glance down the wide chimney, and in the cottage kitchen he saw a comely young woman dandling a rosy-cheeked baby.

Now, when Farquhar had been in his mortal state, he had been very fond of children, and a word of blessing rose to his lips.

"God shield you," he said, as he looked at the mother and child, little guessing what the result of his words would be.

For scarce had the Holy Name crossed his lips than the spell which had held him so long was broken, and he became as he had been before.

Instantly his thoughts flew to his friends at home, and to the new Mistress whom he had left waiting for her sieve, for he felt sure that some weeks must have elapsed since he set out to fetch it. So he made haste to go to the farm.

When he arrived in the neighbourhood everything seemed strange. There were woods where no woods used to be, and walls where no walls used to be. To his amazement, he could not find his way to the farm, and, worst of all, in the place where he expected to find his father's house he found nothing but a crop of rank green nettles.

In great distress he looked about for someone to tell him what it all meant, and he found an old man thatching the roof of a cottage.

This old man was so thin and grey that at first Farquhar took him for a patch of mist, but as he went nearer he saw that he was a human being, and, going close up to the wall and shouting with all his might, for he felt sure that such an ancient man would be deaf, he asked him if he could tell him where his friends had gone to, and what had happened to his father's dwelling.

The old man listened, then he shook his head. "I never heard of him," he answered slowly, "but perhaps my father might be able to tell you."

"Your father!" said Farquhar, in great surprise. "Is it possible that your father is alive?"

"Aye he is," answered the old man, with a little laugh. "If you go into the house you'll find him sitting in the arm-chair by the fire."

Farquhar did as he was bid, and on entering the cottage found another old man, who was so thin and withered and bent that he looked as if he must at least be a hundred years old. He was feebly twisting ropes to bind the thatch on the roof.

"Can you tell me aught of my friends, or where my father's cottage is?" asked Farquhar again, hardly expecting that this second old man would be able to answer him.

"I can't," mumbled this ancient person, "but perhaps my father can."

"Your father!" exclaimed Farquhar, more astonished than ever. "But surely he must be dead long ago."

The old man shook his head with a weird grimace.

"Look there," he said, and pointed with a twisted finger, to a leather purse, or sporran, which was hanging to one of the posts of a wooden bedstead in the corner.

Farquhar approached it, and was almost frightened out of his wits by seeing a tiny, shrivelled face crowned by a red pirnie, looking over the edge of the sporran.

"Tak' him out; he'll no touch ye," chuckled the old man by the fire.

So Farquhar took the little creature out carefully between his finger and thumb, and set him on the palm of his left hand. He was so shrivelled with age that he looked just like a mummy.

"Do know anything of my friends, or where my father's cottage is gone to?" asked Farquhar for the third time, hardly expecting to get an answer.

"They were all dead long before I was born," piped out the tiny figure. "I never saw any of them, but I have heard my father speak of them."

"Then I must be older than you!" cried Farquhar, in great dismay. And he got such a shock at the thought that his bones suddenly dissolved into dust, and he fell, a heap of grey ashes, on the floor.

Habetrot the Spinstress

Habetrot the Spinstress is a Scottish folktale collected and retold by Elizabeth Wilson Grierson in The Scottish Fairy Book (J. B. Lippincott Company, 1910). It tells of a young woman who despises spinning, a chore expected of all diligent girls.

Grierson's version, adapted from older Border traditions, preserves the blend of humour and quiet rebellion found in many Scottish wonder tales. Beneath its charm lies a subtle commentary on labour, class, and women's independence, making Habetrot the Spinstress both a folkloric curiosity and a small act of protest.

In bygone days, in an old farmhouse which stood by a river, there lived a beautiful girl called Maisie. She was tall and straight, with auburn hair and blue eyes, and she was the prettiest girl in all the valley. And one would have thought that she would have been the pride of her mother's heart.

But, instead of this, her mother used to sigh and shake her head whenever she looked at her. And why?

Because, in those days, all men were sensible, and instead of looking out for pretty girls to be their wives, they looked out for girls who could cook and spin, and who gave promise of becoming notable housewives.

Maisie's mother had been an industrious spinster, but alas! to her sore grief and disappointment, her daughter did not take after her.

The girl loved to be out of doors, chasing butterflies and plucking wildflowers, far better than sitting at her spinning-wheel. So when her mother saw one after another of Maisie's companions, who were not nearly so pretty as she was, getting rich husbands, she sighed and said, "Woe's me, child, for methinks no brave wooer will ever pause at our door while they see you so idle and thoughtless." But Maisie only laughed.

At last her mother grew really angry, and one bright Spring morning she laid down three heads of lint on the table, saying sharply, "I will have no more of this dallying. People will say that it is my blame that no wooer comes to seek you. I cannot have you left on my hands to be laughed at, as the idle maid who would not marry. So now you must work, and if you have not these heads of lint spun into seven hanks of thread in three days, I will even speak to the Mother at St. Mary's Convent, and you will go there and learn to be a nun."

Now, though Maisie was an idle girl, she had no wish to be shut up in a nunnery; so she tried not to think of the sunshine outside, but sat down soberly with her distaff.

But, alas! she was so little accustomed to work that she made but slow progress, and although she sat at the spinning-wheel all day, and never once went out of doors, she found at night that she had only spun half a hank of yarn.

The next day it was even worse, for her arms ached so much she could only work very slowly. That night she cried herself to sleep, and next morning, seeing that it was quite hopeless to expect to get her task finished, she threw down her distaff in despair, and ran out of doors.

Near the house was a deep dell, through which ran a tiny stream. Maisie loved this dell; the flowers grew so abundantly there.

This morning she ran down to the edge of the stream, and seated herself on a large stone. It was a glorious morning, the hazel trees were newly covered with leaves, and the branches nodded over her head, and showed like delicate tracery against the blue sky. The primroses and sweet-scented violets peeped out from among the grass, and a little water wagtail came and perched on a stone in the middle of the stream, and bobbed up and down, till it seemed as if he were nodding to Maisie, and as if he were trying to say to her, "Never mind, cheer up."

But the poor girl was in no mood that morning to enjoy the flowers and the birds. Instead of watching them, as she generally did, she hid her face in her hands, and wondered what would become of her. She rocked herself to and fro, as she thought how terrible it would be if her mother fulfilled her threat and shut her up in the Convent of St. Mary, with the grave, solemn-faced sisters, who seemed as if they had completely forgotten what it was like to be young, and run about in the sunshine, and laugh, and pick the fresh Spring flowers.

"Oh, I could not do it, I could not do it," she cried . "It would kill me to be a nun."

"And who wants to make a pretty wench like you into a nun?" asked a queer, cracked voice quite close to her.

Maisie jumped up, and stood staring in front of her as if she had been moonstruck. For, just across the stream from where she had been sitting, there was a curious boulder, with a round hole in the middle of it - for all the world like a big apple with the core taken out.

Maisie knew it well; she had often sat upon it, and wondered how the funny hole came to be there.

It was no wonder that she stared, for, seated on this stone, was the queerest little old woman that she had ever seen in her life. Indeed, had it not been for her silver hair, and the white mutch with the big frill that she wore on her head, Maisie would have taken her for a little girl, she wore such a very short skirt, only reaching down to her knees.

Her face, inside the frill of her cap, was round, and her cheeks were rosy, and she had little black eyes, which twinkled merrily as she looked at the startled maiden. On her shoulders was a black and white checked shawl, and on her legs, which she dangled over the edge of the boulder, she wore black silk stockings and the neatest little shoes, with great silver buckles.

In fact, she would have been quite a pretty old lady had it not been for her lips, which were very long and very thick, and made her look quite ugly in spite of her rosy cheeks and black eyes. Maisie stood and looked at her for such a long time in silence that she repeated her question.

"And who wants to make a pretty wench like you into a nun? More likely that some gallant gentleman should want to make a bride of you."

"Oh, no," answered Maisie, "my mother says no gentleman would look at me because I cannot spin."

"Nonsense," said the tiny woman. "Spinning is all very well for old folks like me - my lips, as you see, are long and ugly because I have spun so much, for I always wet my fingers with them, the easier to draw the thread from the distaff. No, no, take care of your beauty, child; do not waste it over the spinning-wheel, nor yet in a nunnery."

"If my mother only thought as you dost," replied the girl sadly, and, encouraged by the old woman's kindly face, she told her the whole story.

"Well," said the old Dame, "I do not like to see pretty girls weep; what if I were able to help you, and spin the lint for you?"

Maisie thought that this offer was too good to be true, but her new friend bade her run home and fetch the lint, and I need not tell you that she required no second bidding.

When she returned she handed the bundle to the little lady, and was about to ask her where she should meet her in order to get the thread from her when it was spun, when a sudden noise behind her made her look round.

She saw nothing, but what was her horror and surprise when she turned back again, to find that the old woman had vanished entirely, lint and all.

She rubbed her eyes, and looked all round, but she was nowhere to be seen. The girl was utterly bewildered. She wondered if she could have been dreaming, but no that could not be, there were her footprints leading up the bank and down again, where she had gone for the lint, and brought it back, and there was the mark of her foot, wet with dew, on a stone in the middle of the stream, where she had stood when she had handed the lint up to the mysterious little stranger.

What was she to do now? What would her mother say when, in addition to not having finished the task that had been given her, she had to confess to having lost the greater part of the lint also? She ran up and down the little dell, hunting amongst the bushes, and peeping into every nook and cranny of the bank where the little old woman might have hidden herself. It was all in vain, and , tired out with the search, she sat down on the stone once more, and presently fell fast asleep.

When she awoke it was evening. The sun had set, and the yellow glow on the western horizon was fast giving place to the silvery light of the moon. She was sitting thinking of the curious events of the day, and gazing at the great boulder opposite, when it seemed to her as if a distant murmur of voices came from it.

With one bound she crossed the stream, and clambered on to the stone. She was right. Someone was talking underneath it, far down in the ground. She put her ear close to the stone, and listened.

The voice of the queer little old woman came up through the hole. "Ho, ho, my pretty little wench little knows that my name is Habetrot."

Full of curiosity, Maisie put her eye to the opening, and the strangest sight that she had ever seen met her gaze. She seemed to be looking through a telescope into a wonderful little valley. The trees there were brighter and greener than any that she had ever seen before and there were beautiful flowers, quite different from the flowers that grew in her country. The little valley was carpeted with the most exquisite moss, and up and down it walked her tiny friend, busily engaged in spinning.

She was not alone, for round her were a circle of other little old women, who were seated on large white stones, and they were all spinning away as fast as they could.

Occasionally one would look up, and then Maisie saw that they all seemed to have the same long, thick lips that her friend had. She really felt very sorry, as they all looked exceedingly kind, and might have been pretty had it not been for this defect.

One of the Spinstresses sat by herself, and was engaged in winding the thread, which the others had spun, into hanks. Maisie did not think that this little lady looked so nice as the others. She was dressed entirely in grey, and had a big, hooked nose, and great horn spectacles. She seemed to be called Slantlie Mab, for Maisie heard Habetrot address her by that name, telling her to make haste and tie up all the thread, for it was getting late, and it was time that the young girl had it to carry home to her mother.

Maisie did not quite know what to do, or how she was to get the thread, for she did not like to shout down the hole in case the queer little old woman should be angry at being watched.

However, Habetrot, as she had called herself, suddenly appeared on the path beside her, with the hanks of thread in her hand.

"Oh, thank you, thank you," cried Maisie. "What can I do to show you how thankful I am?"

"Nothing," answered the Fairy. "For I do not work for reward. Only do not tell your mother who span the thread for you."

It was now late, and Maisie lost no time in running home with the precious thread upon her shoulder. When she walked into the kitchen she found that her mother had gone to bed. She seemed to have had a busy day, for there, hanging up in the wide chimney, in order to dry, were seven large black puddings.

The fire was low, but bright and clear, and the sight of it and the sight of the puddings suggested to Maisie that she was very hungry, and that fried black puddings were very good.

Flinging the thread down on the table, she hastily pulled off her shoes, so as not to make a noise and awake her mother, and, getting down the frying-pan from the wall, she took one of the black puddings from the chimney, and fried it, and ate it.

Coinnach Oer

Coinnach Oer, adapted from an anonymous tale included in Folk-lore and Legends: Scotland (W. W. Gibbings, London, 1889), recounts the life and strange gift of the Highland seer known as Kenneth Mackenzie, or "Coinnach Odhar" in Gaelic, literally, "the Pale Kenneth." The story blends fact and legend, tracing how this figure from Ross-shire, reputedly of humble birth, became feared and revered for his second sight.

In the Folk-lore and Legends version, the tale carries the cool, fatalistic tone of Highland storytelling, where prophecy feels less like choice than inevitability. The narrator presents Coinnach as a man set apart, cursed by knowledge no one should hold. Whether visionary or madman is left for the reader to decide. As with many Scottish legends, landscape and destiny intertwine: the mist, the sea, and the mountains echo his solitude and the weight of his foresight.

Coinnach Oer, which means Dun Kenneth, was a celebrated man in his generation. He has been called the Isaiah of the North. The prophecies of this man are very frequently alluded to and quoted in various parts of the Highlands; although little is known of the man himself, except in Ross-shire. He was a small farmer in Strathpeffer, near Dingwall, and for many years of his life neither exhibited any talents, nor claimed any intelligence above his fellows. The manner in which he obtained the prophetic gift was told by himself in the following manner:

Still she felt hungry, so she took another, and then another, till they were all gone. Then she crept upstairs to her little bed and fell fast asleep.

Next morning her mother came downstairs before Maisie was awake. In fact, she had not been able to sleep much for thinking of her daughter's careless ways, and had been sorrowfully making up her mind that she must lose no time in speaking to the Abbess of St. Mary's about this idle girl of hers.

What was her surprise to see on the table the seven beautiful hanks of thread, while, on going to the chimney to take down a black pudding to fry for breakfast, she found that every one of them had been eaten. She did not know whether to laugh for joy that her daughter had been so industrious, or to cry for vexation because all her lovely black puddings - which she had expected would last for a week at least - were gone. In her bewilderment she sang out:

"My daughter's spun seven, seven, seven,

My daughter's eaten seven, seven, seven,

And all before daylight."

Now I forgot to tell you that, about half a mile from where the old farmhouse stood, there was a beautiful Castle, where a very rich young nobleman lived. He was both good and brave, as well as rich, and all the mothers who had pretty daughters used to wish that he would come their way, some day, and fall in love with one of them. But he had never done so, and everyone said, "He is too grand to marry any country girl. One day he will go away to London Town and marry a Duke's daughter."

Well, this fine spring morning it chanced that this young nobleman's favourite horse had lost a shoe, and he was so afraid that any of the grooms might ride it along the hard road, and not on the soft grass at the side, that he said that he would take it to the smithy himself.

So it happened that he was riding along by Maisie's garden gate as her mother came into the garden singing these strange lines.

He stopped his horse, and said good-naturedly, "Good day, Madam, and may I ask why you sing such a strange song?"

Maisie's mother made no answer, but turned and walked into the house, and the young nobleman, being very anxious to know what it all meant, hung his bridle over the garden gate, and followed her.

She pointed to the seven hanks of thread lying on the table, and said, "This has my daughter done before breakfast."

Then the young man asked to see the Maiden who was so industrious, and her mother went and pulled Maisie from behind the door, where she had hidden herself when the stranger came in, for she had come downstairs while her mother was in the garden.

She looked so lovely in her fresh morning gown of blue gingham, with her auburn hair curling softly round her brow, and her face all over blushes at the sight of such a gallant young man, that he quite lost his heart, and fell in love with her on the spot.

"Ah," he said, "my dear mother always told me to try and find a wife who was both pretty and useful, and I have succeeded beyond my expectations. Do not let our marriage, I pray you, good Dame, be too long deferred."

Maisie's mother was overjoyed, as you may imagine, at this piece of unexpected good fortune, and busied herself in getting everything ready for the wedding, but Maisie herself was a little perplexed.

She was afraid that she would be expected to spin a great deal when she was married and lived at the Castle, and if that were so, her husband was sure to find out that she was not really such a good spinstress as he thought she was.

In her trouble she went down, the night before her wedding, to the great boulder by the stream in the glen, and, climbing up on it, she laid her head against the stone, and called softly down the hole, "Habetrot, dear Habetrot."

The little old woman soon appeared, and, with twinkling eyes, asked her what was troubling her so much just when she should have been so happy. And Maisie told her.

"Trouble not your pretty head about that," answered the Fairy, "but come here with your bridegroom next week, when the moon is full, and I warrant that he will never ask you to sit at a spinning-wheel again."

Accordingly, after all the wedding festivities were over and the couple had settled down at the Castle, on the appointed evening Maisie suggested to her husband that they should take a walk together in the moonlight.

She was very anxious to see what the little Fairy would do to help her, for that very day he had been showing her all over her new home, and he had pointed out to her the beautiful new spinning-wheel made of ebony, which had belonged to his mother, saying proudly, "To-morrow, little one, I shall bring some lint from the town, and then the maids will see what clever little fingers my wife has."

Maisie had blushed as red as a rose as she bent over the lovely wheel, and then felt quite sick, as she wondered whatever she would do if Habetrot did not help her.

So on this particular evening, after they had walked in the garden, she said that she should like to go down to the little dell and see how the stream looked by moonlight. So to the dell they went.

As soon as they came to the boulder Maisie put her head against it and whispered, "Habetrot, dear Habetrot", and in an instant the little old woman appeared.

She bowed in a stately way, as if they were both strangers to her, and said, "Welcome, Sir and Madam, to the Spinsters' Dell." And then she tapped on the root of a great oak tree with a tiny wand which she held in her hand, and a green door, which Maisie never remembered having noticed before, flew open, and they followed the Fairy through it into the other valley which Maisie had seen through the hole in the great stone.

All the little old women were sitting on their white chucky stones busy at work, only they seemed far uglier than they had seemed at first, and Maisie noticed that the reason for this was, that, instead of wearing red skirts and white mutches as they had done before, they now wore caps and dresses of dull grey, and instead of looking happy, they all seemed to be trying who could look most miserable, and who could push out their long lips furthest, as they wet their fingers to draw the thread from their distaffs.

"Save us and help us! What a lot of hideous old witches," exclaimed her husband. "Whatever could this funny old woman mean by bringing a pretty childlike you to look at them? You will dream of them for a week and a day. Just look at their lips", and, pushing Maisie behind him, he went up to one of them and asked her what had made her mouth grow so ugly.

She tried to tell him, but all the sound that he could hear was something that sounded like SPIN-N-N.

He asked another one, and her answer sounded like this: SPAN-N-N. He tried a third, and hers sounded like SPUN-N-N.

He seized Maisie by the hand and hurried her through the green door. "By my troth," he said, "my mother's spinning-wheel may turn to gold before I let you touch it, if this is what spinning leads to. Rather than that your pretty face should be spoilt, the linen chests at the Castle may get empty, and remain so for ever!"

So it came to pass that Maisie could be out of doors all day wandering about with her husband, and laughing and singing to her heart's content. And whenever there was lint at the Castle to be spun, it was carried down to the big boulder in the dell and left there, and Habetrot and her companions spun it, and there was no more trouble about the matter.

Jock and His Mother

Jock and His Mother, adapted from an anonymous tale in Folk-lore and Legends: Scotland (W. W. Gibbings, London, 1889), is a brief but sharply drawn piece of Scottish moral storytelling. It follows a young man named Jock, whose mother sends him out into the world with a simple injunction to mind his manners and behave wisely

The story's humour lies in its rhythm of repetition and reversal, a familiar pattern in Scottish and wider European folk tradition. Jock's misadventures, whether in greeting people wrongly, handling food, or misunderstanding social custom, show how moral lessons can curdle into absurdity when stripped of judgment or kindness. Beneath the comedy runs a shrewd observation about upbringing and independence: wisdom cannot be handed down whole but must be tested, bent, and sometimes broken.

You see, there was a wife had a son, and they called him Jock, and she said to him, "You are a lazy fellow; you must go away and do something to help me."

"Well," says Jock, "I'll do that." So away he goes, and falls in with a packman.

Says the packman, "If you carry my pack all day, I'll give you a needle at night."

So he carried the pack, and got the needle, and as he was going off home to his mother, Jock cut a bundle of brackens, and put the needle into the heart of them. Off he went home.

Says his mother, "What have you made of yourself today?"

Says Jock, "I fell in with a packman, and carried his pack all day, and he gave me a needle for't, and you may look for it among the brackens."

"Hout," cried' she, "you daft gowk, you should have stuck the needle into your bonnet, man."

"I'll mind that again," said Jock.

Next day he fell in with a man carrying plough socks. "If you help me to carry my socks all day, I'll give you one to yourself' at night."

"I'll do that," said Jock. Jock carried them all day, and got a sock, which he stuck in his bonnet. On the way home, Jock was dry, and took a turn to take a drink out of the burn, and with the weight of the sock, his bonnet fell into the river, and floated away and out of sight.

He went home, and his mother says, "Well, Jock, what have you been doing all day?"

And then he told her.

"Hout," she said, "you should have tied the string to it, and trailed it behind you."

"Well," said Jock, "I'll mind that again."

Away he went the next day, and he fell in with a flesher. "Well," says the flesher, "if you'll be my servant all day, I'll give you a leg of mutton at night."

"I'll be that" said Jock.

He got a leg of mutton at night. He tied a string to it, and trailed it behind him the whole road home.

"What have you been doing?" said his mother.

He told her.

"Hout, you fool, you should have carried it on your shoulder."

"I'll mind that again," said Jock.

Off he went the next day, and met a horse-dealer, who said, "If you will help me with my horses all day, I'll give you one to yourself at night."

"I'll do that," said Jock. So he served him, and got his horse, and he tied its feet, but as he was not able to carry it on his back, he left it lying on the roadside. Home he went, and told his mother.

"Hout, you daft gowk, you'll never turn wise! Could you not have jumped on it, and ridden it?"

"I'll mind that again," said Jock.

Well, there was a grand gentleman, who had a daughter who was very subject to melancholy, and her father gave out that whatever should make her laugh would get her hand in marriage. So it happened that she was sitting at the window one day, musing in her melancholy state, when Jock, according to the advice of his mother, came flying up on a cow's back, with the tail over his shoulder. And she burst out into a fit of laughter. When her father made inquiry about what had made her laugh, it was found to be Jock riding on the cow. Accordingly, Jock was sent for to get his bride.

Well, Jock was married to her, and there was a great supper prepared. Amongst the rest of the things, there was some honey, which Jock was very fond of. After supper, everyone retired, and the old priest that married Jock and his bride sat up all night by the kitchen fireside.

But Jock woke in the night-time, and said, "Oh, would you give me some of yon nice, sweet honey that we got for our supper last night?"

"Oh ay," said his wife, "rise and go into the larder, and you'll get a honey-pig finger of it."

Jock rose, and thrust his hand into the honey-pig for a taste, but he could not get his hand out again. So he came away with the pig in his hand, like a mason's mallet, and cried, "Oh, I can't get my hand out."

"Hoot," said his wife, "go away and break it on the hearth-stone."

By this time, the fire was dark, and the old priest was lying snoring with his head against the chimney-piece, with a huge white wig on. Jock turned up and gave him a whack on the head with the honey-pig, thinking it was the hearth-stone, and knocked the honey-pig all in bits.

The old priest roared out, "Murder!"

Jock ran down the stair as hard as he could bicker, and hid himself among the bee hives.

That night, as luck would have it, some thieves came to steal the bees' hives, and in the hurry of tumbling them into a large grey plaid cloth, they tumbled Jock in along with them. So, off they set, with Jock and the hives on their backs. On the way, they had to cross the burn where Jock lost his bonnet.

One of the thieves cried, "Oh, I have found a bonnet!"

Jock, on hearing that, cried out, "Oh, that's mine!"

The thieves thought they had got the devil on their backs. So they dropped everything in the burn, and Jock, being tied in the plaid, couldn't get out; so he and the bees were all drowned together.

If all tales be true, then this is no lie...

Katherine Crackernuts

Katherine Crackernuts is a lively Scottish folktale that turns the usual fairy-tale pattern neatly on its head. Adapted by Elizabeth Wilson Grierson in The Scottish Fairy Book (J. B. Lippincott, 1910), it tells of two princesses, one beautiful, one less so, whose fortunes are bound by love and loyalty rather than envy.

Grierson's version preserves the rhythm and humour of the old oral tale while emphasising wit and compassion over beauty and fate. It belongs to that rare class of stories in which female intelligence drives the plot and loyalty outweighs vanity. Rooted in older Scottish traditions of fairy abduction and night dancing, the tale carries both pagan echoes and Christian overtones of redemption.

There was once a king whose wife died, leaving him with an only daughter, whom he dearly loved. The little Princess's name was Velvet-Cheek, and she was so good, and bonnie, and kind-hearted that all her father's subjects loved her. But as the King was generally engaged in transacting the business of the State, the poor little maiden had rather a lonely life, and often wished that she had a sister with whom she could play, and who would be a companion to her.

The King, hearing this, made up his mind to marry a middle-aged Countess, whom he had met at a neighbouring Court, who had one daughter, named Katherine, who was just a little younger than the Princess Velvet-Cheek, and who, he thought, would make a nice play-fellow for her.

He did so, and in one way the arrangement turned out very well, for the two girls loved one another dearly, and had everything in common, just as if they had really been sisters.

But in another way it turned out very badly, for the new Queen was a cruel and ambitious woman, and she wanted her own daughter to do as she had done, and make a grand marriage, and perhaps even become a Queen. And when she saw that Princess Velvet-Cheek was growing into a very beautiful young woman - more beautiful by far than her own daughter - she began to hate her, and to wish that in some way she would lose her good looks.

"For," thought she, "what suitor will heed my daughter as long as her step-sister is by her side?"

Now, among the servants and retainers at her husband's Castle there was an old Hen-wife, who, men said, was in league with the Evil Spirits of the air, and who was skilled in the knowledge of charms, and philtres, and love potions.

"Perhaps she could help me to do what I seek to do," said the wicked Queen, and one night, when it was growing dusk, she wrapped a cloak round her, and set out to this old Hen-wife's cottage.

"Send the lassie to me tomorrow morning before she has broken her fast," replied the old Dame when she heard what her visitor had to say. "I will find out a way to mar her beauty." And the wicked Queen went home content.

Next morning she went to the Princess's room while she was dressing, and told her to go out before breakfast and get the eggs that the Hen-wife had gathered. "And see," added she, "that you do not eat anything before you go, for there is nothing that makes the roses bloom on a young maiden's cheeks like going out fasting in the fresh morning air."

Princess Velvet-Cheek promised to do as she was bid, and go and fetch the eggs, but as she was not fond of going out of doors before she had had something to eat, and as, moreover, she suspected that her step-mother had some hidden reason for giving her such an unusual order, and she did not trust her step-mother's hidden reasons, she slipped into the pantry as she went downstairs and helped herself to a large slice of cake. Then, after she had eaten it, she went straight to the Hen-wife's cottage and asked for the eggs.

"Lift the lid of that pot there, your Highness, and you will see them," said the old woman, pointing to the big pot standing in the corner in which she boiled her hens' meat.

The Princess did so, and found a heap of eggs lying inside, which she lifted into her basket, while the old woman watched her with a curious smile.

"Go home to your Lady Mother, Hinny," she said , "and tell her from me to keep the press door better snibbit."

The Princess went home, and gave this extraordinary message to her step-mother, wondering to herself the while what it meant.

But if she did not understand the Hen-wife's words, the Queen understood them only too well. For from them she gathered that the Princess had in some way prevented the old Witch's spell doing what she intended it to do.

So next morning, when she sent her step-daughter once more on the same errand, she accompanied her to the door of the Castle herself, so that the poor girl had no chance of paying a visit to the pantry. But as she went along the road that led to the cottage, she felt so hungry that, when she passed a party of country-folk picking peas by the roadside, she asked them to give her a handful. They did so, and she ate the peas, and so it came about that the same thing happened that had happened yesterday.

The Hen-wife sent her to look for the eggs, but she could work no spell upon her, because she had broken her fast. So the old woman bade her go home again and give the same message to the Queen.

The Queen was very angry when she heard it, for she felt that she was being outwitted by this slip of a girl, and she determined that, although she was not fond of getting up early, she would accompany her next day herself, and make sure that she had nothing to eat as she went.

So next morning she walked with the Princess to the Hen-wife's cottage, and as had happened twice before, the old woman sent the Royal maiden to lift the lid off the pot in the corner in order to get the eggs. And the moment that the Princess did so off jumped her own pretty head, and on jumped that of a sheep.

Then the wicked Queen thanked the cruel old Witch for the service that she had rendered to her, and went home quite delighted with the success of her scheme; while the poor Princess picked up her own head and put it into her basket along with the eggs, and went home crying, keeping behind the hedge all the way, for she felt so ashamed of her sheep's head that she was afraid that anyone saw her.

Now, as I told you, the Princess's step-sister Katherine loved her dearly, and when she saw what a cruel deed had been wrought on her she was so angry that she declared that she would not remain another hour in the Castle. "For," she said, "if my Lady Mother can order one such deed to be done, who can hinder her ordering another. So, methinks, 'twere better for us both to be where she cannot reach us."

So she wrapped a fine shawl round her poor step-sister's head, so that none could tell what it was like, and, putting the real head in the basket, she took her by the hand, and the two set out to seek their fortunes.

They walked and they walked, till they reached a splendid Palace, and when they came to it Katherine made as though she would go boldly up and knock at the door.

"I may perchance find work here," she explained, "and earn enough money to keep us both in comfort."

But the poor Princess would fain have pulled her back. "They will have nothing to do with you," she whispered, "when they see that you have a sister with a sheep's head."

"And who is to know that you have a sheep's head?" asked Katherine. "If you hold your tongue, and keep the shawl well round your face, and leave the rest to me."

So up she went and knocked at the kitchen door, and when the housekeeper came to answer it she asked her if there was any work that she could give her to do. "For," she said, "I have a sick sister, who is sore troubled with the migraine in her head, and I would fain find a quiet lodging for her where she could rest for the night."

"Do you know aught of sickness?" asked the housekeeper, who was greatly struck by Katherine's soft voice and gentle ways.

"Ay, do I," replied Katherine, "for when one's sister is troubled with the migraine, one has to learn to go about softly and not to make a noise."

Now it chanced that the King's eldest son, the Crown Prince, was lying ill in the Palace of a strange disease, which seemed to have touched his brain. For he was so restless, especially at nights, that someone had always to be with him to watch that he did himself no harm, and this state of things had gone on so long that everyone was quite worn out.

And the old housekeeper thought that it would be a good chance to get a quiet night's sleep if this capable-looking stranger could be trusted to sit up with the Prince.

So she left her at the door, and went and consulted the King, and the King came out and spoke to Katherine and he, too, was so pleased with her voice and her appearance that he gave orders that a room should be set apart in the Castle for her sick sister and herself, and he promised that, if she would sit up that night with the Prince, and see that no harm befell him, she would have, as her reward, a bag of silver Pennies in the morning.

Katherine agreed to the bargain readily, "for," thought she, "twill always be a night's lodging for the Princess, and forbye that, a bag of silver Pennies is not to be got every day."

So the Princess went to bed in the comfortable chamber that was set apart for her, and Katherine went to watch by the sick Prince.

He was a handsome, comely young man, who seemed to be in some sort of fever, for his brain was not quite clear, and he tossed and tumbled from side to side, gazing anxiously in front of him, and stretching out his hands as if he were in search of something.

And at twelve o'clock at night, just when Katherine thought that he was going to fall into a refreshing sleep, what was her horror to see him rise from his bed, dress himself hastily, open the door, and slip downstairs, as if he were going to look for somebody.

"There be something strange in this," said the girl to herself. "Methinks I had better follow him and see what happens."

So she stole out of the room after the Prince and followed him safely downstairs, and what was her astonishment to find that apparently he was going some distance, for he put on his hat and riding-coat, and, unlocking the door crossed the courtyard to the stable, and began to saddle his horse.

When he had done so, he led it out, and mounted, and, whistling softly to a hound which lay asleep in a corner, he prepared to ride away.

"I must go too, and see the end of this," said Katherine bravely, "for methinks he is bewitched. These be not the actions of a sick man."

So, just as the horse was about to start, she jumped lightly on its back, and settled herself comfortably behind its rider, all unnoticed by him.

Then this strange pair rode away through the woods, and, as they went, Katherine pulled the hazel-nuts that nodded in great clusters in her face. "For," she said to herself, "Dear only knows where next I may get anything to eat."

On and on they rode, till they left the greenwood far behind them and came out on an open moor. Soon they reached a hillock, and here the Prince drew rein, and, stooping down, cried in a strange, uncanny whisper, "Open, open, Green Hill, and let the Prince, and his horse, and his hound enter."

"And" whispered Katherine quickly, "let his lady enter behind him."

Instantly, to her great astonishment, the top of the knowe seemed to tip up, leaving an aperture large enough for the little company to enter; then it closed gently behind them again.

They found themselves in a magnificent hall, brilliantly lighted by hundreds of candles stuck in sconces round the walls. In the centre of this apartment was a group of the most beautiful maidens that Katherine had ever seen, all dressed in shimmering ball-gowns, with wreaths of roses and violets in their hair. And there were sprightly gallants also, who had been treading a measure with these beauteous damsels to the strains of fairy music.

When the maidens saw the Prince, they ran to him, and led him away to join their revels. And at the touch of their hands all his languor seemed to disappear, and he became the gayest of all the throng, and laughed, and danced, and sang as if he had never known what it was to be ill.

As no one took any notice of Katherine, she sat down quietly on a bit of rock to watch what would befall. And as she watched, she became aware of a wee, wee bairnie, playing with a tiny wand, quite close to her feet.

He was a bonnie bit bairn, and she was just thinking of trying to make friends with him when one of the beautiful maidens passed, and, looking at the wand, said to her partner, in a meaning tone, "Three strokes of that wand would give Katherine's sister back her pretty face."

Here was news indeed! Katherine's breath came thick and fast, and with trembling fingers she drew some of the nuts out of her pocket, and began rolling them carelessly towards the child. Apparently he did not get nuts very often, for he dropped his little wand at once, and stretched out his tiny hands to pick them up.

This was just what she wanted, and she slipped down from her seat to the ground, and drew a little nearer to him. Then she threw one or two more nuts in his way, and, when he was picking these up, she managed to lift the wand unobserved, and to hide it under her apron. After this, she crept cautiously back to her seat again, and not a moment too soon, for just then a cock crew, and at the sound the whole of the dancers vanished - all but the Prince, who ran to mount his horse, and was in such a hurry to be gone that Katherine had much ado to get up behind him before the hillock opened, and he rode swiftly into the outer world once more.

But she managed it, and, as they rode homewards in the grey morning light, she sat and cracked her nuts and ate them as fast as she could, for her adventures had made her marvellously hungry.

When she and her strange patient had once more reached the Castle, she just waited to see him go back to bed, and begin to toss and tumble as he had done before; then she ran to her step-sister's room, and, finding her asleep, with her poor misshapen head lying peacefully on the pillow, she gave it three sharp little strokes with the fairy wand and, lo and behold! the sheep's head vanished, and the Princess's own pretty one took its place.

In the morning the King and the old housekeeper came to inquire what kind of night the Prince had had. Katherine answered that he had had a very good night, for she was very anxious to stay with him longer, for now that she had found out that the Elfin Maidens who dwelt in the Green Knowe had thrown a spell over him, she was resolved to find out also how that spell could be loosed.

And Fortune favoured her, for the King was so pleased to think that such a suitable nurse had been found for the Prince, and he was also so charmed with the looks of her step-sister, who came out of her chamber as bright and bonnie as in the old days, declaring that her migraine was all gone, and that she was now able to do any work that the housekeeper might find for her, that he begged Katherine to stay with his son a little longer, adding that if she would do so, he would give her a bag of gold Bonnet Pieces.

So Katherine agreed readily, and that night she watched by the Prince as she had done the night before. And at twelve o'clock he rose and dressed himself, and rode to the Fairy Knowe, just as she had expected him to do, for she was quite certain that the poor young man was bewitched, and not suffering from a fever, as everyone thought he was.

And you may be sure that she accompanied him, riding behind him all unnoticed, and filling her pockets with nuts as she rode.

When they reached the Fairy Knowe, he spoke the same words that he had spoken the night before. "Open, open, Green Hill, and let the young Prince in with his horse and his hound." And when the Green Hill opened, Katherine added softly, "And his lady behind him." So they all passed in together.

Katherine seated herself on a stone, and looked around her. The same revels were going on as yesternight, and the Prince was soon in the thick of them, dancing and laughing madly. The girl watched him narrowly, wondering if she would ever be able to find out what would restore him to his right mind, and, as she was watching him, the same little bairn who had played with the magic wand came up to her again. Only this time he was playing with a little bird.

And as he played, one of the dancers passed by, and, turning to her partner, said lightly, "Three bites of that birdie would lift the Prince's sickness, and make him as well as he ever was." Then she joined in the dance again, leaving Katherine sitting upright on her stone quivering with excitement.

If only she could get that bird the Prince might be cured! Very carefully she began to shake some nuts out of her pocket, and roll them across the floor towards the child.

He picked them up eagerly, letting go the bird as he did so, and, in an instant, Katherine caught it, and hid it under her apron.

In no long time after that the cock crew, and the Prince and she set out on their homeward ride. But this morning, instead of cracking nuts, she killed and plucked the bird, scattering its feathers all along the road, and the instant she gained the Prince's room, and had seen him safely into bed, she put it on a spit in front of the fire and began to roast it.

And soon it began to frizzle, and get brown, and smell deliciously, and the Prince, in his bed in the corner, opened his eyes and murmured faintly, "How I wish I had a bite of that birdie."

When she heard the words Katherine's heart jumped for joy, and as soon as the bird was roasted she cut a little piece from its breast and popped it into the Prince's mouth.

When he had eaten it his strength seemed to come back somewhat, for he rose on his elbow and looked at his nurse. "Oh! if I had but another bite of that birdie!" he said. And his voice was certainly stronger.

So Katherine gave him another piece, and when he had eaten that he sat right up in bed.

"Oh! if I had but a third bite o' that birdie!" he cried. And now the colour was coming back into his face, and his eyes were shining.

This time Katherine brought him the whole of the rest of the bird, and he ate it up greedily, picking the bones quite clean with his fingers, and when it was finished, he sprang out of bed and dressed himself, and sat down by the fire.

And when the King came in the morning, with his old housekeeper at his back, to see how the Prince was, he found him sitting cracking nuts with his nurse, for Katherine had brought home quite a lot in her apron pocket.

The King was so delighted to find his son cured that he gave all the credit to Katherine Crackernuts, as he called her, and he gave orders at once that the Prince should marry her. "For," he said, "a maiden who is such a good nurse is sure to make a good Queen."

The Prince was quite willing to do as his father bade him, and, while they were talking together, his younger brother came in, leading Princess Velvet-Cheek by the hand, whose acquaintance he had made but yesterday, declaring that he had fallen in love with her, and that he wanted to marry her immediately.

So it all fell out very well, and everybody was quite pleased, and the two weddings took place at once, and, unless they be dead sinsyne, the young couples are living yet.

Michael Scott

The tale of Michael Scott, adapted from an anonymous source and included in Folk-lore and Legends: Scotland (W. W. Gibbings, London, 1889), recounts the exploits of one of Scotland's most enduring semi-historical figures of legend. Michael Scott of Balwearie, a real thirteenth-century scholar and astrologer, became in folklore a powerful wizard whose command over nature, spirits, and even the Devil himself marked him as both revered and feared.

The story reflects the uneasy respect with which medieval Scotland viewed scholars who blurred the line between science and sorcery. While Michael Scott's cunning and erudition bring him great renown, they also isolate him from ordinary people, who whisper that he built bridges in a single night and split mountains with a spell. His legend survives as a cautionary fable about intellect untempered by humility, and about the danger of seeking dominion over mysteries meant to remain unknown.

In the early part of Michael Scott's life he was in the habit of emigrating annually to the Scottish metropolis, for the purpose of being employed in his capacity of mason. One time as he and two companions were journeying to the place of their destination for a similar object, they had occasion to pass over a high hill, the name of which is not mentioned, but which is supposed to have been one of the Grampians, and being fatigued with climbing, they sat down to rest themselves. They had no sooner done so than they were warned to take to their heels by the hissing of a large serpent, which they observed revolving itself towards them with great velocity. Terrified at the sight, Michael's two companions fled, while he, on the contrary, resolved to encounter the reptile. The appalling monster approached Michael Scott with distended mouth and forked tongue, and, throwing itself into a coil at his feet, was raising its head to inflict a mortal sting, when Michael, with one stroke of his stick, severed its body into three pieces. Having re-joined his affrighted comrades, they resumed their journey, and, on arriving at the next public-house, it being late, and the travellers being weary, they took up their quarters at it for the night. In the course of the night's conversation, reference was naturally made to Michael's recent exploit with the serpent, when the landlady of the house, who was remarkable for her "arts," happened to be present. Her curiosity appeared much excited by the conversation, and, after making some inquiries regarding the colour of the serpent, which she was told was white, she offered any of them that would procure her the middle piece such a tempting reward, as induced one of the party instantly to go for it. The distance was not very great, and on reaching the spot, he found the middle and tail piece in the place where Michael left them, but the head piece was gone.

The landlady on receiving the piece, which still vibrated with life, seemed highly gratified at her acquisition, and over and above the promised reward, regaled her lodgers very plentifully with the choicest dainties in her house. Fired with curiosity to know the purpose for which the serpent was intended, the wily Michael Scott was immediately seized with a severe fit of indisposition, which caused him to prefer the request that he might be allowed to sleep beside the fire, the warmth of which, he affirmed, was in the highest degree beneficial to him.

Never suspecting Michael Scott's hypocrisy, and naturally supposing that a person so severely indisposed would feel very little curiosity about the contents of any cooking utensils which might lie around the fire, the landlady allowed his request. As soon as the other inmates of the house were retired to bed, the landlady resorted to her darling occupation, and, in his feigned state of indisposition, Michael had a favourable opportunity of watching most scrupulously all her actions through the keyhole of a door leading to the next apartment where she was. He could see the rites and ceremonies with which the serpent was put into the oven, along with many mysterious ingredients. After which the unsuspicious landlady placed the dish by the fireside, where lay the distressed traveller, to stove till the morning.

Once or twice in the course of the night the "wife of the change-house," under the pretence of inquiring for her sick lodger, and administering to him some renovating cordials, the beneficial effects of which he gratefully acknowledged, took occasion to dip her finger in her saucepan, upon which the cock, perched on his roost, crowed aloud. All Michael's sickness could not prevent him considering very inquisitively the landlady's cantrips, and particularly the influence of the sauce upon the crowing of the cock. Nor could he dissipate some inward desires he felt to follow her example. At the same time, he suspected that Satan had a hand in the pie, yet he thought he would like very much to be at the bottom of the concern, and thus his reason and his curiosity clashed against each other for the space of several hours. At length passion, as is too often the case, became the conqueror. Michael, too, dipped his finger in the sauce, and applied it to the tip of his tongue, and immediately the cock perched on the spardan announced the circumstance in a mournful clarion. Instantly his mind received a new light to which he was formerly a stranger, and the astonished dupe of a landlady now found it her interest to admit her sagacious lodger into a knowledge of the remainder of her secrets.

Endowed with the knowledge of "good and evil," and all the "second sights" that can be acquired, Michael left his lodgings in the morning, with the philosopher's stone in his pocket. By daily perfecting his supernatural attainments, by new series of discoveries, he became more than a match for Satan himself. Having seduced some thousands of Satan's best workmen into his employment, he trained them up so successfully to the architective business, and inspired them with such industrious habits, that he was more than sufficient for all the architectural work of the empire. To establish this assertion, we need only refer to some remains of his workmanship still existing north of the Grampians, some of them, stupendous bridges built by him in one short night, with no other visible agents than two or three workmen.

On one occasion work was getting scarce, as might have been naturally expected, and his workmen, as they were wont, flocked to his doors, perpetually exclaiming, "Work! work! work!" Continually annoyed by their incessant entreaties, he called out to them in derision to go and make a dry road from Fortrose to Arderseir, over the Moray Firth. Immediately their cry ceased, and as Scott supposed it wholly impossible for them to execute his order, he retired to rest, laughing most heartily at the chimerical sort of employment he had given to his industrious workmen. Early in the morning, however, he got up and took a walk at the break of day down to the shore to divert himself at the fruitless labours of his zealous workmen. But on reaching the spot, what was his astonishment to find the formidable piece of work allotted to them only a few hours before already nearly finished. Seeing the great damage the commercial class of the community would sustain from the operation, he ordered the workmen to demolish the most part of their work; leaving, however, the point of Fortrose to show the traveller to this day the wonderful exploit of Michael Scott's fairies.

On being thus again thrown out of employment, their former clamour was resumed, nor could Michael Scott, with all his sagacity, devise a plan to keep them in innocent employment. He at length discovered one. "Go," says he, "and manufacture me ropes that will carry me to the back of the moon, of these materials - miller's-sudds and sea-sand." Michael Scott here obtained rest from his active operators; for, when other work failed them, he always despatched them to their rope manufactory. But though these agents could never make proper ropes of those materials, their efforts to that effect are far from being contemptible, for some of their ropes are seen by the sea-side to this day.

We shall close our notice of Michael Scott by reciting one anecdote of him in the latter part of his life.

In consequence of a violent quarrel which Michael Scott once had with a person whom he conceived to have caused him some injury, he resolved, as the highest punishment he could inflict upon him, to send his adversary to that evil place designed only for Satan and his black companions. He accordingly, by means of his supernatural machinations, sent the poor unfortunate man thither, and had he been sent by any other means than those of Michael Scott, he would no doubt have met with a warm reception. Out of pure spite to Michael, however, when Satan learned who was his billet-master, he would no more receive him than he would receive the Wife of Beth, and instead of treating the unfortunate man with the harshness characteristic of him, he showed him considerable civilities. Introducing him to his "Ben Taigh," he directed her to show the stranger any curiosities he might wish to see, hinting very significantly that he had provided some accommodation for their mutual friend, Michael Scott, the sight of which might afford him some gratification. The polite housekeeper accordingly conducted the stranger through the principal apartments in the house, where he saw fearful sights.

But the bed of Michael Scott! - his greatest enemy could not but feel satiated with revenge at the sight of it. It was a place too horrid to be described, filled promiscuously with all the awful brutes imaginable. Toads and lions, lizards and leeches, and, amongst the rest, not the least conspicuous, a large serpent gaping for Michael Scott, with its mouth wide open. This last sight having satisfied the stranger's curiosity, he was led to the outer gate, and came away. He reached his friends, and, among other pieces of news touching his travels, he was not backward in relating the entertainment that awaited his friend Michael Scott, as soon as he would "stretch his foot" for the other world.

But Michael did not at all appear disconcerted at his friend's intelligence. He affirmed that he would disappoint all his enemies in their expectations - in proof of which he gave the following signs, "When I am just dead," says he, "open my breast and extract my heart. Carry it to some place where the public may see the result. You will then transfix it upon a long pole, and if Satan will have my soul, he will come in the likeness of a black raven and carry it off, and if my soul will be saved it will be carried off by a white dove."

His friends obeyed his instructions. Having exhibited his heart in the manner directed, a large black raven was observed to come from the east with great fleetness, while a white dove came from the west with equal velocity. The raven made a furious dash at the heart, missing which, it was unable to curb its force, till it was considerably past it, and the dove, reaching the spot at the same time, carried off the heart amidst the rejoicing and ejaculations of the spectators.

Peerifool

Peerifool, as retold by Elizabeth Wilson Grierson in The Scottish Fairy Book (J. B. Lippincott Company, 1910), is a Shetland tale of wit triumphing over malice, told in the brisk, matter-of-fact tone common to northern folktales. It centres on Peerifool, a small and seemingly foolish girl whose name itself means "little fool."

The story reflects both the harshness and the humour of Shetland folk tradition: the ever-present tension between human vulnerability and the sly, uncanny world that shadows it. Beneath its playful tone lies a moral about underestimated strength, how patience, humility, and apparent simplicity can outwit brute force and glamour.

There was once a king and a Queen in Rousay who had three daughters. When the young Princesses were just grown up, the King died, and the Crown passed to a distant cousin, who had always hated him, and who paid no heed to the widowed Queen and her daughters.

So they were left very badly off, and they went to live in a tiny cottage, and did all the housework themselves. They had a kailyard in front of the cottage, and a little field behind it, and they had a cow that grazed in the field, and which they fed with the cabbages that grew in the kailyard. For everyone knows that to feed cows with cabbages makes them give a larger quantity of milk.

But they soon discovered that someone was coming at night and stealing the cabbages, and, of course, this annoyed them very much. For they knew that if they had not cabbages to give to the cow, they would not have enough milk to sell.

So the eldest Princess she said would take out a three-legged stool, and wrap herself in a blanket, and sit in the kailyard all night to see if she could catch the thief. And, although it was very cold and very dark, she did so.

At first it seemed as if all her trouble would be in vain, for hour after hour passed and nothing happened. But in the small hours of the morning, just as the clock was striking two, she heard a stealthy trampling in the field behind, as if some very heavy person were trying to tread very softly, and presently a mighty Giant stepped right over the wall into the kailyard.

He carried an enormous creel on his arm, and a large, sharp knife in his hand, and he began to cut the cabbages, and to throw them into the creel as fast as he could.

Now the Princess was no coward, so, although she had not expected to face a Giant, she gathered up her courage, and cried out sharply, "Who gave you liberty to cut our cabbages? Leave off this minute, and go away."

The Giant paid no heed, but went on steadily with what he was doing.

"Do you not hear me?" cried the girl indignantly, for she was the Princess Royal and had always been accustomed to being obeyed.

"If you be not quiet I will take you too," said the Giant grimly, pressing the cabbages down into the creel.

"I should like to see you try," retorted the Princess, rising from her stool and stamping her foot, for she felt so angry that she forgot for a moment that she was only a weak maiden and he was a great and powerful Giant.

And, as if to show her how strong he was, he seized her by her arm and her leg, and put her in his creel on the top of the cabbages, and carried her away bodily.

When he reached his home, which was in a great square house on a lonely moor, he took her out, and set her down roughly on the floor.

"You will be my servant now," he said, "and keep my house, and do my errands for me. I have a cow, which you must drive out every day to the hillside, and see, here is a bag of wool, when you have taken out the cow, you must come back and settle yourself at home, as a good housewife should, and comb, and card it, and spin it into yarn, with which to weave a good thick cloth for my raiment. I am out most of the day, but when I come home I shall expect to find all this done, and a great bicker of porridge boiled besides for my supper."

The poor Princess was very dismayed when she heard these words, for she had never been accustomed to work hard, and she had always had her sisters to help her, but the Giant took no notice of her distress, but went out as soon as it was daylight, leaving her alone in the house to begin her work.

As soon as he had gone she drove the cow to the pasture, as he had told her to do, but she had a good long walk over the moor before she reached the hill, and by the time that she got back to the house she felt very tired.

So she thought that she would put on the porridge pot, and make herself some porridge before she began to card and comb the wool.

She did so, and just as she was sitting down to sup them the door opened, and a crowd of wee, wee Peerie Folk came in.

They were the tiniest men and women that the Princess had ever seen; not one of them would have reached halfway to her knee, and they were dressed in dresses fashioned out of all the colours of the rainbow - scarlet and blue, green and yellow, orange and violet, and the funny thing was, that every one of them had a shock of straw-coloured yellow hair.

They were all talking and laughing with one another, and they hopped up, first on stools, then on chairs, till they reached the top of the table, where they clustered round the bowl, out of which the Princess was eating her porridge.

"We be hungry, we be hungry," they cried, in their tiny shrill voices. "Spare a little porridge for the Peerie Folk."

But the Princess was hungry also, and besides being hungry, she was both tired and cross; so she shook her head and waved them impatiently away with her spoon.

"Little for one, and less for two, and never a grain have I for you", she said sharply, and, to her great delight, for she did not feel quite comfortable with all the Peerie Folk standing on the table looking at her, they vanished in a moment.

After this she finished her porridge in peace; then she took the wool out of the bag, and she set to work to comb and card it. But it seemed as if it were bewitched; it curled and twisted and coiled itself round her fingers so that, try as she would, she could not do anything with it. And when the Giant came home he found her sitting in despair with everything in confusion round her, and the porridge, which she had left for him in the pot, burned to a cinder.

As you may imagine, he was very angry, and raged, and stamped, and used the most dreadful words, and he took her by the heels, and beat her until all her back was skinned and bleeding; then he carried her out to the byre, and threw her up on the joists among the hens. And, although she was not dead, she was so stunned and bruised that she could only lie there motionless, looking down on the backs of the cows.

Time went on, and in the kailyard at home the cabbages were disappearing as fast as ever. So the second Princess said that she would do as her sister had done, and wrap herself in a blanket, and go and sit on a three-legged stool all night, to see what was becoming of them.

She did so, and exactly the same fate befell her that had befallen her elder sister. The Giant appeared with his creel, and he carried her off, and set her to mind the cow and the house, and to make his porridge and to spin, and the little yellow-headed Peerie Folk appeared and asked her for some supper, and she refused to give it to them, and after that, she could not comb or card her wool, and the Giant was angry, and he scolded her, and beat her, and threw her up, half dead, on the joists beside her sister and the hens.

Then the youngest Princess determined to sit out in the kailyard all night, not so much to see what was becoming of the cabbages, as to discover what had happened to her sisters.

And when the Giant came and carried her off, she was not at all sorry, but very glad, for she was a brave and loving little maiden, and now she felt that she had a chance of finding out where they were, and whether they were dead or alive.

So she was quite cheerful and happy, for she felt certain that she was clever enough to outwit the Giant, if only she were watchful and patient; so she lay quite quietly in her creel above the cabbages, but she kept her eyes very wide open to see by which road he was carrying her off.

And when he set her down in his kitchen, and told her all that he expected her to do, she did not look downcast like her sisters, but nodded her head brightly, and said that she felt sure that she could do it.

And she sang to herself as she drove the cow over the moor to pasture, and she ran the whole way back, so that she should have a good long afternoon to work at the wool, and, although she would not have told the Giant this, to search the house.

Before she set to work, however, she made herself some porridge, just as her sisters had done, and, just as she was going to sup them, all the little yellow-haired Peerie Folk trooped in, and climbed up on the table, and stood and stared at her.

"We be hungry, we be hungry," they cried. "Spare a little porridge for the Peerie Folk."

"With all my heart," replied the good-natured Princess. "If you can find dishes little enough for you to sup out of, I will fill them for you. But methinks, if I were to give you all porringers, you would smother yourselves among the porridge."

At her words the Peerie Folk shouted with laughter, till their straw-coloured hair tumbled right over their faces; then they hopped on to the floor and ran out of the house, and presently they came trooping back holding cups of blue-bells, and foxgloves, and saucers of primroses and anemones in their hands, and the Princess put a tiny spoonful of porridge into each saucer, and a tiny drop of milk into each cup, and they ate it all up as daintily as possible with neat little grass spoons, which they had brought with them in their pockets.

When they had finished they all cried out, "Thank you! Thank you!" and ran out of the kitchen again, leaving the Princess alone. And being alone, she went all over the house to look for her sisters, but, of course, she could not find them.

"Never mind, I will find them soon," she said to herself. "To-morrow I will search the byre and the outhouses; in the meantime, I had better get on with my work." So she went back to the kitchen, and took out the bag of wool, which the Giant had told her to make into cloth.

But just as she was doing so the door opened once more, and a Yellow-Haired Peerie Boy entered. He was exactly like the other Peerie Folk who had eaten the Princess's porridge, only he was bigger, and he wore a very rich dress of grass-green velvet. He walked boldly into the middle of the kitchen and looked round him.

"Hast you any work for me to do?" he asked. "I ken grand how to handle wool and turn it into fine thick cloth."

"I have plenty of work for anybody who asks it," replied the Princess, "but I have no money to pay for it, and there are but few folk in this world who will work without wages."

"All the wages that I ask is that you will take the trouble to find out my name, for few folk ken it, and few folk care to ken. But if by any chance you cannot find it out, then must you pay toll of half of your cloth."

The Princess thought that it would be quite an easy thing to find out the Boy's name, so she agreed to the bargain, and, putting all the wool back into the bag, she gave it to him, and he swung it over his shoulder and departed.

She ran to the door to see where he went, for she had made up her mind that she would follow him secretly to his home, and find out from the neighbours what his name was.

But, to her great dismay, though she looked this way and that, he had vanished completely, and she began to wonder what she should do if the Giant came back and found that she had allowed someone, whose name she did not even know, to carry off all the wool.

And, as the afternoon wore on, and she could think of no way of finding out who the boy was, or where he came from, she felt that she had made a great mistake, and she began to grow very frightened.

Just as the gloaming was beginning to fall a knock came at the door, and, when she opened it, she found an old woman standing outside, who begged for a night's lodging.

Now, as I have told you, the Princess was very kind-hearted, and she would fain have granted the poor old Dame's request, but she dared not, for she did not know what the Giant would say. So she told the old woman that she could not take her in for the night, as she was only a servant, and not the mistress of the house, but she made her sit down on a bench beside the door, and brought her out some bread and milk, and gave her some water to bathe her poor, tired feet.

She was so bonnie, and gentle, and kind, and she looked so sorry when she told her that she would need to turn her away, that the old woman gave her blessing, and told her not to vex herself, as it was a fine, dry night, and now that she had had a meal she could easily sit down somewhere and sleep in the shelter of the outhouses.

And, when she had finished her bread and milk, she went and laid down by the side of a green knowe, which rose out of the moor not very far from the byre door.

And, strange to say, as she lay there she felt the earth beneath her getting warmer and warmer, until she was so hot that she was fain to crawl up the side of the hillock, in the hope of getting a mouthful of fresh air.

And as she got near the top she heard a voice, which seemed to come from somewhere beneath her, saying, "TEASE, TEASENS, TEASE; CARD, CARDENS, CARD; SPIN, SPINNENS, SPIN, for PEERIFOOL PEERIFOOL, PEERIFOOL is what men call me." And when she got to the very top, she found that there was a crack in the earth, through which rays of light were coming, and when she put her eye to the crack, what should she see down below her but a brilliantly lighted chamber, in which all the Peerie Folk were sitting in a circle, working away as hard as they could.

Some of them were carding wool, some of them were combing it, some of them were spinning it, constantly wetting their fingers with their lips, in order to twist the yarn fine as they drew it from the distaff, and some of them were spinning the yarn into cloth.

While round and round the circle, cracking a little whip, and urging them to work faster, was a Yellow-Haired Peerie Boy.

"This is a strange thing, and these be queer on-goings," said the old woman to herself, creeping hastily down to the bottom of the hillock again. "I must even go and tell the bonnie lassie in the house yonder. Maybe the knowledge of what I have seen will stand her in good stead someday. When there be Peerie Folk about, it is well to be on one's guard."

So she went back to the house and told the Princess all that she had seen and heard, and the Princess was so delighted with what she had told her that she risked the Giant's wrath and allowed her to go and sleep in the hayloft.

It was not very long after the old woman had gone to rest before the door opened, and the Peerie Boy appeared once more with a number of webs of cloth upon his shoulder. "Here is your cloth," he said, with a sly smile, "and I will put it on the shelf for you the moment that you tell me what my name is."

Then the Princess, who was a merry maiden, thought that she would tease the little follow for a time before she let him know that she had found out his secret.

So she mentioned first one name and then another, always pretending to think that she had hit upon the right one, and all the time the Peerie Boy jumped from side to side with delight, for he thought that she would never find out the right name, and that half of the cloth would be his.

But the Princess grew tired of joking, and she cried out, with a little laugh of triumph, "Do you by any chance ken anyone called PEERIFOOL, little Mannikin?"

Then he knew that in some way she had found out what men called him, and he was so angry and disappointed that he flung the webs of cloth down in a heap on the floor, and ran out at the door, slamming it behind him.

Meanwhile the Giant was coming down the hill in the darkening, and, to his astonishment, he met a troop of little Peerie Folk toiling up it, looking as if they were so tired that they could hardly get along. Their eyes were dim and listless, their heads were hanging on their breasts, and their lips were so long and twisted that the poor little people looked quite hideous.

The Giant asked how this was, and they told him that they had to work so hard all day, spinning for their Master that they were quite exhausted, and that the reason why their lips were so distorted was that they used them constantly to wet their fingers, so that they might pull the wool in very fine strands from the distaff.

"I always thought a great deal of women who could spin," said the Giant, "and I looked out for a housewife that could do so. But after this I will be more careful, for the housewife that I have now is a bonnie little woman, and I would be loath to have her spoil her face in that manner."

And he hurried home in a great state of mind in case he should find that his new servant's pretty red lips had grown long and ugly in his absence.

Great was his relief to see her standing by the table, bonnie and winsome as ever, with all the webs of cloth in a pile in front of her.

"By my troth, you are an industrious maiden," he said, in high good humour, "and, as a reward for working so diligently, I will restore your sisters to you." And he went out to the byre, and lifted the two other Princesses down from the rafters, and brought them in and laid them on the settle.

Their little sister nearly screamed aloud when she saw how ill they looked and how bruised their backs were, but, like a prudent maiden, she held her tongue, and busied herself with applying a cooling ointment to their wounds, and binding them up, and by and by her sisters revived, and, after the Giant had gone to bed, they told her all that had befallen them.

"I will be avenged on him for his cruelty," said the little Princess firmly, and when she spoke like that her sisters knew that she meant what she said.

So next morning, before the Giant was up, she fetched his creel, and put her eldest sister into it, and covered her with all the fine silken hangings and tapestry that she could find, and on the top of all she put a handful of grass, and when the Giant came downstairs she asked him, in her sweetest tone, if he would do her a favour. And the Giant, who was very pleased with her because of the quantity of cloth which he thought she had spun, said that he would.

"Then carry that creelful of grass home to my mother's cottage for her cow to eat," said the Princess. "Twill help to make up for all the cabbages which you have stolen from her kailyard."

And, wonderful to relate, the Giant did as he was bid, and carried the creel to the cottage.

Next morning she put her second sister into another creel, and covered her with all the fine napery she could find in the house, and put an armful of grass on the top of it, and at her bidding the Giant, who was really getting very fond of her, carried it also home to her mother.

The next morning the little Princess told him that she thought that she would go for a long walk after she had done her housework, and that she might not be in when he came home at night, but that she would have another creel of grass ready for him if he would carry it to the cottage as he had done on the two previous evenings. He promised to do so; then, as usual, he went out for the day.

In the afternoon the clever little maiden went through the house, gathering together all the lace, and silver, and jewellery that she could find, and brought them and placed them beside the creel. Then she went out and cut an armful of grass, and brought it in and laid it beside them.

Then she crept into the creel herself, and pulled all the fine things in above her, and then she covered everything up with the grass, which was a very difficult thing to do, seeing she herself was at the bottom of the basket. Then she lay quite still and waited.

Presently the Giant came in, and, obedient to his promise, he lifted the creel and carried it off to the old Queen's cottage. No one seemed to be at home, so he set it down in the entry, and turned to go away. But the little Princess had told her sisters what to do, and they had a great can of boiling water ready in one of the rooms upstairs, and when they heard his steps coming round that side of the house, they threw open the window and emptied it all over his head, and that was the end of him.

Pinkel the Thief

Pinkel the Thief is a lively Hebridean folktale first collected by the Scottish folklorist John Francis Campbell in Popular Tales of the West Highlands (1860–62) and later adapted by Andrew Lang for The Orange Fairy Book in 1906. It tells of Pinkel, the youngest of seven sons of a poor man, whose quick wit and daring make him a classic trickster hero.

Lang's version, adapted from Campbell's Scots Gaelic source, smooths the oral rhythms of the original while keeping its earthy humour and brisk pace. The tale's roots in Gaelic storytelling are evident in its celebration of cleverness over strength and its wry awareness of social class, the poor man's son triumphing through cunning rather than noble birth. Like many Highland tales, it balances danger with comedy, and ends with poetic justice:

Long, long ago there lived a widow who had three sons. The two eldest were grown up, and though they were known to be idle fellows, some of the neighbours had given them work to do on account of the respect in which their mother was held. But at the time this story begins they had both been so careless and idle that their masters declared they would keep them no longer.

So home they went to their mother and youngest brother, of whom they thought little, because he made himself useful about the house, and looked after the hens, and milked the cow. 'Pinkel,' they called him in scorn, and by-and-by 'Pinkel' became his name throughout the village.

The two young men thought it was much nicer to live at home and be idle than to be obliged to do a quantity of disagreeable things they did not like, and they would have stayed by the fire till the end of their lives had not the widow lost patience with them and said that since they would not look for work at home they must seek it elsewhere, for she would not have them under her roof any longer. But she repented bitterly of her words when Pinkel told her that he too was old enough to go out into the world, and that when he had made a fortune he would send for his mother to keep house for him.

The widow wept many tears at parting from her youngest son, but as she saw that his heart was set upon going with his brothers, she did not try to keep him. So the young men started off one morning in high spirits, never doubting that work such as they might be willing to do would be had for the asking, as soon as their little store of money was spent.

But a very few days of wandering opened their eyes. Nobody seemed to want them, or, if they did, the young men declared that they were not able to undertake all that the farmers or millers or woodcutters required of them. The youngest brother, who was wiser, would gladly have done some of the work that the others refused, but he was small and slight, and no one thought of offering him any. Therefore they went from one place to another, living only on the fruit and nuts they could find in the woods, and getting hungrier every day.

One night, after they had been walking for many hours and were very tired, they came to a large lake with an island in the middle of it. From the island streamed a strong light, by which they could see everything almost as clearly as if the sun had been shining, and they perceived that, lying half hidden in the rushes, was a boat.

'Let us take it and row over to the island, where there must be a house,' said the eldest brother, 'and perhaps they will give us food and shelter.' And they all got in and rowed across in the direction of the light. As they drew near the island they saw that it came from a golden lantern hanging over the door of a hut, while sweet tinkling music proceeded from some bells attached to the golden horns of a goat which was feeding near the cottage. The young men's hearts rejoiced as they thought that they would be able to rest their weary limbs, and they entered the hut, but were amazed to see an ugly old woman inside, wrapped in a cloak of gold which lighted up the whole house. They looked at each other uneasily as she came forward with her daughter, as they knew by the cloak that this was a famous witch.

'What do you want?' asked she, at the same time signing to her daughter to stir the large pot on the fire.

'We are tired and hungry, and would fain have shelter for the night,' answered the eldest brother.

'You cannot get it here,' said the witch, 'but you will find both food and shelter in the palace on the other side of the lake. Take your boat and go, but leave this boy with me - I can find work for him, though something tells me he is quick and cunning, and will do me ill.'

'What harm can a poor boy like me do a great Troll like you?' answered Pinkel. 'Let me go, I pray you, with my brothers. I will promise never to hurt you.' And the witch let him go, and he followed his brothers to the boat.

The way was further than they thought, and it was morning before they reached the palace.

Now, , their luck seemed to have turned, for while the two eldest were given places in the king's stables, Pinkel was taken as page to the little prince. He was a clever and amusing boy, who saw everything that passed under his eyes, and the king noticed this, and often employed him in his own service, which made his brothers very jealous.

Things went on this way for some time, and Pinkel every day rose in the royal favour. At length the envy of his brothers became so great that they could bear it no longer, and consulted together how best they might ruin his credit with the king. They did not wish to kill him - though, perhaps, they would not have been sorry if they had heard he was dead - but merely wished to remind him that he was after all only a child, not half so old and wise as they.

Their opportunity soon came. It happened to be the king's custom to visit his stables once a week, so that he might see that his horses were being properly cared for. The next time he entered the stables the two brothers managed to be in the way, and when the king praised the beautiful satin skins of the horses under their charge, and remarked how different was their condition when his grooms had first come across the lake, the young men at once began to speak of the wonderful light which sprang from the lantern over the hut. The king, who had a passion for collection all the rarest things he could find, fell into the trap directly, and inquired where he could get this marvellous lantern.

'Send Pinkel for it, Sire,' said they. 'It belongs to an old witch, who no doubt came by it in some evil way. But Pinkel has a smooth tongue, and he can get the better of any woman, old or young.'

'Then bid him go this very night,' cried the king, 'and if he brings me the lantern I will make him one of the chief men about my person.'

Pinkel was much pleased at the thought of his adventure, and without more ado he borrowed a little boat which lay moored to the shore, and rowed over to the island at once. It was late by the time he arrived, and almost dark, but he knew by the savoury smell that reached him that the witch was cooking her supper. So he climbed softly on to the roof, and, peering, watched till the old woman's back was turned, when he quickly drew a handful of salt from his pocket and threw it into the pot. Scarcely had he done this when the witch called her daughter and bade her lift the pot off the fire and put the stew into a dish, as it had been cooking quite long enough and she was hungry. But no sooner had she tasted it than she put her spoon down, and declared that her daughter must have been meddling with it, for it was impossible to eat anything that was all made of salt.

'Go down to the spring in the valley, and get some fresh water, that I may prepare a fresh supper,' cried she, 'for I feel half-starved.'

'But, mother,' answered the girl, 'how can I find the well in this darkness? For you know that the lantern's rays shed no light down there.'

'Well, then, take the lantern with you,' answered the witch, 'for supper I must have, and there is no water that is nearer.'

So the girl took her pail in one hand and the golden lantern in the other, and hastened away to the well, followed by Pinkel, who took care to keep out of the way of the rays. When she stooped to fill her pail at the well Pinkel pushed her into it, and snatching up the lantern hurried back to his boat and rowed off from the shore.

He was already a long distance from the island when the witch, who wondered what had become of her daughter, went to the door to look for her. Close around the hut was thick darkness, but what was that bobbing light that streamed across the water? The witch's heart sank as all at once it flashed upon her what had happened.

'Is that you, Pinkel?' cried she, and the youth answered:

'Yes, dear mother, it is I!'

'And are you not a knave for robbing me?' she said.

'Truly, dear mother, I am,' replied Pinkel, rowing faster than ever, for he was half afraid that the witch might come after him. But she had no power on the water, and turned angrily into the hut, muttering to herself all the while:

'Take care! take care! A second time you will not escape so easily!'

The sun had not yet risen when Pinkel returned to the palace, and, entering the king's chamber, he held up the lantern so that its rays might fall upon the bed. In an instant the king awoke, and seeing the golden lantern shedding its light upon him, he sprang up, and embraced Pinkel with joy.

'O cunning one,' cried he, 'what treasure have you brought me!' And calling for his attendants he ordered that rooms next his own should be prepared for Pinkel, and that the youth might enter his presence at any hour. And besides this, he was to have a seat on the council.

It may easily be guessed that all this made the brothers more envious than they were before, and they cast about in their minds afresh how best they might destroy him. At length they remembered the goat with golden horns and the bells, and they rejoiced, 'For,' said they, 'THIS time the old woman will be on the watch, and let him be as clever as he likes, the bells on the horns are sure to warn her.' So when, as before, the king came down to the stables and praised the cleverness of their brother, the young men told him of that other marvel possessed by the witch, the goat with the golden horns.

From this moment the king never closed his eyes at night for longing after this wonderful creature. He understood something of the danger that there might be in trying to steal it, now that the witch's suspicions were aroused, and he spent hours in making plans for outwitting her. But somehow he never could think of anything that would do, and , as the brothers had foreseen, he sent for Pinkel.

'I hear,' he said, 'that the old witch on the island has a goat with golden horns from which hang bells that tinkle the sweetest music. That goat I must have! But tell me, how am I to get it? I would give the third part of my kingdom to anyone who would bring it to me.'

'I will fetch it myself,' answered Pinkel.

This time it was easier for Pinkel to approach the island unseen, as there was no golden lantern to thrown its beams over the water. But, on the other hand, the goat slept inside the hut, and would therefore have to be taken from under the very eyes of the old woman. How was he to do it? All the way across the lake he thought and thought, till at length a plan came into his head which seemed as if it might do, though he knew it would be very difficult to carry out.

The first thing he did when he reached the shore was to look about for a piece of wood, and when he had found it he hid himself close to the hut, till it grew quite dark and near the hour when the witch and her daughter went to bed. Then he crept up and fixed the wood under the door, which opened outwards, in such a manner that the more you tried to shut it the more firmly it stuck. And this was what happened when the girl went as usual to bolt the door and make all fast for the night.

'What are you doing?' asked the witch, as her daughter kept tugging at the handle.

'There is something the matter with the door; it won't shut,' answered she.

'Well, leave it alone; there is nobody to hurt us,' said the witch, who was very sleepy, and the girl did as she was bid, and went to bed. Very soon they both might have been heard snoring, and Pinkel knew that his time had come. Slipping off his shoes he stole into the hut on tiptoe, and taking from his pocket some food of which the goat was particularly fond, he laid it under his nose. Then, while the animal was eating it, he stuffed each golden bell with wool which he had also brought with him, stopping every minute to listen, lest the witch should awaken, and he should find himself changed into some dreadful bird or beast. But the snoring still continued, and he went on with his work as quickly as he could. When the last bell was done he drew another handful of food out of his pocket, and held it out to the goat, which instantly rose to its feet and followed Pinkel, who backed slowly to the door, and directly he got outside he seized the goat in his arms and ran down to the place where he had moored his boat.

As soon as he had reached the middle of the lake, Pinkel took the wool out of the bells, which began to tinkle loudly. Their sound awoke the witch, who cried out as before:

'Is that you, Pinkel?'

'Yes, dear mother, it is I,' said Pinkel.

'Have you stolen my golden goat?' asked she.

'Yes, dear mother, I have,' answered Pinkel.

'Are you not a knave, Pinkel?'

'Yes, dear mother, I am,' he replied. And the old witch shouted in a rage:

'Ah! beware how you come hither again, for next time you shall not escape me!'

But Pinkel laughed and rowed on.

The king was so delighted with the goat that he always kept it by his side, night and day, and, as he had promised, Pinkel was made ruler over the third part of the kingdom. As may be supposed, the brothers were more furious than ever, and grew quite thin with rage.

'How can we get rid of him?' said one to the other. And at length they remembered the golden cloak.

'He will need to be clever if he is to steal that!' they cried, with a chuckle. And when next the king came to see his horses they began to speak of Pinkel and his marvellous cunning, and how he had contrived to steal the lantern and the goat, which nobody else would have been able to do.

'But as he was there, it is a pity he could not have brought away the golden cloak,' added they.

'The golden cloak! what is that?' asked the king. And the young men described its beauties in such glowing words that the king declared he should never know a day's happiness till he had wrapped the cloak round his own shoulders.

'And' added he, 'the man who brings it to me shall wed my daughter, and shall inherit my throne.'

'None can get it save Pinkel,' said they, for they did not imagine that the witch, after two warnings, could allow their brother to escape a third time. So Pinkel was sent for, and with a glad heart he set out.

He passed many hours inventing first one plan and then another, till he had a scheme ready which he thought might prove successful.

Thrusting a large bag inside his coat, he pushed off from the shore, taking care this time to reach the island in daylight. Having made his boat fast to a tree, he walked up to the hut, hanging his head, and putting on a face that was both sorrowful and ashamed.

'Is that you, Pinkel?' asked the witch when she saw him, her eyes gleaming savagely.

'Yes, dear mother, it is I,' answered Pinkel.

'So you have dared, after all you have done, to put yourself in my power!' cried she. 'Well, you shan't escape me THIS time!' And she took down a large knife and began to sharpen it.'

'Oh! dear mother, spare me!' shrieked Pinkel, falling on his knees, and looking wildly about him.

'Spare you, indeed, you thief! Where are my lantern and my goat? No! not! there is only one fate for robbers!' And she brandished the knife in the air so that it glittered in the firelight.

'Then, if I must die,' said Pinkel, who, by this time, was getting really rather frightened, 'let me at least choose the manner of my death. I am very hungry, for I have had nothing to eat all day. Put some poison, if you like, into the porridge, but at least let me have a good meal before I die.'

'That is not a bad idea,' answered the woman, 'as long as you do die, it is all one to me.' And ladling out a large bowl of porridge, she stirred some poisonous herbs into it, and set about work that had to be done. Then Pinkel hastily poured all the contents of the bowl into his bag, and make a great noise with his spoon, as if he was scraping up the last morsel.

'Poisoned or not, the porridge is excellent. I have eaten it, every scrap; do give me some more,' said Pinkel, turning towards her.

'Well, you have a fine appetite, young man,' answered the witch, 'however, it is the last time you will ever eat it, so I will give you another bowlful.' And rubbing in the poisonous herbs, she poured him out half of what remained, and then went to the window to call her cat.

In an instant Pinkel again emptied the porridge into the bag, and the next minute he rolled on the floor, twisting himself about as if in agony, uttering loud groans the while. Suddenly he grew silent and lay still.

'Ah! I thought a second dose of that poison would be too much for you,' said the witch looking at him. 'I warned you what would happen if you came back. I wish that all thieves were as dead as you! But why does not my lazy girl bring the wood I sent her for, it will soon be too dark for her to find her way? I suppose I must go and search for her. What a trouble girls are!' And she went to the door to watch if there were any signs of her daughter. But nothing could be seen of her, and heavy rain was falling.

'It is no night for my cloak,' she muttered, 'it would be covered with mud by the time I got back.' So she took it off her shoulders and hung it carefully up in a cupboard in the room. After that she put on her clogs and started to seek her daughter. Directly the last sound of the clogs had ceased, Pinkel jumped up and took down the cloak, and rowed off as fast as he could.

He had not gone far when a puff of wind unfolded the cloak, and its brightness shed gleams across the water. The witch, who was just entering the forest, turned round at that moment and saw the golden rays. She forgot all about her daughter, and ran down to the shore, screaming with rage at being outwitted a third time.

'Is that you, Pinkel?' cried she.

'Yes, dear mother, it is I.'

'Have you taken my gold cloak?'

'Yes, dear mother, I have.'

'Are you not a great knave?'

'Yes, truly dear mother, I am.'

And so indeed he was!

But all the same, he carried the cloak to the king's palace, and in return he received the hand of the king's daughter in marriage. People said that it was the bride who ought to have worn the cloak at her wedding feast, but the king was so pleased with it that he would not part from it, and to the end of his life was never seen without it. After his death, Pinkel became king, and let up hope that he gave up his bad and thievish ways, and ruled his subjects well. As for his brothers, he did not punish them, but left them in the stables, where they grumbled all day long.

Rory MacGILLIVRAY

Rory MacGillivray is a traditional Scottish folktale first printed in Folklore and Legends: Scotland (London: W. W. Gibbings, 1889), where the author or original collector is left unnamed, suggesting an oral origin passed down through local Highland storytelling. The tale centres on Rory MacGillivray, a bold and somewhat reckless Highlander whose courage draws him into contact with the supernatural.

As with many Scottish wonder tales, the story balances delight with warning. Rory's encounter reflects the deep folk belief in the dangerous beauty of the Otherworld and the peril of losing oneself to it. The fairies here are not the gentle sprites of later romantic invention but older, wilder beings tied to the land's ancient powers. The moral thread, that human life cannot coexist for long with the timeless realm of the sith, runs through the story's quiet melancholy.

Once upon a time a tenant in the neighbourhood of Cairngorm, in Strathspey, emigrated with his family and cattle to the forest of Glenavon, which is well known to be inhabited by many fairies as well as ghosts. Two of his sons being out late one night in search of some of their sheep which had strayed, had occasion to pass a fairy turret, or dwelling, of very large dimensions, and what was their astonishment on observing streams of the most refulgent light shining forth through innumerable crevices in the rock - crevices which the sharpest eye in the country had never seen before. Curiosity led them towards the turret, when they were charmed by the most exquisite sounds ever emitted by a fiddle-string, which, joined to the sportive mirth and glee accompanying it, reconciled them in a great measure to the scene, although they knew well enough the inhabitants of the nook were fairies. Nay, overpowered by the enchanting jigs played by the fiddler, one of the brothers had even the hardihood to propose that they should pay the occupants of the turret a short visit. To this motion the other brother, fond as he was of dancing, and animated as he was by the music, would by no means consent, and he earnestly desired his brother to restrain his curiosity. But every new jig that was played, and every new reel that was danced, inspired the adventurous brother with additional ardour, and at length, completely fascinated by the enchanting revelry, leaving all prudence behind, at one leap he entered the "Shian." The poor forlorn brother was now left in a most uncomfortable situation. His grief for the loss of a brother whom he dearly loved suggested to him more than once the desperate idea of sharing his fate by following his example. But, on the other hand, when he coolly considered the possibility of sharing very different entertainment from that which rang upon his ears, and remembered, too, the comforts and convenience of his father's fireside, the idea immediately appeared to him anything but prudent. After a long and disagreeable altercation between his affection for his brother and his regard for himself, he came to the resolution to take a middle course, that is, to shout in at the window a few remonstrances to his brother, which, if he did not attend to, let the consequences be upon his own head. Accordingly, taking his station at one of the crevices, and calling upon his brother three several times by name, as use is, he uttered the most moving pieces of elocution he could think of, imploring him, as he valued his poor parents' life and blessing, to come forth and go home with him, Donald MacGillivray, his thrice affectionate and unhappy brother. But whether it was the dancer could not hear this eloquent harangue, or what is more probable, that he did not choose to attend to it, certain it is that it proved totally ineffectual to accomplish its object, and the consequence was that Donald MacGillivray found it equally his duty and his interest to return home to his family with the melancholy tale of poor Rory's fate. All the prescribed ceremonies calculated to rescue him from the fairy dominion were resorted to by his mourning relatives without effect, and Rory was supposed lost forever, when a "wise man" of the day having learned the circumstance, discovered to his friends a plan by which they might deliver him at the end of twelve months from his entry.

"Return," says the Duin Glichd to Donald, "to the place where you lost your brother a year and a day from the time. You will insert in your garment a Rowan Cross, which will protect you from the fairies' interposition. Enter the turret boldly and resolutely in the name of the Highest, claim your brother, and, if he does not accompany you voluntarily, seize him and carry him off by force - none dare interfere with you."

The experiment appeared to the cautious contemplative brother as one that was fraught with no ordinary danger, and he would have most willingly declined the prominent character allotted to him in the performance but for the importunate entreaty of his friends, who implored him, as he valued their blessing, not to slight such excellent advice. Their entreaties, together with his confidence in the virtues of the Rowan Cross, overcame his scruples, and he at length agreed to put the experiment in practice, whatever the result might be.

Well, then, the important day arrived, when the father of the two sons was destined either to recover his lost son, or to lose the only son he had, and, anxious as the father felt, Donald MacGillivray, the intended adventurer, felt no less so on the occasion. The hour of midnight approached when the drama was to be acted, and Donald MacGillivray, loaded with all the charms and benedictions in his country, took mournful leave of his friends, and proceeded to the scene of his intended enterprise. On approaching the well-known turret, a repetition of that mirth and those ravishing sounds, that had been the source of so much sorrow to himself and family, once more attracted his attention, without at all creating in his mind any extraordinary feelings of satisfaction. On the contrary, he abhorred the sounds most heartily, and felt much greater inclination to recede than to advance. But what was to be done? Courage, character, and everything dear to him were at stake, so that to advance was his only alternative. In short, he reached the "Shian," and, after twenty fruitless attempts, he at length entered the place with trembling footsteps, and amidst the brilliant and jovial scene the not least gratifying spectacle which presented itself to Donald was his brother Rory earnestly engaged at the Highland fling on the floor, at which, as might have been expected, he had greatly improved. Without losing much time in satisfying his curiosity by examining the quality of the company, Donald ran to his brother, repeating, most vehemently, the words prescribed to him by the "wise man," seized him by the collar, and insisted on his immediately accompanying him home to his poor afflicted parents. Rory assented, provided he would allow him to finish his single reel, assuring Donald, very earnestly, that he had not been half an hour in the house. In vain did the latter assure him that, instead of half an hour, he had actually remained twelve months. Nor would he have believed his overjoyed friends when his brother at length got him home, did not the calves, now grown into stots, and the new-born babes, now travelling the house, at length convince him that in his single reel he had danced for a twelvemonth and a day.

The Battle of the Birds

The Battle of the Birds is one of the most enduring Gaelic folktales collected by John Francis Campbell in Popular Tales of the West Highlands (1860–62) and later adapted by Andrew Lang for The Lilac Fairy Book (1910). It opens with the strange image of a great battle among the birds and beasts, a moment of mythic confusion that leads to the meeting between a young prince and a wounded raven.

The story then moves into the deep current of Celtic wonder-tales: spells, transformations, quests through unearthly landscapes. It is a tale of loyalty and loss, told in rhythms that echo ancient myth. Campbell's version preserves the Gaelic cadences and moral gravity of oral storytelling, while Lang's 1910 adaptation softens the language and shapes it for Edwardian readers without losing the strangeness at its heart.

There was to be a great battle between all the creatures of the earth and the birds of the air. News of it went abroad, and the son of the king of Tethertown said that when the battle was fought he would be there to see it, and would bring back word who was to be king. But in spite of that, he was almost too late, and every fight had been fought save the last, which was between a snake and a great black raven. Both struck hard, but in the end the snake proved the stronger, and would have twisted himself round the neck of the raven till he died had not the king's son drawn his sword, and cut off the head of the snake at a single blow. And when the raven beheld that his enemy was dead, he was grateful, and said, 'For your kindness to me this day, I will show you a sight. So come up now on the root of my two wings.' The king's son did as he was bid, and before the raven stopped flying, they had passed over seven bens and seven glens and seven mountain moors.

'Do you see that house yonder?' said the raven . 'Go straight for it, for a sister of mine dwells there, and she will make you right welcome. And if she asks, "Wert you at the battle of the birds?" answer that you were, and if she asks, "Did you see my likeness?" answer that you saw it, but be sure you meet me in the morning at this place.'

The king's son followed what the raven told him and that night he had meat of each meat, and drink of each drink, warm water for his feet, and a soft bed to lie in.

Thus it happened the next day, and the next, but on the fourth meeting, instead of meeting the raven, in his place the king's son found waiting for him the handsomest youth that ever was seen, with a bundle in his hand.

'Is there a raven hereabouts?' asked the king's son, and the youth answered:

'I am that raven, and I was delivered by you from the spells that bound me, and in reward you will get this bundle. Go back by the road you came on, and lie as before, a night in each house, but be careful not to unloose the bundle till you are in the place wherein you would most wish to dwell.'

Then the king's son set out, and thus it happened as it had happened before, till he entered a thick wood near his father's house. He had walked a long way and suddenly the bundle seemed to grow heavier; first he put it down under a tree, and next he thought he would look at it.

The string was easy to untie, and the king's son soon unfastened the bundle. What was it he saw there? Why, a great castle with an orchard all about it, and in the orchard fruit and flowers and birds of very kind. It was all ready for him to dwell in, but instead of being in the midst of the forest, he did wish he had left the bundle unloosed till he had reached the green valley close to his father's palace. Well, it was no use wishing, and with a sigh he glanced up, and beheld a huge giant coming towards him.

'Bad is the place where you have built your house, king's son,' said the giant.

'True; it is not here that I wish to be,' answered the king's son.

'What reward will you give me if I put it back in the bundle?' asked the giant.

'What reward do you ask?' answered the king's son.

'The first boy you have when he is seven years old,' said the giant.

'If I have a boy you shalt get him,' answered the king's son, and as he spoke the castle and the orchard were tied up in the bundle again.

'Now take your road, and I will take mine,' said the giant. 'And if you forget your promise, I will remember it.'

Light of heart the king's son went on his road, till he came to the green valley near his father's palace. Slowly he unloosed the bundle, fearing lest he should find nothing but a heap of stones or rags. But no! all was as it had been before, and as he opened the castle door there stood within the most beautiful maiden that ever was seen.

'Enter, king's son,' she said, 'all is ready, and we will be married at once,' and so they were.

The maiden proved a good wife, and the king's son, now himself a king, was so happy that he forgot all about the giant. Seven years and a day had gone by, when one morning, while standing on the ramparts, he beheld the giant striding towards the castle. Then he remembered his promise, and remembered, too, that he had told the queen nothing about it. Now he must tell her, and perhaps she might help him in his trouble.

The queen listened in silence to his tale, and after he had finished, she only said, 'Leave you the matter between me and the giant,' and as she spoke, the giant entered the hall and stood before them.

'Bring out your son,' cried he to the king, 'as you promised me seven years and a day since.'

The king glanced at his wife, who nodded, so he answered:

'Let his mother first put him in order,' and the queen left the hall, and took the cook's son and dressed him in the prince's clothes, and led him up to the giant, who held his hand, and together they went out along the road. They had not walked far when the giant stopped and stretched out a stick to the boy.

'If your father had that stick, what would he do with it?' asked he.

'If my father had that stick, he would beat the dogs and cats that steal the king's meat,' replied the boy.

'You are the cook's son!' cried the giant. 'Go home to your mother', and turning his back he strode straight to the castle.

'If you seek to trick me this time, the highest stone will soon be the lowest,' he said, and the king and queen trembled, but they could not bear to give up their boy.

'The butler's son is the same age as ours,' whispered the queen, 'he will not know the difference,' and she took the child and dressed him in the prince's clothes, and the giant let him away along the road. Before they had gone far he stopped, and held out a stick.

'If your father had that rod, what would he do with it?' asked the giant.

'He would beat the dogs and cats that break the king's glasses,' answered the boy.

'You are the son of the butler!' cried the giant. 'Go home to your mother', and turning round he strode back angrily to the castle.

'Bring out your son at once,' roared he, 'or the stone that is highest will be lowest,' and this time the real prince was brought.

But though his parents wept bitterly and fancied the child was suffering all kinds of dreadful things, the giant treated him like his own son, though he never allowed him to see his daughters. The boy grew to be a big boy, and one day the giant told him that he would have to amuse himself alone for many hours, as he had a journey to make. So the boy wandered to the top of the castle, where he had never been before. There he paused, for the sound of music broke upon his ears, and opening a door near him, he beheld a girl sitting by the window, holding a harp.

'Haste and begone, I see the giant close at hand,' she whispered hurriedly, 'but when he is asleep, return hither, for I would speak with you.' And the prince did as he was bid, and when midnight struck he crept back to the top of the castle.

'To-morrow,' said the girl, who was the giant's daughter, 'to-morrow you will get the choice of my two sisters to marry, but you must answer that you will not take either, but only me. This will anger him greatly, for he wishes to betroth me to the son of the king of the Green City, whom I like not at all.'

Then they parted, and on the morrow, as the girl had said, the giant called his three daughters to him, and likewise the young prince to whom he spoke.

'Now, Oh son of the king of Tethertown, the time has come for us to part. Choose one of my two elder daughters to wife, and you shalt take her to your father's house the day after the wedding.'

'Give me the youngest instead,' replied the youth, and the giant's face darkened as he heard him.

'Three things must you do first,' he said.

'Say on, I will do them,' replied the prince, and the giant left the house, and bade him follow to the byre, where the cows were kept.

'For a hundred years no man has swept this byre,' said the giant, 'but if by nightfall, when I reach home, you has not cleaned it so that a golden apple can roll through it from end to end, your blood shall pay for it.'

All day long the youth toiled, but he might as well have tried to empty the ocean. At length, when he was so tired he could hardly move, the giant's youngest daughter stood in the doorway.

'Lay down your weariness,' she said, and the king's son, thinking he could only die once, sank on the floor at her bidding, and fell sound asleep. When he woke the girl had disappeared, and the byre was so clean that a golden apple could roll from end to end of it. He jumped up in surprise, and at that moment in came the giant.

'Hast you cleaned the byre, king's son?' asked he.

'I have cleaned it,' answered he.

'Well, since you were so active to-day, to-morrow you will thatch this byre with a feather from every different bird, or else your blood shall pay for it,' and he went out.

Before the sun was up, the youth took his bow and his quiver and set off to kill the birds. Off to the moor he went, but never a bird was to be seen that day. At last he got so tired with running to and fro that he gave up heart.

'There is but one death I can die,' thought he. Then at midday came the giant's daughter.

'You are tired, king's son?' asked she.

'I am,' answered he, 'all these hours have I wandered, and there fell but these two blackbirds, both of one colour.'

'Lay down your weariness on the grass,' she said, and he did as she bade him, and fell fast asleep.

When he woke the girl had disappeared, and he got up, and returned to the byre. As he drew near, he rubbed his eyes hard, thinking he was dreaming, for there it was, beautifully thatched, just as the giant had wished. At the door of the house he met the giant.

'Hast you thatched the byre, king's son?'

'I have thatched it.'

'Well, since you have been so active to-day, I have something else for you! Beside the loch you see over yonder there grows a fir tree. On the top of the fir tree is a magpie's nest, and in the nest are five eggs. You will bring me those eggs for breakfast, and if one is cracked or broken, your blood shall pay for it.'

Before it was light next day, the king's son jumped out of bed and ran down to the loch. The tree was not hard to find, for the rising sun shone red on the trunk, which was five hundred feet from the ground to its first branch. Time after time he walked round it, trying to find some knots, however small, where he could put his feet, but the bark was quite smooth, and he soon saw that if he was to reach the top at all, it must be by climbing up with his knees like a sailor. But then he was a king's son and not a sailor, which made all the difference.

However, it was no use standing there staring at the fir, at least he must try to do his best, and try he did till his hands and knees were sore, for as soon as he had struggled up a few feet, he slid back again. Once he climbed a little higher than before, and hope rose in his heart, then down he came with such force that his hands and knees smarted worse than ever.

'This is no time for stopping,' said the voice of the giant's daughter, as he leant against the trunk to recover his breath.

'Alas! I am no sooner up than down,' answered he.

'Try once more,' she said, and she laid a finger against the tree and bade him put his foot on it. Then she placed another finger a little higher up, and so on till he reached the top, where the magpie had built her nest.

'Make haste now with the nest,' she cried, 'for my father's breath is burning my back,' and down he scrambled as fast as he could, but the girl's little finger had caught in a branch at the top, and she was obliged to leave it there. But she was too busy to pay heed to this, for the sun was getting high over the hills.

'Listen to me,' she said. 'This night my two sisters and I will be dressed in the same garments, and you will not know me. But when my father says, 'Go to your wife, king's son,' come to the one whose right hand has no little finger.'

So he went and gave the eggs to the giant, who nodded his head.

'Make ready for your marriage,' cried he, 'for the wedding shall take place this very night, and I will summon your bride to greet you.' Then his three daughters were sent for, and they all entered dressed in green silk of the same fashion, and with golden circlets round their heads. The king's son looked from one to another. Which was the youngest? Suddenly his eyes fell on the hand of the middle one, and there was no little finger.

'You have aimed well this time too,' said the giant, as the king's son laid his hand on her shoulder, 'but perhaps we may meet some other way', and though he pretended to laugh, the bride saw a gleam in his eye which warned her of danger.

The wedding took place that very night, and the hall was filled with giants and gentlemen, and they danced till the house shook from top to bottom. At last everyone grew tired, and the guests went away, and the king's son and his bride were left alone.

'If we stay here till dawn my father will kill you,' she whispered, 'but you are my husband and I will save you, as I did before,' and she cut an apple into nine pieces, and put two pieces at the head of the bed, and two pieces at the foot, and two pieces at the door of the kitchen, and two at the big door, and one outside the house. And when this was done, and she heard the giant snoring, she and the king's son crept out softly and stole across to the stable, where she led out the blue-grey mare and jumped on its back, and her husband mounted behind her. Not long after, the giant awoke.

'Are you asleep?' asked he.

'Not yet,' answered the apple at the head of the bed, and the giant turned over, and soon was snoring as loudly as before. By and bye he called again.

'Are you asleep?'

'Not yet,' said the apple at the foot of the bed, and the giant was satisfied. After a while, he called a third time, 'Are you asleep?'

'Not yet,' replied the apple in the kitchen, but when in a few minutes, he put the question for the fourth time and received an answer from the apple outside the house door, he guessed what had happened, and ran to the room to look for himself.

The bed was cold and empty!

'My father's breath is burning my back,' cried the girl, 'put your hand into the ear of the mare, and whatever you find there, throw it behind you.' And in the mare's ear there was a twig of sloe tree, and as he threw it behind him there sprung up twenty miles of thornwood so thick that scarce a weasel could go through it. And the giant, who was striding headlong forwards, got caught in it, and it pulled his hair and beard.

'This is one of my daughter's tricks,' he said to himself, 'but if I had my big axe and my wood-knife, I would not be long making a way through this,' and off he went home and brought back the axe and the wood-knife.

It took him but a short time to cut a road through the blackthorn, and then he laid the axe and the knife under a tree.

'I will leave them there till I return,' he murmured to himself, but a hoodie crow, which was sitting on a branch above, heard him.

'If you leave them,' said the hoodie, 'we will steal them.'

'You will,' answered the giant, 'and I must take them home.' So he took them home, and started afresh on his journey.

'My father's breath is burning my back,' cried the girl at midday. 'Put your finger in the mare's ear and throw behind you whatever you find in it,' and the king's son found a splinter of grey stone, and threw it behind him, and in a twinkling twenty miles of solid rock lay between them and the giant.

'My daughter's tricks are the hardest things that ever met me,' said the giant, 'but if I had my lever and my crowbar, I would not be long in making my way through this rock also,' but as he had got them, he had to go home and fetch them. Then it took him but a short time to hew his way through the rock.

'I will leave the tools here,' he murmured aloud when he had finished.

'If you leave them, we will steal them,' said a hoodie who was perched on a stone above him, and the giant answered:

'Steal them if you will; there is no time to go back.'

'My father's breath is burning my back,' cried the girl, 'look in the mare's ear, king's son, or we are lost,' and he looked, and found a tiny bladder full of water, which he threw behind him, and it became a great lock. And the giant, who was striding on so fast, could not stop himself, and he walked right into the middle and was drowned.

The blue-grey mare galloped on like the wind, and the next day the king's son came in sight of his father's house.

'Get down and go in,' said the bride, 'and tell them that you have married me. But take heed that neither man nor beast kiss you, for then you will cease to remember me at all.'

'I will do your bidding,' answered he, and left her at the gate. All who met him bade him welcome, and he charged his father and mother not to kiss him, but as he greeted them his old greyhound leapt on his neck, and kissed him on the mouth. And after that he did not remember the giant's daughter.

All that day she sat on a well which was near the gate, waiting, waiting, but the king's son never came. In the darkness she climbed up into an oak tree that shadowed the well, and there she lay all night, waiting, waiting.

On the morrow, at midday, the wife of a shoemaker who dwelt near the well went to draw water for her husband to drink, and she saw the shadow of the girl in the tree, and thought it was her own shadow.

'How handsome I am, to be sure,' she said, gazing into the well, and as she stopped to behold herself better, the jug struck against the stones and broke in pieces, and she was forced to return to her husband without the water, and this angered him.

'You have turned crazy,' he said in wrath. 'Go you, my daughter, and fetch me a drink,' and the girl went, and the same thing befell her as had befallen her mother.

'Where is the water?' asked the shoemaker, when she came back, and as she held nothing save the handle of the jug he went to the well himself. He too saw the reflection of the woman in the tree, but looked up to discover from where it came, and there above him sat the most beautiful woman in the world.

'Come down,' he said, 'for a while you can stay in my house,' and glad enough the girl was to come.

Now the king of the country was about to marry, and the young men about the court thronged the shoemaker's shop to buy fine shoes to wear at the wedding.

'You have a pretty daughter,' said they when they beheld the girl sitting at work.

'Pretty she is,' answered the shoemaker, 'but no daughter of mine.'

'I would give a hundred pounds to marry her,' said one.

'And I,' 'And I,' cried the others.

'That is no business of mine,' answered the shoemaker, and the young men bade him ask her if she would choose one of them for a husband, and to tell them on the morrow. Then the shoemaker asked her, and the girl said that she would marry the one who would bring his purse with him. So the shoemaker hurried to the youth who had first spoken, and he came back, and after giving the shoemaker a hundred pounds for his news, he sought the girl, who was waiting for him.

'Is it thou?' inquired she. 'I am thirsty, give me a drink from the well that is yonder.' And he poured out the water, but he could not move from the place where he was, and there he stayed till many hours had passed by.

'Take away that foolish boy,' cried the girl to the shoemaker , 'I am tired of him,' and then suddenly he was able to walk, and betook himself to his home, but he did not tell the others what had happened to him.

Next day there arrived one of the other young men, and in the evening, when the shoemaker had gone out and they were alone, she said to him, 'See if the latch is on the door.' The young man hastened to do her bidding, but as soon as he touched the latch, his fingers stuck to it, and there he had to stay for many hours, till the shoemaker came back, and the girl let him go. Hanging his head, he went home, but he told no one what had befallen him.

Then was the turn of the third man, and his foot remained fastened to the floor, till the girl unloosed it. And thankfully, he ran off, and was not seen looking behind him.

'Take the purse of gold,' said the girl to the shoemaker, 'I have no need of it, and it will better you.' And the shoemaker took it and told the girl he must carry the shoes for the wedding up to the castle.

'I would fain get a sight of the king's son before he marries,' sighed she.

'Come with me, then,' answered he, 'the servants are all my friends, and they will let you stand in the passage down which the king's son will pass, and all the company too.'

Up they went to the castle, and when the young men saw the girl standing there, they led her into the hall where the banquet was laid out and poured her out some wine. She was just raising the glass to drink when a flame went up out of it, and out of the flame sprang two pigeons, one of gold and one of silver. They flew round and round the head of the girl, when three grains of barley fell on the floor, and the silver pigeon dived down, and swallowed them.

'If you had remembered how I cleaned the byre, you would have given me my share,' cooed the golden pigeon, and as he spoke three more grains fell, and the silver pigeon ate them as before.

'If you had remembered how I thatched the byre, you would have given me my share,' cooed the golden pigeon again, and as he spoke three more grains fell, and for the third time they were eaten by the silver pigeon.

'If you had remembered how I got the magpie's nest, you would have given me my share,' cooed the golden pigeon.

Then the king's son understood that they had come to remind him of what he had forgotten, and his lost memory came back, and he knew his wife, and kissed her. But as the preparations had been made, it seemed a pity to waste them, so they were married a second time, and sat down to the wedding feast.

The Believing Husbands

The Believing Husbands, as retold by Andrew Lang in The Lilac Fairy Book (1910), originates from J. F. Campbell's Popular Tales from the West Highlands, a cornerstone of Scottish folklore collected in the mid-nineteenth century. The story is a lively and ironic piece in which three credulous husbands, each married to a quick-witted wife, are successively outwitted in a contest of foolishness and deceit.

Lang's adaptation retains Campbell's robust, earthy tone but trims the dialect and simplifies the rhythm for his Edwardian readership. Beneath its comic surface, the story preserves a folk moral common to Celtic and European traditions: that trust without sense is folly, and that wit, often found in the margins of power, will have the final laugh.

Once upon a time there dwelt in the land of Erin a young man who was seeking a wife, and of all the maidens round about none pleased him as well as the only daughter of a farmer. The girl was willing and the father was willing, and very soon they were married and went to live at the farm. By and bye the season came when they must cut the peats and pile them up to dry, so that they might have fires in the winter. So on a fine day the girl and her husband, and the father and his wife all went out upon the moor.

They worked hard for many hours, and at length grew hungry, so the young woman was sent home to bring them food, and also to give the horses their dinner. When she went into the stables, she suddenly saw the heavy pack-saddle of the speckled mare just over her head, and she jumped and said to herself:

'Suppose that pack-saddle were to fall and kill me, how dreadful it would be!' and she sat down just under the pack-saddle she was so much afraid of, and began to cry.

Now the others out on the moor grew hungrier and hungrier.

'What can have become of her?' asked they, and at length the mother declared that she would wait no longer, and must go and see what had happened.

As the bride was nowhere in the kitchen or the dairy, the old woman went into the stable, where she found her daughter weeping bitterly.

'What is the matter, my dove?' and the girl answered, between her sobs:

'When I came in and saw the pack-saddle over my head, I thought how dreadful it would be if it fell and killed me,' and she cried louder than before.

The old woman struck her hands together, 'Ah, to think of it! if that were to be, what should I do?' and she sat down by her daughter, and they both wrung their hands and let their tears flow.

'Something strange must have occurred,' exclaimed the old farmer on the moor, who by this time was not only hungry, but cross. 'I must go after them.' And he went and found them in the stable.

'What is the matter?' asked he.

'Oh!' replied his wife, 'when our daughter came home, did she not see the pack-saddle over her head, and she thought how dreadful it would be if it were to fall and kill her.'

'Ah, to think of it!' exclaimed he, striking his hands together, and he sat down beside them and wept too.

As soon as night fell the young man returned full of hunger, and there they were, all crying together in the stable.

'What is the matter?' asked he.

'When your wife came home,' answered the farmer, 'she saw the pack-saddle over her head, and she thought how dreadful it would be if it were to fall and kill her.'

'Well, but it didn't fall,' replied the young man, and he went off to the kitchen to get some supper, leaving them to cry as long as they liked.

The next morning he got up with the sun, and said to the old man and to the old woman and to his wife:

'Farewell: my foot shall not return to the house till I have found other three people as silly as you,' and he walked away till he came to the town, and seeing the door of a cottage standing open wide, he entered. No man was present, but only some women spinning at their wheels.

'You do not belong to this town,' he said.

'You speak truth,' they answered, 'nor you either?'

'I do not,' replied he, 'but is it a good place to live in?'

The women looked at each other.

'The men of the town are so silly that we can make them believe anything we please,' said they.

'Well, here is a gold ring,' replied he, 'and I will give it to the one amongst you who can make her husband believe the most impossible thing,' and he left them.

As soon as the first husband came home his wife said to him:

'You are sick!'

'Am I?' asked he.

'Yes, you are,' she answered, 'take off your clothes and lie down.'

So he did, and when he was in his bed his wife went to him and said, 'You are dead.'

'Oh, am I?' asked he.

'You are,' she said, 'shut your eyes and stir neither hand nor foot.'

And dead he felt sure he was.

Soon the second man came home, and his wife said to him:

'You are not my husband!'

'Oh, am I not?' asked he.

'No, it is not you,' answered she, so he went away and slept in the wood.

When the third man arrived his wife gave him his supper, and after that he went to bed, just as usual. The next morning a boy knocked at the door, bidding him attend the burial of the man who was dead, and he was just going to get up when his wife stopped him.

'Time enough,' she said, and he lay still till he heard the funeral passing the window.

'Now rise, and be quick,' called the wife, and the man jumped out of bed in a great hurry, and began to look about him.

'Why, where are my clothes?' asked he.

'Silly that you are, they are on your back, of course,' answered the woman.

'Are they?' he said.

'They are,' she said, 'and make haste lest the burying be ended before you get there.'

Then off he went, running hard, and when the mourners saw a man coming towards them with nothing on but his nightshirt, they forgot in their fright what they were there for, and fled to hide themselves. And the naked man stood alone at the head of the coffin.

Very soon a man came out of the wood and spoke to him.

'Do you know me?'

'Not I,' answered the naked man. 'I do not know you.'

'But why are you naked?' asked the first man.

'Am I naked? My wife told me that I had all my clothes on,' answered he.

'And my wife told me that I myself was dead,' said the man in the coffin.

But at the sound of his voice the two men were so terrified that they ran straight home, and the man in the coffin got up and followed them, and it was his wife that gained the gold ring, as he had been sillier than the other two.

The Black Bull of Norroway

The Black Bull of Norroway is one of the most striking Scottish fairy tales, a dark and adventurous story that combines elements of romance, enchantment, and endurance. Adapted from The Scottish Fairy Book (Elizabeth Wilson Grierson, J. B. Lippincott Company, 1910), it tells of a widowed queen whose three daughters set out to seek their fortunes.

The tale is both a test of patience and faith, and a parable of transformation. The heroine's trials mirror the inner work of constancy and love that breaks enchantment. Grierson's 1910 version preserves the cadence and superstition of the oral Scottish tradition while softening some of its harsher folk edges, turning it into a story of quiet heroism rather than vengeance.

Long ago, in the far-off days of kings and castles, there lived a widowed queen who had three daughters. The poor woman had fallen on such hard times that she and her girls often struggled to find enough food to eat. At last, the eldest princess decided to go out into the world to seek her fortune, and her mother agreed. "It's better to work abroad than starve at home," she said sadly.

Now, near the castle lived an old hen-wife who was said to be a witch, able to tell a person's fortune. The queen sent her daughter to ask in which of the four winds she should travel to find the best luck. But when the girl went to the cottage, the old woman shook her head kindly. "You need go no farther than my back door, dearie," she said.

The princess ran to the door and looked out. To her astonishment, she saw a splendid coach drawn by six cream-coloured horses coming up the road. Breathless, she told the hen-wife what she had seen.

"Aye, that's your fortune," said the old woman. "The coach and six have come for you."

Sure enough, the carriage stopped at the castle gate. The second princess came running down to tell her sister to hurry, and, full of delight, the eldest said farewell to her mother and sisters, climbed inside, and was carried away. It's she said went to the palace of a great prince, who married her, but that is another story.

A few weeks later, the second princess decided she would do the same. She visited the hen-wife, hoping her fortune would be as grand as her sister's. When she looked from the back door, another coach and six appeared, even finer than before. The hen-wife smiled and told her to make haste, for this coach was hers. So the second princess too rode away to her destiny, and before long she too became a prince's bride.

The youngest princess was now eager to try her own fortune. That very evening she ran to the old woman's cottage, full of hope. She was told to look from the back door, but when she did, there was no coach, no horses, no sound of wheels. The road lay empty beneath the moon. Disappointed, she returned to the hen-wife.

"Your fortune's not coming today," said the old woman. "Try again tomorrow."

So the next day the princess came back, but again saw nothing. On the third day, however, a strange sight met her eyes. A great black bull came charging along the road, bellowing and tossing its head. Terrified, she slammed the door and ran to the hen-wife.

"Oh dear," cried the old woman, "and who would have thought it! The Black Bull of Norroway is your fate!"

The poor princess turned pale. "But the bull can't be my fortune," she gasped. "I can't go away with a beast!"

"You must," said the hen-wife. "You looked for your fortune, and this is what's come. You'll have to accept it."

The girl ran home weeping to beg her mother to let her stay, but the queen, remembering what had happened with her sisters, she said must go. And so, trembling, the youngest princess was lifted onto the back of the huge black bull, who stood calmly waiting at the castle gate. Once she was seated, he set off at a gallop, the wind streaming past her as she clung to his horns in terror.

They travelled for hours, through forest and moor, until the princess was faint with fear and hunger. Just as she felt she could hold on no longer, the bull turned his great head and spoke in a deep, gentle voice. "Eat from my right ear, drink from my left, and you'll be refreshed."

She reached trembling into his right ear and drew out bread and meat, which she ate gratefully. From the left she took a small flagon of wine, and when she drank, her strength returned. On they travelled until they reached a grand castle.

"That's where we'll rest tonight," said the bull. "It's my brother's house."

A servant opened the door and greeted the bull with respect, helping the princess down and leading her into a magnificent hall. She was treated kindly, given supper, and shown to a golden bedchamber. In the morning, before she left, the lord and lady of the castle gave her a shining apple.

"Keep it safe," they said. "If ever you find yourself in your greatest need, break it, and it will help you."

The princess put the apple in her pocket, mounted the bull again, and continued her strange journey. The next night they came to another castle, even grander than the first, where the bull's second brother lived. There she was given a beautiful pear with the same warning. On the third night, at the house of the youngest brother, she was given a lovely plum.

But on the fourth day there were no castles, only a dark, narrow glen. The bull stopped at its mouth. "You must get down here," he said. "I must fight a great spirit of darkness that lives within this place. Sit upon this stone, and do not move hand or foot, nor speak a word, until I return. If you move, the spirit will have you."

The princess promised to obey. "But how will I know what happens to you?" she asked.

"If everything turns blue, I'll have conquered," he said. "If all turns red, I'll be lost."

Then he disappeared into the shadows. Time passed slowly. At last the sky and earth around her began to turn blue, and she cried out in joy. "He's won!" she thought, and, forgetting herself, crossed one leg over the other.

In that instant she vanished from sight, for she had broken the spell. When the bull, who was in truth a prince released from enchantment, returned, he could not find her, though she was sitting on the very stone where he had left her. The same spell blinded her eyes as well, so that they could not see one another.

When she awoke from a troubled sleep, she found herself alone, and set out wandering, unsure where she went. After a long and weary journey, she came to a hill made entirely of glass. She tried again and again to climb it, but each time she slipped back down. At last, exhausted, she came upon a blacksmith's cottage.

"Good smith," she said, "is there any way across this hill?"

He shook his head. "None, unless you have iron shoes. Only those shod in iron can climb the Mountain of Glass."

"Can you make me such shoes?" she asked eagerly.

"They can't be bought," he said. "They must be earned by service, seven years' service, no less."

And so she stayed and worked for him seven long years, cleaning, cooking, and mending. When her time was done, he forged her a pair of iron shoes, and with these she climbed the glass hill as if it were soft turf.

On the other side she came to the cottage of an old washerwoman and her daughter. The woman told her she could stay the night if she would wash a white mantle belonging to the Black Knight of Norroway. "I've tried and failed to wash out the stains," said the old woman. "Perhaps you'll have better luck."

When the princess heard the name, her heart leapt. "Is he the same as the Black Bull of Norroway?" she asked.

"The very same," said the woman. "A prince once cursed to be a bull, who won back his human form after fighting a spirit of darkness. He speaks often of a maiden he has lost."

The princess washed the mantle, and to the old woman's amazement, it came out pure and white. The washerwoman, suspecting some link between the stranger and the knight, gave her a bed early so that she would be out of sight when the prince arrived. That night, when the Black Knight came to collect his mantle, he was told that the washerwoman's daughter had cleaned it, and he declared that he would marry her the next day, for it had been foretold that the woman who made the mantle white again would be his true bride.

When the princess heard this in the morning, her heart broke. Then she remembered the gifts she had been given, the apple, the pear, and the plum, and broke the apple open. Inside were jewels of great beauty. She offered them to the washerwoman in exchange for one night by the prince's bedside. The old woman agreed and drugged the prince's wine so that he would not wake. All night the princess sang softly:

Seven long years I served for you,

The glassy hill I climbed for you,

The mantle white I washed for you,

And will you not waken, and turn to me?

But he slept on. The next night she broke the pear and found more jewels, richer than the last, and again she bought a night's watch. Again she sang, and again he slept. On the third night she broke the plum, finding the most precious stones of all, and once more she bargained for a chance to see him.

That day, as the prince rode out hunting, his servants whispered among themselves about the mysterious singing they had heard at night. One old huntsman asked him directly, and the prince, puzzled, he said had heard nothing. "Then taste not the old wife's drink tonight," the man urged, "and you'll hear what others have heard."

That evening the prince poured the draught away and pretended to drink it. Later, when the princess crept into his chamber and sang her song once more, he heard her voice . He rose, gathered her into his arms, and asked her to tell him all that had happened. When he learned the truth, he banished the deceitful washerwoman and her daughter, and married the princess who had followed him so faithfully through darkness and enchantment.

And there, they say, they lived happily all their days.

The Blue Mountains

The Blue Mountains is a Scottish tale first collected by John Francis Campbell in his Popular Tales from the West Highlands (1860–62) and later adapted by Andrew Lang for The Yellow Fairy Book (1894). It belongs to the great northern cycle of quest stories in which a young hero must rescue an enchanted princess from the power of trolls or giants.

The tale blends the moral force of Celtic storytelling with the structure of older Norse heroic sagas. It speaks of persistence, humility, and the quiet intelligence of those the world underestimates. Lang's version simplifies Campbell's Gaelic phrasing and makes the plot more compact, but he keeps the atmosphere of chill grandeur, the wide moors, the glittering peaks, the dark halls of the giants. The Blue Mountains themselves become a symbol of the impossible goal that only courage and faith can reach.

There were once a Scotsman and an Englishman and an Irishman serving in the army together, who took it into their heads to run away on the first opportunity they could get. The chance came and they took it. They went on travelling for two days through a great forest, without food or drink, and without coming across a single house, and every night they had to climb up into the trees through fear of the wild beasts that were in the wood. On the second morning the Scotsman saw from the top of his tree a great castle far away. He said to himself that he would certainly die if he stayed in the forest without anything to eat but the roots of grass, which would not keep him alive very long. As soon, then, as he got down out of the tree he set off towards the castle, without so much as telling his companions that he had seen it at all; perhaps the hunger and want they had suffered had changed their nature so much that the one did not care what became of the other if he could save himself. He travelled on most of the day, so that it was quite late when he reached the castle, and to his great disappointment found nothing but closed doors and no smoke rising from the chimneys. He thought there was nothing for it but to die after all, and had lain down beside the wall, when he heard a window being opened high above him. At this he looked up, and saw the most beautiful woman he had ever set eyes on.

'Oh, it is Fortune that has sent you to me,' he said. 'It is indeed,' she said. 'What are you in need of, or what has sent you here?'

'Necessity,' he said. 'I am dying for want of food and drink.' 'Come inside, then,' she said, 'there is plenty of both here.' Accordingly he went in to where she was, and she opened a large room for him, where he saw a number of men lying asleep. She then set food before him, and after that showed him to the room where the others were. He lay down on one of the beds and fell sound asleep. And now we must go back to the two that he left behind him in the wood. When nightfall and the time of the wild beasts came upon these, the Englishman happened to climb up into the very same tree on which the Scotsman was when he got a sight of the castle, and as soon as the day began to dawn and the Englishman looked to the four quarters of heaven, what did he see but the castle too! Off he went without saying a word to the Irishman, and everything happened to him just as it had done to the Scotsman.

The poor Irishman was now left all alone, and did not know where the others had gone to, so he just stayed where he was, very sad and miserable. When night came he climbed up into the same tree as the Englishman had been on the night before. As soon as day came he also saw the castle, and set out towards it, but when he reached it he could see no signs of fire or living being about it. Before long, however, he heard the window opened above his head, looked up, and beheld the most beautiful woman he had ever seen. He asked if she would give him food and drink, and she answered kindly and heartily that she would, if he would only come inside. This he did very willingly, and she set before him food and drink that he had never seen the like of before. In the room there was a bed, with diamond rings hanging at every loop of the curtains, and everything that was in the room besides astonished him so much that he actually forgot that he was hungry. When she saw that he was not eating at all, she asked him what he wanted yet, to which he replied that he would neither eat nor drink until he knew who she was, or where she came from, or who had put her there.

'I shall tell you that,' she said. 'I am an enchanted Princess, and my father has promised that the man who releases me from the spell shall have the third of his kingdom while he is alive, and the whole of it after he is dead, and marry me as well. If ever I saw a man who looked likely to do this, you are the one. I have been here for sixteen years now, and no one who ever came to the castle has asked me who I was, except yourself. Every other man that has come, so long as I have been here, lies asleep in the big room down there.' 'Tell me, then,' said the Irishman, 'what is the spell that has been laid on you, and how you can be freed from it.' 'There is a little room there,' said the Princess, 'and if I could get a man to stay in it from ten o'clock till midnight for three nights on end I should be freed from the spell.

'I am the man for you, then,' he said, 'I will take on hand to do it.'

Thereupon she brought him a pipe and tobacco, and he went into the room, but before long he heard a hammering and knocking on the outside of the door, and was told to open it. 'I won't,' he said.

The next moment the door came flying in, and those outside along with it. They knocked him down, and kicked him, and knelt on his body till it came to midnight, but as soon as the cock crew they all disappeared. The Irishman was little more than alive by this time. As soon as daylight appeared the Princess came, and found him lying full length on the floor, unable to speak a word. She took a bottle, rubbed him from head to foot with something from it, and thereupon he was as sound as ever, but after what he had got that night he was very unwilling to try it a second time. The Princess, however, entreated him to stay, saying that the next night would not be so bad, and in the end he gave in and stayed.

When it was getting near midnight he heard them ordering him to open the door, and there were three of them for every one that there had been the previous evening. He did not make the slightest movement to go out to them or to open the door, but before long they broke it up, and were in on top of him. They laid hold of him, and kept throwing him between them up to the ceiling, or jumping above him, until the cock crew, when they all disappeared. When day came the Princess went to the room to see if he was still alive, and taking the bottle put it to his nostrils, which soon brought him to himself. The first thing he said then was that he was a fool to go on getting himself killed for anyone he ever saw, and was determined to be off and stay there no longer, When the Princess learned his intention she entreated him to stay, reminding him that another night would free her from the spell. 'Besides,' she said, 'if there is a single spark of life in you when the day comes, the stuff that is in this bottle will make you as sound as ever you were.'

With all this the Irishman decided to stay, but that night there were three at him for every one that was there the two nights before, and it looked very unlikely that he would be alive in the morning after all that he got. When morning dawned, and the Princess came to see if he was still alive, she found him lying on the floor as if dead. She tried to see if there was breath in him, but could not quite make it out. Then she put her hand on his pulse, and found a faint movement in it. Accordingly she poured what was in the bottle on him, and before long he rose up on his feet, and was as well as ever he was. So that business was finished, and the Princess was freed from the spell.

The Princess then told the Irishman that she must go away for the present, but would return for him in a few days in a carriage drawn by four grey horses. He told her to 'be aisy,' and not speak like that to him. 'I have paid dear for you for the last three nights,' he said, 'if I have to part with you now;' but in the twinkling of an eye she had disappeared. He did not know what to do with himself when he saw that she was gone, but before she went she had given him a little rod, with which he could, when he pleased, waken the men who had been sleeping there, some of them for sixteen years.

After being thus left alone, he went in and stretched himself on three chairs that were in the room, when what does he see coming in at the door but a little fair-haired lad. 'Where did you come from, my lad?' said the Irishman.

'I came to make ready your food for you,' he said. 'Who told you to do that?' said the Irishman. 'My mistress,' answered the lad - 'the Princess that was under the spell and is now free.'

By this the Irishman knew that she had sent the lad to wait on him. The lad also told him that his mistress wished him to be ready next morning at nine o'clock, when she would come for him with the carriage, as she had promised. He was greatly pleased at this, and next morning, when the time was drawing near, went out into the garden, but the little fair-haired lad took a big pin out of his pocket, and stuck it into the back of the Irishman's coat without his noticing it, whereupon he fell sound asleep.

Before long the Princess came with the carriage and four horses, and asked the lad whether his master was awake. He said that he wasn't. 'It is bad for him,' she said, 'when the night is not long enough for him to sleep. Tell him that if he doesn't meet me at this time tomorrow it is not likely that he will ever see me again all his life.'

As soon as she was gone the lad took the pin out of his master's coat, who instantly awoke. The first word he said to the lad was, 'Have you seen her?'

'Yes,' he said, 'and she bade me tell you that if you don't meet her at nine o'clock to-morrow you will never see her again.' He was very sorry when he heard this, and could not understand why the sleep should have fallen upon him just when she was coming. He decided, however, to go early to bed that night, in order to rise in time nest morning, and so he did. When it was getting near nine o'clock he went out to the garden to wait till she came, and the fair-haired lad along with him, but as soon as the lad got the chance he stuck the pin into his master's coat again and he fell asleep as before. Precisely at nine o'clock came the Princess in the carriage with four horses, and asked the lad if his master had got up yet, but he said 'No, he was asleep, just as he was the day before.' 'Dear! dear!' said the Princess, 'I am sorry for him. Was the sleep he had last night not enough for him? Tell him that he will never see me here again, and here is a sword that you will give him in my name, and my blessing along with it.'

With this she went off, and as soon as she had gone the lad took the pin out of his master's coat. He awoke instantly, and the first word he said was, 'Have you seen her?' The lad said that he had, and there was the sword she had left for him. The Irishman was ready to kill the lad out of sheer vexation, but when he gave a glance over his shoulder not a trace of the fair-haired lad was left.

Being thus left all alone, he thought of going into the room where all the men were lying asleep, and there among the rest he found his two comrades who had deserted along with him. Then he remembered what the Princess had told him - that he had only to touch them with the rod she had given him and they would all awake, and the first he touched were his own comrades. They started to their feet at once, and he gave them as much silver and gold as they could carry when they went away. There was plenty to do before he got all the others wakened, for the two doors of the castle were crowded with them all day long.

The loss of the Princess, however, kept rankling in his mind day and night, till finally he thought he would go about the world to see if he could find anyone to give him news of her. So he took the best horse in the stable and set out. Three years he spent travelling through forests and wildernesses, but could find no one able to tell him anything of the Princess. At last he fell into so great despair that he thought he would put an end to his own life, and for this purpose laid hold of the sword that she had given him by the hands of the fair-haired lad, but on drawing it from its sheath he noticed that there was some writing on one side of the blade. He looked at this, and read there, 'You will find me in the Blue Mountains.' This made him take heart again, and he gave up the idea of killing himself, thinking that he would go on in hope of meeting someone who could tell him where the Blue Mountains were. After he had gone a long way without thinking where he was going, he saw a light far away, and made straight for it. On reaching it he found it came from a little house, and as soon as the man inside heard the noise of the horse's feet he came out to see who was there. Seeing a stranger on horseback, he asked what brought him there and where he was going.

'I have lived here,' he said, 'for three hundred years, and all that time I have not seen a single human being but yourself.' 'I have been going about for the last three years,' said the Irishman, 'to see if I could find anyone who can tell me where the Blue Mountains are.'

'Come in,' said the old man, 'and stay with me all night. I have a book which contains the history of the world, which I shall go through to-night, and if there is such a place as the Blue Mountains in it we shall find it out.'

The Irishman stayed there all night, and as soon as morning came rose to go. The old man he said had not gone to sleep all night for going through the book, but there was not a word about the Blue Mountains in it. 'But I'll tell you what,' he said, 'if there is such a place on earth at all, I have a brother who lives nine hundred miles from here, and he is sure to know where they are, if anyone in this world does.' The Irishman answered that he could never go these nine hundred miles, for his horse was giving in already. 'That doesn't matter,' said the old man, 'I can do better than that. I have only to blow my whistle and you will be at my brother's house before nightfall.'

So he blew the whistle, and the Irishman did not know where on earth he was until he found himself at the other old man's door, who also told him that it was three hundred years since he had seen anyone, and asked him where he was going. 'I am going to see if I can find anyone that can tell me where the Blue Mountains are,' he said.

'If you will stay with me to-night,' said the old man, 'I have a book of the history of the world, and I shall know where they are before daylight, if there is such a place in it at all.'

He stayed there all night, but there was not a word in the book about the Blue Mountains. Seeing that he was rather cast down, the old man told him that he had a brother nine hundred miles away, and that if information could be got about them from anyone it would be from him, 'and I will enable you,' he said, 'to reach the place where he lives before night.' So he blew his whistle, and the Irishman landed at the brother's house before nightfall. When the old man saw him he said had not seen a single man for three hundred years, and was very much surprised to see anyone come to him now.

'Where are you going to?' he said.

'I am going about asking for the Blue Mountains,' said the Irishman.

'The Blue Mountains?' said the old man.

'Yes,' said the Irishman.

'I never heard the name before, but if they do exist I shall find them out. I am master of all the birds in the world, and have only to blow my whistle and every one will come to me. I shall then ask each of them to tell where it came from, and if there is any way of finding out the Blue Mountains that is it.'

So he blew his whistle, and when he blew it then all the birds of the world began to gather. The old man questioned each of them as to where they had come from, but there was not one of them that had come from the Blue Mountains. After he had run over them all, however, he missed a big Eagle that was wanting, and wondered that it had not come. Soon afterwards he saw something big coming towards him, darkening the sky. It kept coming nearer and growing bigger, and what was this after all but the Eagle? When she arrived the old man scolded her, and asked what had kept her so long behind.

'I couldn't help it,' she said, 'I had more than twenty times further to come than any bird that has come here to-day.' 'Where have you come from, then?' said the old man. 'From the Blue Mountains,' she said.

'Indeed!' said the old man, and what are they doing there?' 'They are making ready this very day,' said the Eagle, 'for the marriage of the daughter of the King of the Blue Mountains. For three years now she has refused to marry anyone whatsoever, until she should give up all hope of the coming of the man who released her from the spell. Now she can wait no longer, for three years is the time that she agreed with her father to remain without marrying.'

The Irishman knew that it was for himself she had been waiting so long, but he was unable to make any better of it, for he had no hope of reaching the Blue Mountains all his life. The old man noticed how sad he grew, and asked the Eagle what she would take for carrying this man on her back to the Blue Mountains.

'I must have threescore cattle killed,' she said, 'and cut up into quarters, and every time I look over my shoulder he must throw one of them into my mouth.'

As soon as the Irishman and the old man heard her demand they went out hunting, and before evening they had killed three-score cattle. They made quarters of them, as the Eagle told them, and then the old man asked her to lie down, till they would get it all heaped up on her back. First of all, though, they had to get a ladder of fourteen steps, to enable them to get on to the Eagle's back, and there they piled up the meat as well as they could. Then the old man told the Irishman to mount, and to remember to throw a quarter of beef to her every time she looked round. He went up, and the old man gave the Eagle the word to be off, which she instantly obeyed, and every time she turned her head the Irishman threw a quarter of beef into her mouth.

As they came near the borders of the kingdom of the Blue Mountains, however, the beef was done, and, when the Eagle looked over her shoulder, what was the Irishman at but throwing the stone between her tail and her neck! At this she turned a complete somersault, and threw the Irishman off into the sea, where he fell into the bay that was right in front of the King's Palace. Fortunately the points of his toes just touched the bottom, and he managed to get ashore.

When he went up into the town all the streets were gleaming with light, and the wedding of the Princess was just about to begin. He went into the first house he came to, and this happened to be the house of the King's hen-wife. He asked the old woman what was causing all the noise and light in the town.

'The Princess,' she said, 'is going to be married to-night against her will, for she has been expecting every day that the man who freed her from the spell would come.'

'There is a guinea for you,' he said, 'go and bring her here.'

The old woman went, and soon returned along with the Princess. She and the Irishman recognised each other, and were married, and had a great wedding.

The Bogle

The Bogle, adapted from an anonymous tale included in Folk-lore and Legends: Scotland (W. W. Gibbings, London, 1889), is a concise yet haunting example of Scottish supernatural folklore. The story tells of two travellers who, on a pitch-dark night near the banks of the Ettrick, hear a mournful voice crying from the water, "Lost! Lost!"

Though brief, the tale captures the eerie simplicity and moral undertone characteristic of Scottish ghost and spirit lore. The Bogle, a recurring figure in the nation's storytelling tradition, embodies both the landscape's mystery and its moral ambiguity: a creature neither wholly evil nor benign, but playful, testing human credulity and pride. The story also reflects the deep interweaving of natural geography and the supernatural imagination in rural Scotland, where rivers, glens, and mountains often harbour voices of warning or deceit.

It was a night without a moon, when cloud and hill and sky had merged into a single depth of darkness. The air was heavy with damp, and the Ettrick ran unseen but not unheard, its current muttering beneath the banks. Two men, shepherds returning late across the moor, made their way cautiously toward the river's edge, guided only by the pale glimmer of water through the reeds. Then, from the black heart of the stream, there rose a sound so desolate that they stopped where they stood. They heard a long, wavering cry that carried over the rush of the current.

"Lost! Lost!"

It came again, hollow and human, as if torn from a drowning throat. The men looked at one another, fear sharpening their senses, and then they began to run, stumbling over roots and stones, the mud sucking at their boots. They shouted into the dark, calling out to whoever struggled there, but no answer came, only that same despairing cry, now further off, now closer, as though the river itself were calling. As they pressed on, their hearts pounding, it seemed to them that the voice was no longer rising from the water at all, but drifting ahead of them, drawn upstream into the unseen hills.

For hour after hour they followed the voice, climbing beside the torrent as it narrowed into rocky channels, their lantern flickering and fading against the press of the dark. The ground grew treacherous underfoot, with loose stones, slick heather, and sudden hollows where the burn cut deep into the moor. Still they pressed on, their breath misting in the cold air, certain that just beyond the next bend they would find the lost soul crying for deliverance. But the voice would not be caught. It moved as if borne on the wind, keeping always a few paces ahead, at times echoing from the cliffs, at others drifting faint and far as if from the clouds themselves.

By the time the first thin light touched the horizon, they had reached the high corries where the Ettrick is born. The river there was no more than a thread of water running from the peat, and the men stood bewildered in the grey stillness. Then, from beyond the ridge, the cry sounded again, but now it was descending the far side of the mountain, retreating into the mists below. Weariness overcame them. Their limbs were trembling, and their boots sat heavy with water and mud. They gave up the chase, turning for home in silence. At that moment the voice burst into peals of harsh, exultant laughter, echo upon echo tumbling from the slopes. It was the triumphant cackle of the Bogle of the Ettrick, delighted with the fools who had followed his phantom cry through the night.

The Brownie o' Ferne-Den

The Brownie o' Ferne-Den is one of the most enduring household spirit tales from Elizabeth Wilson Grierson's The Scottish Fairy Book (1910, J. B. Lippincott Company), a collection that drew deeply on Lowland and Border folklore. In this story, a hardworking brownie, one of those ancient domestic spirits known for helping with chores in return for a bowl of cream, takes up residence in the farmhouse of Ferne-Den.

Grierson's retelling preserves the mixture of warmth, superstition, and moral caution that characterises Scottish domestic lore, capturing both the tenderness and the melancholy that cling to tales of the unseen folk who once shared hearth and home with humankind.

There have been many Brownies known in Scotland, and stories have been written about the Brownie o' Bodsbeck and the Brownie o' Blednock, but about neither of them has a prettier story been told than that which I am going to tell you about the Brownie o' Ferne-Den.

Now, Ferne-Den was a farmhouse, which got its name from the glen, or "den," on the edge of which it stood, and through which anyone who wished to reach the dwelling had to pass.

And this glen was believed to be the abode of a Brownie, who never appeared to anyone in the daytime, but who, it was said, was sometimes seen at night, stealing about, like an ungainly shadow, from tree to tree, trying to keep from observation, and never, by any chance, harming anybody.

Indeed, like all Brownies that are properly treated and let alone, so far was he from harming anybody that he was always on the lookout to do a good turn to those who needed his assistance. The farmer often said that he did not know what he would do without him, for if there was any work to be finished in a hurry at the farm -corn to thrash, or winnow, or tie up into bags, turnips to cut, clothes to wash, a kirn to be kirned, a garden to be weeded - all that the farmer and his wife had to do was to leave the door of the barn, or the turnip shed, or the milk house open when they went to bed, and put down a bowl of new milk on the doorstep for the Brownie's supper, and when they woke the next morning the bowl would be empty, and the job finished better than if it had been done by mortal hands.

In spite of all this, however, which might have proved to them how gentle and kindly the Creature really was, everyone about the place was afraid of him, and would rather go a couple of miles round about in the dark, when they were coming home from Kirk or Market, than pass through the glen, and run the risk of catching a glimpse of him.

I said that they were all afraid of him, but that was not true, for the farmer's wife was so good and gentle that she was not afraid of anything on God's earth, and when the Brownie's supper had to be left outside, she always filled his bowl with the richest milk, and added a good spoonful of cream to it, for, she said, "He works so hard for us, and asks no wages, he well deserves the very best meal that we can give him."

One night this gentle lady was taken very ill, and everyone was afraid that she was going to die. Of course, her husband was greatly distressed, and so were her servants, for she had been such a good

Mistress to them that they loved her as if she had been their mother. But they were all young, and none of them knew very much about illness, and everyone agreed that it would be better to send off for an old woman who lived about seven miles away on the other side of the river, who was known to be a very skilful nurse.

But who was to go? That was the question. For it was black midnight, and the way to the old woman's house lay straight through the glen. And whoever travelled that road ran the risk of meeting the dreaded Brownie.

The farmer would have gone only too willingly, but he dare not leave his wife alone, and the servants stood in groups about the kitchen, each one telling the other that he ought to go, yet no one offering to go themselves.

Little did they think that the cause of all their terror, a queer, wee, misshapen little man, all covered with hair, with a long beard, red-rimmed eyes, broad, flat feet, just like the feet of a paddock, and enormous, long arms that touched the ground, even when he stood upright, was within a yard or two of them, listening to their talk, with an anxious face, behind the kitchen door.

For he had come up as usual, from his hiding-place in the glen, to see if there were any work for him to do, and to look for his bowl of milk. And he had seen, from the open door and lit-up windows, that there was something wrong inside the farmhouse, which at that hour was usually to be dark, and still, and silent, and he had crept into the entry to try and find out what the matter was.

When he gathered from the servants' talk that the Mistress, whom he loved so dearly, and who had been so kind to him, was ill, his heart sank within him, and when he heard that the silly servants were so taken up with their own fears that they dared not set out to fetch a nurse for her, his contempt and anger knew no bounds.

"Fools, idiots, dolts!" he muttered to himself, stamping his queer, misshapen feet on the floor. "They speak as if a body were ready to take a bite off them as soon as ever he met them. If they only knew the bother it gives me to keep out of their road they wouldna be so silly. But, by my troth, if they go on like this, the bonnie lady will die amongst their fingers. So it strikes me that Brownie must even gang himself."

So saying, he reached up his hand, and took down a dark cloak which belonged to the farmer, which was hanging on a peg on the wall, and throwing it over his head and shoulders, or as somewhat to hide his ungainly form, he hurried away to the stable, and saddled and bridled the fleetest-footed horse that stood there.

When the last buckle was fastened, he led it to the door and scrambled on its back. "Now, if ever you travelled fleetly, travel fleetly now," he said, and it was as if the creature understood him, for it gave a little whinny and pricked up its ears; then it darted out into the darkness like an arrow from the bow.

In less time than the distance had ever been ridden in before, the Brownie drew rein at the old woman's cottage.

She was in bed, fast asleep, but he rapped sharply on the window, and when she rose and put her old face, framed in its white mutch, close to the pane to ask who was there, he bent forward and told her his errand.

"You must come with me, Goodwife, and that quickly," he commanded, in his deep, harsh voice, "if the Lady of Ferne-Den's life is to be saved, for there is no one to nurse her up-bye at the farm there, save a lot of empty-headed servant wenches."

"But how am I to get there? Have they sent a cart for me?" asked the old woman anxiously; for, as far as she could see, there was nothing at the door save a horse and its rider.

"No, they have sent no cart," replied the Brownie, shortly. "So you must just climb up behind me on the saddle, and hang on tight to my waist, and I'll promise to land you at Ferne-Den safe and sound."

His voice was so masterful that the old woman dare not refuse to do as she was bid; besides, she had often ridden pillion-wise when she was a lassie, so she made haste to dress herself, and when she was ready she unlocked her door, and, mounting the louping-on stone that stood beside it, she was soon seated behind the dark-cloaked stranger, with her arms clasped tightly round him.

Not a word was spoken till they approached the dreaded glen, then the old woman felt her courage giving way. "Do you think that there will be any chance of meeting the Brownie?" she asked timidly. "I would fain not run the risk, for folk say that he is an unchancy creature."

Her companion gave a curious laugh. "Keep up your heart, and dinna talk havers," he said, "for I promise you ye'll see naught uglier this night than the man whom you ride behind."

"Oh, then, I'm fine and safe," replied the old woman, with a sigh of relief, "for although I haven't' seen your face, I warrant that you are a true man, for the care you have taken of a poor old woman."

She relapsed into silence again till the glen was passed and the good horse had turned into the farmyard. Then the horseman slid to the ground, and, turning round, lifted her carefully down in his long, strong arms. As he did so the cloak slipped off him, revealing his short, broad body and his misshapen limbs.

"In a' the world, what kind o' man are ye?" she asked, peering into his face in the grey morning light, which was just dawning. "What makes your eyes so big? And what have you done to your feet? They are more like paddock's webs than aught else."

The queer little man laughed again. "I've wandered many a mile in my time without a horse to help me, and I've heard it said that ower much walking makes the feet unshapely," he replied. "But waste no time in talking, good Dame. Go your way into the house, and hark'ee, if anyone asks you who brought you hither so quickly, tell them that there was a lack of men, so you had even to be content to ride behind the BROWNIE o' FERNE-DEN."

The Death "Bree"

The Death "Bree" is a traditional Scottish folktale, adapted from an anonymous source and included in Folk-lore and Legends: Scotland (W. W. Gibbings, London, 1889). The story tells of a supernatural warning known as the "death bree" or "death blast", a chilling wind believed to carry news of imminent death.

The power of the story lies in its restraint and atmosphere. There are no apparitions, no spoken prophecies, only the unseen touch of the uncanny on the living world. It captures a peculiarly Scottish sensibility, where nature and the supernatural are never far apart, and where grief is bound up with weather and land.

There was once a woman, who lived in the Camp-del-more of Strathavon, whose cattle were seized with a murrain, or some such fell disease, which ravaged the neighbourhood at the time, carrying off great numbers of them daily. All the forlorn fires and hallowed waters failed of their customary effects, and she was at length told by the wise people, whom she consulted on the occasion, that it was evidently the effect of some infernal agency, the power of which could not be destroyed by any other means than the never-failing specific - the juice of a dead head from the churchyard - a nostrum certainly very difficult to be procured, considering that the head must needs be abstracted from the grave at the hour of midnight.

Being, however, a woman of a stout heart and strong faith, native feelings of delicacy towards the sanctuary of the dead had more weight than held fear in restraining her for some time from resorting to this desperate remedy. At length, seeing that her stock would soon be annihilated by the destructive career of the disease, the wife of Camp-del-more resolved to put the experiment in practice, whatever the result might be.

Accordingly, having with considerable difficulty engaged a neighbouring woman as her companion in this hazardous expedition, they set out a little before midnight for the parish churchyard, distant about a mile and a half from her residence, to execute her determination. On arriving at the churchyard her companion, whose courage was not so notable, appalled by the gloomy prospect before her, refused to enter among the habitations of the dead. She, however, agreed to remain at the gate till her friend's business was accomplished.

This circumstance, however, did not stagger the wife's resolution. She, with the greatest coolness and intrepidity, proceeded towards what she supposed an old grave, took down her spade, and commenced her operations. After a good deal of toil she arrived at the object of her labour. Raising the first head, or rather skull, that came in her way, she was about to make it her own property, when a hollow, wild, sepulchral voice exclaimed, "That is my head; let it alone!"

Not wishing to dispute the claimant's title to this head, and supposing she could be otherwise provided, she very good-naturedly returned it and took up another.

"That is my father's head," bellowed the same voice.

Wishing, if possible, to avoid disputes, the wife of Camp-del-more took up another head, when the same voice instantly started a claim to it as his grandfather's head.

"Well," replied the wife, nettled at her disappointments, "although it were your grandmother's head, you shan't get it till I am done with it."

"What do you say, you limmer?" says the ghost, starting up in his awry habiliments. "What do you say, you limmer?" repeated he in a great rage. "By the great oath, you had better leave my grandfather's head."

Upon matters coming this length, the wily wife of Camp-del-more thought it proper to assume a more conciliatory aspect. Telling the claimant the whole particulars of the predicament in which she was placed, she promised faithfully that if his honour would only allow her to carry off his grandfather's skull or head in a peaceable manner, she would restore it again when done with. Here, after some communing, they came to an understanding, and she was allowed to take the head along with her, on condition that she should restore it before cock-crowing, under the heaviest penalties.

On coming out of the churchyard and looking for her companion, she had the mortification to find her "without a mouthful of breath in her body"; for, on hearing the dispute between her friend and the guardian of the grave, and suspecting much that she was likely to share the unpleasant punishments with which he threatened her friend, at the bare recital of them she fell down in a faint, from which it was no easy matter to recover her. This proved no small inconvenience to Camp-del-more's wife, as there were not above two hours to elapse before she had to return the head according to the terms of her agreement.

Taking her friend on her back, she carried her up a steep acclivity to the nearest adjoining house, where she left her for the night; then repaired home with the utmost speed, made dead "bree" of the head before the appointed time had expired, restored the skull to its guardian, and placed the grave in its former condition. It is needless to add that, as a reward for her exemplary courage, the "bree" had its desired effect. The cattle speedily recovered, and, so long as she retained any of the "bree", all sorts of diseases were of short duration.

The Doomed Rider

The Doomed Rider is a traditional Scottish ghost story of fate, guilt, and the uneasy boundary between the living and the dead. The tale tells of a man who, while crossing a lonely stretch of countryside on horseback, encounters a mysterious figure who offers him guidance through storm and darkness.

The version printed in Folk-lore and Legends: Scotland (W. W. Gibbings, London, 1889) is derived from oral traditions whose origins are uncertain, though similar motifs appear throughout the Borders and the Highlands. The anonymous collector or adapter presents the story in the plain, direct style of nineteenth-century folklore compilations, where superstition, moral lesson, and atmosphere intertwine. As with many Scottish tales of the period, The Doomed Rider reflects both the Presbyterian sense of predestined justice and the older, pagan awe of the land itself.

The Conan is as bonny a river as we have in all the north country. There's many a sweet sunny spot on its banks, and many a time have I waded through its shallows, when a boy, to set my little scautling-line for the trouts and the eels, or to gather the big pearl-mussels that lie so thick in the fords. But these bonny wooded banks are places for enjoying the day in - not for passing the night. I know how it is; it's none of your wild streams that wander desolate through a deserted country, like the Aven, or that come rushing down in foam and thunder, over broken rocks, like the Foyers, or that wallow in darkness, deep, deep in the bowels of the earth, like the fearful old Graunt

And yet not one of these rivers has more frightful stories connected with it than the Conan. One can hardly saunter over half-a-mile in its course, from where it leaves Coutin till where it enters the sea, without passing over the scene of some frightful old legend of the kelpie or the water wraith. And one of the most frightful looking of these places is to be found among the woods of Conan House.

You enter a swampy meadow that waves with flags and rushes like a corn-field in harvest, and see a hillock covered with willows rising like an island in the midst. There are thick mirk-woods on either bank; the river, dark and awesome, and whirling round and round in mossy eddies, sweeps away behind it, and there is an old burying-ground, with the broken ruins of an old Papist kirk on the top. One can see among the rougher stones the rose-wrought mullions of an arched window, and the trough that once held the holy water. About two hundred years ago - a wee more maybe, or a wee bit less, for one cannot be very sure of the date of these old stories - the building was entire, and a spot near it, where the wood now grows thickest, was laid out in a corn-field. The marks of the furrows may still be seen among the trees.

A party of Highlanders were busily engaged, all day in harvest, in cutting down the corn of that field, and just about noon, when the sun shone brightest and they were busiest in the work, they heard a voice from the river exclaim, "The hour but not the man has come."

Sure enough, on looking round, there was the kelpie standing in the ford, just in front of the old kirk. There is a deep black pool bath about and below that place, but in the ford there's a bonny ripple, that shows, as one might think, but little depth of water, and just in the middle of that, in a place where a horse might swim, stood the kelpie, and it again repeated its words, "The hour but not the man has come," and then flashing through the water like a drake, it disappeared in the lower pool.

When the folk stood wondering what the creature might mean, they saw a man on horseback come spurring down the hill in hot haste, making straight for the ford. They could then understand her words at once, and four of the stoutest of them sprang out from among the corn to warn him of his danger, and keep him back, and so they told him what they had seen and heard, and urged him either to turn back and take another road, or stay for an hour or so where he was.

But he just would not hear them, for he was both unbelieving and in haste, and would have taken the ford for all they could say, had not the Highlanders, determined on saving him whether he would or no, gathered round him and pulled him from his horse. To make sure of him, they locked him up in the old kirk.

Well, when the hour had gone by - the fatal hour of the kelpie - they flung open the door, and cried to him that he might now go on his journey. Ah! but there was no answer, though, and so they cried a second time, and there was no answer still, and then they went in, and found him lying stiff and cold on the floor, with his face buried in the water of the very stone trough that we may still see among the ruins. His hour had come, and he had fallen in a fit, as 'twould seem, head-foremost into the water of the trough, where he had been smothered, - and so you see, the prophecy of the kelpie availed nothing.

The Draiglin' Hogney

The Draiglin' Hogney is one of the liveliest tales in The Scottish Fairy Book by Elizabeth Wilson Grierson, first published in 1910 by J. B. Lippincott Company. Like many of Grierson's retellings, it blends humour with a moral warning, drawing on the rich folklore of Lowland Scotland.

Grierson's version of the tale captures the oral rhythms and rustic wit of the older fireside stories from which it likely descended. Her language keeps the dialectal flavour, "draiglin'" meaning dragging or trailing, while shaping the chaos into a story fit for print. Beneath the mischief, the tale carries a familiar folkloric lesson: greed and cruelty call down their own undoing, often in the form of the uncanny.

There was once a man who had three sons, and very little money to provide for them. So, when the eldest had grown into a lad, and saw that there was no means of making a livelihood at home, he went to his father and said to him, "Father, if you will give me a horse to ride on, a hound to hunt with, and a hawk to fly, I will go out into the wide world and seek my fortune."

His father gave him what he asked for, and he set out on his travels. He rode and he rode, over mountain and glen, until, just at nightfall, he came to a thick, dark wood. He entered it, thinking that he might find a path that would lead him through it, but no path was visible, and after wandering up and down for some time, he was obliged to acknowledge to himself that he was completely lost.

There seemed to be nothing for it but to tie his horse to a tree, and make a bed of leaves for himself on the ground, but just as he was about to do so he saw a light glimmering in the distance, and, riding on in the direction in which it was, he soon came to a clearing in the wood, in which stood a magnificent Castle.

The windows were all lit up, but the great door was barred, and, after he had ridden up to it, and knocked, and received no answer, the young man raised his hunting horn to his lips and blew a loud blast in the hope of letting the inmates know that he was without.

Instantly the door flew open of its own accord, and the young man entered, wondering very much what this strange thing would mean. And he wondered still more when he passed from room to room, and found that, although fires were burning brightly everywhere, and there was a plentiful meal laid out on the table in the great hall, there did not seem to be a single person in the whole of the vast building.

However, as he was cold, and tired, and wet, he put his horse in one of the stalls of the enormous stable, and taking his hawk and hound along with him, went into the hall and ate a hearty supper. After which he sat down by the side of the fire, and began to dry his clothes.

By this time it had grown late, and he was just thinking of retiring to one of the bedrooms which he had seen upstairs and going to bed, when a clock which was hanging on the wall struck twelve.

Instantly the door of the huge apartment opened, and a most awful-looking Draiglin' Hogney entered. His hair was matted and his beard was long, and his eyes shone like stars of fire from under his bushy eyebrows, and in his hands he carried a queerly shaped club.

He did not seem at all astonished to see his unbidden guest, but, coming across the hall, he sat down upon the opposite side of the fireplace, and, resting his chin on his hands, gazed fixedly at him.

"Does your horse ever kick any?" he said , in a harsh, rough voice.

"Ay, he does," replied the young man, for the only steed that his father had been able to give him was a wild and unbroken colt.

"I have some skill in taming horses," went on the Draiglin' Hogney, "and I will give you something to tame your withal. Throw this over him" - and he pulled one of the long, coarse hairs out of his head and gave it to the young man. And there was something so commanding in the Hogney's voice that he did as he was bid, and went out to the stable and threw the hair over the horse.

Then he returned to the hall, and sat down again by the fire. The moment that he was seated the Draiglin' Hogney asked another question.

"Does your hound ever bite any?"

"Ay, verily," answered the youth, for his hound was so fierce-tempered that no man, save his master, dare lay a hand on him.

"I can cure the wildest tempered dog in Christendom," replied the Draiglin' Hogney. "Take that, and throw it over him." And he pulled another hair out of his head and gave it to the young man, who lost no time in flinging it over his hound.

There was still a third question to follow. "Does ever your hawk peck any?"

The young man laughed. "I have ever to keep a bandage over her eyes, save when she is ready to fly," he said, "else were nothing safe within her reach."

"Things will be safe now," said the Hogney, grimly. "Throw that over her." And for the third time he pulled a hair from his head and handed it to his companion. And as the other hairs had been thrown over the horse and the hound, so this one was thrown over the hawk.

Then, before the young man could draw breath, the fearsome Draiglin' Hogney had given him such a clout on the side of his head with his queer-shaped club that he fell down in a heap on the floor.

And very soon his hawk and his hound tumbled down still and motionless beside him, and, out in the stable, his horse became stark and stiff, as if turned to stone. For the Draiglin's words had meant more than at first appeared when he said that he could make all unruly animals quiet.

Sometime afterwards the second of the three sons came to his father in the old home with the same request that his brother had made. That he should be provided with a horse, a hawk, and a hound, and be allowed to go out to seek his fortune. And his father listened to him, and gave him what he asked, as he had given his brother.

And the young man set out, and in due time came to the wood, and lost himself in it, just as his brother had done; then he saw the light, and came to the Castle, and went in, and had supper, and dried his clothes, just as it all had happened before.

And the Draiglin' Hogney came in, and asked him the three questions, and he gave the same three answers, and received three hairs - one to throw over his horse, one to throw over his hound, and one to throw over his hawk; then the Hogney killed him, just as he had killed his brother.

Time passed, and the youngest son, finding that his two elder brothers never returned, asked his father for a horse, a hawk, and a hound, in order that he might go and look for them. And the poor old man, who was feeling very desolate in his old age, gladly gave them to him.

So he set out on his quest, and at nightfall he came, as the others had done, to the thick wood and the Castle. But, being a wise and cautious youth, he liked not the way in which he found things. He liked not the empty house; he liked not the spread-out feast, and, most of all, he liked not the look of the Draiglin' Hogney when he saw him. And he determined to be very careful what he said or did as long as he was in his company.

So when the Draiglin' Hogney asked him if his horse kicked, he replied that it did, in very few words, and when he got one of the Hogney's hairs to throw over him, he went out to the stable, and pretended to do so, but he brought it back, hidden in his hand, and, when his unchancy companion was not looking, he threw it into the fire. It fizzled up like a tongue of flame with a little hissing sound like that of a serpent.

"What's that fizzling?" asked the Giant suspiciously.

"Tis but the sap of the green wood," replied the young man carelessly, as he turned to caress his hound.

The answer satisfied the Draiglin' Hogney, and he paid no heed to the sound which the hair that should have been thrown over the hound, or the sound which the hair that should have been thrown over the hawk, made, when the young man threw them into the fire, and they fizzled up in the same way that the first had done.

Then, thinking that he had the stranger in his power, he whisked across the hearthstone to strike him with his club, as he had struck his brothers, but the young man was on the outlook, and when he saw him coming he gave a shrill whistle. And his horse, which loved him dearly, came galloping in from the stable, and his hound sprang up from the hearthstone where he had been sleeping, and his hawk, who was sitting on his shoulder, ruffled up her feathers and screamed harshly, and they all fell on the Draiglin' Hogney at once, and he found out only too well how the horse kicked, and the hound bit, and the hawk pecked, for they kicked him, and bit him, and pecked him, till he was as dead as a door nail.

When the young man saw that he was dead, he took his little club from his hand, and, armed with that, he set out to explore the Castle.

As he expected, he found that there were dark and dreary dungeons under it, and in one of them he found his two brothers, lying cold and stiff side by side. He touched them with the club, and instantly they came to life again, and sprang to their feet as well as ever.

Then he went into another dungeon, and there were the two horses, and the two hawks, and the two hounds, lying as if dead, exactly as their masters had lain. He touched them with his magic club, and they, too, came to life again.

Then he called to his two brothers, and the three young men searched the other dungeons, and they found great stores of gold and silver hidden in them, enough to make them rich for life.

So they buried the Draiglin' Hogney, and took possession of the Castle, and two of them went home and brought their old father back with them, and they all were as prosperous and happy as they could be, and, for aught that I know, they are living there still.

The Dwarfie Stone

The Dwarfie Stone, as retold by Elizabeth Wilson Grierson in The Scottish Fairy Book (J. B. Lippincott, 1910), draws its inspiration from one of Orkney's most enigmatic prehistoric monuments, a hollowed block of sandstone lying in a lonely valley on the island of Hoy. In Grierson's version, the great stone is said to have been the dwelling of a dwarf who carved it out himself with only his hammer and chisel.

Grierson's retelling transforms what is, in archaeological terms, a Neolithic rock-cut tomb into a vessel for moral and mythic reflection. Her version belongs to that early twentieth-century movement of Scottish folklore writing which sought to fuse local topography with legend, preserving the character of oral storytelling while making it accessible to a modern readership.

Far up in a green valley in the Island of Hoy stands an immense boulder. It is hollow inside, and the natives of these northern islands call it the Dwarfie Stone, because long centuries ago, so the legend has it, Snorro the Dwarf lived there.

Nobody knew where Snorro came from, or how long he had dwelt in the dark chamber inside the Dwarfie Stone. All that they knew about him was that he was a little man, with a queer, twisted, deformed body and a face of marvellous beauty, which never seemed to look any older, but was always smiling and young.

Men said that this was because Snorro's father had been a Fairy, and not a denizen of earth, who had bequeathed to his son the gift of perpetual youth, but nobody knew whether this were true or not, for the Dwarf had inhabited the Dwarfie Stone long before the oldest man or woman in Hoy had been born.

One thing was certain, however: he had inherited from his mother, whom all men agreed had been mortal, the dangerous qualities of vanity and ambition. And the longer he lived the vainer and more ambitious did he become, until he always carried a mirror of polished steel round his neck, into which he constantly looked in order to see the reflection of his handsome face.

And he would not attend to the country people who came to seek his help unless they bowed themselves humbly before him and spoke to him as if he were a King.

I say that the country people sought his help, for he spent his time, or appeared to spend it, in collecting herbs and simples on the hillsides, which he carried home with him to his dark abode, and distilled medicines and potions from them, which he sold to his neighbours at wondrous high prices.

He was also the possessor of a wonderful leather-covered book, clasped with clasps of brass, over which he would pore for hours together, and out of which he would tell the simple Islanders their fortunes, if they would.

For they feared the book almost as much as they feared Snorro himself, for it was whispered that it had once belonged to Odin, and they crossed themselves for protection as they named the mighty Enchanter. But all the time they never guessed the real reason why Snorro chose to live in the Dwarfie Stone.

I will tell you why he did so. Not very far from the Stone there was a curious hill, shaped exactly like a wart. It was known as the Wart Hill of Hoy, and men said that somewhere in the side of it was hidden a wonderful carbuncle, which, when it was found, would bestow on its finder marvellous magic gifts - Health, Wealth, and Happiness. Everything, in fact, that a human being could desire.

And the curious thing about this carbuncle was, that it was said that it could be seen at certain times, if only the people who were looking for it were at the right spot at the right moment.

Now Snorro had made up his mind that he would find this wonderful stone, so, while he pretended to spend all his time in reading his great book or distilling medicines from his herbs, he was really keeping a keen look-out during his wanderings, noting every tuft of grass or piece of rock under which it might be hidden. And at night, when everyone else was asleep, he would creep out, with pickaxe and spade, to turn over the rocks or dig over the turf, in the hope of finding the long-sought-for treasure underneath them.

He was always accompanied on these occasions by an enormous grey-headed Raven, who lived in the cave along with him, and who was his bosom friend and companion. The Islanders feared this bird of ill omen as much, perhaps, as they feared its Master; for, although they went to consult Snorro in all their difficulties and perplexities, and bought medicines and love-potions from him, they always looked upon him with a certain dread, feeling that there was something weird and uncanny about him.

Now, at the time we are speaking of, Orkney was governed by two Earls, who were half-brothers. Paul, the elder, was a tall, handsome man, with dark hair, and eyes like sloes. All the country people loved him, for he was so skilled in knightly exercises, and had such a sweet and loving nature, that no one could help being fond of him. Old people's eyes would brighten at the sight of him, and the little children would run out to greet him as he rode by their mothers' doors.

And this was the more remarkable because, with all his winning manner, he had such a lack of conversation that men called him Paul the Silent, or Paul the Taciturn.

Harold, on the other hand, was as different from his brother as night is from day. He was fair-haired and blue-eyed, and he had gained for himself the name of Harold the Orator, because he was always free of speech and ready with his tongue.

But for all this he was not a favourite. For he was haughty, and jealous, and quick-tempered, and the old folks' eyes did not brighten at the sight of him, and the babes, instead of toddling out to greet him, hid their faces in their mothers' skirts when they saw him coming.

Harold could not help knowing that the people liked his silent brother best, and the knowledge made him jealous of him, so a coldness sprang up between them.

Now it chanced, one summer, that Earl Harold went on a visit to the King of Scotland, accompanied by his mother, the Countess Helga, and her sister, the Countess Fraukirk.

And while he was at Court he met a charming young Irish lady, the Lady Morna, who had come from Ireland to Scotland to attend upon the Scottish Queen. She was so sweet, and good, and gentle that Earl Harold's heart was won, and he made up his mind that she, and only she, should be his bride.

But although he had paid her much attention, Lady Morna had sometimes caught glimpses of his jealous temper; she had seen an evil expression in his eyes, and had heard him speak sharply to his servants, and she had no wish to marry him. So, to his great amazement, she refused the honour which he offered her, and told him that she would prefer to remain as she was.

Earl Harold ground his teeth in silent rage, but he saw that it was no use pressing his suit at that moment. So what he could not obtain by his own merits he determined to obtain by guile.

Accordingly he begged his mother to persuade the Lady Morna to go back with them on a visit, hoping that when she was alone with him in Orkney, he would be able to overcome her prejudice against him, and induce her to become his wife. And all the while he never remembered his brother Paul; or, if he did, he never thought it possible that he could be his rival.

But that was just the very thing that happened. The Lady Morna, thinking no evil, accepted the Countess Helga's invitation, and no sooner had the party arrived back in Orkney than Paul, charmed with the grace and beauty of the fair Irish Maiden, fell head over ears in love with her. And the Lady Morna, from the very first hour that she saw him, returned his love.

Of course this state of things could not long go on hidden, and when Harold realised what had happened his anger and jealousy knew no bounds. Seizing a dagger, he rushed up to the turret where his brother was sitting in his private apartments, and threatened to stab him to the heart if he did not promise to give up all thoughts of winning the lovely stranger.

But Paul met him with pleasant words, "Calm yourself, Brother," he said. "It is true that I love the lady, but that is no proof that I shall win her. Is it likely that she will choose me, whom all men name Paul the Silent, when she has the chance of marrying you, whose tongue moves so swiftly that to you is given the proud title of Harold the Orator?"

At these words Harold's vanity was flattered, and he thought that, after all, his step-brother was right, and that he had a very small chance, with his meagre gift of speech, of being successful in his suit. So he threw down his dagger, and, shaking hands with him, begged him to pardon his unkind thoughts, and went down the winding stair again in high good-humour with himself and all the world.

By this time it was coming near to the Feast of Yule, and at that Festival it was the custom for the Earl and his Court to leave Kirkwall for some weeks, and go to the great Palace of Orphir, nine miles distant. And in order to see that everything was ready, Earl Paul took his departure some days before the others.

The evening before he left he chanced to find the Lady Morna sitting alone in one of the deep windows of the great hall. She had been weeping, for she was full of sadness at the thought of his departure, and at the sight of her distress the kind-hearted young Earl could no longer contain himself, but, folding her in his arms, he whispered to her how much he loved her, and begged her to promise to be his wife.

She agreed willingly. Hiding her rosy face on his shoulder, she confessed that she had loved him from the very first day that she had seen him, and ever since that moment she had determined that, if she could not wed him, she would wed no other man.

For a little time they sat together, rejoicing in their new-found happiness. Then Earl Paul sprang to his feet.

"Let us go and tell the good news to my mother and my brother," he said. "Harold may be disappointed at first, for I know, Sweetheart, he would fain have had you for his own. But his good heart will soon overcome all that, and he will rejoice with us also."

But the Lady Morna shook her head. She knew, better than her lover, what Earl Harold's feeling would be, and she would fain put off the evil hour.

"Let us hold our peace till after Yule," she pleaded. "It will be a joy to keep our secret to ourselves for a little space; there will be time enough then to let all the world know."

Rather reluctantly, Earl Paul agreed, and next day he set off for the Palace at Orphir, leaving his lady-love behind him.

Little he guessed the danger he was in! For, all unknown to him, his step-aunt, Countess Fraukirk, had chanced to be in the hall, the evening before, hidden behind a curtain, and she had overheard every word that Morna and he had spoken, and her heart was filled with black rage.

For she was a hard, ambitious woman, and she had always hated the young Earl, who was no blood-relation to her, and who stood in the way of his brother, her own nephew; for, if Paul were only dead, Harold would be the sole Earl of Orkney.

And now that he had stolen the heart of the Lady Morna, whom her own nephew loved, her hate and anger knew no bounds. She had hastened off to her sister's chamber as soon as the lovers had parted, and there the two women had remained talking together till the chilly dawn broke in the sky.

Next day a boat went speeding over the narrow channel of water that separates Pomona (on the mainland) from Hoy. In it sat a woman, but who she was, or what she was like, no one could say, for she was covered from head to foot with a black cloak, and her face was hidden behind a thick, dark veil.

Snorro the Dwarf knew her, even before she laid aside her trappings, for Countess Fraukirk was no stranger to him. In the course of her long life she had often had occasion to seek his aid to help her in her evil deeds, and she had always paid him well for his services in yellow gold. He therefore welcomed her gladly, but when he had heard the nature of her errand his smiling face grew grave again, and he shook his head.

"I have served you well, Lady, in the past," he said, "but methinks that this thing goes beyond my courage. For to compass an Earl's death is a weighty matter, especially when he is so well beloved as is the Earl Paul.

"You know why I have taken up my abode in this lonely spot - how I hope someday to light upon the magic carbuncle. You know also how the people fear me, and hate me too, forsooth. And if the young Earl died, and suspicion fell on me, I must needs fly the Island, for my life would not be worth a grain of sand. Then my chance of success would be gone. Nay! I cannot do it, Lady; I cannot do it."

But the wily Countess offered him much gold, and bribed him higher and higher, first with wealth, then with success, and lastly she promised to obtain for him a high post at the Court of the King of Scotland, and at that his ambition stirred within him, his determination gave way, and he consented to do what she asked.

"I will summon my magic loom," he said, "and weave a piece of cloth of finest texture and of marvellous beauty, and before I weave it I will so poison the thread with a magic potion that, when it is fashioned into a garment, whoever puts it on will die before he has worn it many minutes."

"You are a clever knave," answered the Countess, a cruel smile lighting up her evil face, "and you shalt be rewarded. Let me have a couple of yards of this wonderful web, and I will make a bonnie waistcoat for my fine young Earl and give it to him as a Yuletide gift. Then I reckon that he will not see the year out."

"That will he not," said Dwarf Snorro, with a malicious grin, and the two parted, after arranging that the piece of cloth should be delivered at the Palace of Orphir on the day before Christmas Eve.

Now, when the Countess Fraukirk had been away upon her wicked errand, strange things were happening at the Castle at Kirkwall. For Harold, encouraged by his brother's absence, offered his heart and hand once more to the Lady Morna. Once more she refused him, and in order to make sure that the scene should not be repeated, she told him that she had plighted her troth to his brother. When he heard that this was so, rage and fury were like to devour him. Mad with anger, he rushed from her presence, flung himself upon his horse, and rode away in the direction of the seashore.

While he was galloping wildly along, his eyes fell on the snow-clad hills of Hoy rising up across the strip of sea that divided the one island from the other. And his thoughts flew at once to Snorro the Dwarf, who he had had occasion, as well as his step-aunt, to visit in bygone days.

"I have it," he cried. "Stupid fool that I was not to think of it at once. I will go to Snorro, and buy from him a love-potion, which will make my Lady Morna hate my precious brother and turn her thoughts kindly towards me."

So he made haste to hire a boat, and soon he was speeding over the tossing waters on his way to the Island of Hoy. When he arrived there he hurried up the lonely valley to where the Dwarfie Stone stood, and he had no difficulty in finding its uncanny occupant, for Snorro was standing at the hole that served as a door, his raven on his shoulder, gazing placidly at the setting sun.

A curious smile crossed his face when, hearing the sound of approaching footsteps, he turned round and his eyes fell on the young noble.

"What brings you here, Sir Earl?" he asked gaily, for he scented more gold.

"I come for a love-potion," said Harold, and without more ado he told the whole story to the Wizard. "I will pay you for it," he added, "if you will give it to me quickly."

Snorro looked at him from head to foot. "Blind must the maiden be, Sir Orator," he said, "who needs a love-potion to make her fancy so gallant a Knight."

Earl Harold laughed angrily. "It is easier to catch a sunbeam than a woman's roving fancy," he replied. "I have no time for jesting. For, hearken, old man, there is a proverb that saith, 'Time and tide wait for no man,' so I need not expect the tide to wait for me. The potion I must have, and that instantly."

Snorro saw that he was in earnest, so without a word he entered his dwelling, and in a few minutes returned with a small phial in his hand, which was full of a rosy liquid.

"Pour the contents of this into the Lady Morna's wine-cup," he said, "and I warrant you that before four-and-twenty hours have passed she will love you better than you love her now." Then he waved his hand, as if to dismiss his visitor, and disappeared into his dwelling-place.

Earl Harold made all speed back to the Castle, but it was not until one or two days had elapsed that he found a chance to pour the love-potion into the Lady Morna's wine-cup. But , one night at supper, he found an opportunity of doing so, and, waving away the little page-boy, he handed it to her himself.

She raised it to her lips, but she only made a pretence at drinking, for she had seen the hated Earl fingering the cup, and she feared some deed of treachery. When he had gone back to his seat she managed to pour the whole of the wine on the floor, and smiled to herself at the look of satisfaction that came over Harold's face as she put down the empty cup.

His satisfaction increased, for from that moment she felt so afraid of him that she treated him with great kindness, hoping that by doing so she would keep in his good graces until the Court moved to Orphir, and her own true love could protect her.

Harold, on his side, was delighted with her graciousness, for he felt certain that the charm was beginning to work, and that his hopes would soon be fulfilled.

A week later the Court removed to the Royal Palace at Orphir, where Earl Paul had everything in readiness for the reception of his guests.

Of course he was overjoyed to meet Lady Morna again, and she was overjoyed to meet him, for she felt that she was now safe from the unwelcome attentions of Earl Harold.

But to Earl Harold the sight of their joy was as gall and bitterness, and he could scarcely contain himself, although he still trusted in the efficacy of Snorro the Dwarf's love-potion.

As for Countess Fraukirk and Countess Helga, they looked forward eagerly to the time when the magic web would arrive, out of which they hoped to fashion a fatal gift for Earl Paul.

At last, the day before Christmas Eve, the two wicked women were sitting in the Countess Helga's chamber talking of the time when Earl Harold would rule alone in Orkney, when a tap came to the window, and on looking round they saw Dwarf Snorro's grey-headed Raven perched on the sill, a sealed packet in its beak.

They opened the casement, and with a hoarse croak the creature let the packet drop on to the floor; then it flapped its great wings and rose slowly into the air again its head turned in the direction of Hoy.

With fingers that trembled with excitement they broke the seals and undid the packet. It contained a piece of the most beautiful material that anyone could possibly imagine, woven in all the colours of the rainbow, and sparkling with gold and jewels.

"Twill make a bonnie waistcoat," exclaimed Countess Fraukirk, with an unholy laugh. "The Silent Earl will be a braw man when he gets it on."

Then, without more ado, they set to work to cut out and sew the garment. All that night they worked, and all next day, till, late in the afternoon, when they were putting in the last stitches, hurried footsteps were heard ascending the winding staircase, and Earl Harold burst open the door.

His cheeks were red with passion, and his eyes were bright, for he could not but notice that, now that she was safe at Orphir under her true love's protection, the Lady Morna's manner had grown cold and distant again, and he was beginning to lose faith in Snorro's charm.

Angry and disappointed, he had sought his mother's room to pour out his story of vexation to her.

He stopped short, however, when he saw the wonderful waistcoat lying on the table, all gold and silver and shining colours. It was like a fairy garment, and its beauty took his breath away.

"For whom have you purchased that?" he asked, hoping to hear that it was intended for him.

"Tis a Christmas gift for your brother Paul," answered his mother, and she would have gone on to tell him how deadly a thing it was, had he given her time to speak. But her words fanned his fury into madness, for it seemed to him that this hated brother of his was claiming everything.

"Everything is for Paul! I am sick of his very name," he cried. "By my troth, he shall not have this!" and he snatched the vest from the table.

It was in vain that his mother and his aunt threw themselves at his feet, begging him to lay it down, and warning him that there was not a thread in it which was not poisoned. He paid no heed to their words, but rushed from the room, and drawing it on, ran downstairs with a reckless laugh, to show the Lady Morna how fine he was.

Alas! alas! Scarce had he gained the hall than he fell to the ground in great pain.

Everyone crowded round him, and the two Countesses, terrified now by what they had done, tried in vain to tear the magic vest from his body. But he felt that it was too late, the deadly poison had done its work, and, waving them aside, he turned to his brother, who, in great distress, had knelt down and taken him tenderly in his arms.

"I wronged you, Paul," he gasped. "For you have ever been true and kind. Forgive me in your thoughts, and," he added, gathering up his strength for one last effort, and pointing to the two wretched women who had wrought all this misery, "Beware of those two women, for they seek to take your life." Then his head sank back on his brother's shoulder, and, with one long sigh, he died.

When he learned what had happened, and understood where the waistcoat came from, and for what purpose it had been intended, the anger of the Silent Earl knew no bounds. He swore a great oath that he would be avenged, not only on Snorro the Dwarf, but also on his wicked step-mother and her cruel sister.

His vengeance was baulked, however, for in the panic and confusion that followed Harold's death, the two Countesses slipped out of the Palace and fled to the coast, and took boat in haste to Scotland, where they had great possessions, and where they were much looked up to, and where no one would believe a word against them.

But retribution fell on them in the end, as it always does fall, sooner or later, on everyone who is wicked, or selfish, or cruel, for the Norsemen invaded the land, and their Castle was set on fire, and they perished miserably in the flames.

When Earl Paul found that they had escaped, he set out in hot haste for the Island of Hoy, for he was determined that the Dwarf, at least, should not escape. But when he came to the Dwarfie Stone he found it silent and deserted, all trace of its uncanny occupants having disappeared.

No one knew what had become of them; a few people were inclined to think that the Dwarf and his Raven had accompanied the Countess Fraukirk and the Countess Helga on their flight, but the greater part of the Islanders held to the belief, which I think was the true one, that the Powers of the Air spirited Snorro away, and shut him up in some unknown place as a punishment for his wickedness, and that his Raven accompanied him.

At any rate, he was never seen again by any living person, and wherever he went, he lost all chance of finding the magic carbuncle.

As for the Silent Earl and his Irish Sweetheart, they were married as soon as Earl Harold's funeral was over, and for hundreds of years afterwards, when the inhabitants of the Orkney Isles wanted to express great happiness, they said, "As happy as Earl Paul and the Countess Morna."

The Elfin Knight

The Elfin Knight, as retold by Elizabeth Wilson Grierson in The Scottish Fairy Book (J. B. Lippincott Company, 1910), draws on one of the oldest motifs in Scottish balladry: the encounter between a mortal woman and a supernatural suitor.

Grierson's adaptation softens the darker edges of earlier oral and ballad sources such as Child Ballad No. 2, The Elfin Knight, where the encounter has overt tones of seduction and peril. Instead, she frames the story as a contest of wit and resolve between human courage and faerie glamour, written in her clear, rhythmic prose. The tale reflects the Borders' enduring fascination with the dangerous beauty of the Otherworld, its promise of love, power, and loss. and Grierson's retelling preserves that tension while making it accessible to modern readers, especially the young.

There is a lone moor in Scotland, which, in times past, was said to be haunted by an Elfin Knight. This Knight was only seen at rare intervals, once in every seven years or so, but the fear of him lay on all the country round, for every now and then someone would set out to cross the moor and would never be heard of again.

And although men might search every inch of the ground, no trace of him would be found, and with a thrill of horror the searching party would go home again, shaking their heads and whispering to one another that he had fallen into the hands of the dreaded Knight.

So, as a rule, the moor was deserted, for nobody dare pass that way, much less live there, and by and by it became the haunt of all sorts of wild animals, which made their lairs there, as they found that they never were disturbed by mortal huntsmen.

Now in that same region lived two young earls, Earl St. Clair and Earl Gregory, who were such friends that they rode, and hunted, and fought together, if need be.

And as they were both very fond of the chase, Earl Gregory suggested one day that they should go a-hunting on the haunted moor, in spite of the Elfin King.

"Certes, I hardly believe in him at all," cried the young man, with a laugh. "Methinks 'tis but an old wives' tale to frighten the bairns withal, lest they go straying amongst the heather and lose themselves. And 'tis pity that such fine sport should be lost because we - two bearded men - pay heed to such gossip."

But Earl St. Clair looked grave. "Tis ill meddling with unchancy things," he answered, "and 'tis no bairn's tale that travellers have set out to cross that moor who have vanished bodily, and never mair been heard of, but it is, as you say, a pity that so much good sport be lost, all because an Elfin Knight choose to claim the land as his, and make us mortals pay toll for the privilege of planting a foot upon it.

"I have heard tell, however, that one is safe from any power that the Knight may have if one wear the Sign of the Blessed Trinity. So let us bind That on our arm and ride forth without fear."

Sir Gregory burst into a loud laugh at these words. "Do you think that I am one of the bairns," he said, "first to be frightened by an idle tale, and then to think that a leaf of clover will protect me? No, no, carry that Sign if you will; I will trust to my good bow and arrow."

But Earl St. Clair did not heed his companion's words, for he remembered how his mother had told him, when he was a little lad at her knee that whoso carried the Sign of the Blessed Trinity need never fear any spell that might be thrown over him by Warlock or Witch, Elf or Demon.

So he went out to the meadow and plucked a leaf of clover, which he bound on his arm with a silken scarf; then he mounted his horse and rode with Earl Gregory to the desolate and lonely moorland.

For some hours all went well, and in the heat of the chase the young men forgot their fears. Then suddenly both of them reined in their steeds and sat gazing in front of them with affrighted faces. For a horseman had crossed their track, and they both would fain have known who he was and from where he came.

"By my troth, but he rides in haste, whoever he may be," said Earl Gregory , "and tho' I always thought that no steed on earth could match mine for swiftness, I reckon that for every league that mine goes, his would go seven. Let us follow him, and see from what part of the world he comes."

"The Lord forbid that you should stir your horse's feet to follow him," said Earl St. Clair devoutly. "Why, man, 'tis the Elfin Knight! Canst you not see that he does not ride on the solid ground, but flies through the air, and that, although he rides on what seems a mortal steed, he is really carried by mighty pinions, which cleave the air like those of a bird? Follow him forsooth! It will be an evil day for you when you seek to do that."

But Earl St. Clair forgot that he carried a Talisman which his companion lacked, that enabled him to see things as they really were, while the other's eyes were holden, and he was startled and amazed when Earl Gregory said sharply, "Your mind has gone mad over this

Elfin King. I tell you he who passed was a goodly Knight, clad in a green vesture, and riding on a great black jennet. And because I love a gallant horseman, and would fain learn his name and degree, I will follow him till I find him, even if it be at the world's end."

And without another word he put spurs to his horse and galloped off in the direction which the mysterious stranger had taken, leaving Earl St. Clair alone upon the moorland, his fingers touching the sacred Sign and his trembling lips muttering prayers for protection.

For he knew that his friend had been bewitched, and he made up his mind, brave gentleman that he was, that he would follow him to the world's end, if need be, and try to deliver him from the spell that had been cast over him.

Meanwhile Earl Gregory rode on and on, ever following in the wake of the Knight in green, over moor, and burn, and moss, till he came to the most desolate region that he had ever been in in his life; where the wind blew cold, as if from snow-fields, and where the hoar-frost lay thick and white on the withered grass at his feet.

And there, in front of him, was a sight from which mortal man might well shrink back in awe and dread. For he saw an enormous Ring marked out on the ground, inside of which the grass, instead of being withered and frozen, was lush, and rank, and green, where hundreds of shadowy Elfin figures were dancing, clad in loose transparent robes of dull blue, which seemed to curl and twist round their wearers like snaky wreaths of smoke.

These weird Goblins were shouting and singing as they danced, and waving their arms above their heads, and throwing themselves about on the ground, for all the world as if they had gone mad, and when they saw Earl Gregory halt on his horse just outside the Ring they beckoned to him with their skinny fingers.

"Come hither, come hither," they shouted, "come tread a measure with us, and afterwards we will drink to you out of our Monarch's loving cup."

And, strange as it may seem, the spell that had been cast over the young Earl was so powerful that, in spite of his fear, he felt that he must obey the eldritch summons, and he threw his bridle on his horse's neck and prepared to join them.

But just then an old and grizzled Goblin stepped out from among his companions and approached him.

Apparently he dare not leave the charmed Circle, for he stopped at the edge of it; then, stooping down and pretending to pick up something, he whispered in a hoarse whisper:

"I know not whom you are, nor from where you come, Sir Knight, but if you love your life, see to it that you come not within this Ring, nor join with us in our feast. Else will you be forever undone."

But Earl Gregory only laughed. "I vowed that I would follow the Green Knight," he replied, "and I will carry out my vow, even if the venture leads me close to the nethermost world." And with these words he stepped over the edge of the Circle, right in amongst the ghostly dancers.

At his coming they shouted louder than ever, and danced more madly, and sang more lustily; then, all at once, a silence fell upon them, and they parted into two companies, leaving a way through their midst, up which they signed to the Earl to pass.

He walked through their ranks till he came to the middle of the Circle, and there, seated at a table of red marble, was the Knight whom he had come so far to seek, clad in his grass-green robes. And before him, on the table, stood a wondrous goblet, fashioned from an emerald, and set round the rim with blood-red rubies.

And this cup was filled with heather ale, which foamed up over the brim, and when the Knight saw Sir Gregory, he lifted it from the table, and handed it to him with a stately bow, and Sir Gregory, being very thirsty, drank.

And as he drank he noticed that the ale in the goblet never grew less, but ever foamed up to the edge, and for the first time his heart misgave him, and he wished that he had never set out on this strange adventure.

But alas! the time for regrets had passed, for already a strange numbness was stealing over his limbs, and a chill pallor was creeping over his face, and before he could utter a single cry for help the goblet dropped from his nerveless fingers, and he fell down before the Elfin King like a dead man.

Then a great shout of triumph went up from all the company, for if there was one thing which filled their hearts with joy, it was to entice some unwary mortal into their Ring and throw their uncanny spell over him, so that he must needs spend long years in their company.

But soon their shouts of triumphs began to die away, and they muttered and whispered to each other with looks of something like fear on their faces.

For their keen ears heard a sound which filled their hearts with dread. It was the sound of human footsteps, which were so free and untrammelled that they knew at once that the stranger, whoever he was, was as yet untouched by any charm. And if this were so he might work them ill, and rescue their captive from them.

And what they dreaded was true, for it was the brave Earl St. Clair who approached, fearless and strong because of the Holy Sign he bore. And as soon as he saw the charmed Ring and the eldritch dancers, he was about to step over its magic border, when the little grizzled Goblin who had whispered to Earl Gregory, came and whispered to him also.

"Alas! alas!" he exclaimed, with a look of sorrow on his wrinkled face, "hast you come, as your companion came, to pay your toll of years to the Elfin King? Oh! if you have wife or child behind you, I beseech you, by all that you hold sacred, to turn back before it be too late."

"Who are you, and from where have you come?" asked the Earl, looking kindly down at the little creature in front of him.

"I came from the country that you have come from," wailed the Goblin. "For I was once a mortal man, even as you. But I set out over the enchanted moor, and the Elfin King appeared in the guise of a beauteous Knight, and he looked so brave, and noble, and generous that I followed him hither, and drank of his heather ale, and now I am doomed to bide here till seven long years be spent.

"As for your friend, Sir Earl, he, too, has drunk of the accursed draught, and he now lies as dead at our lawful Monarch's feet. He will wake up, 'tis true, but it will be in such a guise as I wear, and to the bondage with which I am bound."

"Is there naught that I can do to rescue him!" cried Earl St. Clair eagerly, "ere he takes on him the Elfin shape? I have no fear of the spell of his cruel captor, for I bear the Sign of One Who is stronger than he. Speak speedily, little man, for time presses."

"There is something that you could do, Sir Earl," whispered the Goblin, "but to essay it were a desperate attempt. For if you fail, then could not even the Power of the Blessed Sign save you."

"And what is that?" asked the Earl impatiently.

"You must remain motionless," answered the old man, "in the cold and frost till dawn break and the hour comes when they sing Matins in the Holy Church. Then must you walk slowly nine times round the edge of the enchanted Circle, and after that you must walk boldly across it to the red marble table where sits the Elfin King. On it you will see an emerald goblet studded with rubies and filled with heather ale. That must you secure and carry away, but whilst you are doing so let no word cross your lips. For this enchanted ground whereon we dance may look solid to mortal eyes, but in reality it is not so. 'Tis but a quaking bog, and under it is a great lake, wherein dwells a fearsome Monster, and if you so much as utter a word while your foot rests upon it, you will fall through the bog and perish in the waters beneath."

So saying the Grisly Goblin stepped back among his companions, leaving Earl St. Clair standing alone on the outskirts of the charmed Ring.

There he waited, shivering with cold, through the long, dark hours, till the grey dawn began to break over the hill tops, and, with its coming, the Elfin forms before him seemed to dwindle and fade away.

And at the hour when the sound of the Matin Bell came softly pealing from across the moor, he began his solemn walk. Round and round the Ring he paced, keeping steadily on his way, although loud murmurs of anger, like distant thunder, rose from the Elfin Shades, and even the very ground seemed to heave and quiver, as if it would shake this bold intruder from its surface. But through the power of the Blessed Sign on his arm Earl St. Clair went on unhurt.

When he had finished pacing round the Ring he stepped boldly on to the enchanted ground, and walked across it, and what was his astonishment to find that all the ghostly Elves and Goblins whom he had seen, were lying frozen into tiny blocks of ice, so that he was sore put to it to walk amongst them without treading upon them.

And as he approached the marble table the very hairs rose on his head at the sight of the Elfin King sitting behind it, stiff and stark like his followers; while in front of him lay the form of Earl Gregory, who had shared the same fate.

Nothing stirred, save two coal-black ravens, who sat, one on each side of the table, as if to guard the emerald goblet, flapping their wings, and croaking hoarsely.

When Earl St. Clair lifted the precious cup, they rose in the air and circled round his head, screaming with rage, and threatening to dash it from his hands with their claws; while the frozen Elves, and even their mighty King himself stirred in their sleep, and half sat up, as if to lay hands on this presumptuous intruder. But the Power of the Holy Sign restrained them, else had Earl St. Clair been foiled in his quest.

As he retraced his steps, awesome and terrible were the sounds that he heard around him. The ravens shrieked, and the frozen Goblins screamed, and up from the hidden lake below came the sound of the deep breathing of the awful Monster who was lurking there, eager for prey.

But the brave Earl heeded none of these things, but kept steadily onwards, trusting in the Might of the Sign he bore. And it carried him safely through all the dangers, and just as the sound of the Matin

Bell was dying away in the morning air he stepped on to solid ground once more, and flung the enchanted goblet from him.

And lo! every one of the frozen Elves vanished, along with their King and his marble table, and nothing was left on the rank green grass save Earl Gregory, who slowly woke from his enchanted slumber, and stretched himself, and stood up, shaking in every limb. He gazed vaguely round him, as if he scarce remembered where he was.

And when, after Earl St. Clair had run to him and had held him in his arms till his senses returned and the warm blood coursed through his veins, the two friends returned to the spot where Earl St. Clair had thrown down the wondrous goblet, they found nothing but a piece of rough grey whinstone, with a drop of dew hidden in a little crevice which was hollowed in its side.

The Enchanted Deer

The Enchanted Deer, as retold by Andrew Lang in The Lilac Fairy Book (1910), originates from John Francis Campbell's Popular Tales of the West Highlands (1860–62), one of the foundational collections of Gaelic folklore. Lang's adaptation smooths Campbell's more literal transcription into a flowing Victorian fairy-tale narrative, but the Highland character of the story remains clear. It tells of a brother and sister whose fates are twisted by enchantment.

As with many of Campbell's sources, the story bears traces of older mythic patterns: transformation through taboo, the protective love between siblings, and the idea that magic is both punishment and protection. Lang's retelling lends the tale a sense of moral gentleness and closure characteristic of his late-Victorian readership, but beneath the polish, The Enchanted Deer still carries the wildness of its Gaelic origins.

A young man was out walking one day in Erin, leading a stout cart-horse by the bridle. He was thinking of his mother and how poor they were since his father, who was a fisherman, had been drowned at sea, and wondering what he should do to earn a living for both of them. Suddenly a hand was laid on his shoulder, and a voice said to him:

'Will you sell me your horse, son of the fisherman?' and looking up he beheld a man standing in the road with a gun in his hand, a falcon on his shoulder, and a dog by his side.

'What will you give me for my horse?' asked the youth. 'Will you give me your gun, and your dog, and your falcon?'

'I will give them,' answered the man, and he took the horse, and the youth took the gun and the dog and the falcon, and went home with them. But when his mother heard what he had done she was very angry, and beat him with a stick which she had in her hand.

'That will teach you to sell my property,' she said, when her arm was quite tired, but Ian her son answered her nothing, and went off to his bed, for he was very sore.

That night he rose softly, and left the house carrying the gun with him. 'I will not stay here to be beaten,' thought he, and he walked and he walked and he walked, till it was day again, and he was hungry and looked about him to see if he could get anything to eat. Not very far off was a farm-house, so he went there, and knocked at the door, and the farmer and his wife begged him to come in, and share their breakfast.

'Ah, you have a gun,' said the farmer as the young man placed it in a corner. 'That is well, for a deer comes every evening to eat my corn, and I cannot catch it. It is fortune that has sent you to me.'

'I will gladly remain and shoot the deer for you,' replied the youth, and that night he hid himself and watched till the deer came to the cornfield; then he lifted his gun to his shoulder and was just going to pull the trigger, when, behold! instead of a deer, a woman with long black hair was standing there. At this sight his gun almost dropped from his hand in surprise, but as he looked, there was the deer eating the corn again. And thrice this happened, till the deer ran away over the moor, and the young man after her.

On they went, on and on and one, till they reached a cottage which was thatched with heather. With a bound the deer sprang on the roof, and lay down where none could see her, but as she did so she called out. 'Go in, fisher's son, and eat and drink while you may.' So he entered and found food and wine on the table, but no man, for the house belonged to some robbers, who were still away at their wicked business.

After Ian, the fisher's son, had eaten all he wanted, he hid himself behind a great cask, and very soon he heard a noise, as of men coming through the heather, and the small twigs snapping under their feet. From his dark corner he could see into the room, and he counted four and twenty of them, all big, cross-looking men.

'Someone has been eating our dinner,' cried they, 'and there was hardly enough for ourselves.'

'It is the man who is lying under the cask,' answered the leader. 'Go and kill him, and then come and eat your food and sleep, for we must be off betimes in the morning.'

So four of them killed the fisher's son and left him, and then went to bed.

By sunrise they were all out of the house, for they had far to go. And when they had disappeared the deer came off the roof, to where the dead man lay, and she shook her head over him, and wax fell from her ear, and he jumped up as well as ever.

'Trust me and eat as you did before, and no harm shall happen to you,' she said. So Ian ate and drank, and fell sound asleep under the cask. In the evening the robbers arrived very tired, and crosser than they had been yesterday, for their luck had turned and they had brought back scarcely anything.

'Someone has eaten our dinner again,' cried they.

'It is the man under the barrel,' answered the captain. 'Let four of you go and kill him, but first slay the other four who pretended to kill him last night and didn't because he is still alive.'

Then Ian was killed a second time, and after the rest of the robbers had eaten, they lay down and slept till morning.

No sooner were their faces touched with the sun's rays than they were up and off. Then the deer entered and dropped the healing wax on the dead man, and he was as well as ever. By this time he did not mind what befell him, so sure was he that the deer would take care of him, and in the evening that which had happened before happened again - the four robbers were put to death and the fisher's son also, but because there was no food left for them to eat, they were nearly mad with rage, and began to quarrel. From quarrelling they went on to fighting, and fought so hard that by and bye they were all stretched dead on the floor.

Then the deer entered, and the fisher's son was restored to life, and bidding him follow her, she ran on to a little white cottage where dwelt an old woman and her son, who was thin and dark.

'Here I must leave you,' said the deer, 'but to-morrow meet me at midday in the church that is yonder.' And jumping across the stream, she vanished into a wood.

Next day he set out for the church, but the old woman of the cottage had gone before him, and had stuck an enchanted stick called 'the spike of hurt' in a crack of the door, so that he would brush against it as he stepped across the threshold. Suddenly he felt so sleepy that he could not stand up, and throwing himself on the ground he sank into a deep slumber, not knowing that the dark lad was watching him. Nothing could waken him, not even the sound of sweetest music, nor the touch of a lady who bent over him. A sad look came on her face, as she saw it was no use, and she gave it up, and lifting his arm, wrote her name across the side, 'the daughter of the king of the town under the waves.'

'I will come to-morrow,' she whispered, though he could not hear her, and she went sorrowfully away.

Then he awoke, and the dark lad told him what had befallen him, and he was very grieved. But the dark lad did not tell him of the name that was written underneath his arm.

On the following morning the fisher's son again went to the church, determined that he would not go to sleep, whatever happened. But in his hurry to enter he touched with his hand the spike of hurt, and sank down where he stood, wrapped in slumber. A second time the air was filled with music, and the lady came in, stepping softly, but though she laid his head on her knee, and combed his hair with a golden comb, his eyes opened not. Then she burst into tears, and placing a beautifully wrought box in his pocket she went her way.

The next day the same thing befell the fisher's son, and this time the lady wept more bitterly than before, for she said it was the last chance, and she would never be allowed to come any more, for home she must go.

As soon as the lady had departed the fisher's son awoke, and the dark lad told him of her visit, and how he would never see her as long as he lived. At this the fisher's son felt the cold creeping up to his heart, yet he knew the fault had not been his that sleep had overtaken him.

'I will search the whole world through till I find her,' cried he, and the dark lad laughed as he heard him. But the fisher's son took no heed, and off he went, following the sun day after day, till his shoes were in holes and his feet were sore from the journey. Nought did he see but the birds that made their nests in the trees, not so much as a goat or a rabbit. On and on and on he went, till suddenly he came upon a little house, with a woman standing outside it.

'All hail, fisher's son!' she said. 'I know what you are seeking; enter in and rest and eat, and tomorrow I will give you what help I can, and send you on your way.'

Gladly did Ian the fisher's son accept her offer, and all that day he rested, and the woman gave him ointment to put on his feet, which healed his sores. At daybreak he got up, ready to be gone, and the woman bade him farewell, saying:

'I have a sister who dwells on the road which you must travel. It is a long road, and it would take you a year and a day to reach it, but put on these old brown shoes with holes all over them, and you will be there before you know it. Then shake them off, and turn their toes to the known, and their heels to the unknown, and they will come home of themselves.'

The fisher's son did as the woman told him, and everything happened just as she had said. But at parting the second sister said to him, as she gave him another pair of shoes, 'Go to my third sister, for she has a son who is keeper of the birds of the air, and sends them to sleep when night comes. He is very wise, and perhaps he can help you.'

Then the young man thanked her, and went to the third sister. The third sister was very kind, but had no counsel to give him, so he ate and drank and waited till her son came home, after he had sent all the birds to sleep. He thought a long while after his mother had told him the young man's story, and he said that he was hungry, and the cow must be killed, as he wanted some supper. So the cow was killed and the meat cooked, and a bag made of its red skin.

'Now get into the bag,' bade the son, and the young man got in and took his gun with him, but the dog and the falcon he left outside. The keeper of the birds drew the string at the top of the bag, and left it to finish his supper, when in flew an eagle through the open door, and picked the bag up in her claws and carried it through the air to an island. There was nothing to eat on the island, and the fisher's son thought he would die of food, when he remembered the box that the lady had put in his pocket. He opened the lid, and three tiny little birds flew out, and flapping their wings they asked,

'Good master, is there anything we can do for you?'

'Bear me to the kingdom of the king under the waves,' he answered, and one little bird flew on to his head, and the others perched on each of his shoulders, and he shut his eyes, and in a moment there he was in the country under the sea. Then the birds flew away, and the young man looked about him, his heart beating fast at the thought that here dwelt the lady whom he had sought all the world over.

He walked on through the streets, and presently he reached the house of a weaver who was standing at his door, resting from his work.

'You are a stranger here, that is plain,' said the weaver, 'but come in, and I will give you food and drink.' And the young man was glad, for he knew not where to go, and they sat and talked till it grew late.

'Stay with me, I pray, for I love company and am lonely,' observed the weaver , and he pointed to a bed in a corner, where the fisher's son threw himself, and slept till dawn.

'There is to be a horse-race in the town to-day,' remarked the weaver, 'and the winner is to have the king's daughter to wife.' The young man trembled with excitement at the news, and his voice shook as he answered:

'That will be a prize indeed, I should like to see the race.'

'Oh, that is quite easy - anyone can go,' replied the weaver. 'I would take you myself, but I have promised to weave this cloth for the king.'

'That is a pity,' returned the young man politely, but in his heart he rejoiced, for he wished to be alone.

Leaving the house, he entered a grove of trees which stood behind, and took the box from his pocket. He raised the lid, and out flew the three little birds.

'Good master, what shall we do for you?' asked they, and he answered, 'Bring me the finest horse that ever was seen, and the grandest dress, and glass shoes.'

'They are here, master,' said the birds, and so they were, and never had the young man seen anything so splendid.

Mounting the horse he rode into the ground where the horses were assembling for the great race, and took his place among them. Many good beasts were there which had won many races, but the horse of the fisher's son left them all behind, and he was first at the winning post. The king's daughter waited for him in vain to claim his prize, for he went back to the wood, and got off his horse, and put on his old clothes, and bade the box place some gold in his pockets. After that he went back to the weaver's house, and told him that the gold had been given him by the man who had won the race, and that the weaver might have it for his kindness to him.

Now as nobody had appeared to demand the hand of the princess, the king ordered another race to be run, and the fisher's son rode into the field still more splendidly dressed than he was before, and easily distanced everybody else. But again he left the prize unclaimed, and so it happened on the third day, when it seemed as if all the people in the kingdom were gathered to see the race, for they were filled with curiosity to know who the winner could be.

'If he will not come of his own free will, he must be brought,' said the king, and the messengers who had seen the face of the victor were sent to seek him in every street of the town. This took many days, and when they found the young man in the weaver's cottage, he was so dirty and ugly and had such a strange appearance, that they declared he could not be the winner they had been searching for, but a wicked robber who had murdered ever so many people, but had always managed to escape.

'Yes, it must be the robber,' said the king, when the fisher's son was led into his presence, 'build a gallows at once and hang him in the sight of all my subjects, that they may behold him suffer the punishment of his crimes.'

So the gallows was built upon a high platform, and the fisher's son mounted the steps up to it, and turned at the top to make the speech that was expected from every doomed man, innocent or guilty. As he spoke he happened to raise his arm, and the king's daughter, who was there at her father's side, saw the name which she had written under it. With a shriek she sprang from her seat, and the eyes of the spectators were turned towards her.

'Stop! stop!' she cried, hardly knowing what she said. 'If that man is hanged there is not a soul in the kingdom but shall die also.' And running up to where the fisher's son was standing, she took him by the hand, saying,

'Father, this is no robber or murderer, but the victor in the three races, and he loosed the spells that were laid upon me.'

Then, without waiting for a reply, she conducted him into the palace, and he bathed in a marble bath, and all the dirt that the fairies had put upon him disappeared like magic, and when he had dressed himself in the fine garments the princess had sent to him, he looked a match for any king's daughter in Erin. He went down into the great hall where she was awaiting him, and they had much to tell each other but little time to tell it in, for the king her father, and the princes who were visiting him, and all the people of the kingdom were still in their places expecting her return.

'How did you find me out?' she whispered as they went down the passage.

'The birds in the box told me,' answered he, but he could say no more, as they stepped out into the open space that was crowded with people. There the princes stopped. 'O kings!' she said, turning towards them, 'if one of you were killed to-day, the rest would fly, but this man put his trust in me, and had his head cut off three times. Because he has done this, I will marry him rather than one of you, who have come hither to wed me, for many kings here sought to free me from the spells, but none could do it save Ian the fisher's son.'

The Fairies of Merlin's Crag

The Fairies of Merlin's Crag, adapted from The Scottish Fairy Book (1910) by Elizabeth Wilson Grierson, is a tale steeped in the folklore of the Scottish Borders, where the mortal and the magical coexist uneasily. It tells of a shepherd who tends his flock near Merlin's Crag, a place long whispered to be haunted by the fair folk.

Grierson's version preserves the moral and atmosphere typical of Scottish fairy lore: the warning against curiosity, the peril of enchantment, and the thin boundary between the seen and unseen worlds. Her prose, while intended for early twentieth-century readers, keeps close to the rhythms of oral storytelling and to the Scots landscape that shaped it.

About two hundred years ago there was a poor man working as a labourer on a farm in Lanarkshire. He was what is known as an "Orra Man"; that is, he had no special work mapped out for him to do, but he was expected to undertake odd jobs of any kind.

One day his master sent him out to cast peats on a piece of moorland that lay on a certain part of the farm. Now this strip of moorland ran up at one end to a curiously shaped crag, known as Merlin's Crag, because, so the country folk said, that famous Enchanter had once taken up his abode there.

The man obeyed, and being a willing fellow, when he arrived at the moor he set to work with all his might and main. He had lifted quite a quantity of peat from near the Crag, when he was startled by the appearance of the very smallest woman that he had ever seen in his life. She was only about two feet high, and she was dressed in a green gown and red stockings, and her long yellow hair was not bound by any ribbon, but hung loosely around her shoulders.

She was such a dainty little creature that the astonished countryman stopped working, stuck his spade into the ground, and gazed at her in wonder.

His wonder increased when she held up one of her tiny fingers and addressed him in these words, "What would you think if I were to send my husband to uncover your house? You mortals think that you can do aught that pleases you." Then, stamping her tiny foot, she added in a voice of command, "Put back that turf instantly, or you shalt rue this day."

Now the poor man had often heard of the Fairy Folk and of the harm that they could work to unthinking mortals who offended them, so in fear and trembling he set to work to undo all his labour, and to place every divot in the exact spot from which he had taken it.

When he was finished he looked round for his strange visitor, but she had vanished completely; he could not tell how, nor where. Putting up his spade, he wended his way homewards, and going straight to his master, he told him the whole story, and suggested that in future the peats should be taken from the other end of the moor.

But the master only laughed. He was a strong, hearty man, and had no belief in Ghosts, or Elves, or Fairies, or any other creature that he could not see, but although he laughed, he was vexed that his servant should believe in such things, so to cure him, as he thought, of his superstition, he ordered him to take a horse and cart and go back at once, and lift all the peats and bring them to dry in the farm steading.

The poor man obeyed with much reluctance, and was greatly relieved, as weeks went on, to find that, in spite of his having done so, no harm befell him. In fact, he began to think that his master was right, and that the whole thing must have been a dream. So matters went smoothly on. Winter passed, and spring, and summer, until autumn came round once more, and the very day arrived on which the peats had been lifted the year before.

That day, as the sun went down, the orra man left the farm to go home to his cottage, and as his master was pleased with him because he had been working very hard lately, he had given him a little can of milk as a present to carry home to his wife.

So he was feeling very happy, and as he walked along he was humming a tune to himself. His road took him by the foot of Merlin's Crag, and as he approached it he was astonished to find himself growing strangely tired. His eyelids dropped over his eyes as if he were going to sleep, and his feet grew as heavy as lead.

"I will sit down and take a rest for a few minutes," he said to himself, "the road home never seemed so long as it does to-day."

So he sat down on a tuft of grass right under the shadow of the Crag, and before he knew where he was he had fallen into a deep and heavy slumber. When he awoke it was near midnight, and the moon had risen on the Crag. And he rubbed his eyes, when by its soft light he became aware of a large band of Fairies who were dancing round and round him, singing and laughing, pointing their tiny fingers at him, and shaking their wee fists in his face.

The bewildered man rose and tried to walk away from them, but turn in whichever direction he would the Fairies accompanied him, encircling him in a magic ring, out of which he could in no wise go.

At last they stopped, and, with shrieks of elfin laughter, led the prettiest and daintiest of their companions up to him, and cried, "Tread a measure, tread a measure, Oh, Man! Then will you not be so eager to escape from our company."

Now the poor labourer was but a clumsy dancer, and he held back with a shamefaced air, but the Fairy who had been chosen to be his partner reached up and seized his hands, and lo! some strange magic seemed to enter into his veins, for in a moment he found himself waltzing and whirling, sliding and bowing, as if he had done nothing else but dance all his life. And strangest thing of all! he forgot about his home and his children, and he felt so happy that he had no longer the slightest desire to leave the Fairies' company.

All night long the merriment went on. The Little Folk danced and danced as if they were mad, and the farm man danced with them, until a shrill sound came over the moor. It was the cock from the farmyard crowing its loudest to welcome the dawn.

In an instant the revelry ceased, and the Fairies, with cries of alarm, crowded together and rushed towards the Crag, dragging the countryman along in their midst. As they reached the rock, a mysterious door, which he never remembered having seen before, opened in it of its own accord, and shut again with a crash as soon as the Fairy Host had all trooped through.

The door led into a large, dimly lighted hall full of tiny couches, and here the Little Folk sank to rest, tired out with their exertions, while the good man sat down on a piece of rock in the corner, wondering what would happen next.

But there seemed to be some kind of spell thrown over his senses, for even when the Fairies awoke and began to go about their household occupations, and to carry out certain curious practices which he had never seen before, and which, as you will hear, he was forbidden to speak of afterwards, he was content to sit and watch them, without in any way attempting to escape.

As it drew toward evening someone touched his elbow, and he turned round with a start to see the little woman with the green dress and scarlet stockings, who had remonstrated with him for lifting the turf the year before, standing by his side.

"The divots which you took from the roof of my house have grown once more," she said, "and it is covered with grass, so you can go home again, for justice is satisfied. Your punishment has lasted long enough. But first must you take your solemn oath never to tell mortal ears what you have seen whilst you have dwelt among us."

The countryman promised gladly, and took the oath with all due solemnity. Then the door was opened, and he was at liberty to depart. His can of milk was standing on the green, just where he had laid it down when he went to sleep, and it seemed to him as if it were only yesternight that the farmer had given it to him.

But when he reached his home he was speedily undeceived. For his wife looked at him as if he were a ghost, and the children whom he had left wee, toddling things were now well-grown boys and girls, who stared at him as if he had been an utter stranger.

"Where have you been these long years?" cried his wife when she had gathered her wits and seen that it was really he, and not a spirit. "How could you leave the bairns and me alone?"

And then he knew that the one day he had passed in Fairy-land had lasted seven whole years, and he realised how heavy the punishment had been which the Wee Folk had laid upon him.

The Fairy Boy of Leith

The Fairy Boy of Leith is a curious and haunting tale, adapted from an anonymous source and included in Folk-lore and Legends: Scotland (W. W. Gibbings, London, 1889). Set around the port town of Leith, it tells of a boy who was often seen playing a small drum and claiming to be taught his music by the fairies.

The tale reflects enduring Scottish beliefs about the permeability of the world between mortals and the sith folk, and it also hints at the thin line between inspiration and possession. Like many of the legends gathered in the Gibbings volume, The Fairy Boy of Leith blends Christian moral overtones with older, animistic superstition, an uneasy coexistence between faith and folklore.

About fifteen years ago, having business that detained me for some time at Leith, which is near Edinburgh, in the kingdom of Scotland, I often met some of my acquaintance at a certain house there, where we used to drink a glass of wine for our refection. The woman which kept the house was of honest reputation among the neighbours, which made me give the more attention to what she told me one day about a fairy boy (as they called him) who lived about that town.

She had given me so strange an account of him, that I desired her I might see him the first opportunity, which she promised, and not long after, passing that way, she told me there was the fairy boy, but a little before I came by, and, casting her eye into the street, said, 'Look you, sir, yonder he is, at play with those other boys', and pointing him out to me, I went, and by smooth words, and a piece of money, got him to come into the house with me; where, in the presence of divers people, I demanded of him several astrological questions, which he answered with great subtlety, and, through all his discourse, carried it with a cunning much above his years, which seemed not to exceed ten or eleven.

He seemed to make a motion like drumming upon the table with his fingers, upon which I asked him whether he could beat a drum? To which he replied, 'Yes, sir, as well as any man in Scotland, for every Thursday night I beat all points to a sort of people that used to meet under yonder hill' (pointing to the great hill between Edinburgh and Leith).

'How, boy?' said I, 'what company have you there?'

'There are, sir,' he said, 'a great company both of men and women, and they are entertained with many sorts of music besides my drum; they have, besides, plenty of variety of meats and wine, and many times we are carried into France or Holland in the night, and return again, and whilst we are there, we enjoy all the pleasures the country does afford.'

I demanded of him how they got under that hill? To which he replied that there was a great pair of gates that opened to them, though they were invisible to others, and that within there were brave large rooms, as well accommodated as most in Scotland.

I then asked him how I should know what he said to be true? Upon which he told me he would read my fortune, saying, I should have two wives, and that he saw the forms of them over my shoulders, and both would be very handsome women.

The woman of the house told me that all the people in Scotland could not keep him from the rendezvous on Thursday night; upon which, by promising him some more money, I got a promise of him to meet me at the same place in the afternoon, the Thursday following, and so dismissed him at that time.

The boy came again at the place and time appointed, and I had prevailed with some friends to continue with me (if possible) to prevent his moving that night. He was placed between us, and answered many questions, until, about eleven of the clock, he was got away unperceived by the company, but I, suddenly missing him, hastened to the door, and took hold of him, and so returned him into the same room. We all watched him, and, of a sudden, he was again got out of doors; I followed him close, and he made a noise in the street, as if he had been set upon, and from that time I could never see him.

The Fiddler and the Bogle of Bogandoran

The Fiddler and the Bogle of Bogandoran is a lively Scottish folk tale drawn from Folk-lore and Legends: Scotland (W. W. Gibbings, London, 1889), though its original collector or author is unknown. It belongs to that enduring Scottish tradition where wit and music triumph over the uncanny. The story tells of a wandering fiddler who, while travelling across the moors near Bogandoran, encounters a bogle.

As with many tales of its kind, humour tempers the haunting. Beneath its comic surface runs a deeper current of belief in the power of art, here, music, to charm, pacify, and outwit the forces of the otherworld.

Late one night, as my grand-uncle, Lachlan Dhu Macpherson, who was well known as the best fiddler of his day, was returning home from a ball, at which he had acted as a musician, he had occasion to pass through the once-haunted Bog of Torrans. Now, it happened at that time that the bog was frequented by a huge bogle or ghost, who was of a most mischievous disposition, and took particular pleasure in abusing every traveller who had occasion to pass through the place betwixt the twilight at night and cock-crowing in the morning.

Suspecting much that he would also come in for a share of his abuse, my grand-uncle made up his mind, in the course of his progress, to return the ghost any civilities which he might think meet to offer him. On arriving on the spot, he found his suspicions were too well grounded, for whom did he see but the ghost of Bogandoran apparently ready waiting him, and seeming by his ghastly grin not a little overjoyed at the meeting.

Marching up to my grand-uncle, the bogle clapped a huge club into his hand, and furnishing himself with one of the same dimensions, he put a spittle in his hand, and deliberately commenced the combat. My grand-uncle returned the salute with equal spirit, and so ably did both parties ply their batons that for a while the issue of the combat was extremely doubtful.

At length, however, the fiddler could easily discover that his opponent's vigour was much in the fagging order. Picking up renewed courage in consequence, he plied the ghost with renewed force, and after a stout resistance, in the course of which both parties were seriously handled, the ghost of Bogandoran thought it prudent to give up the night.

At the same time, filled no doubt with great indignation at this signal defeat, it seems the ghost resolved to re-engage my grand-uncle on some other occasion, under more favourable circumstances. Not long after, as my grand-uncle was returning home quite unattended from another ball in the Braes of the country, he had just entered the hollow of Auldichoish, well known for its 'eerie' properties, when, lo! who presented himself to his view on the adjacent eminence but his old friend of Bogandoran, advancing as large as the gable of a house, and putting himself in the most threatening and fighting attitudes.

Looking at the very dangerous nature of the ground where they had met, and feeling no anxiety for a second encounter with a combatant of his weight, in a situation so little desirable, the fiddler would have willingly deferred the settlement of their differences till a more convenient season. He, accordingly, assuming the most submissive aspect in the world, endeavoured to pass by his champion in peace, but in vain. Longing, no doubt, to retrieve the disgrace of his late discomfiture, the bogle instantly seized the fiddler, and attempted with all his might to pull the latter down the precipice, with the diabolical intention, it is supposed, of drowning him in the river Avon below.

In this pious design the bogle was happily frustrated by the intervention of some trees which grew on the precipice, and to which my unhappy grand-uncle clung with the zeal of a drowning man. The enraged ghost, finding it impossible to extricate him from those friendly trees, and resolving, at all events, to be revenged upon him, fell upon maltreating the fiddler with his hands and feet in the most inhuman manner.

Such gross indignities my worthy grand-uncle was not accustomed to, and being incensed beyond all measure at the liberties taken by Bogandoran, he resolved again to try his mettle, whether life or death should be the consequence. Having no other weapon wherewith to defend himself but his dirk, which, considering the nature of his opponent's constitution, he suspected would be of little use to him - I say, in the absence of any other weapon, he sheathed the dirk three times in the ghost of Bogandoran's body. And what was the consequence? Why, to the great astonishment of my courageous forefather, the ghost fell down cold dead at his feet, and was never more seen or heard of.

The Fisherman and the Merman

The Fisherman and the Merman, adapted from an anonymous source and included in Folk-lore and Legends: Scotland (W. W. Gibbings, London, 1889), is one of those quiet, moral tales that inhabit the shoreline between superstition and faith. The story tells of a fisherman who hauls from the sea not the expected catch but a living merman, a strange and sorrowful being half-human, half-sea-creature.

Like many coastal legends collected in the late nineteenth century, the tale reflects both the peril and the sanctity of the sea in Scottish imagination. The merman is not merely a creature of fancy but a voice for moral order, reminding humans of their smallness against the elements and their dependence upon mercy.

Of Mermen and Merwomen many strange stories are told in the Shetland Isles. Beneath the depths of the ocean, according to these stories, an atmosphere exists adapted to the respiratory organs of certain beings, resembling, in form, the human race, possessed of surpassing beauty, of limited supernatural powers, and liable to the incident of death. They dwell in a wide territory of the globe, far below the region of fishes, over which the sea, like the cloudy canopy of our sky, loftily rolls, and they possess habitations constructed of the pearl and coral productions of the ocean.

Having lungs not adapted to a watery medium, but to the nature of atmospheric air, it would be impossible for them to pass through the volume of waters that intervenes between the submarine and supramarine world, if it were not for the extraordinary power they inherit of entering the skin of some animal capable of existing in the sea, which they are enabled to occupy by a sort of demoniacal possession.

One shape they put on, is that of an animal human above the waist, yet terminating below in the tail and fins of a fish, but the most favourite form is that of the larger seal or Haaf-fish; for, in possessing an amphibious nature, they are enabled not only to exist in the ocean, but to land on some rock, where they frequently lighten themselves of their sea-dress, resume their proper shape, and with much curiosity examine the nature of the upper world belonging to the human race.

Unfortunately, however, each merman or merwoman possesses but one skin, enabling the individual to ascend the seas, and if, on visiting the abode of man, the garb be lost, the hapless being must unavoidably become an inhabitant of the earth.

A story is told of a boat's crew who landed for the purpose of attacking the seals lying in the hollows of the crags at one of the sea stacks. The men stunned a number of the animals, and while they were in this state stripped them of their skins, with the fat attached to them. Leaving the carcasses on the rock, the crew were about to set off for the shore of Papa Stour, when such a tremendous swell arose that everyone flew quickly to the boat. All succeeded in entering it except one man, who had imprudently lingered behind. The crew were unwilling to leave a companion to perish on the skerries, but the surge increased so fast, that after many unsuccessful attempts to bring the boat close into the stack the unfortunate wight was left to his fate.

A stormy night came on, and the deserted Shetlander saw no prospect before him but that of perishing from cold and hunger, or of being washed into the sea by the breakers which threatened to dash over the rocks. At length, he perceived many of the seals, who, in their flight had escaped the attack of the boatmen, approach the skerry, disrobe themselves of their amphibious hides, and resume the shape of the sons and daughters of the ocean.

Their first object was to assist in the recovery of their friends, who having been stunned by clubs, had, while in that state, been deprived of their skins. When the flayed animals had regained their sensibility, they assumed their proper form of mermen or merwomen, and began to lament in a mournful lay, wildly accompanied by the storm that was raging around, the loss of their sea-dress, which would prevent them from again enjoying their native azure atmosphere, and coral mansions that lay below the deep waters of the Atlantic.

But their chief lamentation was for Ollavitinus, the son of Gioga, who, having been stripped of his seal's skin, would be forever parted from his mates, and condemned to become an outcast inhabitant of the upper world. Their song was at length broken off, by observing one of their enemies viewing, with shivering limbs and looks of comfortless despair, the wild waves that dashed over the stack.

Gioga immediately conceived the idea of rendering subservient to the advantage of the son the perilous situation of the man. She addressed him with mildness, proposing to carry him safe on her back across the sea to Papa Stour, on condition of receiving the seal-skin of Ollavitinus. A bargain was struck, and Gioga clad herself in her amphibious garb, but the Shetlander, alarmed at the sight of the stormy main that he was to ride through, prudently begged leave of the matron, for his better preservation, that he might be allowed to cut a few holes in her shoulders and flanks, in order to procure, between the skin and the flesh, a better fastening for his hands and feet. The request being complied with, the man grasped the neck of the seal, and committing himself to her care, she landed him safely at Acres Gio in Papa Stour; from which place he immediately repaired to a skeo (dry stone hut) at Hamna Voe, where the skin was deposited, and honourably fulfilled his part of the contract, by affording Gioga the means whereby her son could again revisit the ethereal space over which the sea spread its green mantle.

The Fishermen of Shetland

The Fishermen of Shetland, adapted from Peter Henry Emerson's Fairy-Tales & Other Stories (1894), is a stark and atmospheric tale drawn from the maritime folklore of Scotland's northern isles. It follows the lives of Shetland fishermen whose work brings them into daily intimacy with the sea, at once their sustainer and their doom.

In this tale, the sea itself becomes a moral and spiritual force, unpredictable and alive, mirroring the inner lives of the men who depend on it. The Fishermen of Shetland stands as both a record of a vanishing maritime culture and a meditation on humanity's fragile compact with nature, one that the islanders honour each time they put out to sea.

There was a snug little cove in one of the Shetland Islands. At the head of the cove stood a fishing hamlet, containing some twenty huts. In these huts lived the fisher-folk, ruled by one man - their chief - who was the father of two beautiful daughters.

Now these fishermen for some years had been very lucky, for a fairy queen and her fairies had settled there, and she had given her power over to a merman, who was the chief of a large family of mermaids. The fairy queen had made the merman a belt of seaweed, which he always wore round his body. The merman used to turn the water red, green, and white, at noon each day, so that the fishermen knew that if they cast their nets into the coloured waters they would make good hauls.

Amongst these fishermen were two brave brothers, who courted the chief's daughters, but the old man would not let them get married until they became rich men. Whenever the fishermen went off in the boats the merman was used to sit on a rock, and watch them fishing.

Close by the hamlet was a great wood, in which lived a wicked old witch and a dwarf.

Now this witch wished to get possession of the merman's belt, and so gain the fairy's power. Telling her scheme to the dwarf, she said to him, "Now you must trap the merman when he is sitting on the rocks watching the fishing fleet. But I must change you into a bee, when you must suck of the juice in this magic basin, then fly off and alight on the merman's head, when he will fall asleep."

So the dwarf agreed, and it happened as she had said, and the merman fell asleep, and the dwarf stole the belt and brought it to the witch.

"Now you must wear the belt," said the witch to the dwarf, "and you will have the power and the fairy will lose her power."

They then carried the sleeping merman to the forest and laid him before the hut, when the witch got a copper vessel, saying, "We must bury him in this."

Then she got the magic pot, and told the dwarf to take a ladleful of the fluid in the pot, and pour it over the merman, which he did, and immediately the merman turned into smoke, that settled in the copper vessel. Then they sealed the copper vessel tightly.

"Now take this vessel, and heave it into the sea fifty miles from the land," said the witch, and the dwarf did as he was bid.

"Now we'll starve those old fishermen out this winter," said the witch, and it happened as she had said - they could catch nothing.

In the spring the queen fairy came to one of the young fishermen who was courting one of the chief's daughters, and said, "You must venture for the sake of your love, and for the lives of the fishermen, or you will all starve - but I will be with you. Will you run the risk?"

"I will," said the brave fisherman.

"Well, the dwarf has got my belt, he stole it from the merman, and so I have lost power over the world for twelve months and a day, but if you get back the belt I can settle the witch; if not, you will all starve and catch no fish."

So the bold fisherman agreed to try.

"Now I must transform you into a bear, and you'll have to watch the witch and the dwarf, and take your chance of getting the belt, and you must watch where he hides his treasure, for he is using the belt as a means to get gold, which he hides in a cave."

And so the sailor was turned into a bear, and he went to the wood and watched the dwarf, and saw that he hid his treasure in a cave in some crags.

The bear had been given the power of making himself invisible, by sitting on his haunches and rubbing his ears with his paws.

One night, when it was very boisterous, the bear felt like going to see his sweetheart. So he went, and knocked at the door. The girl opened the door, and shrieked when she saw the bear.

"Oh, let him in," he said her old mother.

So the bear came in and asked for shelter from the storm, for he could speak. And he went and sat by the fire, and asked his sweetheart to brush the snow from his coat, which she did.

"I won't do you any harm," he said, "let me sleep by the fire."

He came again the next night, and they gave him some gruel, and played with him, for he was just like a dog.

So he came every night until the springtime, when, one morning, as he was going away, he said, "You mustn't expect me anymore. Spring has come, and the snows have melted. I can't come again till the summer is over."

So he returned to the wood and watched the dwarf, but he could never catch him without his belt, until one day he saw him fishing for salmon without the belt, and at the same time his sweetheart and her sister came by picking flowers.

So the bear went up to the dwarf, and the dwarf, when he saw him coming, said, "Ah! good bear! good bear! let me go. These two girls will be a daintier morsel for you."

But the bear smote him with his paw and killed him, and immediately the bear was turned into his former self, and the girls ran up and kissed him, and talked.

Then he took the two girls to the dwarf's cave, and gave each of them a bag of treasure, keeping one for himself. And taking the belt, he put it on, and they all walked back to the hamlet, when he told the fishermen that their troubles would soon be over - but that he must kill the witch first.

Then he turned the belt three times, and said, "I wish for the queen fairy."

And she came, and was delighted, and said, "Now you must come and slay the witch," and she handed him a bow and arrow, telling him to use it right and tight when he got to the hut.

So he went off to the wood, and found the witch in her hut, and she begged for mercy. "Oh no, you have done too much mischief," he said, and he shot her.

Then the queen fairy appeared, and sent him to gather dry wood to make a fire. When the fire was made she sent him to fetch the witch's wand, which she cast into the flames, saying, "Now, mark my word, all the devils of hell will be here."

And when the wand began to burn all the devils came and tried to snatch it from the fire, but the queen raised her wand, saying, "Through this powerful wand that I hold in my hand, through this bow and arrow, I have caused her to be slain, that she may leave our domain. Now take her up high into the sky, and let her burst asunder as a clap of thunder. Then take her to hell and there let her dwell, to all eternity." And the wand was burnt, and the devils carried the witch off in a noise like thunder.

The twelve months were up on that day, and the fairy said to the fisherman, "Take your chief and your brother, and put out to sea half-a-mile, where you'll see a red spot, bright as the sun on the water; cast in your net on the sea-side of the spot, and pull to the shore."

They did as the queen commanded, and when they pulled the net on the shore they found the copper vessel.

"Now open it," said the queen to the fisherman with the belt, "but cover your belt with your coat first."

And he did so, and when he opened the copper a ball of smoke rose into the air, and suddenly the merman stood before them, and said, "The first four months that I was in prison, I swore I'd make the man as rich as a king, the man who released me. But there was no release, no release, no release. The second four months that I was in prison,

I swore I'd make the water run red, but there was no release, no release, no release. The last four months that I was in prison, I swore in my wrath I'd take my deliverer's life, whoever he might be."

Whereupon the fisherman opened his coat and showed him the belt. Then the merman immediately cooled down, and said, "Oh, that's how I came into this trouble."

Then he asked the fisherman with the belt what had happened, and he told him the whole story.

Then the queen told the fisherman to take the girdle off and put it back on the merman, and he did so, and suddenly the merman took to the sea, and began to sing from a rock:

"As I sit upon the rock,

I am like a statue block,

And I straighten my hair,

That is so long and fair.

And now my eyes look bright,

For I am in great delight,

Because I am free in glee,

To roam over the sea."

After that the hamlet was joyful again, for the fishermen began to catch plenty of fish, for the merman showed them where to cast their nets, by colouring the water as of old.

And the two brothers married the chief's two beautiful daughters, and they lived happily ever afterwards.

The Fox and the Wolf

The Fox and the Wolf, adapted by Andrew Lang in The Orange Fairy Book (1906) from John Francis Campbell's Popular Tales from the West Highlands (1860–62), is a lively Scottish folktale built around cunning and reversal. It follows a wily fox and a rather gullible wolf who set out together to steal food from a farm.

Lang's retelling keeps much of Campbell's earthy tone and rhythm but refines the structure and phrasing for a younger, late-Victorian readership. His version remains brisk and moral without sermonising, part of his wider project to preserve Celtic and European oral material in polished literary English. Beneath the simple animal farce lies a reflection of older Highland storytelling, its sympathy for the underdog, its mistrust of brute power, and its appreciation of cunning as a means of survival in a hard landscape.

At the foot of some high Scottish mountains there was, once upon a time, a small village, and a little way off two roads met, one of them going to the east and the other to the west. The villagers were quiet, hard-working folk, who toiled in the fields all day, and in the evening set out for home when the bell began to ring in the little church. In the summer mornings they led out their flocks to pasture, and were happy and contented from sunrise to sunset.

One summer night, when a round full moon shone down upon the white road, a great wolf came trotting round the corner.

'I positively must get a good meal before I go back to my den,' he said to himself, 'it is nearly a week since I have tasted anything but scraps, though perhaps no one would think it to look at my figure! Of course there are plenty of rabbits and hares in the mountains, but indeed one needs to be a greyhound to catch them, and I am not so young as I was! If I could only dine off that fox I saw a fortnight ago, curled up into a delicious hairy ball, I should ask nothing better; I would have eaten her then, but unluckily her husband was lying beside her, and one knows that foxes, great and small, run like the wind. Really it seems as if there was not a living creature left for me to prey upon but a wolf, and, as the proverb says, "One wolf does not bite another." However, let us see what this village can produce. I am as hungry as a schoolmaster.'

Now, while these thoughts were running through the mind of the wolf, the very fox he had been thinking of was galloping along the other road.

'The whole of this day I have listened to those village hens clucking till I could bear it no longer,' murmured she as she bounded along, hardly seeming to touch the ground. 'When you are fond of fowls and eggs it is the sweetest of all music. As sure as there is a sun in heaven I will have some of them this night, for I have grown so thin that my very bones rattle, and my poor babies are crying for food.' And as she spoke she reached a little plot of grass, where the two roads joined, and flung herself under a tree to take a little rest, and to settle her plans. At this moment the wolf came up.

At the sight of the fox lying within his grasp his mouth began to water, but his joy was somewhat checked when he noticed how thin she was. The fox's quick ears heard the sound of his paws, though they were soft as velvet, and turning her head she said politely, 'Is that you, neighbour? What a strange place to meet in! I hope you are quite well?'

'Quite well as regards my health,' answered the wolf, whose eye glistened greedily, 'at least, as well as one can be when one is very hungry. But what is the matter with you? A fortnight ago you were as plump as heart could wish!'

'I have been ill - very ill,' replied the fox, 'and what you say is quite true. A worm is fat in comparison with me.'

'He is. Still, you are good enough for me, for "to the hungry no bread is hard."'

'Oh, you are always joking! I'm sure you are not half as hungry as I!'

'That we shall soon see,' cried the wolf, opening his huge mouth and crouching for a spring.

'What are you doing?' exclaimed the fox, stepping backwards.

'What am I doing? What I am going to do is to make my supper off you, in less time than a cock takes to crow.'

'Well, I suppose you must have your joke,' answered the fox lightly, but never removing her eye from the wolf, who replied with a snarl which showed all his teeth, 'I don't want to joke, but to eat!'

'But surely a person of your talents must perceive that you might eat me to the very last morsel and never know that you had swallowed anything at all!'

'In this world the cleverest people are always the hungriest,' replied the wolf.

'Ah! how true that is, but - '

'I can't stop to listen to your "buts" and "yets," broke in the wolf rudely, 'let us get to the point, and the point is that I want to eat you and not talk to you.'

'Have you no pity for a poor mother?' asked the fox, putting her tail to her eyes, but peeping slyly out of them all the same.

'I am dying of hunger,' answered the wolf, doggedly, 'and you know,' he added with a grin, 'that charity begins at home.'

'Quite so,' replied the fox, 'it would be unreasonable of me to object to your satisfying your appetite at my expense. But if the fox resigns herself to the sacrifice, the mother offers you one last request.'

'Then be quick and don't waste my time, for I can't wait much longer. What is it you want?'

'You must know,' said the fox, 'that in this village there is a rich man who makes in the summer enough cheeses to last him for the whole year, and keeps them in an old well, now dry, in his courtyard. By the well hang two buckets on a pole that were used, in former days, to draw up water. For many nights I have crept down to the palace, and have lowered myself in the bucket, bringing home with me enough cheese to feed the children. All I beg of you is to come with me, and, instead of hunting chickens and such things, I will make a good meal off cheese before I die.'

'But the cheeses may be all finished by now?'

'If you were only to see the quantities of them!' laughed the fox. 'And even if they were finished, there would always be ME to eat.'

'Well, I will come. Lead the way, but I warn you that if you try to escape or play any tricks you are reckoning without your host - that is to say, without my legs, which are as long as yours!'

All was silent in the village, and not a light was to be seen but that of the moon, which shone bright and clear in the sky. The wolf and the fox crept softly along, when suddenly they stopped and looked at each other; a savoury smell of frying bacon reached their noses, and reached the noses of the sleeping dogs, who began to bark greedily.

'Is it safe to go on, think you?' asked the wolf in a whisper. And the fox shook her head.

'Not while the dogs are barking,' she said, 'someone might come out to see if anything was the matter.' And she signed to the wolf to curl himself up in the shadow beside her.

In about half an hour the dogs grew tired of barking, or perhaps the bacon was eaten up and there was no smell to excite them. Then the wolf and the fox jumped up, and hastened to the foot of the wall.

'I am lighter than he is,' thought the fox to herself, 'and perhaps if I make haste I can get a start, and jump over the wall on the other side before he manages to spring over this one.' And she quickened her pace. But if the wolf could not run he could jump, and with one bound he was beside his companion.

'What were you going to do, comrade?'

'Oh, nothing,' replied the fox, much vexed at the failure of her plan.

'I think if I were to take a bit out of your haunch you would jump better,' said the wolf, giving a snap at her as he spoke. The fox drew back uneasily.

'Be careful, or I shall scream,' she snarled. And the wolf, understanding all that might happen if the fox carried out her threat, gave a signal to his companion to leap on the wall, where he immediately followed her.

Once on the top they crouched down and looked about them. Not a creature was to be seen in the courtyard, and in the furthest corner from the house stood the well, with its two buckets suspended from a pole, just as the fox had described it. The two thieves dragged themselves noiselessly along the wall till they were opposite the well, and by stretching out her neck as far as it would go the fox was able to make out that there was only very little water in the bottom, but just enough to reflect the moon, big, and round and yellow.

'How lucky!' cried she to the wolf. 'There is a huge cheese about the size of a mill wheel. Look! look! did you ever see anything so beautiful!'

'Never!' answered the wolf, peering over in his turn, his eyes glistening greedily, for he imagined that the moon's reflection in the water was really a cheese.

'And now, unbeliever, what have you to say?' and the fox laughed gently.

'That you are a woman - I mean a fox - of your word,' replied the wolf.

'Well, then, go down in that bucket and eat your fill,' said the fox.

'Oh, is that your game?' asked the wolf, with a grin. 'No! no! The person who goes down in the bucket will be you! And if you don't go down your head will go without you!'

'Of course I will go down, with the greatest pleasure,' answered the fox, who had expected the wolf's reply.

'And be sure you don't eat all the cheese, or it will be the worse for you,' continued the wolf. But the fox looked up at him with tears in her eyes.

'Farewell, suspicious one!' she said sadly. And climbed into the bucket.

In an instant she had reached the bottom of the well, and found that the water was not deep enough to cover her legs.

'Why, it is larger and richer than I thought,' cried she, turning towards the wolf, who was leaning over the wall of the well.

'Then be quick and bring it up,' commanded the wolf.

'How can I, when it weighs more than I do?' asked the fox.

'If it is so heavy bring it in two bits, of course,' he said.

'But I have no knife,' answered the fox. 'You will have to come down yourself, and we will carry it up between us.'

'And how am I to come down?' inquired the wolf.

'Oh, you are really very stupid! Get into the other bucket that is nearly over your head.'

The wolf looked up, and saw the bucket hanging there, and with some difficulty he climbed into it. As he weighed at least four times as much as the fox the bucket went down with a jerk, and the other bucket, in which the fox was seated, came to the surface.

As soon as he understood what was happening, the wolf began to speak like an angry wolf, but was a little comforted when he remembered that the cheese still remained to him.

'But where is the cheese?' he asked of the fox, who in her turn was leaning over the parapet watching his proceedings with a smile.

'The cheese?' answered the fox, 'why I am taking it home to my babies, who are too young to get food for themselves.'

'Ah, traitor!' cried the wolf, howling with rage. But the fox was not there to hear this insult, for she had gone off to a neighbouring fowl-house, where she had noticed some fat young chickens the day before.

'Perhaps I did treat him rather badly,' she said to herself. 'But it seems getting cloudy, and if there should be heavy rain the other bucket will fill and sink to the bottom, and his will go up - at least it may!'

The Ghosts of Craig-Aulnaic

The Ghosts of Craig-Aulnaic, adapted from an anonymous nineteenth-century source and reprinted in Folk-lore and Legends: Scotland (W. W. Gibbings, London, 1889), is a classic Highland ghost story that blends the chill of the supernatural with the moral atmosphere of older Scottish tradition. Set near the river Spey, it tells of a traveller who seeks shelter for the night in the ruined house of Craig-Aulnaic, long shunned by locals for its reputation as a haunt of restless spirits.

Stories such as this one echo the Highland fascination with place, guilt, and endurance. The haunting is not random but bound to the landscape, suggesting that human deeds leave permanent traces on the land. Though the author remains unknown, the piece reflects the late-Victorian taste for moralised ghost tales that blurred folklore with Gothic fiction.

Two celebrated ghosts existed, once upon a time, in the wilds of Craig-Aulnaic, a romantic place in the district of Strathdown, Banffshire. The one was a male and the other a female. The male was called Fhuna Mhoir Ben Baynac, after one of the mountains of Glenavon, where at one time he resided, and the female was called Clashnichd Aulnaic, from her having had her abode in Craig-Aulnaic. But although the great ghost of Ben Baynac was bound by the common ties of nature and of honour to protect and cherish his weaker companion, Clashnichd Aulnaic, yet he often treated her in the most cruel and unfeeling manner. In the dead of night, when the surrounding hamlets were buried in deep repose, and when nothing else disturbed the solemn stillness of the midnight scene, oft would the shrill shrieks of poor Clashnichd burst upon the sleeper's ears, and awake them to anything but pleasant reflections.

But of all those who were incommoded by the noisy and unseemly quarrels of these two ghosts, James Owre or Gray, the tenant of the farm of Balbig of Delnabo, was the greatest sufferer. From the proximity of his abode to their haunts, it was the misfortune of himself and family to be the nightly audience of Clashnichd's cries and lamentations, which they considered anything but agreeable entertainment.

One day as James Gray was on his rounds looking after his sheep, he happened to fall in with Clashnichd, the ghost of Aulnaic, with whom he entered into a long conversation. In the course of it he took occasion to remonstrate with her on the very disagreeable disturbance she caused himself and family by her wild and unearthly cries - cries which, he said, few mortals could relish in the dreary hours of midnight.

Poor Clashnichd, by way of apology for her conduct, gave James Gray a sad account of her usage, detailing at full length the series of cruelties committed upon her by Ben Baynac. From this account, it appeared that her living with the latter was by no means a matter of choice with Clashnichd; on the contrary, it seemed that she had, for a long time, lived apart with much comfort, residing in a snug dwelling, as already mentioned, in the wilds of Craig-Aulnaic, but Ben Baynac having unfortunately taken into his head to pay her a visit, took a fancy, not to herself, but her dwelling, of which, in his own name and authority, he took immediate possession, and soon after he expelled poor Clashnichd, with many stripes, from her natural inheritance. Not satisfied with invading and depriving her of her just rights, he was in the habit of following her into her private haunts, not with the view of offering her any endearments, but for the purpose of inflicting on her person every torment which his brain could invent.

Such a moving relation could not fail to affect the generous heart of James Gray, who determined from that moment to risk life and limb in order to vindicate the rights and avenge the wrongs of poor Clashnichd, the ghost of Craig-Aulnaic. He, therefore, took good care to interrogate his new protégée touching the nature of her oppressor's constitution, whether he was of that killable species of ghost that could be shot with a silver sixpence, or if there was any other weapon that could possibly accomplish his annihilation.

Clashnichd informed him that she had occasion to know that Ben Baynac was wholly invulnerable to all the weapons of man, with the exception of a large mole on his left breast, which was no doubt penetrable by silver or steel, but that, from the specimens she had of his personal prowess and strength, it were vain for mere man to attempt to combat him. Confiding, however, in his expertness as an archer - for he was allowed to be the best marksman of the age - James Gray told Clashnichd he did not fear him with all his might, that he was a man, and desired her, moreover, next time the ghost chose to repeat his incivilities to her, to apply to him, James Gray, for redress.

It was not long before he had an opportunity of fulfilling his promises. Ben Baynac having one night, in the want of better amusement, entertained himself by inflicting an inhuman castigation on Clashnichd, she lost no time in waiting on James Gray, with a full and particular account of it. She found him smoking his cutty, for it was night when she came to him, but, notwithstanding the inconvenience of the hour, James needed no great persuasion to induce him to proceed directly along with Clashnichd to hold a communing with their friend, Ben Baynac, the great ghost.

Clashnichd was stout and sturdy, and understood the knack of travelling much better than our women do. She expressed a wish that, for the sake of expedition, James Gray would suffer her to bear him along, a motion to which the latter agreed, and a few minutes brought them close to the scene of Ben Baynac's residence. As they approached his haunt, he came forth to meet them, with looks and gestures which did not at all indicate a cordial welcome. It was a fine moonlight night, and they could easily observe his actions. Poor Clashnichd was now sorely afraid of the great ghost.

Apprehending instant destruction from his fury, she exclaimed to James Gray that they would be both dead people, and that immediately, unless James Gray hit with an arrow the mole which covered Ben Baynac's heart. This was not so difficult a task as James had hitherto apprehended it. The mole was as large as a common bonnet, and yet nowise disproportioned to the natural size of the ghost's body, for he certainly was a great and a mighty ghost.

Ben Baynac cried out to James Gray that he would soon make eagle's meat of him, and certain it is, such was his intention, had not the shepherd so effectually stopped him from the execution of it. Raising his bow to his eye when within a few yards of Ben Baynac, he took deliberate aim; the arrow flew - it hit - a yell from Ben Baynac announced the result. A hideous howl re-echoed from the surrounding mountains, responsive to the groans of a thousand ghosts, and Ben Baynac, like the smoke of a shot, vanished into air.

Clashnichd, the ghost of Aulnaic, now found herself emancipated from the most abject state of slavery, and restored to freedom and liberty, through the invincible courage of James Gray. Overpowered with gratitude, she fell at his feet, and vowed to devote the whole of her time and talents towards his service and prosperity. Meanwhile, being anxious to have her remaining goods and furniture removed to her former dwelling, where she had been so iniquitously expelled by Ben Baynac, the great ghost, she requested of her new master the use of his horses to remove them.

James observing on the adjacent hill a flock of deer, and wishing to have a trial of his new servant's sagacity or expertness, told her those were his horses - she was welcome to the use of them; desiring that when she had done with them, she would enclose them in his stable. Clashnichd then proceeded to make use of the horses, and James Gray returned home to enjoy his night's rest.

Scarce had he reached his arm-chair, and reclined his cheek on his hand, to ruminate over the bold adventure of the night, when Clashnichd entered, with her "breath in her throat," and venting the bitterest complaints at the unruliness of his horses, which had broken one-half of her furniture, and caused her more trouble in the stabling of them than their services were worth.

"Oh! they are stabled, then?" inquired James Gray. Clashnichd replied in the affirmative. "Very well," re-joined James, "they shall be tame enough to-morrow."

From this specimen of Clashnichd, the ghost of Craig-Aulnaic's expertness, it will be seen what a valuable acquisition her service proved to James Gray and his young family. They were, however, speedily deprived of her assistance by a most unfortunate accident. From the sequel of the story, from which the foregoing is an extract, it appears that poor Clashnichd was deeply addicted to propensities which at that time rendered her kin so obnoxious to their human neighbours. She was constantly in the habit of visiting her friends much oftener than she was invited, and, in the course of such visits, was never very scrupulous in making free with any eatables which fell within the circle of her observation.

One day, while engaged on a foraging expedition of this description, she happened to enter the Mill of Delnabo, which was inhabited in those days by the miller's family. She found his wife engaged in roasting a large gridiron of fine savoury fish, the agreeable smell proceeding from which perhaps occasioned her visit. With the usual inquiries after the health of the miller and his family, Clashnichd proceeded with the greatest familiarity and good-humour to make herself comfortable at their expense. But the miller's wife, enraged at the loss of her fish, and not relishing such unwelcome familiarity, punished the unfortunate Clashnichd rather too severely for her freedom. It happened that there was at the time a large cauldron of boiling water suspended over the fire, and this cauldron the enraged wife overturned in Clashnichd's bosom!

Scalded beyond recovery, she fled up the wilds of Craig-Aulnaic, uttering the melancholiest lamentations, nor has she been ever heard of since.

The Hoodie-Crow

The Hoodie-Crow is a Scottish folktale adapted by Andrew Lang in The Lilac Fairy Book (1910), drawn from J. F. Campbell's Popular Tales from the West Highlands (1860–62). It belongs to that class of Celtic wonder tales where enchantment and transformation test loyalty and love. The story follows a young princess who encounters a hooded crow that can take on human form.

Lang's version preserves the rhythm and imagery of Campbell's Gaelic original but tempers some of its darker turns for a younger readership. Still, its heart remains thoroughly Highland: a landscape alive with magic, curses, and the thin border between the human and the otherworldly. As in many Scottish variants of the "animal bridegroom" theme, endurance and faith are central virtues, and love is portrayed not as sentiment but as persistence against impossible odds.

Once there lived a farmer who had three daughters, and good useful girls they were, up with the sun, and doing all the work of the house. One morning they all ran down to the river to wash their clothes, when a hoodie came round and sat on a tree close by.

'Will you wed me, you farmer's daughter?' he said to the eldest.

'Indeed I won't wed you,' she answered, 'an ugly brute is the hoodie.' And the bird, much offended, spread his wings and flew away. But the following day he came back again, and said to the second girl:

'Will you wed me, farmer's daughter?'

'Indeed, I will not,' answered she, 'an ugly brute is the hoodie.' And the hoodie was angrier than before and went away in a rage. However, after a night's rest he was in a better temper and thought that he might be luckier the third time, so back he went to the old place.

'Will you wed me, farmer's daughter?' he said to the youngest.

'Indeed I will wed you; a pretty creature is the hoodie,' answered she, and on the morrow they were married.

'I have something to ask you,' said the hoodie when they were far away in his own house. 'Would you rather I should be a hoodie by day and a man by night, or a man by day and a hoodie by night?'

The girl was surprised at his words, for she did not know that he could be anything but a hoodie at all times.

Still she said nothing of this, and only replied, 'I would rather you were a man by day and a hoodie by night,' And so he was, and a handsomer man or a more beautiful hoodie never was seen. The girl loved them both, and never wished for things to be different.

By and bye they had a son, and very pleased they both were. But in the night soft music was heard stealing close towards the house, and every man slept, and the mother slept also. When they woke again it was morning, and the baby was gone. High and low they looked for it, but nowhere could they find it, and the farmer, who had come to see his daughter, was greatly grieved, as he feared it might be thought that he had stolen it, because he did not want the hoodie for a son-in-law.

The next year the hoodie's wife had another son, and this time a watch was set at every door. But it was no use. In vain they determined that, come what might, they would not close their eyes; at the first note of music they all fell asleep, and when the farmer arrived in the morning to see his grandson, he found them all weeping, for while they had slept the baby had vanished.

Well, the next year it all happened again, and the hoodie's wife was so unhappy that her husband resolved to take her away to another house he had, and her sisters with her for company. So they set out in a coach which was big enough to hold them, and had not gone very far when the hoodie suddenly said, 'You are sure you have not forgotten anything?'

'I have forgotten my coarse comb,' answered the wife, feeling in her pocket, and as she spoke the coach changed into a withered faggot, and the man became a hoodie again, and flew away.

The two sisters returned home, but the wife followed the hoodie. Sometimes she would see him on a hill-top, and then would hasten after him, hoping to catch him. But by the time she had got to the top of the hill, he would be in the valley on the other side. When night came, and she was tired, she looked about for some place to rest, and glad she was to see a little house full of light straight in front of her, and she hurried towards it as fast as she could.

At the door stood a little boy, and the sight of him filled her heart with pleasure, she did not know why. A woman came out, and bade her welcome, and set before her food, and gave her a soft bed to lie on. And the hoodie's wife lay down, and so tired was she, that it seemed to her but a moment before the sun rose, and she awoke again. From hill to hill she went after the hoodie, and sometimes she saw him on the top, but when she got to the top, he had flown into the valley, and when she reached the valley he was on the top of another hill - and so it happened till night came round again. Then she looked round for some place to rest in, and she beheld a little house of light before her, and fast she hurried towards it. At the door stood a little boy, and her heart was filled with pleasure at the sight of him, she did not know why. After that a woman bade her enter, and set food before her, and gave her a soft bed to lie in. And when the sun rose she got up, and left the house, in search of the hoodie. This day everything befell as on the two other days, but when she reached the small house, the woman bade her keep awake, and if the hoodie flew into the room, to try to seize him.

But the wife had walked far, and was very tired, and strive as she would, she fell sound asleep. Many hours she slept, and the hoodie entered through a window, and let fall a ring on her hand. The girl awoke with a start, and leant forward to grasp him, but he was already flying off, and she only seized a feather from his wing. And when dawn came, she got up and told the woman.

'He has gone over the hill of poison,' she said, 'and there you cannot follow him without horseshoes on your hands and feet. But I will help you. Put on this suit of men's clothes, and go down this road till you come to the smithy, and there you can learn to make horseshoes for yourself.'

The girl thanked her, and put on the cloths and went down the road to do her bidding. So hard did she work, that in a few days she was able to make the horse-shoes. Early one morning she set out for the hill of poison. On her hands and feet she went, but even with the horse-shoes on she had to be very careful not to stumble, lest some poisoned thorns should enter into her flesh, and she should die. But when she was over, it was only to hear that her husband was to be married that day to the daughter of a great lord.

Now there was to be a race in the town, and everyone meant to be there, except the stranger who had come over the hill of poison - everyone, that is, but the cook, who was to make the bridal supper. Greatly he loved races, and sore was his heart to think that one should be run without his seeing it, so when he beheld a woman whom he did not know coming along the street, hope sprang up in him.

'Will you cook the wedding feast in place of me?' he said, 'and I will pay you well when I return from the race.'

Gladly she agreed, and cooked the feast in a kitchen that looked into the great hall, where the company were to eat it. After that she watched the seat where the bridegroom was sitting, and taking a plateful of the broth, she dropped the ring and the feather into it, and set if herself before him.

With the first spoonful he took up the ring, and a thrill ran through him; in the second he beheld the feather and rose from his chair.

'Who has cooked this feast?' asked he, and the real cook, who had come back from the race, was brought before him.

'He may be the cook, but he did not cook this feast,' said the bridegroom, and then inquiry was made, and the girl was summoned to the great hall.

'That is my married wife,' he declared, 'and no one else will I have,' and at that very moment the spells fell off him, and never more would he be a hoodie. Happy indeed were they to be together again, and little did they mind that the hill of poison took long to cross, for she had to go some way forwards, and then throw the horse-shoes back for him to put on. Still, they were over, and they went back the way she had come, and stopped at the three houses in order to take their little sons to their own home.

But the story never says who had stolen them, nor what the coarse comb had to do with it.

The King of the Waterfalls

The King of the Waterfalls is a Scottish folk tale retold by Andrew Lang in The Lilac Fairy Book (1910), adapted from J. F. Campbell's Popular Tales from the West Highlands (1860–62). The story follows a young man who wins the love of a princess after helping her with a magical task, but his happiness is short-lived.

In Campbell's original collection, the story reflects the Gaelic tradition of water-spirits and enchanted kings tied to the wild landscape of the Highlands, beings who blur the boundary between benevolent guardians and deadly forces of nature. Lang's retelling softens some of the darker folkloric edges, bringing a romantic, moral clarity to the tale, typical of his late-Victorian adaptations.

When the young king of Easaidh Ruadh came into his kingdom, the first thing he thought of was how he could amuse himself best. The sports that all his life had pleased him best suddenly seemed to have grown dull, and he wanted to do something he had never done before. At last his face brightened.

'I know!' he said. 'I will go and play a game with the Gruagach.' Now the Gruagach was a kind of wicked fairy, with long curly brown hair, and his house was not very far from the king's house.

But though the king was young and eager, he was also prudent, and his father had told him on his deathbed to be very careful in his dealings with the 'good people,' as the fairies were called. Therefore before going to the Gruagach the king sought out a wise man of the countryside.

'I am wanting to play a game with the curly-haired Gruagach,' he said.

'Are you, indeed?' replied the wizard. 'If you take my counsel, you will play with someone else.'

'No; I will play with the Gruagach,' persisted the king.

'Well, if you must, you must, I suppose,' answered the wizard, 'but if you win that game, ask as a prize the ugly crop-headed girl that stands behind the door.'

'I will,' said the king.

So before the sun rose he got up and went to the house of the Gruagach, who was sitting outside.

'O king, what has brought you here to-day?' asked the Gruagach. 'But right welcome you are, and more welcome will you be still if you will play a game with me.'

'That is just what I want,' said the king, and they played, and sometimes it seemed as if one would win, and sometimes the other, but in the end it was the king who was the winner.

'And what is the prize that you will choose?' inquired the Gruagach.

'The ugly crop-headed girl that stands behind the door,' replied the king.

'Why, there are twenty others in the house, and each fairer than she!' exclaimed the Gruagach.

'Fairer they may be, but it is she whom I wish for my wife, and none other,' and the Gruagach saw that the king's mind was set upon her, so he entered his house, and bade all the maidens in it come out one by one, and pass before the king.

One by one they came; tall and short, dark and fair, plump and thin, and each said 'I am she whom you want. You will be foolish indeed if you do not take me.'

But he took none of them, neither short nor tall, dark nor fair, plump nor thin, till at the last the crop-headed girl came out.

'This is mine,' said the king, though she was so ugly that most men would have turned from her. 'We will be married at once, and I will carry you home.' And married they were, and they set forth across a meadow to the king's house. As they went, the bride stooped and picked a sprig of shamrock, which grew amongst the grass, and when she stood upright again her ugliness had all gone, and the most beautiful woman that ever was seen stood by the king's side.

The next day, before the sun rose, the king sprang from his bed, and told his wife he must have another game with the Gruagach.

'If my father loses that game, and you win it,' she said, 'accept nothing for your prize but the shaggy young horse with the stick saddle.'

'I will do that,' answered the king, and he went.

'Does your bride please you?' asked the Gruagach, who was standing at his own door.

'Ah! does she not!' answered the king quickly. 'Otherwise I should be hard indeed to please. But will you play a game to-day?'

'I will,' replied the Gruagach, and they played, and sometimes it seemed as if one would win, and sometimes the other, but in the end the king was the winner.

'What is the prize that you will choose?' asked the Gruagach.

'The shaggy young horse with the stick saddle,' answered the king, but he noticed that the Gruagach held his peace, and his brow was dark as he led out the horse from the stable. Rough was its mane and dull was its skin, but the king cared nothing for that, and throwing his leg over the stick saddle, rode away like the wind.

On the third morning the king got up as usual before dawn, and as soon as he had eaten food he prepared to go out, when his wife stopped him. 'I would rather,' she said, 'that you did not go to play with the Gruagach, for though twice you have won yet some day he will win, and then he will put trouble upon you.'

'Oh! I must have one more game,' cried the king, 'just this one.' And he went off to the house of the Gruagach.

Joy filled the heart of the Gruagach when he saw him coming, and without waiting to talk they played their game. Somehow or other, the king's strength and skill had departed from him, and soon the Gruagach was the victor.

'Choose your prize,' said the king, when the game was ended, 'but do not be too hard on me, or ask what I cannot give.'

'The prize I choose,' answered the Gruagach, 'is that the crop-headed creature should take your head and your neck, if you do not get for me the Sword of Light that hangs in the house of the king of the oak windows.'

'I will get it,' replied the young man bravely, but as soon as he was out of sight of the Gruagach he pretended no more, and his face grew dark and his steps lagging.

'You have brought nothing with you to-night,' said the queen, who was standing on the steps awaiting him. She was so beautiful that the king was fain to smile when he looked at her, but then he remembered what had happened, and his heart grew heavy again.

'What is it? What is the matter? Tell me your sorrow that I may bear it with you, or, it may be, help you!' Then the king told her everything that had befallen him, and she stroked his hair the while.

'That is nothing to grieve about,' she said when the tale was finished. 'You have the best wife in Erin, and the best horse in Erin. Only do as I bid you, and all will go well.' And the king suffered himself to be comforted.

He was still sleeping when the queen rose and dressed herself, to make everything ready for her husband's journey, and the first place she went to was the stable, where she fed and watered the shaggy brown horse and put the saddle on it. Most people thought this saddle was of wood, and did not see the little sparkles of gold and silver that were hidden in it. She strapped it lightly on the horse's back, and then led it down before the house, where the king waited.

'Good luck to you, and victories in all your battles,' she said, as she kissed him before he mounted. 'I need not be telling you anything. Take the advice of the horse, and see you obey it.'

So he waved his hand and set out on his journey, and the wind was not swifter than the brown horse - no, not even the March wind which raced it and could not catch it. But the horse never stopped nor looked behind, till in the dark of the night he reached the castle of the king of the oak windows.

'We are at the end of the journey,' said the horse, 'and you will find the Sword of Light in the king's own chamber. If it comes to you without scrape or sound, the token is a good one. At this hour the king is eating his supper, and the room is empty, so none will see you. The sword has a knob at the end, and take heed that when you grasp it, you draw it softly out of its sheath. Now go! I will be under the window.'

Stealthily the young man crept along the passage, pausing now and then to make sure that no man was following him, and entered the king's chamber. A strange white line of light told him where the sword was, and crossing the room on tiptoe, he seized the knob, and drew it slowly out of the sheath. The king could hardly breathe with excitement lest it should make some noise, and bring all the people in the castle running to see what the matter was. But the sword slid swiftly and silently along the case till only the point was left touching it. Then a low sound was heard, as of the edge of a knife touching a silver plate, and the king was so startled that he nearly dropped the knob.

'Quick! quick!' cried the horse, and the king scrambled hastily through the small window, and leapt into the saddle.

'He has heard and he will follow,' said the horse, 'but we have a good start,' And on they sped, on and on, leaving the winds behind them.

At length the horse slackened its pace. 'Look and see who is behind you,' it said, and the young man looked.

'I see a swarm of brown horses racing madly after us,' he answered.

'We are swifter than those,' said the horse, and flew on again.

'Look again, Oh king! Is anyone coming now?'

'A swarm of black horses, and one has a white face, and on that horse a man is seated. He is the king of the oak windows.'

'That is my brother, and swifter still than I,' said the horse, 'and he will fly past me with a rush. Then you must have your sword ready, and take off the head of the man who sits on him, as he turns and looks at you. And there is no sword in the world that will cut off his head, save only that one.'

'I will do it,' replied the king, and he listened with all his might, till he judged that the white-faced horse was close to him. Then he sat up very straight and made ready.

The next moment there was a rushing noise as of a mighty tempest, and the young man caught a glimpse of a face turned towards him. Almost blindly he struck, not knowing whether he had killed or only wounded the rider. But the head rolled off, and was caught in the brown horse's mouth.

'Jump on my brother, the black horse, and go home as fast as you can, and I will follow as quickly as I may,' cried the brown horse, and leaping forward the king alighted on the back of the black horse, but so near the tail that he almost fell off again. But he stretched out his arm and clutched wildly at the mane and pulled himself into the saddle.

Before the sky was streaked with red he was at home again, and the queen was sitting waiting till he arrived, for sleep was far from her eyes. Glad was she to see him enter, but she said little, only took her harp and softly sang the songs which he loved, till he went to bed, soothed and happy.

It was broad day when he woke, and he sprang up saying, 'Now I must go to the Gruagach, to find out if the spells he laid on me are loose.'

'Have a care,' answered the queen, 'for it is not with a smile as on the other days that he will greet you. Furiously he will meet you, and will ask you in his wrath if you have got the sword, and you will reply that you have got it. Next he will want to know how you got it, and to this you must say that but for the knob you had not got it at all. Then he will raise his head to look at the knob, and you must stab him in the mole which is on the right side of his neck, but take heed, for if you miss the mole with the point of the sword, then my death and your death are certain. He is brother to the king of the oak windows, and sure will he be that the king must be head, or the sword would not be in your hands.' After that she kissed him, and bade him good speed.

'Did you get the sword?' asked the Gruagach when they met in the usual place.

'I got the sword.'

'And how did you get it?'

'If it had not had a knob on the top, then I had not got it,' answered the king.

'Give me the sword to look at,' said the Gruagach, peering forward, but like a flash the king had drawn it from under his nose and pierced the mole, so that the Gruagach rolled over on the ground.

'Now I shall be at peace,' thought the king. But he was wrong, for when he reached home he found his servants tied together back-to-back with cloths bound round their mouths, so that they could not speak. He hastened to set them free, and he asked who had treated them in so evil a manner.

'No sooner had you gone than a great giant came, and dealt with us as you see, and carried off your wife and your two horses,' said the men.

'Then my eyes will not close nor will my head lay itself down till I fetch my wife and horses home again,' answered he, and he stopped and noted the tracks of the horses on the grass, and followed after them till he arrived at the wood, when the darkness fell.

'I will sleep here,' he said to himself, 'but first I will make a fire,' And he gathered together some twigs that were lying about, and then took two dry sticks and rubbed them together till the fire came, and he sat by it.

The twigs cracked and the flame blazed up, and a slim yellow dog pushed through the bushes and laid his head on the king's knee, and the king stroked his head.

'Wuf, wuf,' said the dog. 'Sore was the plight of your wife and your horses when the giant drove them last night through the forest.'

'That is why I have come,' answered the king, and suddenly his heart seemed to fail him and he felt that he could not go on.

'I cannot fight that giant,' he cried, looking at the dog with a white face. 'I am afraid, let me turn homewards.'

'No, don't do that,' replied the dog. 'Eat and sleep, and I will watch over you.' So the king ate and lay down, and slept till the sun waked him.

'It is time for you to start on your way,' said the dog, 'and if danger presses, call on me, and I will help you.'

'Farewell, then,' answered the king, 'I will not forget that promise,' and on he went, and on, and on, till he reached a tall cliff with many sticks lying about.

'It is almost night,' he thought, 'I will make a fire and rest,' and thus he did, and when the flames blazed up, the hoary hawk of the grey rock flew on to a bough above him.

'Sore was the plight of your wife and your horses when they passed here with the giant,' said the hawk.

'Never shall I find them,' answered the king, 'and nothing shall I get for all my trouble.'

'Oh, take heart,' replied the hawk, 'things are never so bad but what they might be worse. Eat and sleep and I will watch you,' and the king did as he was bidden by the hawk, and by the morning he felt brave again.

'Farewell,' said the bird, 'and if danger presses call to me, and I will help you.'

On he walked, and on and on, till as dusk was falling he came to a great river, and on the bank there were sticks lying about.

'I will make myself a fire,' he thought, and thus he did, and by and bye a smooth brown head peered at him from the water, and a long body followed it.

'Sore was the plight of your wife and your horses when they passed the river last night,' said the otter.

'I have sought them and not found them,' answered the king, 'and nought shall I get for my trouble.'

'Be not so downcast,' replied the otter, 'before noon to-morrow you shalt behold your wife. But eat and sleep and I will watch over you.' So the king did as the otter bid him, and when the sun rose he woke and saw the otter lying on the bank.

'Farewell,' cried the otter as he jumped into the water, 'and if danger presses, call to me and I will help you.'

For many hours the king walked, and at length he reached a high rock, which was rent into two by a great earthquake. Throwing himself on the ground he looked over the side, and right at the very bottom he saw his wife and his horses. His heart gave a great bound, and all his fears left him, but he was forced to be patient, for the sides of the rock were smooth, and not even a goat could find foothold. So he got up again, and made his way round through the wood, pushing by trees, scrambling over rocks, wading through streams, till he was on flat ground again, close to the mouth of the cavern.

His wife gave a shriek of joy when he came in, and then burst into tears, for she was tired and very frightened. But her husband did not understand why she wept, and he was tired and bruised from his climb, and a little cross too.

'You give me but a sorry welcome,' grumbled he, 'when I have half-killed myself to get to you.'

'Do not heed him,' said the horses to the weeping woman, 'put him in front of us, where he will be safe, and give him food, for he is weary.' And she did as the horses told her, and he ate and rested, till by and bye a long shadow fell over them, and their hearts beat with fear, for they knew that the giant was coming.

'I smell a stranger,' cried the giant, as he entered, but it was dark inside the chasm, and he did not see the king, who was crouching down between the feet of the horses.

'A stranger, my lord! no stranger ever comes here, not even the sun!' and the king's wife laughed gaily as she went up to the giant and stroked the huge hand which hung down by his side.

'Well, I perceive nothing, certainly,' answered he, 'but it is very odd. However, it is time that the horses were fed;' and he lifted down an armful of hay from a shelf of rock and held out a handful to each animal, who moved forward to meet him, leaving the king behind. As soon as the giant's hands were near their mouths they each made a snap, and began to bit them, so that his groans and shrieks might have been heard a mile off. Then they wheeled round and kicked him till they could kick no more. At length the giant crawled away, and lay quivering in a corner, and the queen went up to him.

'Poor thing! poor thing!' she said, 'they seem to have gone mad; it was awful to behold.'

'If I had had my soul in my body they would certainly have killed me,' groaned the giant.

'It was lucky indeed,' answered the queen, 'but tell me, where is your soul, that I may take care of it?'

'Up there, in the Bonnach stone,' answered the giant, pointing to a stone which was balanced loosely on an edge of rock. 'But now leave me, that I may sleep, for I have far to go to-morrow.'

Soon snores were heard from the corner where the giant lay, and then the queen lay down too, and the horses, and the king was hidden between them, so that none could see him.

Before the dawn the giant rose and went out, and immediately the queen ran up to the Bonnach stone, and tugged and pushed at it till it was quite steady on its ledge, and could not fall over. And so it was in the evening when the giant came home, and when they saw his shadow, the king crept down in front of the horses.

'Why, what have you done to the Bonnach stone?' asked the giant.

'I feared lest it should fall over, and be broken, with your soul in it,' said the queen, 'so I put it further back on the ledge.'

It is not there that my soul is,' answered he, 'it is on the threshold. But it is time the horses were fed;' and he fetched the hay, and gave it to them, and they bit and kicked him as before, till he lay half dead on the ground.

Next morning he rose and went out, and the queen ran to the threshold of the cave, and washed the stones, and pulled up some moss and little flowers that were hidden in the crannies, and by and bye when dusk had fallen the giant came home.

'You have been cleaning the threshold,' he said.

'And was I not right to do it, seeing that your soul is in it?' asked the queen.

'It is not there that my soul is,' answered the giant. 'Under the threshold is a stone, and under the stone is a sheep, and in the sheep's body is a duck, and in the duck is an egg, and in the egg is my soul. But it is late, and I must feed the horses;' and he brought them the hay, but they only bit and kicked him as before, and if his soul had been within him, they would have killed him outright.

It was still dark when the giant got up and went his way, and then the king and the queen ran forward to take up the threshold, while the horses looked on. But sure enough! just as the giant had said, underneath the threshold was the flagstone, and they pulled and tugged till the stone gave way. Then something jumped out so suddenly, that it nearly knocked them down, and as it fled past, they saw it was a sheep.

'If the slim yellow dog of the greenwood were only here, he would soon have that sheep,' cried the king, and as he spoke, the slim yellow dog appeared from the forest, with the sheep in his mouth. With a blow from the king, the sheep fell dead, and they opened its body, only to be blinded by a rush of wings as the duck flew past.

'If the hoary hawk of the rock were only here, he would soon have that duck,' cried the king, and as he spoke the hoary hawk was seen hovering above them, with the duck in his mouth. They cut off the duck's head with a swing of the king's sword, and took the egg out of its body, but in his triumph the king held it carelessly, and it slipped from his hand, and rolled swiftly down the hill right into the river.

'If the brown otter of the stream were only here, he would soon have that egg,' cried the king, and the next minute there was the brown otter, dripping with water, holding the egg in his mouth. But beside the brown otter, a huge shadow came stealing along - the shadow of the giant.

The king stood staring at it, as if he were turned into stone, but the queen snatched the egg from the otter and crushed it between her two hands. And after that the shadow suddenly shrank and was still, and they knew that the giant was dead, because they had found his soul.

Next day they mounted the two horses and rode home again, visiting their friends the brown otter and the hoary hawk and the slim yellow dog by the way.

The Laird O' Co'

The Laird O' Co' is one of the livelier tales from Elizabeth Wilson Grierson's The Scottish Fairy Book (J. B. Lippincott, 1910), a collection that reimagines oral traditions from across Scotland in the clear, rhythmic prose of the early twentieth century. The story belongs to that class of Borders folk narratives where pride and mischief meet the uncanny. It tells of a boastful laird who scorns the warnings of the supernatural and learns, as so many mortals do in Scottish legend, that the "good folk" or fairies are not to be taken lightly.

Grierson's version captures both the humour and the quiet dread of rural superstition. Her laird is neither villain nor fool, but a man undone by disbelief in a world still alive with older forces. Through him, the story preserves a distinctly Scottish tension between reason and the unseen, between the worldly confidence of land and title, and the humbler wisdom of those who know to leave offerings by the hearth or the hill.

It was a fine summer morning, and the Laird o' Co' was having a dander on the green turf outside the Castle walls. His real name was the Laird o' Colzean, and his descendants to-day bear the proud title of Marquises of Ailsa, but all up and down Ayrshire nobody called him anything else than the Laird o' Co'; because of the Co's, or caves, which were to be found in the rock on which his Castle was built.

He was a kind man, and a courteous, always ready to be interested in the affairs of his poorer neighbours, and willing to listen to any tale of woe.

So when a little boy came across the green, carrying a small can in his hand, and, pulling his forelock, asked him if he might go to the Castle and get a little ale for his sick mother, the Laird gave his consent at once, and, patting the little fellow on the head, told him to go to the kitchen and ask for the butler, and tell him that he, the Laird, had given orders that his can was to be filled with the best ale that was in the cellar.

Away the boy went, and found the old butler, who, after listening to his message, took him down into the cellar, and proceeded to carry out his master's orders.

There was one cask of particularly fine ale, which was kept entirely for the Laird's own use, which had been opened some time before, and which was now about half full.

"I will fill the bairn's can out o' this," thought the old man to himself. "Tis both nourishing and light - the very thing for sick folk." So, taking the can from the child's hand, he proceeded to draw the ale.

But what was his astonishment to find that, although the ale flowed freely enough from the barrel, the little can, which could not have held more than a quarter of a gallon, remained always just half full.

The ale poured into it in a clear amber stream, until the big cask was quite empty, and still the quantity that was in the little can did not seem to increase. The butler could not understand it. He looked at the cask, and then he looked at the can; then he looked down at the floor at his feet to see if he had not spilt any.

No, the ale had not disappeared in that way, for the cellar floor was as white, and dry, and clean, as possible.

"Plague on the can; it must be bewitched," thought the old man, and his short, stubby hair stood up like porcupine quills round his bald head, for if there was anything on earth of which he had a mortal dread, it was Warlocks, and Witches, and such like Bogles.

"I'm not going to broach another barrel," he said gruffly, handing back the half-filled can to the little lad. "So you may just go home with what is there; the Laird's ale is too good to waste on a smatchet like you."

But the boy stoutly held his ground. A promise was a promise, and the Laird had both promised, and sent orders to the butler that the can was to be filled, and he would not go home till it was filled.

It was in vain that the old man first argued, and then grew angry - the boy would not stir a step.

"The Laird had said that he was to get the ale, and the ale he must have."

At last the perturbed butler left him standing there, and hurried off to his master to tell him he was convinced that the can was bewitched, for it had swallowed up a whole half cask of ale, and after doing so it was only half full, and to ask if he would come down himself, and order the lad off the premises.

"Not I," said the genial Laird, "for the little fellow is quite right. I promised that he should have his can full of ale to take home to his sick mother, and he shall have it if it takes all the barrels in my cellar to fill it. So haste you to the house again, and open another cask."

The butler dare not disobey; so he reluctantly retraced his steps, but, as he went, he shook his head sadly, for it seemed to him that not only the boy with the can, but his master also, was bewitched.

When he reached the cellar he found the bairn waiting patiently where he had left him, and, without wasting further words, he took the can from his hand and broached another barrel.

If he had been astonished before, he was more astonished now. Scarce had a couple of drops fallen from the tap, than the can was full to the brim.

"Take it, laddie, and begone, with all the speed you can," he said, glad to get the can out of his fingers, and the boy did not wait for a second bidding. Thanking the butler most earnestly for his trouble, and paying no attention to the fact that the old man had not been so civil to him as he might have been, he departed. Nor, though the butler took pains to ask all round the country-side, could he ever hear of him again, nor of anyone who knew anything about him, or anything about his sick mother.

Years passed by, and sore trouble fell upon the House o' Co'. For the Laird went to fight in the wars in Flanders, and chancing to be taken prisoner, he was shut up in prison, and condemned to death. Alone, in a foreign country, he had no friends to speak for him, and escape seemed hopeless.

It was the night before his execution, and he was sitting in his lonely cell, thinking sadly of his wife and children, whom he never expected to see again. At the thought of them the picture of his home rose clearly in his mind - the grand old Castle standing on its rock, and the bonnie daisy-spangled stretch of greensward which lay before its gates, where he had been used to take a dander in the sweet summer mornings. Then, all unbidden, a vision of the little lad carrying the can, who had come to beg ale for his sick mother, and whom he had long ago forgotten, rose up before him.

The vision was so clear and distinct that he felt almost as if he were acting the scene over again, and he rubbed his eyes to get rid of it, feeling that, if he had to die tomorrow, it was time that he turned his thoughts to better things.

But as he did so the door of his cell flew noiselessly open, and there, on the threshold, stood the self-same little lad, looking not a day older, with his finger on his lip, and a mysterious smile upon his face.

"Laird o' Co', rise and go!" he whispered, beckoning to him to follow him. Needless to say, the Laird did so, too much amazed to think of asking questions.

Through the long passages of the prison the little lad went, the Laird close at his heels, and whenever he came to a locked door, he had but to touch it, and it opened before them, so that in no long time they were safe outside the walls.

The overjoyed Laird would have overwhelmed his little deliverer with words of thanks had not the boy held up his hand to stop him. "Get on my back," he said shortly, "for you are not safe till you are out of this country."

The Laird did as he was bid, and, marvellous as it seems, the boy was quite able to bear his weight. As soon as he was comfortably seated the pair set off, over sea and land, and never stopped till, in almost less time than it takes to tell it, the boy set him down, in the early dawn, on the daisy-spangled green in front of his Castle, just where he had spoken first to him so many years before.

Then he turned, and laid his little hand on the Laird's big one. "One good turn deserves another, take this for being so kind to my old mother," he said, and vanished. And from that day to this he has never been seen again.

The Laird of Balmachie's Wife

The Laird of Balmachie's Wife is a grim Scottish folktale of jealousy, cruelty, and uneasy retribution. Set in Angus, it tells of a laird who, convinced by false whispers that his wife has been unfaithful, murders her in a fit of rage.

In later retellings, including the version printed in Folk-lore and Legends: Scotland (W. W. Gibbings, London, 1889), the story acquires a spectral turn. It stands as both a local cautionary tale and a fragment of a wider moral pattern found throughout Scottish folk tradition: the warning that injustice done in haste, especially against the innocent, draws its own relentless haunting.

In the olden times, when it was the fashion for gentlemen to wear swords, the Laird of Balmachie went one day to Dundee, leaving his wife at home ill in bed. Riding home in the twilight, he had occasion to leave the high road, and when crossing between some little romantic knolls, called the Cur-hills, in the neighbourhood of Carlungy, he encountered a troop of fairies supporting a kind of litter, upon which some person seemed to be borne. Being a man of dauntless courage, and, as he said, impelled by some internal impulse, he pushed his horse close to the litter, drew his sword, laid it across the vehicle, and in a firm tone exclaimed, "In the name of God, release your captive."

The tiny troop immediately disappeared, dropping the litter on the ground. The laird dismounted, and found that it contained his own wife, dressed in her bedclothes. Wrapping his coat around her, he placed her on the horse before him, and, having only a short distance to ride, arrived safely at home.

Placing her in a room under the care of an attentive friend, he immediately went to the chamber where he had left his wife in the morning, and there to all appearance she still lay, very sick of a fever. She was fretful, discontented, and complained much of having been neglected in his absence, at all of which the laird affected great concern, and pretending much sympathy, insisted upon her rising to have her bed made. She said that she was unable to rise, but her husband was peremptory, and having ordered a large wood fire to warm the room, he lifted the impostor from the bed, and bearing her across the floor he threw her on the fire, from which she bounced like a sky-rocket, and went through the ceiling, and out at the roof of the house, leaving a hole among the slates.

He then brought in his own wife, a little recovered from her alarm, who said, that sometime after sunset, the nurse having left her for the purpose of preparing a little candle, a multitude of elves came in at the window, thronging like bees from a hive. They filled the room, and having lifted her from the bed carried her through the window, after which she recollected nothing further, till she saw her husband standing over her on the Cur-hills, at the back of Carlungy.

The hole in the roof, by which the female fairy made her escape, was mended, but could never be kept in repair, as a tempest of wind happened always once a year, which uncovered that particular spot, without injuring any other part of the roof.

The Mermaid Wife

Adapted from a story by an unknown author or collector and taken from Folk-lore and Legends: Scotland, published in London by W. W. Gibbings in 1889. The book is a compact anthology of traditional Scottish tales compiled by Charles John Tibbits. It belongs to a wider late-Victorian series that also included volumes devoted to Ireland, England, and Germany, aimed at bringing the old folk narratives of Europe to a general readership. The Scottish volume gathers stories of fairies, brownies, ghosts, and other spirits thought to haunt the country's hills and lochs. Its tone is shaped by the era's fascination with the picturesque and the supernatural, reflecting the belief that Scotland's rugged landscapes and remote communities fostered a particularly vivid popular imagination.

A story is told of an inhabitant of Unst, who, in walking on the sandy margin of a Voe, saw a number of mermen and mermaids dancing by moonlight, and several seal-skins strewed beside them on the ground. At his approach they immediately fled to secure their garbs, and, taking upon themselves the form of seals, plunged immediately into the sea.

But as the Shetlander perceived that one skin lay close to his feet, he snatched it up, bore it swiftly away, and placed it in concealment. On returning to the shore he met the fairest damsel that was ever gazed upon by mortal eyes, lamenting the robbery, by which she had become an exile from her submarine friends, and a tenant of the upper world.

Vainly she implored the restitution of her property; the man had drunk deeply of love, and was inexorable, but he offered her protection beneath his roof as his betrothed spouse. The merlady, perceiving that she must become an inhabitant of the earth, found that she could not do better than accept of the offer.

This strange attachment subsisted for many years, and the couple had several children. The Shetlander's love for his merwife was unbounded, but his affection was coldly returned. The lady would often steal alone to the desert strand, and, on a signal being given, a large seal would make his appearance, with whom she would hold, in an unknown tongue, an anxious conference.

Years had thus glided away, when it happened that one of the children, in the course of his play, found concealed beneath a stack of corn a seal's skin, and, delighted with the prize, he ran with it to his mother. Her eyes glistened with rapture - she gazed upon it as her own - as the means by which she could pass through the ocean that led to her native home.

She burst forth into an ecstasy of joy, which was only moderated when she beheld her children, whom she was now about to leave, and, after hastily embracing them, she fled with all speed towards the sea-side.

The husband immediately returned, learned the discovery that had taken place, ran to overtake his wife, but only arrived in time to see her transformation of shape completed - to see her, in the form of a seal, bound from the ledge of a rock into the sea. The large animal of the same kind with whom she had held a secret converse soon appeared, and evidently congratulated her, in the most tender manner, on her escape. But before she dived to unknown depths, she cast a parting glance at the wretched Shetlander, whose despairing looks excited in her breast a few transient feelings of commiseration.

"Farewell!" she said to him, "and may all good attend you. I loved you very well when I resided upon earth, but I always loved my first husband much better."

The Milk-White Doo

The Milk-White Doo, adapted from The Scottish Fairy Book (1910) by Elizabeth Wilson Grierson, is a tender and mournful Scottish folktale of love, faith, and transformation beyond death. It tells of a young woman betrayed and murdered by her jealous sister.

Grierson's version retains the moral starkness and lyrical sadness of older oral variants found in the Borders and Lowlands, while softening the supernatural edge into something more spiritual than eerie. Her prose reflects her characteristic blend of Christian symbolism and folk imagery, the doo as a soul at peace, not a ghost in torment.

There was once a man who got his living by working in the fields. He had one little son, called Curly-Locks, and one little daughter, called Golden-Tresses, but his wife was dead, and, as he had to be out all day, these children were often left alone. So, as he was afraid that some evil might befall them when there was no one to look after them, he, in an ill day, married again.

I say, "in an ill day," for his second wife was a most deceitful woman, who really hated children, although she pretended, before her marriage, to love them. And she was so unkind to them, and made the house so uncomfortable with her bad temper, that her poor husband often sighed to himself, and wished that he had let well alone, and remained a widower.

But it was no use crying over spilt milk; the deed was done, and he had just to try to make the best of it. So things went on for several years, until the children were beginning to run about the doors and play by themselves.

Then one day the Goodman chanced to catch a hare, and he brought it home and gave it to his wife to cook for the dinner.

Now his wife was a very good cook, and she made the hare into a pot of delicious soup, but she was also very greedy, and while the soup was boiling she tasted it, and tasted it, till she discovered that it was almost gone. Then she was in a fine state of mind, for she knew that her husband would soon be coming home for his dinner, and that she would have nothing to set before him.

So what do you think the wicked woman did? She went out to the door, where her little step-son, Curly-Locks, was playing in the sun, and told him to come in and get his face washed. And while she was washing his face, she struck him on the head with a hammer and stunned him, and popped him into the pot to make soup for his father's dinner.

By and by the Goodman came in from his work, and the soup was dished up, and he, and his wife, and his little daughter, Golden-Tresses, sat down to sup it.

"Where's Curly-Locks?" asked the Goodman. "It's a pity he is not here as long as the soup is hot."

"How should I ken?" answered his wife crossly. "I have other work to do than to run about after a mischievous laddie all the morning."

The Goodman went on supping his soup in silence for some minutes; then he lifted up a little foot in his spoon.

"This is Curly-Locks' foot," he cried in horror. "There has been ill work here."

"Hoots, havers," answered his wife, laughing, pretending to be very much amused. "What should Curly-Locks' foot be doing in the soup? 'Tis the hare's forefoot, which is very like that of a bairn."

But presently the Goodman took something else up in his spoon. "This is Curly-Locks' hand," he said shrilly. "I ken it by the crook in its little finger."

"The man's demented," retorted his wife, "not to ken the hind foot of a hare when he sees it!"

So the poor father did not say any more, but went away out to his work, sorely perplexed in his mind; while his little daughter, Golden-Tresses, who had a shrewd suspicion of what had happened, gathered all the bones from the empty plates, and, carrying them away in her apron, buried them beneath a flat stone, close by a white rose tree that grew by the cottage door.

And, lo and behold! those poor bones, which she buried with such care:

"Grew and grew,

To a milk-white Doo,

That took its wings,

And away it flew."

And it lighted on a tuft of grass by a burnside, where two women were washing clothes. It sat there cooing to itself for some time; then it sang this song softly to them:

"Pew, pew,

My mimmie me slew,

My daddy me chew,

My sister gathered my banes,

And put them between two milk-white stanes.

And I grew and grew

To a milk-white Doo,

And I took to my wings and away I flew."

The women stopped washing and looked at one another in astonishment. It was not every day that they came across a bird that could sing a song like that, and they felt that there was something not canny about it.

"Sing that song again, my bonnie bird," said one of them , "and we'll give you all these clothes!"

So the bird sang its song over again, and the washerwomen gave it all the clothes, and it tucked them under its right wing, and flew on.

Presently it came to a house where all the windows were open, and it perched on one of the window-sills, and inside it saw a man counting out a great heap of silver.

And, sitting on the window-sill, it sang its song to him:

"Pew, pew,

My mimmie me slew,

My daddy me chew,

My sister gathered my banes,

And put them between two milk-white stanes.

And I grew and grew

To a milk-white Doo,

And I took to my wings and away I flew."

The man stopped counting his silver, and listened. He felt, like the washerwomen, that there was something not canny about this Doo. When it had finished its song, he said, "Sing that song again, my bonnie bird, and I'll give you all this silver in a bag."

So the Doo sang its song over again, and got the bag of silver, which it tucked under its left wing. Then it flew on.

It had not flown very far, however, before it came to a mill where two millers were grinding corn. And it settled down on a sack of meal and sang its song to them:

"Pew, pew,

My mimmie me slew,

My daddy me chew,

My sister gathered my banes,

And put them between two milk-white stanes.

And I grew and grew

To a milk-white Doo,

And I took to my wings and away I flew."

The millers stopped their work, and looked at one another, scratching their heads in amazement.

"Sing that song over again, my bonnie bird!" exclaimed both of them together when the Doo had finished, "and we will give you this millstone."

So the Doo repeated its song, and got the millstone, which it asked one of the millers to lift on its back; then it flew out of the mill, and up the valley, leaving the two men staring after it dumb with astonishment.

As you may think, the Milk-White Doo had a heavy load to carry, but it went bravely on till it came within sight of its father's cottage, and lighted down on the thatched roof.

Then it laid its burdens on the thatch, and, flying down to the courtyard, picked up a number of little chuckie stones. With them in its beak it flew back to the roof, and began to throw them down the chimney.

By this time it was evening, and the Goodman and his wife, and his little daughter, Golden-Tresses, were sitting round the table eating their supper. And you may be sure that they were all very much startled when the stones came rattling down the chimney, bringing such a cloud of soot with them that they were like to be smothered.

They all jumped up from their chairs, and ran outside to see what the matter was.

And Golden-Tresses, being the littlest, ran the fastest, and when she came out at the door the Milk-White Doo flung the bundle of clothes down at her feet.

And the father came out next, and the Milk-White Doo flung the bag of silver down at his feet.

But the wicked stepmother, being somewhat stout came out last, and the Milk-White Doo threw the millstone right down on her head and killed her.

Then it spread its wings and flew away, and has never been seen again, but it had made the Goodman and his daughter rich for life, and it had rid them of the cruel stepmother, so that they lived in peace and plenty for the remainder of their days.

The Minister and the Fairy

The Minister and the Fairy is a brief but striking Scottish folktale, adapted from an anonymous source and first collected in Folk-Lore and Legends: Scotland (W. W. Gibbings, London, 1889). The story reflects the old tension between the spiritual authority of the Church and the lingering power of the supernatural in rural Scotland. It tells of a stern minister who encounters a fairy woman intent on tempting or testing him.

What makes this tale memorable is its ambiguity. The fairy is not wholly malign; she embodies charm, intelligence, and a strange moral neutrality, forcing the minister to confront the limits of his certainty. In its few paragraphs the story captures a larger truth about the coexistence of belief systems in nineteenth-century Scottish life, the pulpit and the hill, sermon and spell.

Not long since, a pious clergyman was returning home, after administering spiritual consolation to a dying member of his flock. It was late of the night, and he had to pass through a good deal of uncanny land. He was, however, a good and a conscientious minister of the Gospel, and feared not all the spirits in the country.

On his reaching the end of a lake which stretched along the roadside for some distance, he was a good deal surprised at hearing the most melodious strains of music. Overcome by pleasure and curiosity, the minister coolly sat down to listen to the harmonious sounds, and try what new discoveries he could make with regard to their nature and source.

He had not sat many minutes before he could distinguish the approach of the music, and also observe a light in the direction from where it proceeded gliding across the lake towards him. Instead of taking to his heels, as any faithless wight would have done, the pastor fearlessly determined to await the issue of the phenomenon.

As the light and music drew near, the clergyman could at length distinguish an object resembling a human being walking on the surface of the water, attended by a group of diminutive musicians, some of them bearing lights, and others instruments of music, from which they continued to evoke those melodious strains which first attracted his attention. The leader of the band dismissed his attendants, landed on the beach, and afforded the minister the amplest opportunities of examining his appearance.

He was a little primitive-looking grey-headed man, clad in the most grotesque habit the clergyman had ever seen, and such as led him at once to suspect his real character. He walked up to the minister, whom he saluted with great grace, offering an apology for his intrusion. The pastor returned his compliments, and, without further explanation, invited the mysterious stranger to sit down by his side. The invitation was complied with, upon which the minister proposed the following question, "Who are you, stranger, and from where?"

To this question the fairy, with downcast eye, replied that he was one of those sometimes called Doane Shee, or men of peace, or good men, though the reverse of this title was a more fit appellation for them. Originally angelic in his nature and attributes, and once a sharer of the indescribable joys of the regions of light, he was seduced by Satan to join him in his mad conspiracies, and, as a punishment for his transgression, he was cast down from those regions of bliss, and was now doomed, along with millions of fellow-sufferers, to wander through seas and mountains, until the coming of the Great Day. What their fate would be then they could not divine, but they apprehended the worst.

"And" continued he, turning to the minister, with great anxiety, "the object of my present intrusion on you is to learn your opinion, as an eminent divine, as to our final condition on that dreadful day."

Here the venerable pastor entered upon a long conversation with the fairy, touching the principles of faith and repentance. Receiving rather unsatisfactory answers to his questions, the minister desired the "sheech" to repeat after him the Paternoster, in attempting to do which, it was not a little remarkable that he could not repeat the word "art," but said "were," in heaven.

Inferring from every circumstance that their fate was extremely precarious, the minister resolved not to puff the fairies up with presumptuous, and, perhaps, groundless expectations. Accordingly, addressing himself to the unhappy fairy, who was all anxiety to know the nature of his sentiments, the reverend gentleman told him that he could not take it upon him to give them any hopes of pardon, as their crime was of so deep a hue as scarcely to admit of it. On this the unhappy fairy uttered a shriek of despair, plunged headlong into the loch, and the minister resumed his course to his home.

The Page-Boy and the Silver Goblet

The Page-Boy and the Silver Goblet is one of the gentler moral tales from Elizabeth Wilson Grierson's The Scottish Fairy Book (J. B. Lippincott, 1910). Set within a world of castles, lords, and loyal servants, it tells the story of a humble page-boy whose honesty and courage are tested when a priceless silver goblet goes missing.

As with much of Grierson's work, the tale blends Scottish domestic realism with the cadence of traditional folklore. Her prose softens older oral motifs into a form suitable for early twentieth-century readers, focusing on ethical trials rather than enchantments.

There was once a little page-boy, who was in service in a stately Castle. He was a very good-natured little fellow, and did his duties so willingly and well that everybody liked him, from the great Earl whom he served every day on bended knee, to the fat old butler whose errands he ran.

Now the Castle stood on the edge of a cliff overlooking the sea, and although the walls at that side were very thick, in them there was a little postern door, which opened on to a narrow flight of steps that led down the face of the cliff to the seashore, so that anyone who liked could go down there in the pleasant summer mornings and bathe in the shimmering sea.

On the other side of the Castle were gardens and pleasure grounds, opening on to a long stretch of heather-covered moorland, which, , met a distant range of hills.

The little page-boy was very fond of going out on this moor when his work was done, for then he could run about as much as he liked, chasing bumble-bees, and catching butterflies, and looking for birds' nests when it was nesting time.

And the old butler was very pleased that he should do so, for he knew that it was good for a healthy little lad to have plenty of fun in the open air. But before the boy went out the old man always gave him one warning.

"Now, mind my words, laddie, and keep far away from the Fairy Knowe, for the Little Folk are not to trust to."

This Knowe of which he spoke was a little green hillock, which stood on the moor not twenty yards from the garden gate, and folk said that it was the abode of Fairies, who would punish any rash mortal who came too near them. And because of this the country people would walk a good half-mile out of their way, even in broad daylight, rather than run the risk of going too near the Fairy Knowe and bringing down the Little Folks' displeasure upon them. And at night they would hardly cross the moor at all, for everyone knows that Fairies come abroad in the darkness, and the door of their dwelling stands open, so that any luckless mortal who does not take care may find himself inside.

Now, the little page-boy was an adventurous wight, and instead of being frightened of the Fairies, he was very anxious to see them, and to visit their abode, just to find out what it was like.

So one night, when everyone else was asleep, he crept out of the Castle by the little postern door, and stole down the stone steps, and along the seashore, and up on to the moor, and went straight to the Fairy Knowe.

To his delight he found that what everyone said was true. The top of the Knowe was tipped up, and from the opening that was thus made, rays of light came streaming out. His heart was beating fast with excitement, but, gathering his courage, he stooped down and slipped inside the Knowe.

He found himself in a large room lit by numberless tiny candles, and there, seated round a polished table, were scores of the Tiny Folk, Fairies, and Elves, and Gnomes, dressed in green, and yellow, and pink; blue, and lilac, and scarlet; in all the colours, in fact, that you can think of.

He stood in a dark corner watching the busy scene in wonder, thinking how strange it was that there should be such a number of these tiny beings living their own lives all unknown to men, at such a little distance from them, when suddenly someone - he could not tell who it was - gave an order.

"Fetch the Cup," cried the owner of the unknown voice, and instantly two little Fairy pages, dressed all in scarlet livery, darted from the table to a tiny cupboard in the rock, and returned staggering under the weight of a most beautiful silver cup, richly embossed and lined inside with gold.

He placed it in the middle of the table, and, amid clapping of hands and shouts of joy, all the Fairies began to drink out of it in turn. And the page could see, from where he stood, that no one poured wine into it, and yet it was always full, and that the wine that was in it was not always the same kind, but that each Fairy, when he grasped its stem, wished for the wine that he loved best, and lo! in a moment the cup was full of it.

"Twould be a fine thing if I could take that cup home with me," thought the page. "No one will believe that I have been here except I have something to show for it." So he bided his time, and watched.

Presently the Fairies noticed him, and, instead of being angry at his boldness in entering their abode, as he expected that they would be, they seemed very pleased to see him, and invited him to a seat at the table. But by and by they grew rude and insolent, and jeered at him for being content to serve mere mortals, telling him that they saw everything that went on at the Castle, and making fun of the old butler, whom the page loved with all his heart. And they laughed at the food he ate, saying that it was only fit for animals, and when any fresh dainty was set on the table by the scarlet-clad pages, they would push the dish across to him, saying, "Taste it, for you will not have the chance of tasting such things at the Castle."

At last he could stand their teasing remarks no longer; besides, he knew that if he wanted to secure the cup he must lose no time in doing so.

So he suddenly stood up, and grasped the stem of it tightly in his hand. "I'll drink to you all in water," he cried, and instantly the ruby wine was turned to clear cold water.

He raised the cup to his lips, but he did not drink from it. With a sudden jerk he threw the water over the candles, and instantly the room was in darkness. Then, clasping the precious cup tightly in his arms, he sprang to the opening of the Knowe, through which he could see the stars glimmering clearly.

He was just in time, for it fell to with a crash behind him, and soon he was speeding along the wet, dew-spangled moor, with the whole troop of Fairies at his heels. They were wild with rage, and from the shrill shouts of fury which they uttered, the page knew well that, if they overtook him, he need expect no mercy at their hands.

And his heart began to sink, for, fleet of foot though he was, he was no match for the Fairy Folk, who gained on him steadily. All seemed lost when a mysterious voice sounded out of the darkness:

"If you would gain the Castle door,

Keep to the black stones on the shore."

It was the voice of some poor mortal, who, for some reason or other, had been taken prisoner by the Fairies - who were really very malicious Little Folk - and who did not want a like fate to befall the adventurous page-boy, but the little fellow did not know this.

He had once heard that if anyone walked on the wet sands, where the waves had come over them, the Fairies could not touch him, and this mysterious sentence brought the saying into his mind.

So he turned, and dashed panting down to the shore. His feet sank in the dry sand, his breath came in little gasps, and he felt as if he must give up the struggle, but he persevered, and , just as the foremost Fairies were about to lay hands on him, he jumped across the water-mark on to the firm, wet sand, from which the waves had just receded, and then he knew that he was safe.

For the Little Folk could go no step further, but stood on the dry sand uttering cries of rage and disappointment, while the triumphant page-boy ran safely along the shore, his precious cup in his arms, and climbed lightly up the steps in the rock and disappeared through the postern. And for many years after, long after the little page-boy had grown up and become a stately butler, who trained other little page-boys to follow in his footsteps, the beautiful cup remained in the Castle as a witness of his adventure.

The Princess Bella-Flor

The Princess Bella-Flor, as retold by Andrew Lang in The Orange Fairy Book (1906), originates from J. F. Campbell's Popular Tales from the West Highlands, part of his celebrated nineteenth-century collection of Gaelic folk narratives. It is a romantic and questing tale of enchantment, following a young prince who dreams of the beautiful Princess Bella-Flor and sets out to find her.

Lang's adaptation preserves much of Campbell's rhythm and imagery but smooths the idiom for his Edwardian readership. The result is a distinctly Victorian-era retelling, romantic, elegant, and slightly moralising, yet still rooted in the raw imaginative soil of Gaelic myth.

Once upon a time there lived a man who had two sons. When they grew up the elder went to seek his fortune in a far country, and for many years no one heard anything about him. Meanwhile the younger son stayed at home with his father, who died in a good old age, leaving great riches behind him.

For some time the son who stayed at home spent his father's wealth freely, believing that he alone remained to enjoy it. But, one day, as he was coming downstairs, he was surprised to see a stranger enter the hall, looking about as if the house belonged to him.

'Have you forgotten me?' asked the man.

'I can't forget a person I have never known,' was the rude answer.

'I am your brother,' replied the stranger, 'and I have returned home without the money I hoped to have made. And what is worse, they tell me in the village that my father is dead. I would have counted my lost gold as nothing if I could have seen him once more.'

'He died six months ago,' said the rich brother, 'and he left you, as your portion, the old wooden chest that stands in the loft. You had better go there and look for it; I have no more time to waste.' And he went his way.

So the wanderer turned his steps to the loft, which was at the top of the storehouse, and there he found the wooden chest, so old that it looked as if it were dropping to pieces.

'What use is this old thing to me?' he said to himself. 'Oh, well, it will serve to light a fire at which I can warm myself; so things might be worse after all.'

Placing the chest on his back, the man, whose name was Jose, set out for his inn, and, borrowing a hatchet, began to chop up the box. In doing so he discovered a secret drawer, and in it lay a paper. He opened the paper, not knowing what it might contain, and was astonished to find that it was the acknowledgment of a large debt that was owing to his father. Putting the precious writing in his pocket, he hastily inquired of the landlord where he could find the man whose name was written inside, and he ran out at once in search of him.

The debtor proved to be an old miser, who lived at the other end of the village. He had hoped for many months that the paper he had written had been lost or destroyed, and, indeed, when he saw it, was very unwilling to pay what he owed. However, the stranger threatened to drag him before the king, and when the miser saw that there was no help for it he counted out the coins one by one. The stranger picked them up and put them in his pocket, and went back to his inn feeling that he was now a rich man.

A few weeks after this he was walking through the streets of the nearest town, when he met a poor woman crying bitterly. He stopped and asked her what the matter was, and she answered between her sobs that her husband was dying, and, to make matters worse, a creditor whom he could not pay was anxious to have him taken to prison.

'Comfort yourself,' said the stranger kindly, 'they shall neither send your husband to prison nor sell your goods. I will not only pay his debts but, if he dies, the cost of his burial also. And now go home, and nurse him as well as you can.'

And so she did, but, in spite of her care, the husband died, and was buried by the stranger. But everything cost more than he expected, and when all was paid he found that only three gold pieces were left.

'What am I to do now?' he said to himself. 'I think I had better go to court, and enter into the service of the king.'

At first he was only a servant, who carried the king the water for his bath, and saw that his bed was made in a particular fashion. But he did his duties so well that his master soon took notice of him, and in a short time he rose to be a gentleman of the bedchamber.

Now, when this happened the younger brother had spent all the money he had inherited, and did not know how to make any for himself. He then bethought him of the king's favourite, and went whining to the palace to beg that his brother, whom he had so ill-used, would give him his protection, and find him a place. The elder, who was always ready to help everyone spoke to the king on his behalf, and the next day the young man took up is work at court.

Unfortunately, the new-comer was by nature spiteful and envious, and could not bear anyone to have better luck than himself. By dint of spying through keyholes and listening at doors, he learned that the king, old and ugly though he was, had fallen in love with the Princess Bella-Flor, who would have nothing to say to him, and had hidden herself in some mountain castle, no one knew where.

'That will do nicely,' thought the scoundrel, rubbing his hands. 'It will be quite easy to get the king to send my brother in search of her, and if he returns without finding her, his head will be the forfeit. Either way, he will be out of MY path.'

So he went at once to the Lord High Chamberlain and craved an audience of the king, to whom he declared he wished to tell some news of the highest importance. The king admitted him into the presence chamber without delay, and bade him state what he had to say, and to be quick about it.

'Oh, sire! the Princess Bella-Flor...' answered the man, and then stopped as if afraid.

'What of the Princess Bella-Flor?' asked the king impatiently.

'I have heard - it is whispered at court - that your majesty desires to know where she lies in hiding.'

'I would give half my kingdom to the man who will bring her to me,' cried the king, eagerly. 'Speak on, knave; has a bird of the air revealed to you the secret?'

'It is not I, but my brother, who knows,' replied the traitor, 'if your majesty would ask him - ' But before the words were out of his mouth the king had struck a blow with his sceptre on a golden plate that hung on the wall.

'Order Jose to appear before me instantly,' he shouted to the servant who ran to obey his orders, so great was the noise his majesty had made, and when Jose entered the hall, wondering what in the world could be the matter, the king was nearly dumb from rage and excitement.

'Bring me the Princess Bella-Flor this moment,' stammered he, 'for if you return without her I will have you drowned!' And without another word he left the hall, leaving Jose staring with surprise and horror.

'How can I find the Princess Bella-Flor when I have never even seen her?' thought he. 'But it is no use staying here, for I shall only be put to death.' And he walked slowly to the stables to choose himself a horse.

There were rows upon rows of fine beasts with their names written in gold above their stalls, and Jose was looking uncertainly from one to the other, wondering which he should choose, when an old white horse turned its head and signed to him to approach.

'Take me,' it said in a gentle whisper, 'and all will go well.'

Jose still felt so bewildered with the mission that the king had given him that he forgot to be astonished at hearing a horse talk. Mechanically he laid his hand on the bridle and led the white horse out of the stable. He was about to mount on his back, when the animal spoke again, 'Pick up those three loaves of bread which you see there, and put them in your pocket.'

Jose did as he was told, and being in a great hurry to get away, asked no questions, but swung himself into the saddle.

They rode far without meeting any adventures, but at length they came to an ant-hill, and the horse stopped.

'Crumble those three loaves for the ants,' he said. But Jose hesitated.

'Why, we may want them ourselves!' answered he.

'Never mind that; give them to the ants all the same. Do not lose a chance of helping others.' And when the loaves lay in crumbs on the road, the horse galloped on.

By-and-by they entered a rocky pass between two mountains, and here they saw an eagle which had been caught in a hunter's net.

'Get down and cut the meshes of the net, and set the poor bird free,' said the horse.

'But it will take so long,' objected Jose, 'and we may miss the princess.'

'Never mind that; do not lose a chance of helping others,' answered the horse. And when the meshes were cut, and the eagle was free, the horse galloped on.

The had ridden many miles, and they came to a river, where they beheld a little fish lying gasping on the sand, and the horse said, 'Do you see that little fish? It will die if you do not put it back in the water.'

'But, really, we shall never find the Princess Bella-Flor if we waste our time like this!' cried Jose.

'We never waste time when we are helping others,' answered the horse. And soon the little fish was swimming happily away.

A little while after they reached a castle, which was built in the middle of a very thick wood, and right in front was the Princess Bella-Flor feeding her hens.

'Now listen,' said the horse. 'I am going to give all sorts of little hops and skips, which will amuse the Princess Bella-Flor. Then she will tell you that she would like to ride a little way, and you must help her to mount. When she is seated I shall begin to neigh and kick, and you must say that I have never carried a woman before, and that you had better get up behind so as to be able to manage me. Once on my back we will go like the wind to the king's palace.'

Jose did exactly as the horse told him, and everything fell out as the animal prophesied; so that it was not until they were galloping breathlessly towards the palace that the princess knew that she was taken captive. She said nothing, however, but quietly opened her apron which contained the bran for the chickens, and in a moment it lay scattered on the ground.

'Oh, I have let fall my bran!' cried she, 'please get down and pick it up for me.'

But Jose only answered, 'We shall find plenty of bran where we are going.' And the horse galloped on.

They were now passing through a forest, and the princess took out her handkerchief and threw it upwards, so that it stuck in one of the topmost branches of a tree.

'Dear me; how stupid! I have let my handkerchief blow away,' she said. 'Will you climb up and get it for me?' But Jose answered:

'We shall find plenty of handkerchiefs where we are going.' And the horse galloped on.

After the wood they reached a river, and the princess slipped a ring off her finger and let it roll into the water.

'How careless of me,' gasped she, beginning to sob. 'I have lost my favourite ring; DO stop for a moment and look if you can see it.' But Jose answered:

'You will find plenty of rings where you are going.' And the horse galloped on.

At last they entered the palace gates, and the king's heart bounded with joy at beholding his beloved Princess Bella-Flor. But the princess brushed him aside as if he had been a fly, and locked herself into the nearest room, which she would not open for all his entreaties.

'Bring me the three things I lost on the way, and perhaps I may think about it,' was all she would say. And, in despair, the king was driven to take counsel of Jose.

'There is no remedy that I can see,' said his majesty, 'but that you, who know where they are, should go and bring them back. And if you return without them I will have you drowned.'

Poor Jose was much troubled at these words. He thought that he had done all that was required of him, and that his life was safe. However, he bowed low, and went out to consult his friend the horse.

'Do not vex yourself,' said the horse, when he had heard the story, 'jump up, and we will go and look for the things.' And Jose mounted at once.

They rode on till they came to the ant-hill, and then the horse asked, 'Would you like to have the bran?'

'What is the use of liking?' answered Jose.

'Well, call the ants, and tell them to fetch it for you, and, if some of it has been scattered by the wind, to bring in its stead the grains that were in the cakes you gave them.' Jose listened in surprise. He did not much believe in the horse's plan, but he could not think of anything better, so he called to the ants, and bade them collect the bran as fast as they could.

Then he saw under a tree and waited, while his horse cropped the green turf.

'Look there!' said the animal, suddenly raising its head, and Jose looked behind him and saw a little mountain of bran, which he put into a bag that was hung over his saddle.

'Good deeds bear fruit sooner or later,' observed the horse, 'but mount again, as we have far to go.'

When they arrived at the tree, they saw the handkerchief fluttering like a flag from the topmost branch, and Jose's spirits sank again.

'How am I to get that handkerchief?' cried he, 'why I should need Jacob's ladder!' But the horse answered:

'Do not be frightened; call to the eagle you set free from the net, he will bring it to you.'

So Jose called to the eagle, and the eagle flew to the top of the tree and brought back the handkerchief in its beak. Jose thanked him, and vaulting on his horse they rode on to the river.

A great deal of rain had fallen in the night, and the river, instead of being clear as it was before, was dark and troubled.

'How am I to fetch the ring from the bottom of this river when I do not know exactly where it was dropped, and cannot even see it?' asked Jose. But the horse answered, 'Do not be frightened; call the little fish whose life you saved, and she will bring it to you.'

So he called to the fish, and the fish dived to the bottom and slipped behind big stones, and moved little ones with its tail till it found the ring, and brought it to Jose in its mouth.

Well pleased with all he had done, Jose returned to the palace, but when the king took the precious objects to Bella-Flor, she declared that she would never open her door till the bandit who had carried her off had been fried in oil.

'I am very sorry,' said the king to Jose, 'I really would rather not, but you see I have no choice.'

While the oil was being heated in the great caldron, Jose went to the stables to inquire of his friend the horse if there was no way for him to escape.

'Do not be frightened,' said the horse. 'Get on my back, and I will gallop till my whole body is wet with perspiration, then rub it all over your skin, and no matter how hot the oil may be you will never feel it.'

Jose did not ask any more questions but did as the horse bade him, and men wondered at his cheerful face as they lowered him into the caldron of boiling oil. He was left there till Bella-Flor cried that he must be cooked enough. Then out came a youth so young and handsome, that everyone fell in love with him, and Bella-Flor most of all.

As for the old king, he saw that he had lost the game, and in despair he flung himself into the caldron, and was fried instead of Jose. Then Jose was proclaimed king, on condition that he married Bella-Flor which he promised to do the next day. But first he went to the stables and sought out the horse, and said to him, 'It is to you that I owe my life and my crown. Why have you done all this for me?'

And the horse answered, 'I am the soul of that unhappy man for whom you spent all your fortune. And when I saw you in danger of death I begged that I might help you, as you had helped me. For, as I told you, Good deeds bear their own fruit!'

The Red Etin

The Red Etin, as retold by Elizabeth Wilson Grierson in The Scottish Fairy Book (1910), is a classic Scottish folktale of courage, destiny, and the redemptive power of kindness. It tells of three sons who set out from home to seek their fortunes.

Grierson's adaptation captures the cadence and moral rhythm of traditional Border storytelling, blending the supernatural with homely wisdom. The tale bears the familiar hallmarks of Scottish oral tradition: the power of courtesy, the dangers of pride, and the victory of clear-hearted persistence over brute strength.

There were once two widows who lived in two cottages which stood not very far from one another. And each of those widows possessed a piece of land on which she grazed a cow and a few sheep, and in this way she made her living.

One of these poor widows had two sons, the other had one, and as these three boys were always together, it was natural that they should become great friends.

At last the time arrived when the eldest son of the widow who had two sons, must leave home and go out into the world to seek his fortune. And the night before he went away his mother told him to take a can and go to the well and bring back some water, and she would bake a cake for him to carry with him.

"But remember," she added, "the size of the cake will depend on the quantity of water that you bring back. If you bring much, then will it be large, and, if you bring little, then will it be small. But, big or little, it is all that I have to give you."

The lad took the can and went off to the well, and filled it with water, and came home again. But he never noticed that the can had a hole in it, and was running out; so that, by the time that he arrived at home, there was very little water left. So his mother could only bake him a very little cake.

But, small as it was, she asked him, as she gave it to him, to choose one of two things. Either to take the half of it with her blessing, or the whole of it with her malison. "For," she said, "you cannot have both the whole cake and a blessing along with it."

The lad looked at the cake and hesitated. It would have been pleasant to have left home with his mother's blessing upon him, but he had far to go, and the cake was little; the half of it would be a mere mouthful, and he did not know when he would get any more food. So he made up his mind to take the whole of it, even if he had to bear his mother's malison.

Then he took his younger brother aside, and gave him his hunting-knife, saying, "Keep this by you, and look at it every morning. For as long as the blade remains clear and bright, you will know that it is well with me, but should it grow dim and rusty, then know you that some evil has befallen me."

After this he embraced them both and set out on his travels. He journeyed all that day, and all the next, and on the afternoon of the third day he came to where an old shepherd was sitting beside a flock of sheep.

"I will ask the old man whose sheep they are," he said to himself, "for mayhap his master might engage me also as a shepherd." So he went up to the old man, and asked him to whom the sheep belonged. And this was all the answer he got:

"The Red-Etin of Ireland

Ance lived in Ballygan,

And stole King Malcolm's daughter,

The King of fair Scotland.

He beats her, he binds her,

He lays her on a band,

And every day he dings her

With a bright silver wand.

Like Julian the Roman,

He's one that fears no man.

It's said there's one predestinate

To be his mortal foe,

But that man is yet unborn,

And lang may it be so."

"That does not tell me much, but somehow I do not fancy this Red-Etin for a master," thought the youth, and he went on his way.

He had not gone very far, however, when he saw another old man, with snow-white hair, herding a flock of swine, and as he wondered to whom the swine belonged, and if there was any chance of him getting a situation as a swineherd, he went up to the countryman, and asked who the owner of the animals was.

He got the same answer from the swineherd that he had got from the shepherd:

"The Red-Etin of Ireland

Ance lived in Ballygan,

And stole King Malcolm's daughter,

The King of fair Scotland.

He beats her, he binds her,

He lays her on a band,

And every day he dings her

With a bright silver wand.

Like Julian the Roman,

He's one that fears no man.

It's said there's one predestinate

To be his mortal foe,

But that man is yet unborn,

And lang may it be so."

"Plague on this old Red-Etin; I wonder when I will get out of his domains," he muttered to himself, and he journeyed still further.

Presently he came to a very, very old man - so old, indeed, that he was quite bent with age - and he was herding a flock of goats.

Once more the traveller asked to whom the animals belonged, and once more he got the same answer:

"The Red-Etin of Ireland

Ance lived in Ballygan,

And stole King Malcolm's daughter,

The King of fair Scotland.

He beats her, he binds her,

He lays her on a band,

And every day he dings her

With a bright silver wand.

Like Julian the Roman,

He's one that fears no man.

It's said there's one predestinate

To be his mortal foe,

But that man is yet unborn,

And lang may it be so."

But this ancient goatherd added a piece of advice at the end of his rhyme. "Beware, stranger," he said, "of the next herd of beasts that you shall meet. Sheep, and swine, and goats will harm nobody, but the creatures you shall now encounter are of a sort that you have never met before, and they are not harmless."

The young man thanked him for his counsel, and went on his way, and he had not gone very far before he met a herd of very dreadful creatures, unlike anything that he had ever dreamed of in all his life.

For each of them had three heads, and on each of its three heads it had four horns, and when he saw them he was so frightened that he turned and ran away from them as fast as he could.

Up hill and down dale he ran, until he was well-nigh exhausted, and, just when he was beginning to feel that his legs would not carry him any further, he saw a great Castle in front of him, the door of which was standing wide open.

He was so tired that he went straight in, and after wandering through some magnificent halls, which appeared to be quite deserted, he reached the kitchen, where an old woman was sitting by the fire.

He asked her if he might have a night's lodging, as he had come a long and weary journey, and would be glad of somewhere to rest.

"You can rest here, and welcome, for me," said the old Dame, "but for your own sake I warn you that this is an ill house to bide in, for it is the Castle of the Red-Etin, who is a fierce and terrible Monster with three heads, and he spares neither man nor woman, if he can get hold of them."

Tired as he was, the young man would have made an effort to escape from such a dangerous abode had he not remembered the strange and awful beasts from which he had just been fleeing, and he was afraid that, as it was growing dark, if he set out again he might chance to walk right into their midst. So he begged the old woman to hide him in some dark corner, and not to tell the Red-Etin that he was in the Castle.

"For," thought he, "if I can only get shelter until the morning, I will then be able to avoid these terrible creatures and go on my way in peace."

So the old Dame hid him in a press under the back stairs, and, as there was plenty of room in it, he settled down quite comfortably for the night.

But just as he was going off to sleep he heard an awful roaring and trampling overhead. The Red-Etin had come home, and it was plain that he was searching for something.

And the terrified youth soon found out what the "Something" was, for very soon the horrible Monster came into the kitchen, crying out in a voice like thunder:

"Seek but, and seek ben,

I smell the smell of an earthly man!

Be he living, or be he dead,

His heart this night I shall eat with my bread."

And it was not very long before he discovered the poor young man's hiding-place and pulled him roughly out of it.

Of course, the lad begged that his life might be spared, but the Monster only laughed at him.

"It will be spared if you can answer three questions," he said, "if not, it is forfeited."

The first of these three questions was, "Whether Ireland or Scotland was first inhabited?"

The second, "How old was the world when Adam was made?"

And the third, "Whether men or beasts were created first?"

The lad was not skilled in such matters, having had but little book-learning, and he could not answer the questions. So the Monster struck him on the head with a queer little hammer which he carried, and turned him into a piece of stone.

Now every morning since he had left home his younger brother had done as he had promised, and had carefully examined his hunting-knife.

On the first two mornings it was bright and clear, but on the third morning he was very much distressed to find that it was dull and rusty. He looked at it for a few moments in great dismay; then he ran straight to his mother, and held it out to her.

"By this token I know that some mischief has befallen my brother," he said, "so I must set out at once to see what evil has come upon him."

"First must you go to the well and fetch me some water," said his mother, "that I may bake you a cake to carry with you, as I baked a cake for him who is gone. And I will say to you what I said to him. That the cake will be large or small according as you bring much or little water back with you."

So the lad took the can, as his brother had done, and went off to the well, and it seemed as if some evil spirit directed him to follow his example in all things, for he brought home little water, and he chose the whole cake and his mother's malison, instead of the half and her blessing, and he set out and met the shepherd, and the swineherd, and the goatherd, and they all gave the same answers to him which they had given to his brother. And he also encountered the same fierce beasts, and ran from them in terror, and took shelter from them in the Castle, and the old woman hid him, and the Red-Etin found him, and, because he could not answer the three questions, he, too, was turned into a pillar of stone.

And no more would ever have been heard of these two youths had not a kind Fairy, who had seen all that had happened, appeared to the other widow and her son, as they were sitting at supper one night in the gloaming, and told them the whole story, and how their two poor young neighbours had been turned into pillars of stone by a cruel enchanter called Red-Etin.

Now the third young man was both brave and strong, and he determined to set out to see if he could in anywise help his two friends. And, from the very first moment that he had made up his mind to do so, things went differently with him than they had with them. I think, perhaps, that this was because he was much more loving and thoughtful than they were.

For, when his mother sent him to fetch water from the well so that she might bake a cake for him, just as the other mother had done for her sons, a raven, flying above his head, croaked out that his can was leaking, and he, wishing to please his mother by bringing her a good supply of water, patched up the hole with clay, and so came home with the can quite full.

Then, when his mother had baked a big bannock for him, and giving him his choice between the whole cake and her malison, or half of it and her blessing, he chose the latter, "for," he said, throwing his arms round her neck, "I may light on other cakes to eat, but I will never light on another blessing such as yours. "

And the curious thing was, that, after he had said this, the half cake which he had chosen seemed to spread itself out, and widen, and broaden, till it was bigger by far than it had been at first.

Then he started on his journey, and, after he had gone a good way he began to feel hungry. So he pulled it out of his pocket and began to eat it.

Just then he met an old woman, who seemed to be very poor, for her clothing was thin, and worn, and old, and she stopped and spoke to him.

"Of your charity, kind Master," she said, stretching out one of her withered hands, "spare me a bit of the cake that you are eating."

Now the youth was very hungry, and he could have eaten it all himself, but his kind heart was touched by the woman's pinched face, so he broke it in two, and gave her half of it.

Instantly she was changed into the Fairy who had appeared to his mother and himself as they had sat at supper the night before, and she smiled graciously at the generous lad, and held out a little wand to him.

"Though you know it not, your mother's blessing and your kindness to an old and poor woman has gained you many blessings, brave boy," he said. "Keep that as your reward; you will need it before your errand be done." Then, bidding him sit down on the grass beside her, she told him all the dangers that he would meet on his travels, and the way in which he could overcome them, and then, in a moment, before he could thank her, she vanished out of his sight.

But with the little wand, and all the instructions that she had given him, he felt that he could face fearlessly any danger that he might be called on to meet, so he rose from the grass and went his way, full of a cheerful courage.

After he had walked for many miles further, he came, as each of his friends had done, to the old shepherd herding his sheep. And, like them, he asked to whom the sheep belonged. And this time the old man answered:

"The Red-Etin of Ireland

Ance lived in Ballygan,

And stole King Malcolm's daughter,

The King of fair Scotland.

He beats her, he binds her,

He lays her on a band,

And every day he dings her

With a bright silver wand.

Like Julian the Roman,

He's one that fears no man.

But now I fear his end is near,

And destiny at hand;

And you're to be, I plainly see,

The heir of all his land."

Then the young man went on, and he came to the swineherd, and to the goatherd, and each of them in turn repeated the same words to him.

And, when he came to where the droves of monstrous beasts were, he was not afraid of them, and when one came running up to him with its mouth wide open to devour him, he just struck it with his wand, and it dropped down dead at his feet.

At last he arrived at the Red-Etin's Castle, and he knocked boldly at the door. The old woman answered his knock, and, when he had told her his errand, warned him gravely not to enter.

"Your two friends came here before you," she said, "and they are now turned into two pillars of stone; what advantage is it to you to lose your life also?"

But the young man only laughed. "I have knowledge of an art of which they knew nothing," he said. "And methinks I can fight the Red-Etin with his own weapons."

So, much against her will, the old woman let him in, and hid him where she had hidden his friends.

It was not long before the Monster arrived, and, as on former occasions, he came into the kitchen in a furious rage, crying:

"Seek but, and seek ben,

I smell the smell of an earthly man!

Be he living, or be he dead,

His heart this night I shall eat with my bread."

Then he peered into the young man's hiding-place, and called to him to come out. And after he had come out, he put to him the three questions, never dreaming that he could answer them, but the Fairy had told the youth what to say, and he gave the answers as pat as any book.

Then the Red-Etin's heart sank within him for fear, for he knew that someone had betrayed him, and that his power was gone.

And gone in very truth it was. For when the youth took an axe and began to fight with him, he had no strength to resist, and, before he knew where he was, his heads were cut off. And that was the end of the Red-Etin.

As soon as he saw that his enemy was really dead, the young man asked the old woman if what the shepherd, and the swineherd, and the goatherd had told him were true, and if King Malcolm's daughter were really a prisoner in the Castle.

The old woman nodded. "Even with the Monster lying dead at my feet, I am almost afraid to speak of it," she said. "But come with me, my gallant gentleman, and you will see what dule and misery the Red-Etin has caused to many a home."

She took a huge bunch of keys, and led him up a long flight of stairs, which ended in a passage with a great many doors on each side of it. She unlocked these doors with her keys, and, as she opened them, she put her head into every room and said, "You have naught to fear now, Madam, the Predestinated Deliverer has come, and the Red-Etin is dead."

And behold, with a cry of joy, out of every room came a beautiful lady who had been stolen from her home, and shut up there, by the Red-Etin.

Among them was one who was more beautiful and statelier than the rest, and all the others bowed down to her and treated her with such great reverence that it was clear to see that she was the Royal Princess, King Malcolm's daughter.

And when the youth stepped forward and did reverence to her also, she spoke so sweetly to him, and greeted him so gladly, and called him her Deliverer, in such a low, clear voice, that his heart was taken captive at once.

But, for all that, he did not forget his friends. He asked the old woman where they were, and she took him into a room at the end of the passage, which was so dark that one could scarcely see in it, and so low that one could scarcely stand upright. In this dismal chamber stood two blocks of stone.

"One can unlock doors, young Master," said the old woman, shaking her head forebodingly, "but 'tis hard work to try to turn cold stone back to flesh and blood."

"Nevertheless, I will do it," said the youth, and, lifting his little wand, he touched each of the stone pillars lightly on the top.

Instantly the hard stone seemed to soften and melt away, and the two brothers started into life and form again. Their gratitude to their friend, who had risked so much to save them, knew no bounds, while he, on his part, was delighted to think that his efforts had been successful.

The next thing to do was to convey the Princess and the other ladies (who were all noblemen's daughters) back to the King's Court, and this they did next day.

King Malcolm was so overjoyed to see his dearly loved daughter, whom he had given up for dead, safe and sound, and so grateful to her deliverer, that he said that he should become his son-in-law and marry the Princess, and come and live with them at Court. Which all came to pass in due time; while as for the two other young men, they married noblemen's daughters, and the two old mothers came to live near their sons, and everyone was as happy as they could possibly be.

The Seal-Catcher and the Merman

The Seal-Catcher and the Merman is one of the more striking tales from Elizabeth Wilson Grierson's The Scottish Fairy Book (J. B. Lippincott Company, 1910), a collection that gathers traditional Scottish folk and fairy lore for a younger early-twentieth-century audience. The story tells of a seal-hunter from the northern coasts who makes his living by trapping and skinning seals, creatures long believed in Gaelic and Norse tradition to be the seal-folk or selkies, beings that could cast off their skins and live for a time among humans.

Grierson's retelling preserves the moral clarity and eerie restraint typical of Scottish coastal folklore. The natural world is never neutral; it watches and remembers. Her prose conveys both the harsh realism of a life tied to the sea and the mythic grandeur of its unseen depths. As in many selkie legends, the tale ends with uneasy reconciliation rather than triumph: the hunter learns that every act of cruelty toward the sea carries a price.

Once upon a time there was a man who lived not very far from John O'Groats house, which, as everyone knows, is in the very north of Scotland. He lived in a little cottage by the sea-shore, and made his living by catching seals and selling their fur, which is very valuable.

He earned a good deal of money in this way, for these creatures used to come out of the sea in large numbers, and lie on the rocks near his house basking in the sunshine, so that it was not difficult to creep up behind them and kill them.

Some of those seals were larger than others, and the country people used to call them "Roane," and whisper that they were not seals at all, but Mermen and Merwomen, who came from a country of their own, far down under the ocean, who assumed this strange disguise in order that they might pass through the water, and come up to breathe the air of this earth of ours.

But the seal catcher only laughed at them, and said that those seals were most worth killing, for their skins were so big that he got an extra price for them.

Now it chanced one day, when he was pursuing his calling, that he stabbed a seal with his hunting-knife, and whether the stroke had not been sure enough or not, I cannot say, but with a loud cry of pain the creature slipped off the rock into the sea, and disappeared under the water, carrying the knife along with it.

The seal catcher, much annoyed at his clumsiness, and also at the loss of his knife, went home to dinner in a very downcast frame of mind. On his way he met a horseman, who was so tall and so strange-looking and who rode on such a gigantic horse, that he stopped and looked at him in astonishment, wondering who he was, and from what country he came.

The stranger stopped also, and asked him his trade and on hearing that he was a seal catcher, he immediately ordered a great number of seal skins. The seal catcher was delighted, for such an order meant a large sum of money to him. But his face fell when the horseman added that it was absolutely necessary that the skins should be delivered that evening.

"I cannot do it," he said in a disappointed voice, "for the seals will not come back to the rocks again until tomorrow morning."

"I can take you to a place where there are any number of seals," answered the stranger, "if you will mount behind me on my horse and come with me."

The seal catcher agreed to this, and climbed up behind the rider, who shook his bridle rein, and off the great horse galloped at such a pace that he had much ado to keep his seat.

On and on they went, flying like the wind, until they came to the edge of a huge precipice, the face of which went sheer down to the sea. Here the mysterious horseman pulled up his steed with a jerk.

"Get off now," he said shortly.

The seal catcher did as he was bid, and when he found himself safe on the ground, he peeped cautiously over the edge of the cliff, to see if there were any seals lying on the rocks below.

To his astonishment he saw no rocks, only the blue sea, which came right up to the foot of the cliff. "Where are the seals that you spoke of?" he asked anxiously, wishing that he had never set out on such a rash adventure.

"You will see presently," answered the stranger, who was attending to his horse's bridle.

The seal catcher was now thoroughly frightened, for he felt sure that some evil was about to befall him, and in such a lonely place he knew that it would be useless to cry out for help.

And it seemed as if his fears would prove only too true, for the next moment the stranger's hand was laid upon his shoulder, and he felt himself being hurled bodily over the cliff, and then he fell with a splash into the sea.

He thought that his last hour had come, and he wondered how anyone could work such a deed of wrong upon an innocent man.

But, to his astonishment, he found that some change must have passed over him, for instead of being choked by the water, he could breathe quite easily, and he and his companion, who was still close at his side, seemed to be sinking as quickly down through the sea as they had flown through the air.

Down and down they went, nobody knows how far, till they came to a huge arched door, which appeared to be made of pink coral, studded over with cockle-shells. It opened, of its own accord, and when they entered they found themselves in a huge hall, the walls of which were formed of mother-of-pearl, and the floor of which was of sea-sand, smooth, and firm, and yellow.

The hall was crowded with occupants, but they were seals, not men, and when the seal catcher turned to his companion to ask him what it all meant, he was aghast to find that he, too, had assumed the form of a seal. He was still more aghast when he caught sight of himself in a large mirror that hung on the wall, and saw that he also no longer bore the likeness of a man, but was transformed into a nice, hairy, brown seal.

"Ah, woe to me," he said to himself, "for no fault of mine own this artful stranger has laid some baneful charm upon me, and in this awful guise will I remain for the rest of my natural life."

At first none of the huge creatures spoke to him. For some reason or other they seemed to be very sad, and moved gently about the hall, talking quietly and mournfully to one another, or lay sadly upon the sandy floor, wiping big tears from their eyes with their soft furry fins.

But presently they began to notice him, and to whisper to one another, and presently his guide moved away from him, and disappeared through a door at the end of the hall. When he returned he held a huge knife in his hand.

"Did you ever see this before?" he asked, holding it out to the unfortunate seal catcher, who, to his horror, recognised his own hunting knife with which he had struck the seal in the morning, and which had been carried off by the wounded animal.

At the sight of it he fell upon his face and begged for mercy, for he at once came to the conclusion that the inhabitants of the cavern, enraged at the harm which had been wrought upon their comrade, had, in some magic way, contrived to capture him, and to bring him down to their subterranean abode, in order to wreak their vengeance upon him by killing him.

But, instead of doing so, they crowded round him, rubbing their soft noses against his fur to show their sympathy, and implored him not to put himself about, for no harm would befall him, and they would love him all their lives long if he would only do what they asked him.

"Tell me what it is," said the seal catcher, "and I will do it, if it lies within my power."

"Follow me," answered his guide, and he led the way to the door through which he had disappeared when he went to seek the knife.

The seal catcher followed him. And there, in a smaller room, he found a great brown seal lying on a bed of pale pink seaweed, with a gaping wound in his side.

"That is my father," said his guide, "whom you wounded this morning, thinking that he was one of the common seals who live in the sea, instead of a Merman who has speech, and understanding, as you mortals have. I brought you hither to bind up his wounds, for no other hand than yours can heal him."

"I have no skill in the art of healing," said the seal catcher, astonished at the forbearance of these strange creatures, whom he had so unwittingly wronged, "but I will bind up the wound to the best of my power, and I am only sorry that it was my hands that caused it."

He went over to the bed, and stooping over the wounded Merman, washed and dressed the hurt as well as he could, and the touch of his hands appeared to work like magic, for no sooner had he finished than the wound seemed to deaden and die, leaving only the scar, and the old seal sprang up, as well as ever.

Then there was great rejoicing throughout the whole Palace of the Seals. They laughed, and they talked, and they embraced each other in their own strange way, crowding round their comrade, and rubbing their noses against his, as if to show him how delighted they were at his recovery.

But all this while the seal catcher stood alone in a corner, with his mind filled with dark thoughts, for although he saw now that they had no intention of killing him, he did not relish the prospect of spending the rest of his life in the guise of a seal, fathoms deep under the ocean.

But presently, to his great joy, his guide approached him, and said, "Now you are at liberty to return home to your wife and children. I will take you to them, but only on one condition."

"And what is that?" asked the seal catcher eagerly, overjoyed at the prospect of being restored safely to the upper world, and to his family.

"That you will take a solemn oath never to wound a seal again."

"That will I do right gladly," he replied, for although the promise meant giving up his means of livelihood, he felt that if only he regained his proper shape he could always turn his hand to something else.

So he took the required oath with all due solemnity, holding up his fin as he swore, and all the other seals crowded round him as witnesses. And a sigh of relief went through the halls when the words were spoken, for he was the most noted seal catcher in the North.

Then he bade the strange company farewell, and, accompanied by his guide, passed once more through the outer doors of coral, and up, and up, and up, through the shadowy green water, until it began to grow lighter and lighter and they emerged into the sunshine of earth.

Then, with one spring, they reached the top of the cliff, where the great black horse was waiting for them, quietly nibbling the green turf.

When they left the water their strange disguise dropped from them, and they were now as they had been before, a plain seal catcher and a tall, well-dressed gentleman in riding clothes.

"Get up behind me," said the latter, as he swung himself into his saddle. The seal catcher did as he was bid, taking tight hold of his companion's coat, for he remembered how nearly he had fallen off on his previous journey.

Then it all happened as it happened before. The bridle was shaken, and the horse galloped off, and it was not long before the seal catcher found himself standing in safety before his own garden gate.

He held out his hand to say "goodbye," but as he did so the stranger pulled out a huge bag of gold and placed it in it.

"You have done your part of the bargain - we must do ours," he said. "Men shall never say that we took away an honest man's work without making reparation for it, and here is what will keep you in comfort to your life's end."

Then he vanished, and when the astonished seal catcher carried the bag into his cottage, and turned the gold out on the table, he found that what the stranger had said was true, and that he would be a rich man for the remainder of his days.

The Shifty Lad

The Shifty Lad is a lively Scottish tale of trickery and mischief, first recorded by the folklorist John Francis Campbell in his Popular Tales of the West Highlands (1860–62) and later retold by Andrew Lang in The Lilac Fairy Book (1910). The story follows a clever young thief known only as the Shifty Lad, whose wits and quick tongue keep him one step ahead of the law and his companions alike.

Beneath the comedy, the tale explores the ambiguous morality of cunning: the Shifty Lad's intelligence is admirable, yet his trickery leads inevitably to downfall. The story, like many from Campbell's collections, bridges older oral traditions with the literary fairy-tale revival of the late nineteenth and early twentieth centuries, showing how Scottish folklore's dark wit and moral complexity survived into modern retellings.

In the land of Erin there dwelt long ago a widow who had an only son. He was a clever boy, so she saved up enough money to send him to school, and, as soon as he was old enough, to apprentice him to any trade that he would choose. But when the time came, he said would not be bound to any trade, and that he meant to be a thief.

Now his mother was very sorrowful when she heard of this, but she knew quite well that if she tried to stop his having his own way he would only grow more determined to get it. So all the answer she made was that the end of thieves was hanging at the bridge of Dublin, and then she left him alone, hoping that when he was older he might become more sensible.

One day she was going to church to hear a sermon from a great preacher, and she begged the Shifty Lad, as the neighbours called him from the tricks he played, to come with her. But he only laughed and declared that he did not like sermons, adding:

'However, I will promise you this, that the first trade you hear named after you come out from church shall be my trade for the rest of my life.'

These words gave a little comfort to the poor woman, and her heart was lighter than before as she bade him farewell.

When the Shifty Lad thought that the hour had nearly come for the sermon to be over, he hid himself in some bushes in a little path that led straight to his mother's house, and, as she passed along, thinking of all the good things she had heard, a voice shouted close to her ear 'Robbery! Robbery! Robbery!' The suddenness of it made her jump. The naughty boy had managed to change his voice, so that she did not know it for his, and he had concealed himself so well that, though she peered about all round her, she could see no one. As soon as she had turned the corner the Shifty Lad came out, and by running very fast through the wood he contrived to reach home before his mother, who found him stretched out comfortably before the fire.

'Well, have you got any news to tell me?' asked he.

'No, nothing, for I left the church at once, and did not stop to speak to anyone.'

'Oh, then no one has mentioned a trade to you?' he said in tones of disappointment.

'Ye - es,' she replied slowly. 'At least, as I walked down the path a voice cried out "Robbery! Robbery! Robbery!" but that was all.'

'And quite enough too,' answered the boy. 'What did I tell you? That is going to be my trade.'

'Then your end will be hanging at the bridge of Dublin,' she said. But there was no sleep for her that night, for she lay in the dark thinking about her son.

'If he is to be a thief at all, he had better be a good one. And who is there that can teach him?' the mother asked herself. But an idea came to her, and she arose early, before the sun was up, and set off for the home of the Black Rogue, or Gallows Bird, who was such a wonderful thief that, though all had been robbed by him, no one could catch him.

'Good-morning to you,' said the woman as she reached the place where the Black Gallows Bird lived when he was not away on his business. 'My son has a fancy to learn your trade. Will you be kind enough to teach him?'

'If he is clever, I don't mind trying,' answered the Black Gallows Bird, 'and, of course, if ANY one can turn him into a first-rate thief, it is I. But if he is stupid, it is of no use at all; I can't bear stupid people.'

'No, he isn't stupid,' said the woman with a sigh. 'So to-night, after dark, I will send him to you.'

The Shifty Lad jumped for joy when his mother told him where she had been.

'I will become the best thief in all Erin!' he cried, and paid no heed when his mother shook her head and murmured something about 'the bridge of Dublin.'

Every evening after dark the Shifty Lad went to the home of the Black Gallows Bird, and many were the new tricks he learned. By-

and-by he was allowed to go out with the Bird and watch him at work, and there came a day when his master though that he had grown clever enough to help in a big robbery.

'There is a rich farmer up there on the hill, who has just sold all his fat cattle for much money and has bought some lean ones which will cost him little. Now it happens that, while he has received the money for the fat cattle, he has not yet paid the price of the thin ones, which he has in the cowhouse. To-morrow he will go to the market with the money in his hand, so to-night we must get at the chest. When all is quiet we will hide in the loft.'

There was no moon, and it was the night of Halloween, and everyone was burning nuts and catching apples in a tub of water with their hands tied, and playing all sorts of other games, till the Shifty Lad grew quite tired of waiting for them to get to bed. The Black Gallows Bird, who was more accustomed to the business, tucked himself up on the hay and went to sleep, telling the boy to wake him when the merry-makers had departed. But the Shifty Lad, who could keep still no longer, crept down to the cowshed and loosened the heads of the cattle which were tied, and they began to kick each other and bellow, and made such a noise that the company in the farmhouse ran out to tie them up again. Then the Shifty Lad entered the room and picked up a big handful of nuts, and returned to the loft, where the Black Rogue was still sleeping. At first the Shifty Lad shut his eyes too, but very soon he sat up, and taking a big needle and thread from his pocket, he sewed the hem of the Black Gallows Bird's coat to a heavy piece of bullock's hide that was hanging at his back.

By this time the cattle were all tied up again, but as the people could not find their nuts they sat round the fire and began to tell stories.

'I will crack a nut,' said the Shifty Lad.

'You shall not,' cried the Black Gallows Bird, 'they will hear you.'

'I don't care,' answered the Shifty Lad. 'I never spend Halloweven yet without cracking a nut', and he cracked one.

'Someone is cracking nuts up there,' said one of the merry-makers in the farmhouse. 'Come quickly, and we will see who it is.'

He spoke loudly, and the Black Gallows Bird heard, and ran out of the loft, dragging the big leather hide after him which the Shifty Lad had sewed to his coat.

'He is stealing my hide!' shouted the farmer, and they all darted after him, but he was too swift for them, and he managed to tear the hide from his coat, and then he flew like a hare till he reached his old hiding-place. But all this took a long time, and meanwhile the Shifty Lad got down from the loft, and searched the house till he found the chest with the gold and silver in it, concealed behind a load of straw and covered with loaves of bread and a great cheese. The Shifty Lad slung the money bags round his shoulders and took the bread and the cheese under his arm, then set out quietly for the Black Rogue's house.

'Here you are , you villain!' cried his master in great wrath. 'But I will be revenged on you.'

'It is all right,' replied the Shifty Lad calmly. 'I have brought what you wanted', and he laid the things he was carrying down on the ground.

'Ah! you are the better thief,' said the Black Rogue's wife, and the Black Rogue added:

'Yes, it is you who are the clever boy', and they divided the spoil and the Black Gallows Bird had one half and the Shifty Lad the other half.

A few weeks after that the Black Gallows Bird had news of a wedding that was to be held near the town, and the bridegroom had many friends and everybody sent him a present. Now a rich farmer who lived up near the moor thought that nothing was so useful to a young couple when they first began to keep house as a fine fat sheep, so he bade his shepherd go off to the mountain where the flock were feeding, and bring him back the best he could find. And the shepherd chose out the largest and fattest of the sheep and the one with the whitest fleece; then he tied its feet together and put it across his shoulder, for he had a long way to go.

That day, the Shifty Lad happened to be wandering over the moor, when he saw the man with the sheep on his shoulder walking along the road which led past the Black Rogue's house. The sheep was heavy and the man was in no hurry, so he came slowly and the boy knew that he himself could easily get back to his master before the shepherd was even in sight.

'I will wager,' he cried, as he pushed quickly through the bushes which hid the cabin, 'I will wager that I will steal the sheep from the man that is coming before he passes here.'

'Will you indeed?' said the Gallows Bird. 'I will wager you a hundred silver pieces that you can do nothing of the sort.'

'Well, I will try it, anyway,' replied the boy, and disappeared in the bushes. He ran fast till he entered a wood through which the shepherd must go, and then he stopped, and taking off one of his shoes smeared it with mud and set it in the path. When this was done he slipped behind a rock and waited.

Very soon the man came up, and seeing the shoe lying there, he stooped and looked at it.

'It is a good shoe,' he said to himself, 'but very dirty. Still, if I had the fellow, I would be at the trouble of cleaning it'; so he threw the shoe down again and went on.

The Shifty Lad smiled as he heard him, and, picking up the shoe, he crept round by a short way and laid the other shoe on the path. A few minutes after the shepherd arrived, and beheld the second shoe lying on the path.

'Why, that is the fellow of the dirty shoe!' he exclaimed when he saw it. 'I will go back and pick up the other one, and then I shall have a pair of good shoes,' and he put the sheep on the grass and returned to fetch the shoe. Then the Shifty Lad put on his shoes, and, picking up the sheep, carried it home. And the Black Rogue paid him the hundred marks of his wager.

When the shepherd reached the farmhouse that night he told his tale to his master, who scolded him for being stupid and careless, and bade him go the next day to the mountain and fetch him a kid, and he would send that as a wedding gift. But the Shifty Lad was on the look-out, and hid himself in the wood, and the moment the man drew near with the kid on his shoulders began to bleat like a sheep, and no one, not even the sheep's own mother, could have told the difference.

'Why, it must have got its feet loose, and have strayed after all,' thought the man, and he put the kid on the grass and hurried off in the direction of the bleating. Then the boy ran back and picked up the kid, and took it to the Black Gallows Bird.

The shepherd could hardly believe his eyes when he returned from seeking the sheep and found that the kid had vanished. He was afraid to go home and tell the same tale that he had told yesterday; so he searched the wood through and through till night had nearly come.

Then he felt that there was no help for it, and he must go home and confess to his master.

Of course, the farmer was very angry at this second misfortune, but this time he told him to drive one of the big bulls from the mountain, and warned him that if he lost THAT he would lose his place also. Again the Shifty Lad, who was on the watch, perceived him pass by, and when he saw the man returning with the great bull he cried to the Black Rogue:

'Be quick and come into the wood, and we will try to get the bull also.'

'But how can we do that?' asked the Black Rogue.

'Oh, quite easily! You hide yourself out there and baa like a sheep, and I will go in the other direction and bleat like a kid. It will be alright, I assure you.'

The shepherd was walking slowly, driving the bull before him, when he suddenly heard a loud baa amongst the bushes far away on one side of the path, and a feeble bleat answering it from the other side.

'Why, it must be the sheep and the kid that I lost,' he said. 'Yes, surely it must', and tying the bull hastily to a tree, he went off after the sheep and the kid, and searched the wood till he was tired. Of course by the time he came back the two thieves had driven the bull home and killed him for meat, so the man was obliged to go to his master and confess that he had been tricked again.

After this the Black Rogue and the Shifty Lad grew bolder and bolder, and stole great quantities of cattle and sold them and grew quite rich. One day they were returning from the market with a large sum of money in their pockets when they passed a gallows erected on the top of a hill.

'Let us stop and look at that gallows,' exclaimed the Shifty Lad. 'I have never seen one so close before. Yet some say that it is the end of all thieves.'

There was no one in sight, and they carefully examined every part of it.

'I wonder how it feels to be hanged,' said the Shifty Lad. 'I should like to know in case they ever catch me. I'll try first, and then you can do so.'

As he spoke he fastened the loose cord about his neck, and when it was quite secure he told the Black Rogue to take the other end of the rope and draw him up from the ground.

'When I am tired of it I will shake my legs, and then you must let me down,' he said.

The Black Rogue drew up the rope, but in half a minute the Shifty Lad's legs began to shake, and he quickly let it down again.

'You can't imagine what a funny feeling hanging gives you,' murmured the Shifty Lad, who looked rather purple in the face and spoke in an odd voice. 'I don't think you have every tried it, or you wouldn't have let me go up first. Why, it is the pleasantest thing I have ever done. I was shaking my legs from sheer delight, and if you had been there you would have shaken your legs too.'

'Well, let me try, if it is so nice,' answered the Black Rogue. 'But be sure you tie the knot securely, for I don't want to fall down and break my neck.'

'Oh, I will see to that!' replied the Shifty Lad. 'When you are tired, just whistle, and I'll let you down.'

So the Black Rogue was drawn up, and as soon as he was as high as the rope would allow him to go the Shifty Lad called to him:

'Don't forget to whistle when you want to come down, but if you are enjoying yourself as I did, shake your legs.'

And in a moment the Black Rogue's legs began to shake and to kick, and the Shifty Lad stood below, watching him and laughing heartily.

'Oh, how funny you are! If you could only see yourself! Oh, you ARE funny! But when you have had enough, whistle and you shall be let down', and he rocked again with laughter.

But no whistle came, and soon the legs ceased to shake and to kick, for the Black Gallows Bird was dead, as the Shifty Lad intended he should be.

Then he went home to the Black Rogue's wife, and told her that her husband was dead, and that he was ready to marry her if she liked. But the woman had been fond of the Black Rogue, thief though he was, and she shrank from the Shifty Lad in horror, and set the people after him, and he had to fly to another part of the country where none knew of his doings.

Perhaps if the Shifty Lad's mother knew anything of this, she may have thought that by this time her son might be tired of stealing, and ready to try some honest trade. But in reality he loved the tricks and danger, and life would have seemed very dull without them. So he went on just as before, and made friends whom he taught to be as wicked as himself, till they took to robbing the king's storehouses, and by the advice of the Wise Man the king sent out soldiers to catch the band of thieves.

For a long while they tried in vain to lay hands on them. The Shifty Lad was too clever for them all, and if they laid traps he laid better ones. At last one night he stole upon some soldiers while they were asleep in a barn and killed them, and persuaded the villagers that if they did not kill the other soldiers before morning they would certainly be killed themselves. Thus it happened that when the sun rose not a single soldier was alive in the village.

Of course this news soon reached the king's ears, and he was very angry, and summoned the Wise Man to take counsel with him. And this was the counsel of the Wise Man - that he should invite all the people in the countryside to a ball, and among them the bold and impudent thief would be sure to come, and would be sure to ask the king's daughter to dance with him.

'Your counsel is good,' said the king, who made his feast and prepared for his ball, and all the people of the countryside were present, and the Shifty Lad came with them.

When everyone had eaten and drunk as much as they wanted they went into the ballroom. There was a great throng, and while they were pressing through the doorway the Wise Man, who had a bottle of black ointment hidden in his robes, placed a tiny dot on the cheek of the Shifty Lad near his ear. The Shifty Lad felt nothing, but as he approached the king's daughter to ask her to be his partner he caught sight of the black dot in a silver mirror. Instantly he guessed who had put it there and why, but he said nothing, and danced so beautifully that the princess was quite delighted with him. At the end of the dance he bowed low to his partner and left her, to mingle with the crowd that was filling the doorway. As he passed the Wise Man he contrived not only to steal the bottle but to place two black dots on his face, and one on the faces of twenty other men. Then he slipped the bottle back in the Wise Man's robe.

By-and-by he went up to the king's daughter again, and begged for the honour of another dance. She consented, and while he was stooping to tie the ribbons on his shoe she took out from her pocket another bottle, which the Wizard had given her, and put a black dot on his cheek. But she was not as skilful as the Wise Man, and the Shifty Lad felt the touch of her fingers; so as soon as the dance was over he contrived to place a second black dot on the faces of the twenty men and two more on the Wizard, after which he slipped the bottle into her pocket.

At length the ball came to an end, and then the king ordered all the doors to be shut, and search made for a man with two black dots on his cheek. The chamberlain went among the guests, and soon found such a man, but just as he was going to arrest him and bring him before the king his eye fell on another with the same mark, and another, and another, till he had counted twenty - besides the Wise Man - on whose face were found spots.

Not knowing what to do, the chamberlain hurried back with his tale to the king, who immediately sent for the Wise Man, and then for his daughter.

'The thief must have stolen your bottle,' said the king to the Wizard.

'No, my lord, it is here,' answered the Wise Man, holding it out.

'Then he must have got yours,' he cried, turning to his daughter.

'Indeed, father, it is safe in my pocket,' replied she, taking it out as she spoke, and they all three looked at each other and remained silent.

'Well,' said the king , 'the man who has done this is cleverer than most men, and if he will make himself known to me he shall marry the princess and govern half my kingdom while I am alive, and the whole of it when I am dead. Go and announce this in the ballroom,' he added to an attendant, 'and bring the fellow hither.'

So the attendant went into the ballroom and did as the king had bidden him, when, to his surprise, not one man, but twenty, stepped forward, all with black dots on their faces.

'I am the person you want,' they all exclaimed at once, and the attendant, as much bewildered as the chamberlain had been, desired them to follow him into the king's presence.

But the question was too difficult for the king to decide, so he called together his council. For hours they talked, but to no purpose, and in the end they hit upon a plan which they might just as well have thought of at the beginning.

And this was the plan. A child was to be brought to the palace, and next the king's daughter would give her an apple. Then the child was to take the apple and be led into a room where the twenty men with the black dots were sitting in a ring. And to whomsoever the child gave the apple, that man should marry the king's daughter.

'Of course,' said the king, 'it may not be the right man, after all, but then again it MAY be. Anyhow, it is the best we can do.'

The princess herself led the child into the room where the twenty men were now seated. She stood in the centre of the ring for a moment, looking at one man after another, and then held out the apple to the Shifty Lad, who was twisting a shaving of wood round his finger, and had the mouthpiece of a bagpipe hanging from his neck.

'You ought not to have anything which the others have not got,' said the chamberlain, who had accompanied the princess, and he bade the child stand outside for a minute, while he took away the shaving and the mouthpiece, and made the Shifty Lad change his place. Then he called the child in, but the little girl knew him again, and went straight up to him with the apple.

'This is the man whom the child has twice chosen,' said the chamberlain, signing to the Shifty Lad to kneel before the king. 'It was all quite fair; we tried it twice over.' In this way the Shifty Lad won the king's daughter, and they were married the next day.

A few days later the bride and bridegroom were walking together, and the path led down to the river, and over the river was a bridge.

'And what bridge may this be?' asked the Shifty Lad, and the princess told him that this was the bridge of Dublin.

'Is it indeed?' cried he. 'Well, now, many is the time that my mother has said, when I played her a trick, that my end would be that I should hang on the bridge of Dublin.'

'Oh, if you want to fulfil her prophecies,' laughed the princess, 'you have only to let me tie my handkerchief around your ankle, and I will hold you as you hang over the wall of the bridge.'

'That would be fine fun,' he said, 'but you are not strong enough to hold me up.'

'Oh, yes, I am,' said the princess, 'just try.' So he let her bind the handkerchief around his ankle and hang him over the wall, and they both laughed and jested at the strength of the princess.

'Now pull me up again,' called he, but as he spoke a great cry arose that the palace was burning. The princess turned round with a start, and let go her handkerchief, and the Shifty Lad fell, and struck his head on a stone, and died in an instant. So his mother's prophecy had come true, after all.

The Sprightly Tailor

The Sprightly Tailor is one of the most memorable tales from Celtic Fairy Tales, edited by Joseph Jacobs and first published in 1892 by David Nutt, London. The story is rooted in Scottish folklore and tells of a clever tailor who accepts the challenge of sewing a pair of trews for the laird of Duffus Castle while sitting alone at night in the haunted church of Tomnahurich, near Inverness.

Jacobs's version, drawn from Scottish oral tradition and possibly influenced by Campbell's Popular Tales of the West Highlands, celebrates human cleverness over brute strength, a recurring theme in Celtic storytelling. The tale combines eerie atmosphere, dry humour, and the triumph of quick thinking, and like many of Jacobs's selections, it preserves a distinctly local flavour while echoing universal patterns found across European folklore.

A sprightly tailor was employed by the great Macdonald, in his castle at Saddell, in order to make the laird a pair of trews, used in olden time. And trews being the vest and breeches united in one piece, and ornamented with fringes, were very comfortable, and suitable to be worn in walking or dancing. And Macdonald had said to the tailor, that if he would make the trews by night in the church, he would get a handsome reward. For it was thought that the old, ruined church was haunted, and that fearsome things were to be seen there at night.

The tailor was well aware of this, but he was a sprightly man, and when the laird dared him to make the trews by night in the church, the tailor was not to be daunted, but took it in hand to gain the prize. So, when night came, away he went up the glen, about half a mile distance from the castle, till he came to the old church. Then he chose him a nice gravestone for a seat and he lighted his candle, and put on his thimble, and set to work at the trews; plying his needle nimbly, and thinking about the hire that the laird would have to give him.

For some time he got on pretty well, until he felt the floor all of a tremble under his feet, and looking about him, but keeping his fingers at work, he saw the appearance of a great human head rising up through the stone pavement of the church. And when the head had risen above the surface, there came from it a great, great voice. And the voice said, "Do you see this great head of mine?"

"I see that, but I'll sew this!" replied the sprightly tailor, and he stitched away at the trews.

Then the head rose higher up through the pavement, until its neck appeared. And when its neck was shown, the thundering voice came again and said, "Do you see this great neck of mine?"

"I see that, but I'll sew this!" said the sprightly tailor, and he stitched away at his trews.

Then the head and neck rose higher still, until the great shoulders and chest were shown above the ground. And again the mighty voice thundered, "Do you see this great chest of mine?"

And again the sprightly tailor replied, "I see that, but I'll sew this!" and stitched away at his trews.

And still it kept rising through the pavement, until it shook a great pair of arms in the tailor's face, and said, "Do you see these great arms of mine?"

"I see those, but I'll sew this!" answered the tailor, and he stitched hard at his trews, for he knew that he had no time to lose.

The sprightly tailor was taking the long stitches, when he saw it gradually rising and rising through the floor, until it lifted out a great leg, and stamping with it upon the pavement, said in a roaring voice, "Do you see this great leg of mine?"

"Aye, aye, I see that, but I'll sew this!" cried the tailor, and his fingers flew with the needle, and he took such long stitches, that he had just come to the end of the trews, when it was taking up its other leg. But before it could pull it out of the pavement, the sprightly tailor had finished his task, and, blowing out his candle, and springing from off his gravestone, he buckled up, and ran out of the church with the trews under his arm. Then the fearsome thing gave a loud roar, and stamped with both his feet upon the pavement, and out of the church he went after the sprightly tailor.

Down the glen they ran, faster than the stream when the flood rides it, but the tailor had got the start and a nimble pair of legs, and he did not choose to lose the laird's reward. And though the thing roared to him to stop, yet the sprightly tailor was not the man to be beholden to a monster. So he held his trews tight, and let no darkness grow under his feet, until he had reached Saddell Castle. He had no sooner got inside the gate, and shut it, than the apparition came up to it, and, enraged at losing his prize, struck the wall above the gate, and left there the mark of his five great fingers. You may see them plainly to this day, if ye'll only peer close enough.

But the sprightly tailor gained his reward: for Macdonald paid him handsomely for the trews, and never discovered that a few of the stitches were somewhat long.

The Story of John O'Groats

The Story of John O'Groats, as adapted from Peter Henry Emerson's Fairy-Tales & Other Stories (1894), recounts the origins of the northernmost dwelling in mainland Scotland, a site that came to bear the name of its founder.

Emerson's retelling preserves the story's air of quiet wisdom, emphasising the values of fairness, civility, and pragmatic peace, qualities that reflect the moral tone of late-Victorian folklore collections. His version, while rooted in a Scottish legend, reads like a moral fable of temperance and reason triumphing over pride. In later years, the site of John o' Groats became a symbolic point of extremity in the British imagination, the farthest north, the edge of the map, and Emerson's story offers the human origin behind that geography.

He was an old seaman, with weather-beaten face and black eyes, that had looked upon many lands and many sights.

"Well, indeed, I'll tell you about Johnny Groats as it was told to me one night in the trades," he said, blowing a whiff of smoke from his wheezy pipe. "Well, in olden times there was a rich lord, who owned all the property looking on to the Pentlands - an awful place in bad weather; indeed, in any weather. He was a lone man, for his wife was dead, and his son had turned out to be a rake and a spendthrift, spending all his substance upon harlots and entertainments.

"Now this lord had a factor, by name John o' Scales, a stingy, cunning man, who robbed his master all he could during the week, and prayed hard for forgiveness on the Sabbath. The lord, who was getting very old, was much grieved on account of his son's behaviour. 'He'll spend everything when I am gone, and the estates will go into other hands,' the old man said to himself."

One fine morning in summer the factor received orders to build a hut by the sea, and plant bushes and trees round about it. 'But don't make the door to fit close; leave the space of a foot at the bottom, so the leaves can blow in, for I want the hut to shoot sea-fowl as they flight, and it is cold standing on the bare ground,' said the old man.

The factor carried out his master's instructions, but not without suspicion of ulterior motives on his master's part. However, when he saw my lord shooting the birds and stuffing many of them his suspicions were allayed, and the factor thought that, after all, though his master wanted the hut for flight-shooting, still he must be getting softening of the brain, for it was very eccentric that he should take up this new hobby in his old age.

So the old lord was never disturbed in his hut by curious and ill-timed visits. After a time the lord died, and was laid with his fathers, the prodigal inheriting the property.

The old castle was then the scene of perpetual feastings and card parties, so that in a few years the property was heavily mortgaged, the old factor advancing the money.

Things went apace, until one day the factor informed the young spendthrift that he had spent everything, and the estates were no longer his, so he gave him a few pounds, and turned him out.

When the news spread round the countryside his old friends began to drop off, until the spendthrift found every door closed against him.

When he had spent his last penny, the prodigal thought of the key which his father had given him, saying, 'When you have spent everything, take this key, and go to the hut.'

But he had lost the key long before.

Nevertheless, he went to the hut. It had a deserted appearance, being overgrown with moss and lichens.

He managed to squeeze himself under the door, and when he stood up he saw a rope, with a noose hanging from the centre of the roof. Pursuing his investigations, he found a parchment nailed to the back of the door, and in one corner stood an old three-legged stool. There was nothing else in the damp, mouldy room, so he began to read the parchment.

'You have come to beggary; end your miserable existence, for it is your father's wish,' he read.

He was dazed, and looked from the parchment to the rope, and from the rope to the parchment, saying to himself, 'Well, I have come to that, I must follow my father's wish.'

So he got the stool and put it under the noose, and standing upon it, adjusted the rope with trembling fingers round his neck, when he said, hoarsely, 'Father, I do your bidding,' and he kicked the stool from under him.

Immediately he heard a crash, and found himself lying upon the leaves, with a feeling that his neck had been jerked off. However, he soon recovered, and, taking the noose from his neck, he looked up and saw an open trap-door in the ceiling. Placing the stool beneath the opening, he got on to it, and lifted himself through the trap-door, when he found himself in a loft, a parchment nailed to the wall facing him, and on the parchment was written, 'This has been prepared, for your end was foreseen, and your foolish father buried three chests of gold one foot below the surface of the floor of the hut. Go and take it and buy back your estate: marry, and beget an heir.'

'Good God! is this a ghastly joke?' said the prodigal. But the words looked truthful; so he tore down the parchment, dropped through the trap-door, shut it, and readjusted the rope. He left the hut and borrowed a pick and shovel, and returning to the hut, he began to dig, and found one chest full of gold. When he made this discovery he closed the chest, filled in the hole, and spread leaves over the spot. He then ran off to his father's best friend, and told him of his good luck. They then called in two other friends, and consulted together how the old lord's wish was best to be carried out. 'I'll tell you,' said his father's oldest friend. 'Mr. John o' Scales gives a great dinner party once a month, and three of us here are invited as usual. You must come in in the middle of dinner in your ordinary beggar clothes and beg humbly for some food, when he will give orders to have you turned out. Then you must begin to call him a liar and a thief, and accuse him of robbing your father and yourself of your inheritance. You'll see he'll get angry, and offer to let you have it back.'

So the prodigal dug up the chests, and carted the money away in canvas bags, storing it at his friend's house."

When the night of the dinner party came, the prodigal drove up to the castle in a cart filled with canvas bags. Jumping off his seat by the driver, he went into the feast in his beggar's clothes, and going up to the host, he begged humbly for some food.

'Go from this house! What business have you here?' asked the host.

Most of the gentlemen and ladies began to frown upon him, and murmur against him, as he walked to the lady of the house and begged her to give him some food, but she replied:

'Oh, you spendthrift! you fool of fools! if all fools were hanged, as they ought to be, you'd be the first.'

Then the beggar's countenance changed, a deep flush of anger overspread his features, and drawing himself up to his full height, he said, with solemn voice, addressing the host:

'You have robbed my father all the days of his life, and you have robbed the orphan. May the curse of God be upon you!'

The host grew furious; then he looked ashamed, and shouted angrily:

'Bring me £40,000, and you shall have your estate back. I never robbed you, but you lost your inheritance by your own follies.'

'Gentlemen,' said the beggar, 'I take you all to witness that this thief says I can have my estate back for £40,000.'

The people murmured, and the three friends said, 'We are witnesses.'

The beggar ran out into the night, and returned with a man laden with sacks, and they began to count out £40,000 upon a side-table, where a haunch of venison still smoked.

When they had counted out the money, the beggar said, 'There is your £40,000; sign this receipt.'

The amazed factor drew back, when the three friends said, 'You must sign; you are a gentleman of your word, of course.'

Mechanically John O'Scales signed the paper.

'And now,' said the former beggar, 'leave my house at once, with your wife - you coward! you cur! You robbed my father, and then cheated me when I was a spendthrift. Begone, and may your name be accursed in the land!'

And the son turned all out except his three friends.

In a few months he married the daughter of one of his friends, but he never gambled again, only entertaining his three friends and their families, who came and went as they liked.

And from that day John o' Scales was called John O'Groats."

The Three Crowns

The Three Crowns, as adapted by Andrew Lang in The Lilac Fairy Book (1910), originates from John Francis Campbell's Popular Tales of the West Highlands (1860–62), one of the foundational collections of Scottish Gaelic folklore. The story bears the distinctive Highland blend of magic, hardship, and moral trial that Campbell gathered from oral storytellers across the western isles and glens. Lang's retelling streamlines Campbell's denser oral phrasing into a smoother narrative suited to his Edwardian readership, but the bones of the Gaelic tale remain clear.

There was once a king who had three daughters. The two eldest were very proud and quarrelsome, but the youngest was as good as they were bad. Well, three princes came to court them, and two of them were exactly like the eldest ladies, and one was just as lovable as the youngest. One day they were all walking down to a lake that lay at the bottom of the lawn when they met a poor beggar. The king wouldn't give him anything, and the eldest princesses wouldn't give him anything, nor their sweethearts, but the youngest daughter and her true love did give him something, and kind words along with it, and that was better than all.

When they got to the edge of the lake what did they find but the most beautiful boat you ever saw in your life, and says the eldest, 'I'll take a sail in this fine boat', and says the second eldest, 'I'll take a sail in this fine boat', and says the youngest, 'I won't take a sail in that fine boat, for I am afraid it's an enchanted one.' But the others persuaded her to go in, and her father was just going in after her, when up sprung on the deck a little man only seven inches high, and ordered him to stand back. Well, all the men put their hands to their swords, and if the same swords were only playthings, they weren't able to draw them, for all strength that was left their arms. Seven Inches loosened the silver chain that fastened the boat, and pushed away, and after grinning at the four men, says he to them. 'Bid your daughters and your brides farewell for a while. You,' says he to the youngest, 'needn't fear, you'll recover your princess all in good time, and you and she will be as happy as the day is long. Bad people, if they were rolling stark naked in gold, would not be rich. Good-bye.' Away they sailed, and the ladies stretched out their hands, but weren't able to say a word.

Well, they weren't crossing the lake while a cat 'ud be lickin' her ear, and the poor men couldn't stir hand or foot to follow them. They saw Seven Inches handing the three princesses out of the boat, and letting them down by a basket into a draw-well, but king nor princes ever saw an opening before in the same place. When the last lady was out of sight, the men found the strength in their arms and legs again. Round the lake they ran, and never drew rein till they came to the well and windlass, and there was the silk rope rolled on the axle, and the nice white basket hanging to it. 'Let me down,' says the youngest prince. 'I'll die or recover them again.' 'No,' says the second daughter's sweetheart, 'it is my turn first.' And says the other, 'I am the eldest.' So they gave way to him, and in he got into the basket, and down they let him. First they lost sight of him, and then, after winding off a hundred perches of the silk rope, it slackened, and they stopped turning. They waited two hours, and then they went to dinner, because there was no pull made at the rope.

Guards were set till next morning, and then down went the second prince, and sure enough, the youngest of all got himself let down on the third day. He went down perches and perches, while it was as dark about him as if he was in a big pot with a cover on. At last he saw a glimmer far down, and in a short time he felt the ground. Out he came from the big lime-kiln, and, lo! and behold you, there was a wood, and green fields, and a castle in a lawn, and a bright sky over all. 'It's in Tir-na-n-Oge I am,' says he. 'Let's see what sort of people are in the castle.' On he walked, across fields and lawn, and no one was there to keep him out or let him into the castle, but the big hall-door was wide open. He went from one fine room to another that was finer, and he reached the handsomest of all, with a table in the middle. And such a dinner as was laid upon it! The prince was hungry enough, but he was too mannerly to eat without being invited. So he sat by the fire, and he did not wait long till he heard steps, and in came Seven Inches with the youngest sister by the hand. Well, prince and princess flew into one another's arms, and says the little man, says he, 'Why aren't you eating?' 'I think, sir,' says the prince, 'it was only good manner to wait to be asked.' 'The other princes didn't think so,' says he. 'Each o' them fell to without leave, and only gave me the rough words when I told them they were making more free than welcome. Well, I don't think they feel much hunger now. There they are, good marble instead of flesh and blood,' says he, pointing to two statues, one in one corner, and the other in the other corner of the room. The prince was frightened, but he was afraid to say anything, and Seven Inches made him sit down to dinner between himself and his bride, and he'd be as happy as the day is long, only for the sight of the stone men in the corner. Well, that day went by, and when the next came, says Seven Inches to him, 'Now, you'll have to set out that way,' pointing to the sun, 'and you'll find the second princess in a giant's castle this evening, when you'll be tired and hungry, and the eldest princess tomorrow evening, and you may as well bring them here with you. You need not ask leave of their masters, and perhaps if they ever get home, they'll look on poor people as if they were flesh and blood like themselves.'

Away went the prince, and bedad! it's tired and hungry he was when he reached the first castle, at sunset. Oh, wasn't the second princess glad to see him! And what a good supper she gave him. But she heard the giant at the gate, and she hid the prince in a closet. Well, when he came in, he snuffed, an' he snuffed, and says he, 'By the life, I smell fresh meat.' 'Oh,' says the princess, 'it's only the calf I got killed to-day.' 'Ay, ay,' says he, 'is supper ready?' 'It is,' says she, and before he rose from the table he ate three-quarters of a calf, and a flask of wine. 'I think,' says he when all was done, 'I smell fresh meat still.' 'It's sleepy you are,' says she, 'go to bed.' 'When will you marry me?' says the giant. 'You're putting me off too long.' 'St. Tibb's Eve,' says she. 'I wish I knew how far off that is,' says he, and he fell asleep, with his head in the dish.

Next day, he went out after breakfast, and she sent the prince to the castle where the eldest sister was. The same thing happened there, but when the giant was snoring, the princess wakened up the prince, and they saddled two steeds in the stables and rode into the field on them. But the horses' heels struck the stones outside the gate, and up got the giant and strode after them. He roared and he shouted, and the more he shouted, the faster ran the horses, and just as the day was breaking he was only twenty perches behind. But the prince didn't leave the castle of Seven Inches without being provided with something good. He reined in his steed, and flung a short, sharp knife over his shoulder, and up sprung a thick wood between the giant and themselves. They caught the wind that blew before them, and the wind that blew behind them did not catch them. At last they were near the castle where the other sister lived, and there she was, waiting for them under a high hedge, and a fine steed under her.

But the giant was now in sight, roaring like a hundred lions, and the other giant was out in a moment, and the chase kept on. For every two springs the horses gave, the giants gave three, and they were only seventy perches off. Then the prince stopped again, and flung the second knife behind him. Down went all the flat field, till there was a quarry between them a quarter of a mile deep, and the bottom filled with black water, and before the giants could get round it, the prince and princesses were inside the kingdom of the great magician, where the high thorny hedge opened of itself to everyone that he chose to let in. There was joy enough between the three sisters, till the two eldest saw their lovers turned into stone. But while they were shedding tears for them, Seven Inches came in, and touched them with his rod. So they were flesh, and blood, and life once more, and there was great hugging and kissing, and all sat down to breakfast, and Seven Inches sat at the head of the table.

When breakfast was over, he took them into another room, where there was nothing but heaps of gold, and silver, and diamonds, and silks, and satins, and on a table there was lying three sets of crowns: a gold crown was in a silver crown, and that was lying in a copper crown. He took up one set of crowns, and gave it to the eldest princess, and another set, and gave it to the second youngest princess, and another, and gave it to the youngest of all, and says he, 'Now you may all go to the bottom of the pit, and you have nothing to do but stir the basket, and the people that are watching above will draw you up. But remember, ladies, you are to keep your crows safe, and be married in them, all the same day. If you be married separately, or if you be married without your crowns, a curse will follow - mind what I say.'

So they took leave of him with great respect, and walked arm-in-arm to the bottom of the draw-well. There was a sky and a sun over them, and a great high wall, covered with ivy, rose before them, and was so high they could not see to the top of it, and there was an arch in this wall, and the bottom of the draw-well was inside the arch. The youngest pair went last, and says the princess to the prince, 'I'm sure the two princes don't mean any good to you. Keep these crowns under your cloak, and if you are obliged to stay last, don't get into the basket, but put a big stone, or any heavy thing inside, and see what will happen.'

As soon as they were inside the dark cave, they put in the eldest princess first, and stirred the basket, and up she went. Then the basket was let down again, and up went the second princess, and then up went the youngest, but first she put her arms round her prince's neck, and kissed him, and cried a little. At last it came to the turn of the youngest prince, and instead of going into the basket he put in a big stone. He drew on one side and listened, and after the basket was drawn up about twenty perches, down came it and the stone like thunder, and the stone was broken into little bits.

Well, the poor prince had nothing for it but to walk back to the castle, and through it and round it he walked, and the finest of eating and drinking he got, and a bed of bog-down to sleep on, and long walks he took through gardens and lawns, but not a sight could he get, high or low, of Seven Inches. He, before a week, got tired of it, he was so lonesome for his true love, and at the end of a month he didn't know what to do with himself.

One morning he went into the treasure room, and took notice of a beautiful snuff-box on the table that he didn't remember seeing there before. He took it in his hands and opened it, and out Seven Inches walked on the table. 'I think, prince,' says he, 'you're getting a little tired of my castle?' 'Ah!' says the other, 'if I had my princess here, and could see you now and then, I'd never know a dismal day.' 'Well, you're long enough here now, and you're wanted there above. Keep your bride's crowns safe, and whenever you want my help, open this snuff-box. Now take a walk down the garden, and come back when you're tired.'

The prince was going down a gravel walk with a quickset hedge on each side, and his eyes on the ground, and he was thinking of one thing and another. At last he lifted his eyes, and there he was outside of a smith's gate that he often passed before, about a mile away from the palace of his betrothed princess. The clothes he had on him were as ragged as you please, but he had his crowns safe under his old cloak.

Then the smith came out, and says he, 'It's a shame for a strong, big fellow like you to be lazy, and so much work to be done. Are you any good with hammer and tongs? Come in and bear a hand, and I'll give you diet and lodging, and a few pence when you earn them.' 'Never say't twice,' says the prince. 'I want nothing but to be busy.' So he took the hammer, and pounded away at the red-hot bar that the smith was turning on the anvil to make into a set of horseshoes.

They hadn't been long at work when a tailor came in, and he sat down and began to talk. 'You all heard how the two princess were loath to be married till the youngest would be ready with her crowns and her sweetheart. But after the windlass loosened accidentally when they were pulling up her bridegroom that was to be, there was no more sign of a well, or a rope, or a windlass, than there is on the palm of your hand. So the princes that were courting the eldest ladies wouldn't give peace or ease to their lovers nor the king till they got consent to the marriage, and it was to take place this morning. Myself went down out o' curiosity, and to be sure I was delighted with the grand dresses of the two brides, and the three crowns on their heads - gold, silver, and copper, one inside the other. The youngest was standing by mournful enough, and all was ready. The two bridegrooms came in as proud and grand as you please, and up they were walking to the altar rails, when the boards opened two yards wide under their feet, and down they went among the dead men and the coffins in the vaults. Oh, such shrieks as the ladies gave! and such running and racing and peeping down as there was! but the clerk soon opened the door of the vault, and up came the two princes, their fine clothes covered an inch thick with cobwebs and mould.

So the king said they should put off the marriage. 'For,' says he, 'I see there is no use in thinking of it till the youngest gets her three crowns, and is married with the others. I'll give my youngest daughter for a wife to whoever brings three crowns to me like the others, and if he doesn't care to be married, some other one will, and I'll make his fortune.'

'I wish,' says the smith, 'I could do it, but I was looking at the crowns after the princesses got home, and I don't think there's a black or a white smith on the face of the earth that could imitate them.' 'Faint heart never won fair lady,' says the prince. 'Go to the palace and ask for a quarter of a pound of gold, a quarter of a pound of silver, and a quarter of a pound of copper. Get one crown for a pattern, and my head for a pledge, I'll give you out the very things that are wanted in the morning.' 'Are you in earnest?' says the smith. 'Faith, I am so,' says he. 'Go! you can't do worse than lose.'

To make a long story short, the smith got the quarter of a pound of gold, and the quarter of a pound of silver, and the quarter of a pound of copper, and gave them and the pattern crown to the prince. He shut the forge door at nightfall, and the neighbours all gathered in the yard, and they heard him hammering, hammering, hammering, from that to daybreak, and every now and then he'd throw out through the window bits of gold, silver, and copper, and the idlers scrambled for them, and cursed one another, and prayed for the good luck of the workman.

Well, just as the sun was thinking to rise, he opened the door, and brought out the three crowns he got from his true love, and such shouting and huzzaing as there was! The smith asked him to go along with him to the palace, but he refused; so off set the smith, and the whole townland with him, and wasn't the king rejoiced when he saw the crowns! 'Well,' says he to the smith, 'you're a married man. What's to be done?' 'Faith, your majesty, I didn't make them crowns at all. It was a big fellow that took service with me yesterday.' 'Well, daughter, will you marry the fellow that made these crowns?' 'Let me see them first, father,' she said, but when she examined them she knew them right well, and guessed it was her true love that sent them. 'I will marry the man that these crowns came from,' says she.

'Well,' says the king to the elder of the two princes, 'go up to the smith's forge, take my best coaches, and bring home the bridegroom.' He did not like doing this, he was so proud, but he could not refuse. When he came to the forge he saw the prince standing at the door, and beckoned him over to the coach. 'Are you the fellow,' says he, 'that made these crowns?' 'Yes,' says the other. 'Then,' says he, 'maybe you'd give yourself a brushing, and get into that coach; the king wants to see you. I pity the princess.' The young prince got into the carriage, and while they were on the way he opened the snuff-box, and out walked Seven Inches, and stood on his thigh. 'Well,' says he, 'what trouble is on you now?' 'Master,' says the other, 'please let me go back to my forge, and let this carriage be filled with paving stones.' No sooner said than done. The prince was sitting in his forge, and the horses wondered what was after happening to the carriage.

When they came into the palace yard, the king himself opened the carriage door, for respect to his new son-in-law. As soon as he turned the handle, a shower of small stones fell on his powdered wig and his silk coat, and down he fell under them. There was great fright and some laughter, and the king, after he wiped the blood from his forehead, looked very cross at the eldest prince. 'My lord,' says he, 'I'm very sorry for this accident, but I'm not to blame. I saw the young smith get into the carriage, and we never stopped a minute since.' 'It's uncivil you were to him. Go,' says he to the other prince, 'and bring the young smith here, and be polite.' 'Never fear,' says he.

But there's some people that couldn't be good-natured if they tried, and not a bit civiler was the new messenger than the old, and when the king opened the carriage door a second time, it's shower of mud that came down on him. 'There's no use,' says he, 'going on this way. The fox never got a better messenger than himself.'

So he changed his clothes, and washed himself, and out he set to the prince's forge and asked him to sit along with himself. The prince begged to be allowed to sit in the other carriage, and when they were half-way he opened his snuff-box. 'Master,' says he, 'I'd wish to be dressed now according to my rank.' 'You shall be that' says Seven Inches. 'And now I'll bid you farewell. Continue as good and kind as you always were; love your wife, and that's all the advice I'll give you.' So Seven Inches vanished, and when the carriage door was opened in the yard, out walks the prince as fine as hands could make him, and the first thing he did was to run over to his bride and embrace her.

Everyone was full of joy but the two other princes. There was not much delay about the marriages, and they were all celebrated on the one day. Soon after, the two elder couples went to their own courts, but the youngest pair stayed with the old king, and they were as happy as the happiest married couple you ever heard of in a story.

The Wedding of Robin Redbreast and Jenny Wren

The Wedding of Robin Redbreast and Jenny Wren is one of the most charming and lightly humorous tales in Elizabeth Wilson Grierson's The Scottish Fairy Book (1910, J. B. Lippincott Company). Drawing on traditional children's verse and animal lore, Grierson transforms a familiar nursery rhyme motif into a miniature fable of courtship, ceremony, and community.

In Grierson's retelling, the tone remains playful but threaded with the old moral sense that marks much Scottish folk tradition: harmony, companionship, and the fleeting joy of celebration against the backdrop of nature's cycles. Though slight in plot, the story carries the grace of an old fireside tale, shaped by rhythm and repetition rather than drama.

There was once an old grey Pussy Baudrons, and she went out for a stroll one Christmas morning to see what she could see. And as she was walking down the burnside she saw a little Robin Redbreast hopping up and down on the branches of a briar bush.

"What a tasty breakfast he would make," thought she to herself. "I must try to catch him."

So, "Good morning, Robin Redbreast," she said, sitting down on her tail at the foot of the briar bush and looking up at him. "And where may you be going so early on this cold winter's day?"

"I'm on my road to the King's Palace," answered Robin cheerily, "to sing him a song this merry Yule morning."

"That's a pious errand to be travelling on, and I wish you good success," replied Pussy slyly, "but just hop down a minute before you go, and I will show you what a bonnie white ring I have round my neck. 'Tis few cats that are marked like me."

Then Robin cocked his head on one side, and looked down on Pussy Baudrons with a twinkle in his eye. "Ha, ha! grey Pussy Baudrons," he said. "Ha, ha! for I saw you worry the little grey mouse, and I have no wish that you should worry me."

And with that he spread his wings and flew away. And he flew, and he flew, till he lighted on an old sod dyke, and there he saw a greedy old gled (common Kite) sitting, with all his feathers ruffled up as if he felt cold.

"Good morning, Robin Redbreast," cried the greedy old gled, who had had no food since yesterday, and was therefore very hungry. "And where may you be going to, this cold winter's day?"

"I'm on my road to the King's Palace," answered Robin, "to sing to him a song this merry Yule morning." And he hopped away a yard or two from the gled, for there was a look in his eye that he did not quite like.

"You are a friendly little fellow," remarked the gled sweetly, "and I wish you good luck on your errand, but before you go on, come nearer me, I prith'ee, and I will show you what a curious feather I have in my wing. 'Tis said that no other gled in the country-side has one like it."

"Like enough," re-joined Robin, hopping still further away, "but I will take your word for it, without seeing it. For I saw you pluck the feathers from the wee lintie, and I have no wish that you should pluck the feathers from me. So I will bid you good day, and go on my journey."

The next place on which he rested was a piece of rock that overhung a dark, deep glen, and here he saw a sly old fox looking out of his hole not two yards below him.

"Good morning, Robin Redbreast," said the sly old fox, who had tried to steal a fat duck from a farmyard the night before, and had barely escaped with his life. "And where may you be going so early on this cold winter's day?"

"I'm on my road to the King's Palace, to sing him a song this merry Yule morning," answered Robin, giving the same answer that he had given to the grey Pussy Baudrons and the greedy gled.

"You will get a right good welcome, for His Majesty is fond of music," said the wily fox. "But before you go, just come down and have a look at a black spot which I have on the end of my tail. 'Tis said that there is not a fox 'twixt here and the Border that has a spot on his tail like mine."

"Very like, very like," replied Robin, "but I chanced to see you worrying the wee lambie up on the braeside yonder, and I have no wish that you should try your teeth on me. So I will even go on my way to the King's Palace, and you can show the spot on your tail to the next passer-by."

So the little Robin Redbreast flew away once more, and never rested till he came to a bonnie valley with a little burn running through it, and there he saw a rosy-cheeked boy sitting on a log eating a piece of bread and butter. And he perched on a branch and watched him.

"Good morning, Robin Redbreast, and where may you be going so early on this cold winter's day?" asked the boy eagerly, for he was making a collection of stuffed birds, and he had still to get a Robin Redbreast.

"I'm on my way to the King's Palace to sing him a song this merry Yule morning," answered Robin, hopping down to the ground, and keeping one eye fixed on the bread and butter.

"Come a bit nearer, Robin," said the boy, "and I will give you some crumbs."

"Na, na, my wee man," chirped the cautious little bird, "for I saw you catch the goldfinch, and I have no wish to give you the chance to catch me."

At last he came to the King's Palace and lighted on the window-sill, and there he sat and sang the very sweetest song that he could sing, for he felt so happy because it was the Blessed Yuletide, that he wanted everyone else to be happy too. And the King and the Queen were so delighted with his song, as he peeped in at them at their open window, that they asked each other what they could give him as a reward for his kind thought in coming so far to greet them.

"We can give him a wife," replied the Queen, "who will go home with him and help him to build his nest."

"And who will you give him for a bride?" asked the King. "Methinks 'twould need to be a very tiny lady to match his size."

"Why, Jenny Wren, of course," answered the Queen. "She has looked somewhat dowie of late, this will be the very thing to brighten her up."

Then the King clapped his hands, and praised his wife for her happy thought, and wondered that the idea had not struck him before.

So Robin Redbreast and Jenny Wren were married, amid great rejoicings, at the King's Palace, and the King and Queen and all the fine Nobles and Court Ladies danced at their wedding. Then they flew away home to Robin's own country-side, and built their nest in the roots of the briar bush, where he had spoken to Pussy Baudrons. And you will be glad to hear that Jenny Wren proved the best little housewife in the world.

The Wee Bannock

The Wee Bannock is a lively Scottish folk tale, retold by Elizabeth Wilson Grierson in The Scottish Fairy Book (1910). It belongs to that mischievous family of stories where everyday life and enchantment collide, turning the homely into the uncanny. The tale begins in a crofting kitchen, where an old wife, weary of hunger, bakes a bannock, an oatcake, small and round, yet full of life.

Grierson's version, adapted from oral and printed sources, preserves the humour and vernacular texture of the old folk tradition while shaping it for early twentieth-century readers. The wee bannock becomes more than a trick of magic; it is a symbol of stubborn independence and wit, the spirit of something small refusing to yield to a world of giants.

"Some tell about their sweethearts,

How they tirled them to the winnock,

But I'll tell you a bonnie tale

About a good oatmeal bannock."

There was once an old man and his wife, who lived in a dear little cottage by the side of a burn. They were a very canty and contented couple, for they had enough to live on, and enough to do. Indeed, they considered themselves quite rich, for, besides their cottage and their garden, they possessed two sleek cows, five hens and a cock, an old cat, and two kittens.

The old man spent his time looking after the cows, and the hens, and the garden; while the old woman kept herself busy spinning.

One day, just after breakfast, the old woman thought that she would like an oatmeal bannock for her supper that evening, so she took down her baking board, and put on her girdle, and baked a couple of fine cakes, and when they were ready she put them down before the fire to harden.

While they were toasting, her husband came in from the byre, and sat down to take a rest in his great arm-chair. Presently his eyes fell on the bannocks, and, as they looked very good, he broke one through the middle and began to eat it.

When the other bannock saw this it determined that it should not have the same fate, so it ran across the kitchen and out of the door as fast as it could. And when the old woman saw it disappearing, she ran after it as fast as her legs would carry her, holding her spindle in one hand and her distaff in the other.

But she was old, and the bannock was young, and it ran faster than she did, and escaped over the hill behind the house. It ran, and it ran, and it ran, until it came to a large newly thatched cottage, and, as the door was open, it took refuge inside, and ran right across the floor to a blazing fire, which was burning in the first room that it came to.

Now, it chanced that this house belonged to a tailor, and he and his two apprentices were sitting cross-legged on the top of a big table by the window, sewing away with all their might, while the tailor's wife was sitting beside the fire carding lint.

When the wee bannock came trundling across the floor, all three tailors got such a fright that they jumped down from the table and hid behind the Master Tailor's wife.

"Hoot," she said, "what a set of cowards you be! 'Tis but a nice wee bannock. Get hold of it and divide it between you, and I'll fetch you all a drink of milk."

So she jumped up with her lint and her lint cards, and the tailor jumped up with his great shears, and one apprentice grasped the line measure, while another took up the saucer full of pins, and they all tried to catch the wee bannock. But it dodged them round and round the fire, and it got safely out of the door and ran down the road, with one of the apprentices after it, who tried to snip it in two with his shears.

It ran too quickly for him, however, and he stopped and went back to the house, while the wee bannock ran on until it came to a tiny cottage by the roadside. It trundled in at the door, and there was a weaver sitting at his loom, with his wife beside him, winding a clue of yarn.

"What's that, Tibby?" said the weaver, with a start as the little cake flew past him.

"Oh!" cried she in delight, jumping to her feet, "tis a wee bannock. I wonder where it came from?"

"Dinna bother your head about that, Tibby," he said, "but grip it, my woman, grip it."

But it was not so easy to get hold of the wee bannock. It was in vain that the Goodwife threw her clue at it, and that the Goodman tried to chase it into a corner and knock it down with his shuttle. It dodged, and turned, and twisted, like a thing bewitched, till it flew out at the door again, and vanished down the hill, "for all the world," as the old woman said, "like a new tarred sheep, or a daft cow."

In the next house that it came to it found the Goodwife in the kitchen, kirning. She had just filled her kirn, and there was still some cream standing in the bottom of her cream jar.

"Come away, little bannock," she cried when she saw it. "You have come in just the nick of time, for I am beginning to feel hungry, and I'll have cakes and cream for my dinner."

But the wee bannock hopped round to the other side of the kirn, and the Goodwife after it. And she was in such a hurry that she nearly upset the kirn, and by the time that she had put it right again, the wee bannock was out at the door and half-way down the brae to the mill.

The miller was sifting meal in the trough, but he straightened himself up when he saw the little cake. "It's a sign of plenty when bannocks are running about with no one to look after them," he said, "but I like bannocks and cheese, so just come in, and I will give you a night's lodging."

But the little bannock had no wish to be eaten up by the miller, so it turned and ran out of the mill, and the miller was so busy that he did not trouble himself to run after it.

After this it ran on, and on, and on, till it came to the smithy, and it popped in there to see what it could see. The smith was busy at the anvil making horse-shoe nails, but he looked up as the wee bannock entered.

"If there be one thing I am fond of, it is a glass of ale and a well-toasted cake," he cried. "So come in by here, and welcome to ye."

But as soon as the little bannock heard of the ale, it turned and ran out of the smithy as fast as it could, and the disappointed smith picked up his hammer and ran after it. And when he saw that he could not catch it, he flung his heavy hammer at it, in the hope of knocking it down, but, luckily for the little cake, he missed his aim.

After this the bannock came to a farmhouse, with a great stack of peats standing at the back of it. In it went, and ran to the fireside. In this house the master had all the lint spread out on the floor, and was cloving it with an iron rod, while the mistress was heckling what he had already cloven.

"Oh, Janet," cried the Goodman in surprise, "here comes in a little bannock. It looks rare and good to eat. I'll have one half of it."

"And I'll have the other half," cried the Goodwife. "Hit it over the back with your cloving-stick, Sandy, and knock it down. Quick, or it will be out at the door again."

But the bannock played "joke-about," and dodged behind a chair. "Hoot!" cried Janet contemptuously, for she thought that her husband might easily have hit it, and she threw her heckle at it.

But the heckle missed it, just as her husband's cloving-rod had done, for it played "joke-about" again, and flew out of the house.

This time it ran up a burnside till it came to a little cottage standing among the heather. Here the Goodwife was making porridge for the supper in a pot over the fire, and her husband was sitting in a corner plaiting ropes of straw with which to tie up the cow.

"Oh, Jock! come here, come here," cried the Goodwife. "You are aye crying for a little bannock for your supper; come here, histie, quick, and help me to catch it."

"Ay, ay," assented Jock, jumping to his feet and hurrying across the little room. "But where is it? I cannot see it."

"There, man, there," cried his wife, "under that chair. Run you to that side; I will keep to this."

So Jock ran into the dark corner behind the chair, but, in his hurry, he tripped and fell, and the wee bannock jumped over him and flew laughing out at the door.

Through the whins and up the hillside it ran, and over the top of the hill, to a shepherd's cottage on the other side. The inmates were just sitting down to their porridge, and the Goodwife was scraping the pan.

"Save us and help us," she exclaimed, stopping with the spoon halfway to her mouth. "There's a wee bannock come in to warm itself at our fireside."

"Sneck the door," cried the husband, "and we'll try to catch it. It would come in handy after the porridge."

But the bannock did not wait until the door was sneckit. It turned and ran as fast as it could, and the shepherd and his wife and all the bairns ran after it, with their spoons in their hands, in hopes of catching it.

And when the shepherd saw that it could run faster than they could, he threw his bonnet at it, and almost struck it, but it escaped all these dangers, and soon it came to another house, where the folk were just going to bed.

The Goodman was half undressed, and the Goodwife was raking the cinders carefully out of the fire.

"What's that?" he said, "for the bowl of brose that I had at supper-time wasna' very big."

"Catch it, then," answered his wife, "and I'll have a bit, too. Quick! quick! Throw your coat over it or it will be away."

So the Goodman threw his coat right on the top of the little bannock, and almost managed to smother it, but it struggled bravely, and got out, breathless and hot, from under it. Then it ran out into the grey light again, for night was beginning to fall, and the Goodman ran out after it, without his coat. He chased it and chased it through the stockyard and across a field, and in amongst a fine patch of whins. Then he lost it, and, as he was feeling cold without his coat, he went home.

As for the poor little bannock, it thought that it would creep under a whin bush and lie there till morning, but it was so dark that it never saw that there was a fox's hole there. So it fell down the fox's hole, and the fox was very glad to see it, for he had had no food for two days.

"Oh, welcome, welcome," he cried, and he snapped it through the middle with his teeth, and that was the end of the poor wee bannock.

And if a moral be wanted for this tale, here it is: That people should never be too uplifted or too cast down over anything, for all the good folk in the story thought that they were going to get the bannock, and, lo and behold! the fox got it after all.

The Weird of the Three Arrows

The Weird of the Three Arrows is drawn from Folk-Lore and Legends: Scotland (W. W. Gibbings, 1889), an anonymous Victorian anthology that gathered older oral traditions into print for a general readership. The word weird here carries its older meaning of fate or destiny, and the story follows a Highland chieftain who seeks to outwit a prophecy foretelling ruin to his house.

As preserved in Folk-Lore and Legends: Scotland, this story is part moral reflection, part heroic lament. Its anonymous adapter gives it a sombre, almost bardic tone, emphasising pride, prophecy, and the futility of resisting the old powers that govern life and death.

Sir James Douglas, the companion of Robert The Bruce, and well known by his appellation of the "Black Douglas," was once, during the hottest period of the exterminating war carried on by him and his colleague Randolph, against the English, stationed at Linthaughlee, near Jedburgh. He was resting, himself and his men after the toils of many days' fighting-marches through Teviotdale, and, according to his custom, had walked round the tents, previous to retiring to the unquiet rest of a soldier's bed.

He stood for a few minutes at the entrance to his tent contemplating the scene before him, rendered more interesting by a clear moon, whose silver beams fell, in the silence of a night without a breath of wind, calmly on the slumbers of mortals destined to mix in the mêlée of dreadful war, perhaps on the morrow. As he stood gazing, irresolute whether to retire to rest or indulge longer in a train of thought not very suitable to a warrior who delighted in the spirit-stirring scenes of his profession, his eye was attracted by the figure of an old woman, who approached him with a trembling step, leaning on a staff, and holding in her left hand three English cloth-shaft arrows.

"You are he who is called the good Sir James?" said the old woman.

"I am, good woman," replied Sir James. "Why have you wandered from the sutler's camp?"

"I dinna belong to the camp o' the hoblers," answered the woman. "I have been living in Linthaughlee since the day when King Alexander passed the door o' my cottage with his bonny French bride, who was terrified away from Jedburgh by the death's-head whilk that appeared to her on the day o' her marriage." The old woman looked down at three arrow heads that she held in her hand. "What I have suffered since that day lies between me and heaven."

"Some of your sons have been killed in the wars, I presume?" said Sir James.

"You have guessed a part o' my woes," replied the woman. "That arrow" (holding out one of the three) "carries on its point the blood o' my first born; that is stained with the stream that poured from the heart o' my second, and that is red with the gore in which my youngest weltered, as he gave up the life that made me childless. They were all shot by English hands, in different armies, in different battles. I am an honest woman, and wish to return to the English what belongs to the English, but that in the same fashion in which they were sent. The Black Douglas has the strongest arm and the surest eye in old Scotland, and who can execute my commission better than he?"

"I do not use the bow, good woman," replied Sir James. "I love the grasp of the dagger or the battle-axe. You must apply to some other individual to return your arrows."

"I canna take them home again," said the woman, laying them down at the feet of Sir James. "You'll see me again on St. James' Eve". The old woman departed as she said these words.

Sir James took up the arrows, and placed them in an empty quiver that lay amongst his baggage. He retired to rest, but not to sleep. The figure of the old woman and her strange request occupied his thoughts, and produced trains of meditation which ended in nothing but restlessness and disquietude.

Getting up at daybreak, he met a messenger at the entrance of his tent, who informed him that Sir Thomas de Richmont, with a force of ten thousand men, had crossed the Borders, and would pass through a narrow defile, which he mentioned, where he could be attacked with great advantage. Sir James gave instant orders to march to the spot, and, with that genius for scheming, for which he was so remarkable, commanded his men to twist together the young birch-trees on either side of the passage to prevent the escape of the enemy. This finished, he concealed his archers in a hollow way, near the gorge of the pass.

The enemy came on, and when their ranks were embarrassed by the narrowness of the road, and it was impossible for the cavalry to act with effect, Sir James rushed upon them at the head of his horsemen, and the archers, suddenly discovering themselves, poured in a flight of arrows on the confused soldiers, and put the whole army to flight. In the heat of the onset, Douglas killed Sir Thomas de Richmont with his dagger.

Not long after this, Edmund de Cailon, a knight of Gascony, and Governor of Berwick, who had been heard to vaunt that he had sought the famous Black Knight, but could not find him, was returning to England, loaded with plunder, the fruit of an inroad on Teviotdale. Sir James thought it a pity that a Gascon's vaunt should be heard unpunished in Scotland, and made long forced marches to satisfy the desire of the foreign knight, by giving him a sight of the dark countenance he had made a subject of reproach. He soon succeeded in gratifying both himself and the Gascon. Coming up in his terrible manner, he called to Cailon to stop, and, before he proceeded into England, receive the respects of the Black Knight he had come to find, but hitherto had not met. The Gascon's vaunt was now changed, but shame supplied the place of courage, and he ordered his men to receive Douglas's attack. Sir James assiduously sought his enemy. He succeeded, and a single combat ensued, of a most desperate character. But whoever escaped the arm of Douglas when fairly opposed to him in single conflict? Cailon was killed; he had met the Black Knight .

"So much," cried Sir James, "for the vaunt of a Gascon!"

Similar in every respect to the fate of Cailon, was that of Sir Ralph Neville. He, too, on hearing the great fame of Douglas's prowess, from some of Gallon's fugitive soldiers, openly boasted that he would fight with the Scottish Knight, if he would come and show his banner before Berwick. Sir James heard the boast and rejoiced in it. He marched to that town, and caused his men to ravage the country in front of the battlements, and burn the villages. Neville left Berwick with a strong body of men, and, stationing himself on a high ground, waited till the rest of the Scots should disperse to plunder, but Douglas called in his detachment and attacked the knight. After a desperate conflict, in which many were slain, Douglas, as was his custom, succeeded in bringing the leader to a personal encounter, and the skill of the Scottish knight was again successful. Neville was slain, and his men utterly discomfited.

Having retired one night to his tent to take some rest after so much pain and toil, Sir James Douglas was surprised by the reappearance of the old woman whom he had seen at Linthaughlee.

"This is the feast o' St. James," she said, as she approached him. "I said I would see you again this night, and I'm as good as my word. Have you returned the arrows I left with you to the English who sent them to the hearts o' my sons?"

"No," replied Sir James. "I told you I did not fight with the bow. Wherefore do you importune me thus?"

"Give me back the arrows then," said the woman.

Sir James went to bring the quiver in which he had placed them. On taking them out, he was surprised to find that they were all broken through the middle.

"How has this happened?" he said. "I put these arrows in this quiver entire, and now they are broken."

"The weird is fulfilled!" cried the old woman, laughing eldritchly, and clapping her hands. "That broken shaft came from a soldier o' Richmont's; that from one o' Cailon's, and that from one o' Neville's. They are all dead, and I am revenged!"

The old woman then departed, scattering, as she went, the broken fragments of the arrows on the floor of the tent.

The Well o' the World's End

The Well o' the World's End, as retold by Elizabeth Wilson Grierson in The Scottish Fairy Book (1910), is one of those old wonder tales in which hardship gives rise to grace. It tells of a young girl, mistreated by her cruel stepmother, who is sent on an impossible errand to fetch water from the fabled well at the world's edge

Grierson's adaptation draws upon older versions recorded in Lowland oral tradition and in Joseph Jacobs's English Fairy Tales (1890), yet hers carries the distinct texture of the Scottish tongue and countryside. The imagery of the well itself, clear, unreachable, and restorative, belongs to a much older mythic pattern linking water with purity, trial, and rebirth.

There was once an old widow woman, who lived in a little cottage with her only daughter, who was such a bonnie lassie that everyone liked to look at her.

One day the old woman took a notion into her head to bake a girdleful of cakes. So she took down her bakeboard, and went to the girnel and fetched a basinful of meal, but when she went to seek a jug of water to mix the meal with, she found that there was none in the house.

So she called to her daughter, who was in the garden, and when the girl came she held out the empty jug to her, saying, "Run, like a good lassie, to the Well o' the World's End and bring me a jug of water, for I have long found that water from the Well o' the World's End makes the best cakes."

So the lassie took the jug and set out on her errand.

Now, as its name shows, it is a long road to that well, and many a weary mile had the poor maid to go before she reached it. But she arrived there , and what was her disappointment to find it dry.

She was so tired and so vexed that she sat down beside it and began to cry, for she did not know where to get any more water, and she felt that she could not go back to her mother with an empty jug.

While she was crying, a nice yellow Paddock, with very bright eyes, came jump-jump-jumping over the stones of the well, and squatted down at her feet, looking up into her face.

"And why are you greeting, my bonnie maid?" he asked. "Is there aught that I can do to help you?"

"I am greeting because the well is empty," she answered, "and I cannot get any water to carry home to my mother."

"Listen," said the Paddock softly. "I can get you water in plenty, if so be you will promise to be my wife."

Now the lassie had but one thought in her head, and that was to get the water for her mother's oat-cakes, and she never for a moment thought that the Paddock was in earnest, so she promised gladly enough to be his wife, if he would get her a jug of water.

No sooner had the words passed her lips than the beastie jumped down the mouth of the well, and in another moment it was full to the brim with water.

The lassie filled her jug and carried it home, without troubling any more about the matter. But late that night, just as her mother and she were going to bed, something came with a faint "thud, thud," against the cottage door, and then they heard a tiny little wee voice singing:

"Oh, open the door, my hinnie, my heart,

Oh, open the door, my ain true love;

Remember the promise that you and I made

Down in the meadow, where we two met."

"Wheesht," said the old woman, raising her head. "What noise is that at the door?"

"Oh," said her daughter, who was feeling rather frightened, "it's only a yellow Paddock."

"Poor bit beastie," said the kind-hearted old mother. "Open the door and let him in. It's cold work sitting on the doorstep."

So the lassie, very unwillingly opened the door, and the Paddock came jump-jump-jumping across the kitchen, and sat down at the fireside. And while he sat there he began to sing this song:

"Oh, give me my supper, my hinnie, my heart,

Oh, give me my supper, my ain true love;

Remember the promise that you and I made

Down in the meadow, where we two met."

"Give the poor beast his supper," said the old woman. "He's an uncommon Paddock that can sing like that."

"Tut," replied her daughter crossly, for she was growing more and more frightened as she saw the creature's bright black eyes fixed on her face. "I'm not going to be so silly as to feed a wet, sticky Paddock."

"Don't be ill-natured and cruel," he said her mother. "Who knows how far the little beastie has travelled? And I warrant that it would like a saucerful of milk."

Now, the lassie could have told her that the Paddock had travelled from the Well o' the World's End, but she held her tongue, and went ben to the milk-house, and brought back a saucerful of milk, which she set down before the strange little visitor.

"Now chap off my head, my hinnie, my heart,

Now chap off my head, my ain true love,

Remember the promise that you and I made

Down in the meadow, where we two met."

"Hout, havers, pay no heed, the creature's daft," exclaimed the old woman, running forward to stop her daughter, who was raising the axe to chop off the Paddock's head. But she was too late; down came the axe, off went the head, and lo, and behold! on the spot where the little creature had sat, stood the handsomest young Prince that had ever been seen.

He wore such a noble air, and was so richly dressed, that the astonished girl and her mother would have fallen on their knees before him had he not prevented them by a movement of his hand.

"Tis I that should kneel to you, Sweetheart," he said, turning to the blushing girl, "for you have delivered me from a fearful spell, which was cast over me in my infancy by a wicked Fairy, who at the same time slew my father. For long years I have lived in that well, the Well o' the World's End, waiting for a maiden to appear, who should take pity on me, even in my loathsome disguise, and promise to be my wife, and who would also have the kindness to let me into her house, and the courage, at my bidding, to cut off my head.

"Now I can return and claim my father's Kingdom, and you, most gracious maiden, will go with me, and be my bride, for you well deserve the honour."

And this was how the lassie who went to fetch water from the Well o' the World's End became a Princess.

The Witch of Fife

The Witch of Fife, as retold by Elizabeth Wilson Grierson in The Scottish Fairy Book (1910), draws on one of Scotland's oldest and most evocative folk motifs: the nocturnal flight of witches.

Grierson's version draws from earlier oral and literary tellings, including those found in Robert Kirk's Secret Commonwealth (1691) and local Fife witch lore. Her adaptation softens the cruelty often found in older witch stories, focusing instead on mischief, domestic tension, and wonder.

In the kingdom of Fife, in the days of long ago, there lived an old man and his wife. The old man was a douce, quiet body, but the old woman was lightsome and flighty, and some of the neighbours were apt to look at her askance, and whisper to each other that they sorely feared that she was a Witch.

And her husband was afraid of it, too, for she had a curious habit of disappearing in the gloaming and staying out all night, and when she returned in the morning she looked quite white and tired, as if she had been travelling far, or working hard.

He used to try and watch her carefully, in order to find out where she went, or what she did, but he never managed to do so, for she always slipped out of the door when he was not looking, and before he could reach it to follow her, she had vanished utterly.

At last, one day, when he could stand the uncertainty no longer, he asked her to tell him straight out whether she were a Witch or no.

And his blood ran cold when, without the slightest hesitation, she answered that she was, and if he would promise not to let anyone know, the next time that she went on one of her midnight expeditions she would tell him all about it.

The Goodman promised, for it seemed to him just as well that he should know all about his wife's cantrips. He had not long to wait before he heard of them. For the very next week the moon was new, which is, as everybody knows, the time of all others when Witches like to stir abroad, and on the first night of the new moon his wife vanished. Nor did she return till daybreak next morning.

And when he asked her where she had been, she told him, in great glee, how she and four like-minded companions had met at the old Kirk on the moor and had mounted branches of the green bay tree and stalks of hemlock, which had instantly changed into horses, and how they had ridden, swift as the wind, over the country, hunting the foxes, and the weasels, and the owls, and how they had swam the Forth and come to the top of Bell Lomond. And how there they had dismounted from their horses, and drunk beer that had been brewed in no earthly brewery, out of horn cups that had been fashioned by no mortal hands.

And how, after that, a wee, wee man had jumped up from under a great mossy stone, with a tiny set of bagpipes under his arm, and how he had piped such wonderful music, that, at the sound of it, the very trouts jumped out of the Loch below, and the stoats crept out of their holes, and the corby crows and the herons came and sat on the trees in the darkness, to listen. And how all the Witches danced until they were so weary that, when the time came for them to mount their steeds again, if they would be home before cock-crow, they could scarce sit on them for fatigue.

The Goodman listened to this long story in silence, shaking his head meanwhile, and, when it was finished, all that he answered was, "And what the better are you for all your dancing? Ye'd have been a deal more comfortable at home."

At the next new moon the old wife went off again for the night, and when she returned in the morning she told her husband how, on this occasion, she and her friends had taken cockle-shells for boats, and had sailed away over the stormy sea till they reached Norway. And there they had mounted invisible horses of wind, and had ridden and ridden, over mountains and glens, and glaciers, till they reached the land of the Lapps lying under its mantle of snow.

And here all the Elves, and Fairies, and Mermaids of the North were holding festival with Warlocks, and Brownies, and Pixies, and even the Phantom Hunters themselves, who are never looked upon by mortal eyes. And the Witches from Fife held festival with them, and danced, and feasted, and sang with them, and what was of more consequence, they learned from them certain wonderful words, which, when they uttered them, would bear them through the air, and would undo all bolts and bars, and so gain them admittance to any place so ever where they wanted to be. And after that they had come home again, delighted with the knowledge which they had acquired.

"What took you to siccan a land as that?" asked the old man, with a contemptuous grunt. "You would hae been a sight warmer in your bed."

But when his wife returned from her next adventure, he showed a little more interest in her doings.

For she told him how she and her friends had met in the cottage of one of their number, and how, having heard that the Lord Bishop of Carlisle had some very rare wine in his cellar, they had placed their feet on the crook from which the pot hung, and had pronounced the magic words which they had learned from the Elves of Lapland. And, lo and behold! they flew up the chimney like whiffs of smoke, and sailed through the air like little wreathes of cloud, and in less time than it takes to tell they landed at the Bishop's Palace at Carlisle.

And the bolts and the bars flew loose before them, and they went down to his cellar and sampled his wine, and were back in Fife, fine, sober, old women by cock-crow.

When he heard this, the old man started from his chair in right earnest, for he loved good wine above all things, and it was but seldom that it came his way.

"By my troth, but you are a wife to be proud of!" he cried. "Tell me the words, Woman! and I will even go and sample his Lordship's wine for myself."

But the Goodwife shook her head. "Na, na! I cannot do that," she said, "for if I did, an' you told it over again, 'twould turn the whole world upside down. For everybody would be leaving their own lawful work, and flying about the world after other folk's business and other folk's dainties. So just bide content, Goodman. You get on fine with the knowledge you already possess."

And although the old man tried to persuade her with all the soft words he could think of, she would not tell him her secret.

But he was a sly old man, and the thought of the Bishop's wine gave him no rest. So night after night he went and hid in the old woman's cottage, in the hope that his wife and her friends would meet there, and although for a long time it was all in vain, his trouble was rewarded. For one evening the whole five old women assembled, and in low tones and with chuckles of laughter they recounted all that had befallen them in Lapland. Then, running to the fireplace, they, one after another, climbed on a chair and put their feet on the sooty crook. Then they repeated the magic words, and, hey, presto! they were up the lum and away before the old man could draw his breath.

"I can do that, too," he said to himself, and he crawled out of his hiding-place and ran to the fire. He put his foot on the crook and repeated the words, and up the chimney he went, and flew through the air after his wife and her companions, as if he had been a Warlock born.

And, as Witches are not in the habit of looking over their shoulders, they never noticed that he was following them, until they reached the Bishop's Palace and went down into his cellar, then, when they found that he was among them, they were not too well pleased.

However, there was no help for it, and they settled down to enjoy themselves. They tapped this cask of wine, and they tapped that, drinking a little of each, but not too much, for they were cautious old women, and they knew that if they wanted to get home before cock-crow it behoved them to keep their heads clear.

But the old man was not so wise, for he sipped, and he sipped, until he became quite drowsy, and lay down on the floor and fell fast asleep.

And his wife, seeing this, thought that she would teach him a lesson not to be so curious in the future. So, when she and her four friends thought that it was time to be gone, she departed without waking him.

He slept peacefully for some hours, until two of the Bishop's servants, coming down to the cellar to draw wine for their master's table, almost fell over him in the darkness. Greatly astonished at his presence there, for the cellar door was fast locked, they dragged him up to the light and shook him, and cuffed him, and asked him how he came to be there.

And the poor old man was so confused at being awakened in this rough way, and his head seemed to whirl round so fast, that all he could stammer out was, "that he came from Fife, and that he had travelled on the midnight wind."

As soon as they heard that, the men servants cried out that he was a Warlock, and they dragged him before the Bishop, and, as Bishops in those days had a holy horror of Warlocks and Witches, he ordered him to be burned alive.

When the sentence was pronounced, you may be very sure that the poor old man wished with all his heart that he had stayed quietly at home in bed, and never hankered after the Bishop's wine.

But it was too late to wish that now, for the servants dragged him out into the courtyard, and put a chain around his waist, and fastened it to a great iron stake, and they piled faggots of wood round his feet and set them alight.

As the first tiny little tongue of flame crept up, the poor old man thought that his last hour had come. But when he thought that, he forgot completely that his wife was a Witch.

For, just as the little tongue of flame began to singe his breeches, there was a swish and a flutter in the air, and a great Grey Bird, with outstretched wings, appeared in the sky, and swooped down suddenly, and perched for a moment on the old man's shoulder.

And in this Grey Bird's mouth was a little red pirnie, which, to everyone's amazement, it popped on to the prisoner's head. Then it gave one fierce croak, and flew away again, but to the old man's ears that croak was the sweetest music that he had ever heard.

For to him it was the croak of no earthly bird, but the voice of his wife whispering words of magic to him. And when he heard them he jumped for joy, for he knew that they were words of deliverance, and he shouted them aloud, and his chains fell off, and he mounted in the air - up and up - while the onlookers watched him in awestruck silence.

He flew right away to the Kingdom of Fife, without as much as saying good-bye to them, and when he found himself once more safely at home, you may be very sure that he never tried to find out his wife's secrets again, but left her alone to her own devices.

Thomas the Rhymer

Thomas the Rhymer, as retold by Elizabeth Wilson Grierson in The Scottish Fairy Book (1910), draws on one of Scotland's most enduring legends, blending folklore, prophecy, and the uneasy traffic between the mortal and the faerie worlds. Based on the medieval figure Thomas of Erceldoune, also known as Thomas Learmonth, a 13th-century laird and reputed seer, the tale begins when Thomas encounters the Queen of Elfland beneath the Eildon Tree near Melrose.

Grierson's adaptation draws heavily from the Border ballads collected in The Minstrelsy of the Scottish Border (edited by Sir Walter Scott, 1802–03) while softening the archaic language and emphasising the moral undertones familiar to her early twentieth-century readership. Her Thomas the Rhymer captures both the enchantment and the melancholy of a man caught between worlds, gifted with truth but robbed of ordinary life.

Of all the young gallants in Scotland in the thirteenth century, there was none more gracious and debonair than Thomas Learmont, Laird of the Castle of Ercildoune, in Berwickshire.

He loved books, poetry, and music, which were uncommon tastes in those days, and, above all, he loved to study nature, and to watch the habits of the beasts and birds that made their abode in the fields and woods round about his home.

Now it chanced that, one sunny May morning, Thomas left his Tower of Ercildoune, and went wandering into the woods that lay about the Huntly Burn, a little stream that came rushing down from the slopes of the Eildon Hills. It was a lovely morning - fresh, and bright, and warm, and everything was so beautiful that it looked like Paradise might look.

The tender leaves were bursting out of their sheaths, and covering all the trees with a fresh soft mantle of green, and amongst the carpet of moss under the young man's feet, yellow primroses and starry anemones were turning up their faces to the morning sky.

The little birds were singing like to burst their throats, and hundreds of insects were flying backwards and forwards in the sunshine; while down by the burnside the bright-eyed water-rats were poking their noses out of their holes, as if they knew that summer had come, and wanted to have a share in all that was going on.

Thomas felt so happy with the gladness of it all, that he threw himself down at the root of a tree, to watch the living things around him. As he was lying there, he heard the trampling of a horse's hooves, as it forced its way through the bushes, and, looking up, he saw the most beautiful lady that he had ever seen coming riding towards him on a grey palfrey.

She wore a hunting dress of glistening silk, the colour of the fresh spring grass, and from her shoulders hung a velvet mantle, which matched the riding-skirt exactly. Her yellow hair, like rippling gold, hung loosely around her shoulders, and on her head sparkled a diadem of precious stones, which flashed like fire in the sunlight.

Her saddle was of pure ivory, and her saddle-cloth of blood-red satin, while her saddle girths were of corded silk and her stirrups of cut crystal. Her horse's reins were of beaten gold, all hung with little silver bells, so that, as she rode along, she made a sound like fairy music.

Apparently she was bent on the chase, for she carried a hunting-horn and a sheaf of arrows, and she led seven greyhounds along in a leash, while as many scenting hounds ran loose at her horse's side.

As she rode down the glen, she lilted a bit of an old Scotch song, and she carried herself with such a queenly air, and her dress was so magnificent, that Thomas was like to kneel by the side of the path and worship her, for he thought that it must be the Blessed Virgin herself.

But when the rider came to where he was, and understood his thoughts, she shook her head sadly. "I am not that Blessed Lady, as you think," she said. "Men call me Queen, but it is of a far other country, for I am the Queen of Fairy-land, and not the Queen of Heaven."

And certainly it seemed as if what she said were true; for, from that moment, it was as if a spell were cast over Thomas, making him forget prudence, and caution, and common-sense itself.

For he knew that it was dangerous for mortals to meddle with Fairies, yet he was so entranced with the Lady's beauty that he begged her to give him a kiss. This was just what she wanted, for she knew that if she once kissed him she had him in her power.

And, to the young man's horror, as soon as their lips had met, an awful change came over her. For her beautiful mantle and riding-skirt of silk seemed to fade away, leaving her clad in a long grey garment, which was just the colour of ashes. Her beauty seemed to fade away also, and she grew old and wan, and, worst of all, half of her abundant yellow hair went grey before his very eyes. She saw the poor man's astonishment and terror, and she burst into a mocking laugh.

"I am not so fair to look on now as I was at first," she said, "but that matters little, for you have sold yourself, Thomas, to be my servant for seven long years. For whoso kisses the Fairy Queen must even go with her to Fairy-land, and serve her there till that time is past."

When he heard these words poor Thomas fell on his knees and begged for mercy. But mercy he could not obtain. The Elfin Queen only laughed in his face, and brought her dapple-grey palfrey close up to where he was standing.

"No, no," she said, in answer to his entreaties. "You did ask the kiss, and now you must pay the price. So dally no longer, but mount behind me, for it is full time that I was gone."

So Thomas, with many a sigh and groan of terror, mounted behind her, and as soon as he had done so, she shook her bridle rein, and the grey steed galloped off.

On and on they went, going swifter than the wind; till they left the land of the living behind, and came to the edge of a great desert, which stretched before them, dry, and bare, and desolate, to the edge of the far horizon.

At least, so it seemed to the weary eyes of Thomas of Ercildoune, and he wondered if he and his strange companion had to cross this desert, and, if so, if there were any chance of reaching the other side of it alive.

But the Fairy Queen suddenly tightened her rein, and the grey palfrey stopped short in its wild career. "Now must you descend to earth, Thomas," said the Lady, glancing over her shoulder at her unhappy captive, "and lout down, and lay your head on my knee, and I will show you hidden things, which cannot be seen by mortal eyes."

So Thomas dismounted, and louted down, and rested his head on the Fairy Queen's knee, and lo, as he looked once more over the desert, everything seemed changed. For he saw three roads leading across it now, which he had not noticed before, and each of these three roads was different.

One of them was broad, and level, and even, and it ran straight on across the sand, so that no one who was travelling by it could possibly lose his way. And the second road was as different from the first as it well could be. It was narrow, and winding, and long, and there was a thorn hedge on one side of it, and a briar hedge on the other, and those hedges grew so high, and their branches were so wild and tangled, that those who were travelling along that road would have some difficulty in persevering on their journey at all.

And the third road was unlike any of the others. It was a bonnie, bonnie road, winding up a hillside among brackens, and heather, and golden-yellow whins, and it looked as if it would be pleasant travelling, to pass that way.

"Now," said the Fairy Queen, "as' you will, I shall tell you where these three roads lead to. The first road, as you see, is broad, and even, and easy, and there be many that choose it to travel on. But though it be a good road, it leads to a bad end, and the folk that choose it repent their choice for ever.

"And as for the narrow road, all hampered and hindered by the thorns and the briars, there be few that be troubled to ask where that leads to. But did they ask, perchance more of them might be stirred up to set out along it. For that is the Road of Righteousness, and, although it be hard and irksome, yet it ends in a glorious City, which is called the City of the Great King.

"And the third road - the bonnie road - that runs up the brae among the ferns, and leads no mortal kens where, but I ken where it leads, Thomas - for it leads unto fair Elf-land, and that road take we.

"And mark 'ee, Thomas, if ever you hope to see your own Tower of Ercildoune again, take care of your tongue when we reach our journey's end, and speak no single word to anyone save me - for the mortal who opens his lips rashly in Fairy-land must bide there forever."

Then she bade him mount her palfrey again, and they rode on. The ferny road was not so bonnie all the way as it had been at first, however. For they had not ridden along it very far before it led them into a narrow ravine, which seemed to go right down under the earth, where there was no ray of light to guide them, and where the air was dank and heavy. There was a sound of rushing water everywhere, and the grey palfrey plunged right into it, and it crept up, cold and chill, first over Thomas's feet, and then over his knees.

His courage had been slowly ebbing ever since he had been parted from the daylight, but now he gave himself up for lost, for it seemed to him certain that his strange companion and he would never come safe to their journey's end.

He fell forward in a kind of swoon, and, if it had not been that he had tight hold of the Fairy's ash-grey gown, I warrant he had fallen from his seat, and had been drowned.

But all things, be they good or bad, pass in time, and the darkness began to lighten, and the light grew stronger, until they were back in broad sunshine.

Then Thomas took courage, and looked up, and lo, they were riding through a beautiful orchard, where apples and pears, dates and figs and wine-berries grew in great abundance. And his tongue was so parched and dry, and he felt so faint, that he longed for some of the fruit to restore him.

He stretched out his hand to pluck some of it, but his companion turned in her saddle and forbade him. "There is nothing safe for you to eat here," she said, "save an apple, which I will give you presently. If you touch aught else you are bound to remain in Fairyland for ever."

So poor Thomas had to restrain himself as best he could, and they rode slowly on, until they came to a tiny tree all covered with red apples. The Fairy Queen bent down and plucked one, and handed it to her companion.

"This I can give you," she said, "and I do it gladly, for these apples are the Apples of Truth, and whoso eats them gains this reward, that his lips will never more be able to frame a lie."

Thomas took the apple, and ate it, and for evermore the Grace of Truth rested on his lips, and that is why, in after years, men called him "True Thomas."

They had only a little way to go after this, before they came in sight of a magnificent Castle standing on a hillside.

"Yonder is my abode," said the Queen, pointing to it proudly. "There dwells my Lord and all the Nobles of his court, and, as my Lord has an uncertain temper and shows no liking for any strange gallant whom he sees in my company, I pray you, both for your sake and mine, to utter no word to anyone who speaks to you, and, if anyone should ask me who and what you are, I will tell them that you are dumb. So will you pass unnoticed in the crowd."

With these words the Lady raised her hunting-horn, and blew a loud and piercing blast, and, as she did so, a marvellous change came over her again, for her ugly ash-covered gown dropped off her, and the grey in her hair vanished, and she appeared once more in her green riding-skirt and mantle, and her face grew young and fair.

And a wonderful change passed over Thomas also; for, as he chanced to glance downwards, he found that his rough country clothes had been transformed into a suit of fine brown cloth, and that on his feet he wore satin shoon.

Immediately the sound of the horn rang out, the doors of the Castle flew open, and the King hurried out to meet the Queen, accompanied by such a number of Knights and Ladies, Minstrels and Page-boys, that Thomas, who had slid from his palfrey, had no difficulty in obeying her wishes and passing into the Castle unobserved.

Everyone seemed very glad to see the Queen back again, and they crowded into the Great Hall in her train, and she spoke to them all graciously, and allowed them to kiss her hand. Then she passed, with her husband, to a dais at the far end of the huge apartment, where two thrones stood, on which the Royal pair seated themselves to watch the revels which now began.

Poor Thomas, meanwhile, stood far away at the other end of the Hall, feeling very lonely, yet fascinated by the extraordinary scene on which he was gazing.

For, although all the fine Ladies, and Courtiers, and Knights were dancing in one part of the Hall, there were huntsmen coming and going in another part, carrying in great antlered deer, which apparently they had killed in the chase, and throwing them down in heaps on the floor. And there were rows of cooks standing beside the dead animals, cutting them up into joints, and bearing away the joints to be cooked.

Altogether it was such a strange, fantastic scene that Thomas took no heed of how the time flew, but stood and gazed, and gazed, never speaking a word to anybody. This went on for three long days, then the Queen rose from her throne, and, stepping from the dais, crossed the Hall to where he was standing.

"Tis time to mount and ride, Thomas," she said, "if you would ever see the fair Castle of Ercildoune again."

Thomas looked at her in amazement. "You spoke of seven long years, Lady," he exclaimed, "and I have been here but three days."

The Queen smiled. "Time passes quickly in Fairy-land, my friend," she replied. "You think that you have been here but three days. 'Tis seven years since we two met. And now it is time for you to go. I would fain have had your presence with me longer, but I dare not, for your own sake. For every seventh year an Evil Spirit comes from the Regions of Darkness, and carries back with him one of our followers, whomsoever he chances to choose. And, as you are a goodly fellow, I fear that he might choose you.

"So, as I would be loath to let harm befall you, I will take you back to your own country this very night."

Once more the grey palfrey was brought, and Thomas and the Queen mounted it, and, as they had come, so they returned to the Eildon Tree near the Huntly Burn.

Then the Queen bade Thomas farewell, and, as a parting gift, he asked her to give him something that would let people know that he had really been to Fairy-land.

"I have already given you the Gift of Truth," she replied. "I will now give you the Gifts of Prophecy and Poesie; so that you will be able to foretell the future, and also to write wondrous verses. And, besides these unseen gifts, here is something that mortals can see with their own eyes - a Harp that was fashioned in Fairyland. Fare you well, my friend. Someday, perchance, I will return for you again."

With these words the Lady vanished, and Thomas was left alone, feeling a little sorry, if the truth must be told, at parting with such a radiant Being and coming back to the ordinary haunts of men.

After this he lived for many a long year in his Castle of Ercildoune, and the fame of his poetry and of his prophecies spread all over the country, so that people named him True Thomas, and Thomas the Rhymer.

I cannot write down for you all the prophecies which Thomas uttered, and which most surely came to pass, but I will tell you one or two.

He foretold the Battle of Bannockburn in these words:

"The Burn of Breid

Shall rin fou reid,"

which came to pass on that terrible day when the waters of the little Bannockburn were reddened by the blood of the defeated English.

He also foretold the Union of the Crowns of England and Scotland, under a Prince who was the son of a French Queen, and who yet bore the blood of Bruce in his veins.

"A French Queen shall bearre the Sonne;

Shall rule all Britainne to the sea,

As neere as is the ninth degree,"

which thing came true in 1603, when King James, son of Mary, Queen of Scots, became Monarch of both countries.

*

Fourteen long years went by, and people were beginning to forget that Thomas the Rhymer had ever been in Fairy-land, but a day came when Scotland was at war with England, and the Scottish army was resting by the banks of the Tweed, not far from the Tower of Ercildoune.

And the Master of the Tower determined to make a feast, and invite all the Nobles and Barons who were leading the army to sup with him.

That feast was long remembered, for the Laird of Ercildoune took care that everything was as magnificent as it could possibly be, and when the meal was ended he rose in his place, and, taking his Elfin Harp, he sang song after song of the days of long ago to his assembled guests.

The guests listened breathlessly, for they felt that they would never hear such wonderful music again. And so it fell out.

For that very night, after all the Nobles had gone back to their tents, a soldier on guard saw, in the moonlight, a snow-white Hart and Hind moving slowly down the road that ran past the camp.

There was something so unusual about the animals that he called to his officer to come and look at them. And the officer called to his brother officers, and soon there was quite a crowd softly following the dumb creatures, who paced solemnly on, as if they were keeping time to music unheard by mortal ears.

"There is something uncanny about this," said one soldier . "Let us send for Thomas of Ercildoune, perchance he may be able to tell us if it be an omen or no."

"Ay, send for Thomas of Ercildoune," cried everyone at once. So a little page was sent in haste to the old Tower to rouse the Rhymer from his slumbers.

When he heard the boy's message, the Seer's face grew grave and rapt. "Tis a summons," he said softly, "a summons from the Queen of Fairy-land. I have waited long for it, and it has come ."

And when he went out, instead of joining the little company of waiting men, he walked straight up to the snow-white Hart and Hind. As soon as he reached them they paused for a moment as if to greet him. Then all three moved slowly down a steep bank that sloped to the little river Leader, and disappeared in its foaming waters, for the stream was in full flood.

And, although a careful search was made, no trace of Thomas of Ercildoune was found, and to this day the country folk believe that the Hart and the Hind were messengers from the Elfin Queen, and that he went back to Fairy-land with them.

Whippety-Stourie

Whippety-Stourie, as retold by Elizabeth Wilson Grierson in The Scottish Fairy Book (1910), is a sharp and spirited tale of cunning, pride, and supernatural mischief, drawn from older Borders and Lowlands folk traditions. The story centres on a proud widow whose only son is stolen away by a malicious fairy creature known as Whippety-Stourie.

Grierson's adaptation reflects her talent for balancing the eerie with the homely, preserving the tale's Scots cadence and dry humour while making it accessible. The story stands as an example of how Scottish folklore celebrates wit over brute strength, and how the boundaries between the mortal world and the Otherworld remain thin and treacherous.

I am going to tell you a story about a poor young widow woman, who lived in a house called Kittlerumpit, though whereabouts in Scotland the house of Kittlerumpit stood nobody knows.

Some folk think that it stood in the neighbourhood of the Debatable Land, which, as all the world knows, was on the Borders, where the old Border Reivers were constantly coming and going; the Scotch stealing from the English, and the English from the Scotch. Be that as it may, the widowed Mistress of Kittlerumpit was sorely to be pitied.

For she had lost her husband, and no one quite knew what had become of him. He had gone to a fair one day, and had never come back again, and although everybody believed that he was dead, no one knew how he died.

Some people said that he had been persuaded to enlist, and had been killed in the wars; others, that he had been taken away to serve as a sailor by the press-gang, and had been drowned at sea.

At any rate, his poor young wife was sorely to be pitied, for she was left with a little baby-boy to bring up, and, as times were bad, she had not much to live on.

But she loved her baby dearly, and worked all day amongst her cows, and pigs, and hens, in order to earn enough money to buy food and clothes for both her and him.

Now, on the morning of which I am speaking, she rose very early and went out to feed her pigs, for rent-day was coming on, and she intended to take one of them, a great, big, fat creature, to the market that very day, as she thought that the price that it would fetch would go a long way towards paying her rent.

And because she thought so, her heart was light, and she hummed a little song to herself as she crossed the yard with her bucket on one arm and her baby-boy on the other.

But the song was quickly changed into a cry of despair when she reached the pig-sty, for there lay her cherished pig on its back, with its legs in the air and its eyes shut, just as if it were going to breathe its last breath.

"What shall I do? What shall I do?" cried the poor woman, sitting down on a big stone and clasping her boy to her breast, heedless of the fact that she had dropped her bucket, and that the pig's-meat was running out, and that the hens were eating it.

"First I lost my husband, and now I am going to lose my finest pig. The pig that I hoped would fetch a deal of money."

Now I must explain to you that the house of Kittlerumpit stood on a hillside, with a great fir wood behind it, and the ground sloping down steeply in front.

And as the poor young thing, after having a good cry to herself, was drying her eyes, she chanced to look down the hill, and who should she see coming up it but an Old Woman, who looked like a lady born.

She was dressed all in green, with a white apron, and she wore a black velvet hood on her head, and a steeple-crowned beaver hat over that, something like those, as I have heard tell, that the women wear in Wales. She walked very slowly, leaning on a long staff, and she gave a bit hirple now and then, as if she were lame.

As she drew near, the young widow felt it was becoming to rise and curtsey to the Gentlewoman, for such she saw her to be.

"Madam," she said, with a sob in her voice, "I bid you welcome to the house of Kittlerumpit, although you find its Mistress one of the most unfortunate women in the world."

"Hout-tout," answered the old Lady, in such a harsh voice that the young woman started, and grasped her baby tighter in her arms. "You have little need to say that. You have lost your husband, I grant ye, but there were waur losses at Shirra-Muir. And now your pig is like to die - I could, maybe, remedy that. But I must first hear how much you would give me if I cured him."

"Anything that your Ladyship's Madam likes to ask," replied the widow, too much delighted at having the animal's life saved to think that she was making rather a rash promise.

"Very good," said the old Dame, and without wasting any more words she walked straight into the pigsty.

She stood and looked at the dying creature for some minutes, rocking to and fro and muttering to herself in words which the widow could not understand; at least, she could only understand four of them, and they sounded something like this:

"Pitter-patter,

Holy water."

Then she put her hand into her pocket and drew out a tiny bottle with a liquid that looked like oil in it. She took the cork out, and dropped one of her long lady-like fingers into it; then she touched the pig on the snout and on his ears, and on the tip of his curly tail.

No sooner had she done so than up the beast jumped, and, with a grunt of contentment, ran off to its trough to look for its breakfast.

A joyful woman was the Mistress of Kittlerumpit when she saw it do this, for she felt that her rent was safe, and in her relief and gratitude she would have kissed the hem of the strange Lady's green gown, if she would have allowed it, but she would not.

"No, no," she said, and her voice sounded harsher than ever. "Let us have no fine meanderings, but let us stick to our bargain. I have done my part, and mended the pig; now you must do yours, and give me what I like to ask - your son."

Then the poor widow gave a piteous cry, for she knew now what she had not guessed before - that the Green-clad Lady was a Fairy, and a Wicked Fairy too, else had she not asked such a terrible thing.

It was too late now, however, to pray, and beseech, and beg for mercy; the Fairy stood her ground, hard and cruel.

"You promised me what I liked to ask, and I have asked your son, and your son I will have," she replied, "so it is useless making such a din about it. But one thing I may tell you, for I know well that the knowledge will not help you. By the laws of Fairy-land, I cannot take the bairn till the third day after this, and if by that time you have found out my name I cannot take him even then. But you will not be able to find it out, of that I am certain. So I will call back for the boy in three days."

And with that she disappeared round the back of the pigsty, and the poor mother fell down in a dead faint beside the stone.

All that day, and all the next, she did nothing but sit in her kitchen and cry, and hug her baby tighter in her arms, but on the day before that on which the Fairy said that she was coming back, she felt as if she must get a little breath of fresh air, so she went for a walk in the fir wood behind the house.

Now in this fir wood there was an old quarry hole, in the bottom of which was a bonnie spring well, the water of which was always sweet and pure. The young widow was walking near this quarry hole, when, to her astonishment, she heard the whirr of a spinning-wheel and the sound of a voice lilting a song. At first she could not think where the sound came from; then, remembering the quarry, she laid down her child at a tree root, and crept noiselessly through the bushes on her hands and knees to the edge of the hole and peeped over.

She could hardly believe her eyes! For there, far below her, at the bottom of the quarry, beside the spring well, sat the cruel Fairy, dressed in her green frock and tall felt hat, spinning away as fast as she could at a tiny spinning-wheel.

And what should she be singing but:

"Little kens our guid dame at hame,

Whippety-Stourie is my name."

The widow woman almost cried aloud for joy, for now she had learned the Fairy's secret, and her child was safe. But she dare not, in case the wicked old Dame heard her and threw some other spell over her.

So she crept softly back to the place where she had left her child; then, catching him up in her arms, she ran through the wood to her house, laughing, and singing, and tossing him in the air in such a state of delight that, if anyone had met her, they would have been in danger of thinking that she was mad.

Now this young woman had been a merry-hearted maiden, and would have been merry-hearted still, if, since her marriage, she had not had so much trouble that it had made her grow old and sober-minded before her time, and she began to think what fun it would be to tease the Fairy for a few minutes before she let her know that she had found out her name.

So next day, at the appointed time, she went out with her boy in her arms, and seated herself on the big stone where she had sat before, and when she saw the old Dame coming up the hill, she crumpled up her nice clean cap, and screwed up her face, and pretended to be in great distress and to be crying bitterly.

The Fairy took no notice of this, however, but came close up to her, and said, in her harsh, merciless voice, "Good wife of Kittlerumpit, you ken the reason of my coming; give me the bairn."

Then the young mother pretended to be in sorer distress than ever, and fell on her knees before the wicked old woman and begged for mercy.

"Oh, sweet Madam Mistress," she cried, "spare me my bairn, and take, an' you will, the pig instead."

"We have no need of bacon where I come from," answered the Fairy coldly, "so give me the laddie and let me begone - I have no time to waste in this wise."

"Oh, dear Lady mine," pleaded the Goodwife, "if you will not have the pig, will you not spare my poor bairn and take me myself?"

The Fairy stepped back a little, as if in astonishment. "Art you mad, woman," she cried contemptuously, "that you propose such a thing? Who in all the world would care to take a plain-looking, red-eyed, dowdy wife like you with them?"

Now the young Mistress of Kittlerumpit knew that she was no beauty, and the knowledge had never vexed her, but something in the Fairy's tone made her feel so angry that she could contain herself no longer.

"In troth, fair Madam, I might have had the wit to know that the like of me is not fit to tie the shoe-string of the High and Mighty Princess, WHIPPETY-STOURIE!"

If there had been a charge of gunpowder buried in the ground, and if it had suddenly exploded beneath her feet, the Wicked Fairy could not have jumped higher into air.

And when she came down again she simply turned round and ran down the brae, shrieking with rage and disappointment, for all the world, as an old book says, "like an owl chased by witches."

Historical Notes

This section contains some brief biographical notes about the original collectors and their books featured in this collection. These notes have been adapted from those primarily on Wikipedia along with other supporting sources and notes.

Andrew Lang

Andrew Lang (1844–1912) was a Scottish poet, novelist, literary critic, and anthropologist, best known for his prolific literary output and his contributions to the field of folklore studies.

Andrew Lang was born on March 31, 1844, in Selkirk, Scotland, to John Lang, a town clerk, and Jane Plenderleath Sellar Lang. He was the eldest of eight siblings. Lang received his early education at the Selkirk Grammar School before attending the Edinburgh Academy and later the University of St. Andrews, where he studied classics and modern literature.

Lang began his literary career as a journalist and editor, contributing articles, essays, and reviews to various newspapers and magazines. He gained recognition for his literary criticism, demonstrating a keen intellect and a deep understanding of literature, folklore, and mythology.

Lang's interests were diverse, and he wrote extensively on a wide range of subjects, including poetry, fiction, history, anthropology, and psychology. He was a prolific author, producing numerous works across multiple genres throughout his lifetime.

One of Lang's most significant contributions to scholarship was his work in the field of folklore studies. He was deeply fascinated by the oral traditions and folk beliefs of different cultures, and he devoted much of his career to collecting, researching, and analysing folktales, myths, and legends from around the world.

Lang's "Fairy Books" series, which included collections such as "The Blue Fairy Book" (1889), "The Red Fairy Book" (1890), and "The Green Fairy Book" (1892), among others, became immensely popular and influential. These collections featured fairy tales from various cultural traditions, translated and adapted for English-speaking audiences, and helped to preserve and popularize many classic folk stories.

In addition to his contributions to folklore studies, Lang wrote numerous other books on diverse subjects. He authored poetry collections, such as "Ballads and Lyrics of Old France, " (1872) and "Rhymes à la Mode, " (1884), which showcased his talent for verse.

Lang also wrote historical works, biographies, literary histories, and novels, including "The Monk of Fife, " (1895), a historical novel set in the time of Joan of Arc. He was a versatile writer, capable of tackling both fiction and non-fiction with equal skill and enthusiasm.

In 1875, Andrew Lang married Leonora Blanche Alleyne, with whom he had four children. Blanche, as she was commonly known, was a talented author and translator in her own right, and she often collaborated with Lang on his literary projects.

Andrew Lang's legacy as a writer, folklorist, and scholar endures through his extensive body of work, which continues to be studied, admired, and enjoyed by readers around the world. His contributions to folklore studies helped to popularize the study of folk traditions and fairy tales, shaping the way these stories are understood and appreciated to this day. Lang's influence on literature, anthropology, and cultural studies remains significant, and his works remain important sources for scholars and enthusiasts interested in the rich tapestry of human culture and imagination.

Selected Bibliography:

Fairy Books - Lang's "Coloured Fairy Books" are among his most celebrated works, each named after a different colour:

- The Blue Fairy Book (1889)
- The Red Fairy Book (1890)
- The Green Fairy Book (1892
- The Yellow Fairy Book (1894)
- The Pink Fairy Book (1897)
- The Grey Fairy Book (1900)
- The Violet Fairy Book (1901)
- The Crimson Fairy Book (1903
- The Brown Fairy Book (1904)
- The Orange Fairy Book (1906)
- The Olive Fairy Book (1907)
- The Lilac Fairy Book (1910)

Other Notable Works:

- The Blue Poetry Book (1891): A collection of poems suitable for children.
- The True Story Book (1893): A compilation of historical narratives presented in a storytelling format.
- The Red True Story Book (1895): Continuation of historical tales aimed at younger readers.

- The Animal Story Book (1896): Stories centred around animals, blending fact and fiction.
- The Arabian Nights Entertainments (1898): Lang's rendition of the classic Middle Eastern tales.
- The Book of Romance (1902): A collection of romantic tales from various traditions.
- The Red Book of Animal Stories (1899): Further animal-centric tales for children.

Scholarly and Literary Criticism:

- Custom and Myth (1884): Essays exploring the origins of various customs and myths.
- Myth, Ritual and Religion (1887): A two-volume work examining the connections between mythology, rituals, and religious practices.
- Books and Bookmen (1886): Essays on literary topics and book collecting.
- Letters to Dead Authors (1886): Imaginary letters addressed to famous authors of the past.
- Homer and the Epic (1893): A study of Homer's works and their place in epic literature.

Translations:

- The Odyssey of Homer (1879): Prose translation in collaboration with S.H. Butcher.
- The Iliad of Homer (1883): Prose translation with Walter Leaf and Ernest Myers.

Elizabeth W. Grierson

Elizabeth Wilson Grierson (1869–1943) was born at Whitchesters Farm near Hawick in the Scottish Borders, a landscape of rough pasture and low hills. The rhythms of rural life, together with the persistence of storytelling and superstition in small communities, seem to have shaped her imagination from an early age. She belonged to a generation that stood between the oral and the printed word, when local tales were still being told by firesides but were beginning to be gathered, written down, and circulated to wider audiences. Grierson's own writing sits firmly in that movement, attentive to authenticity, yet conscious of style and readership.

Over the course of a long career she produced more than thirty books. Her interests ranged from retellings of Scottish fairy and folk tales to collections of ballads and travel books exploring the character of places such as Edinburgh and Florence. This breadth hints at both curiosity and discipline: a writer who loved the particular textures of place but also wanted to make them legible to outsiders. Her travel writing, though lighter in tone, carries the same observational care that marks her folklore work.

In 1910 she published *The Scottish Fairy Book*, a collection of roughly thirty tales drawn from across the country. Grierson arranged and framed the material with a quiet authority, distinguishing between two principal traditions of Scottish storytelling: the ancient "Celtic" quest narratives of the Highlands and Islands, and the more domestic fairy tales of the Lowlands, populated by goblins, brownies, and the "sith" folk said to haunt moor and glen. Her introductions and linking passages reveal an awareness of both the literary and the anthropological interest in such tales, yet her prose remains lucid and unpretentious. She wrote not for scholars but for readers who still felt the pulse of wonder.

Grierson's retellings are marked by restraint. She keeps the bones of the stories intact, but smooths the transitions, clarifies motives, and restores moral or emotional coherence where the oral versions had become fragmentary. In doing so she performs a kind of translation, not from one language to another, but from an oral imagination into print. That act of mediation gives *The Scottish Fairy Book* its lasting charm. The book feels rooted yet readable, Scottish in idiom but universal in appeal.

Although her name rarely appears in academic folklore studies, her work has endured in print and online for more than a century. The continued presence of *The Scottish Fairy Book* in libraries, reprints and public-domain archives testifies to its quiet influence. Grierson's Borders background, combined with her sympathy for the landscapes and voices of rural Scotland, lent her writing an integrity that readers still recognise. She stands as one of those early twentieth-century figures who carried the spoken lore of a people across the threshold of modernity, preserving its spirit while giving it shape on the page.

Selected Bibliography:

- The Scottish Fairy Book (1910), a collection of Scottish fairy-tales, compiled and retold by Grierson.
- Tales from Scottish Ballads (1906), a collection of Scottish ballads retold in short story form.
- Peeps at Many Lands: Scotland (1907), part of her travel-guide interest; offering views of Scotland.
- Hereford (1911), travel/local interest, describing the city/cathedral region.

- The Book of Celtic Stories (1922), a later work gathering Celtic-type tales.
- Things Seen in Florence (1922), another travel-oriented title.

Joseph Jacobs

Joseph Jacobs was an Australian-born folklorist, literary critic, historian, and social scientist whose work helped shape the modern understanding of English and European folk traditions. Born in Sydney in 1854 to a Jewish family of Prussian descent, Jacobs was educated first in Australia and later in England, where he attended St. John's College, Cambridge. From early on, he showed a keen interest in history, languages, and the stories that bind cultures together.

Though he trained as a scholar of literature and history, Jacobs is best remembered as one of the foremost collectors and editors of English folklore. His work revived and popularised many of the world's best-loved fairy tales, including *Jack and the Beanstalk*, *Goldilocks and the Three Bears*, *The Three Little Pigs*, *Jack the Giant Killer*, and *The History of Tom Thumb*. These tales first appeared in *English Fairy Tales* (1890) and *More English Fairy Tales* (1893), collections that combined careful research with vivid retelling. His editions became definitive for generations of English-speaking readers, shaping how these stories are still told today.

Jacobs's passion for comparative folklore led him beyond England's borders. He compiled and edited collections of Jewish, Celtic, Indian, and European fairy tales, introducing readers to the breadth of the world's oral traditions. His work was distinguished by a desire to preserve the tone, humour, and moral imagination of the original storytellers, rather than smoothing them into Victorian gentility. In this, Jacobs differed from contemporaries like the Brothers Grimm or Andrew Lang, striving instead for authenticity and cultural respect.

Beyond his collections of tales, Jacobs was an active editor and scholar. He produced critical editions of *The Fables of Bidpai* and *The Fables of Aesop*, wrote extensively on the migration and transformation of folklore motifs, and edited several versions of *The Thousand and One Nights*. He was deeply involved with The Folklore Society in England and served as editor of its journal, *Folklore*. His expertise and editorial rigor helped to formalize folklore studies as a serious academic discipline.

Jacobs also made important contributions to Jewish scholarship and cultural history. In 1896, he travelled to the United States to lecture on The Philosophy of Jewish History at Gratz College in Philadelphia and before audiences of the Council of Jewish Women in New York, Philadelphia, and Chicago. Four years later, he moved permanently to America to take up the role of revising editor for the monumental *Jewish Encyclopaedia* (1901–1906), overseeing contributions from more than six hundred writers and scholars. He also worked closely with the Jewish Publication Society and the American Jewish Historical Society, helping to advance Jewish intellectual life in the English-speaking world.

Joseph Jacobs married Georgina Horne, with whom he had two sons and a daughter. He continued writing and editing until his death at his home in Yonkers, New York, on 30 January 1916, aged sixty-two.

During his lifetime, Jacobs was recognized as one of the leading folklorists of his generation, a scholar who bridged cultures and preserved voices from the deep past. His collections remain some of the most beloved in the English language, cherished both for their storytelling charm and their deep respect for the traditions they represent.

Selected Bibliography

- English Fairy Tales (1890)
- Celtic Fairy Tales (1892)
- More English Fairy Tales (1893)
- Indian Fairy Tales (1892)
- The Fables of Aesop (1894)
- Europa's Fairy Book (1916)
- Jewish Fairy Tales and Legends (1919, posthumous)
- The Fables of Bidpai (1895)
- The Thousand and One Nights (editor, various editions)
- The Story of Geographical Discovery: How the World Became Known (1899)
- The Jews of Angevin England: Documents and Records from Latin and Hebrew Sources (1893)
- Studies in Biblical Archaeology (1894)
- An Inquiry into the Sources of the History of the Jews in Spain (1894)

Peter Henry Emerson

Peter Henry Emerson was a British photographer, writer, and theorist whose pioneering ideas helped to establish photography as a legitimate art form. His deeply naturalistic images of rural life in East Anglia, along with his writings on photographic theory, marked him as one of the key figures in the late nineteenth-century debate over photography's artistic purpose and expressive limits.

Emerson was born in 1856 on La Palma Estate, a sugar plantation near Encrucijada, Cuba. His father, Henry Ezekiel Emerson, was an American planter, and his mother, Jane Emerson, was British. Through his father's family, Emerson was distantly related to both Samuel Morse, inventor of the telegraph, and Ralph Waldo Emerson, the American transcendentalist. His early childhood was spent in Cuba, but the outbreak of the American Civil War brought the family temporarily to Wilmington, Delaware. After his father's death, Emerson moved with his mother to England in 1869.

Educated at Cranleigh School, where he excelled both academically and athletically, Emerson later attended King's College London before transferring to Clare College, Cambridge, earning his medical degree in 1885. Though trained as a surgeon, he soon turned away from medicine to pursue his growing passion for photography, writing, and natural history. In 1881 he married Edith Amy Ainsworth, and during their honeymoon he began drafting his first book. The couple eventually had five children.

Emerson's introduction to photography came through his interest in ornithology, which he shared with his friend, the naturalist A. T. Evans. What began as an attempt to document birds and landscapes soon became a lifelong exploration of photography as a form of fine art. By 1885, he had helped to found the Camera Club of London and was elected to the Council of the Photographic Society. That same year, he abandoned his medical career to devote himself fully to artistic photography and writing.

Influenced by the naturalistic principles of contemporary French painting, Emerson argued that photography should represent the world as the eye perceives it, naturally, with selective focus and atmospheric realism, rather than the artificial clarity of studio compositions. His first major work, *Life and Landscape on the Norfolk Broads* (1886), contained forty platinum prints depicting rural life in East Anglia. The images captured the quiet rhythms of the countryside, reed-cutters, fishermen, and farmers, in compositions that celebrated both the dignity of labour and the beauty of the natural world.

Over the next decade, Emerson published a series of photographic volumes, each more refined than the last. He experimented with focus and printing techniques, seeking to balance precision with the soft tonal gradations that he believed better reflected human vision. His publications, including *Pictures of East Anglian Life* (1888), *Wild Life on a Tidal Water* (1890), and *On English Lagoons* (1893), combined photography with his own lyrical essays and observations on landscape and character. His final photographic work, *Marsh Leaves* (1895), is often regarded as his masterpiece, a melancholic meditation on nature, solitude, and impermanence, printed in delicate photogravure by Emerson himself after frustrations with commercial printers.

After *Marsh Leaves*, Emerson withdrew from photography, disillusioned by ongoing disputes with the photographic establishment and the technical constraints of the medium. Nonetheless, he continued to write prolifically. His later works included novels, essays, and studies on subjects as diverse as genealogy, the history of artistic photography, and the game of billiards. In 1924 he began his final major work, a comprehensive history of artistic photography, which he completed shortly before his death in Falmouth, Cornwall, on 12 May 1936.

Emerson's influence on modern photography is profound. His insistence on photography as an art rooted in natural observation anticipated later movements toward realism and expressive authenticity. Though he was often at odds with the photographic establishment of his time, his writings laid the intellectual foundation for pictorialism and, ultimately, for photography's recognition as a fine art. In 1979, he was posthumously inducted into the International Photography Hall of Fame.

Selected Bibliography

Photographic Works

- Life and Landscape on the Norfolk Broads (1886)
- Pictures of East Anglian Life (1888)
- Wild Life on a Tidal Water: The Adventures of a House-Boat and Her Crew (1890)
- On English Lagoons: Being an Account of the Voyage of Two Amateur Wherrymen on the Norfolk and Suffolk Rivers and Broads (1893)
- Marsh Leaves (1895)

Theoretical and Critical Works

- Naturalistic Photography for Students of the Art (1889)
- The Death of Naturalistic Photography (1891)
- Photography: A Pictorial History of the Art from 1839 to 1925 (manuscript completed 1936, posthumously published)

Other Writings

- Birds, Beasts and Fishes of the Norfolk Broads (1895)
- Welsh Rarebit Tales (1899, fiction)
- Sporting Days and Sporting Ways (1902)
- Essays and shorter works on genealogy, meteorology, and billiards

Maud Isabel Ebbutt

Maud Isabel Ebbutt was a British writer and folklorist best known for her 1910 collection *Hero-Myths and Legends of the British Race*, a sweeping retelling of the legendary and heroic tales that shaped the cultural imagination of Britain. Although relatively little is known about her personal life, Ebbutt's writing places her firmly among the early twentieth-century authors who sought to make the mythic past vivid and accessible to general readers, particularly at a time when Britain was rediscovering its Celtic, Anglo-Saxon, and Norse heritage through scholarship, art, and literature.

Born in 1867, likely in England, Ebbutt came of age during a period of intense interest in folklore and national identity. The late Victorian and Edwardian eras saw a flourishing of mythological studies, with writers such as Andrew Lang, Charles Squire, and Joseph Jacobs adapting traditional tales for new audiences. Ebbutt's contribution to this tradition is distinctive for its intellectual depth and for the moral and philosophical reflections that accompany her storytelling.

Her best-known work, *Hero-Myths and Legends of the British Race* (1910), blends literary retelling with historical and cultural commentary. The book draws upon sources ranging from the Beowulf epic and the Arthurian romances to medieval chronicles and Norse sagas, presenting them as expressions of the ideals and values of the peoples who told them. Ebbutt viewed myth not merely as entertainment but as a moral and cultural mirror, reflecting the evolving character of a nation and its people.

In her introduction, she quotes Thomas Carlyle's dictum, "Hero-worship endures forever while man endures," using it as the guiding principle for her study of heroism through the ages. For Ebbutt, each generation's heroes revealed the spirit of their age: the Saxons' admiration for strength, the Normans' reverence for loyalty, and the English yeoman's love for justice embodied in the figure of Robin Hood. Her prose combines scholarly precision with romantic idealism, suggesting that myth endures because it speaks to the timeless human need for moral exemplars and stories that elevate the spirit.

Hero-Myths and Legends of the British Race was published as part of the popular *Myth and Legend in Literature and Art* series by George G. Harrap & Co., which aimed to present the world's mythologies in an accessible form for general readers and students. Ebbutt's volume remains one of the finest examples in the series for its elegant narrative and thoughtful introduction. Her work stood at the crossroads of literature and cultural history, bridging Victorian moral earnestness with Edwardian curiosity and early twentieth-century scholarship.

As she herself wrote, "To every age, and to every nation, there is a peculiar ideal of heroism, and in the popular legends of each age this ideal may be found."

Selected Bibliography

- Hero-Myths and Legends of the British Race (London: George G. Harrap & Co., 1910) – Part of the Myth and Legend in Literature and Art series.
- "Introduction to Hero-Myths and Legends of the British Race," in which Ebbutt discusses heroism, national identity, and moral philosophy (1910).

- Myths and Legends of the Middle Ages (attributed, London: Harrap, c. 1911), possibly a companion or derivative volume within the same series, though attribution remains uncertain.
- Articles and essays on British folklore and mythology (uncollected, early twentieth century; several reprinted in educational anthologies of myth and legend during the 1910s–1920s).

John Francis Campbell

John Francis Campbell of Islay (1821–1885) was one of the foremost collectors of Scottish Gaelic folklore and one of the first to treat oral tradition with the rigour of a natural science. Born in Islay, Argyllshire, into a distinguished Highland family, he was educated at Eton and the University of Edinburgh, later studying law at the University of Bonn. Though trained for the civil service, Campbell's interests were always broader: languages, geology, meteorology, and the intricate relationship between culture and environment. He grew up speaking both Gaelic and English, a dual inheritance that gave him access to worlds few of his contemporaries could navigate.

After early service in the British administration, including a post as private secretary to George Grey, the governor of New Zealand, Campbell returned to Britain with a growing fascination for the disappearing oral traditions of the Highlands. By the mid-nineteenth century, industrial change and the decline of Gaelic-speaking communities had begun to erode the living folk culture of the region. Campbell saw that what survived in memory and speech would soon be lost if not written down. From this conviction came his major work, *Popular Tales of the West Highlands* (four volumes, 1860–62), a monumental collection of Gaelic stories transcribed directly from storytellers, often through his assistant Alexander Carmichael and a network of native speakers who acted as collectors.

The Popular Tales were groundbreaking in method and scope. Campbell insisted on accuracy and fidelity to oral performance, recording stories in Gaelic before translating them into English. He annotated his texts meticulously, comparing them with Norse, Germanic, and Eastern analogues, and so positioned Gaelic narrative within a wider Indo-European tradition. His notes revealed a mind as interested in linguistic and mythological patterns as in the stories themselves. He treated folklore not as quaint relic but as evidence of shared human imagination, governed by recurring structures and motifs. In this respect, Campbell anticipated later developments in comparative mythology and ethnology, even if his contemporaries did not always grasp the breadth of his vision.

Beyond the *Popular Tales*, Campbell's intellectual range was striking. He produced *Leabhar na Féinne* (1872), a compilation of heroic ballads from oral and manuscript sources, and gathered an immense corpus of unprinted material later published as *The Campbell Collections* by the School of Scottish Studies. His curiosity extended far beyond folklore: he made scientific observations on ocean currents and glacial formations, publishing *Frost and Fire* (1865), an ambitious two-volume work linking natural phenomena to the shaping of myth and legend. The book's speculative tone divided readers, yet it showed his determination to understand both nature and narrative as interwoven systems.

Campbell's travels were extensive, he visited Iceland, Norway, and the Mediterranean, studying languages and customs wherever he went. He moved easily between the drawing rooms of London and the croft houses of the Hebrides, his notebooks filled with sketches, phonetic jottings, and reflections on landscape. Despite his privileged background, he regarded Highland storytellers with genuine respect, crediting them as the true authors of their tales. This sense of equality between collector and informant distinguished him from many Victorian folklorists, who often romanticised or patronised their sources.

In later life he suffered from ill health, but he continued to correspond with scholars across Europe, sharing insights and encouraging others to study oral tradition with the same seriousness as written literature. He died in Cannes in 1885, leaving behind a body of work that would become foundational to Celtic studies and folklore scholarship. His collections influenced later figures such as Alfred Nutt and Joseph Jacobs, and through them shaped the modern understanding of how Scottish, Irish, and wider European story traditions connect.

Selected Bibliography:

- Popular Tales of the West Highlands (Edinburgh: Edmonston & Douglas 1860-62), his most-famous folklore collection.
- Leabhar na Féinne: Gaelic Texts. Heroic Gaelic Ballads collected in Scotland chiefly from 1512 to 1871 (Edinburgh: Spottiswoode, 1872), a significant ballad collection.
- Frost and Fire: Natural Engines, Tool-Marks and Chips; with Sketches Taken at Home and Abroad by a Traveller (Edinburgh: Edmonston & Douglas, 1865), showing his interest in natural history and geology alongside folklore.
- A Short American Tramp in the Fall of 1864 (Edmonston & Douglas, 1865), travel-notes from his time in America.
- My Circular Notes: Extracts from journals, letters sent home, geological and other notes, written while travelling westwards round the world, from July 6, 1874, to July 6, 1875 (Macmillan, London, 1876.
- Canntaireachd: Articulate Music (dedicated to the Islay Association) (1880), reflecting his interest in Gaelic music.
- Thermography (1883), on meteorology/recording temperature and sunshine, part of his scientific side.
- The Celtic Dragon Myth (posthumously published Edinburgh: J. G. Grant, 1911), his final major work on mythic/dragon-motifs in Celtic tradition.

- Life in Normandy: Sketches of French Fishing, Farming, Cooking, Natural History, and Politics, Drawn from Nature (Edmonston & Douglas, 1863), edited from his father's work but published under his name.

Robert Kirk

Robert Kirk (1644–1692) was a seventeenth-century Scottish minister, biblical scholar, and folklorist whose name has become inseparable from *The Secret Commonwealth of Elves, Fauns and Fairies,* a seminal text in the study of Scottish folklore and the supernatural. Born in 1644 in the village of Aberfoyle, Perthshire, Kirk was the seventh son of Reverend James Kirk, minister of the parish, and his wife, Margaret Newton. He studied at the University of St Andrews, where he graduated with a Master of Arts degree in 1661, and continued his education at Edinburgh, where he developed a strong grounding in theology and languages. His scholarly aptitude and deep curiosity about the unseen world would later define both his ministry and his enduring legend.

Kirk became minister of Balquhidder in 1664 and later returned to Aberfoyle in 1685, succeeding his father in the parish. During his ministry, he was admired for his piety, intellect, and learning, particularly his facility with Hebrew, in which he produced one of the earliest printed translations of the Psalms directly from the original language (*The Psalms of David in Meeter*, 1684). Yet alongside his clerical duties, Kirk was drawn increasingly to the folklore and beliefs of the Highland people among whom he lived. He collected tales of "the good people," the fair folk or sith, who were believed to inhabit the hills and glens around Loch Katrine and Doon Hill. Kirk's sympathetic and detailed record of these traditions was unique for its time. He treated fairy lore not as superstition to be condemned, but as a cultural and metaphysical system worthy of serious attention.

Around 1691, Kirk completed *The Secret Commonwealth of Elves, Fauns and Fairies*, a remarkable compendium of Highland belief. Written in a lucid, scholarly style, it describes the invisible world of fairies, spirits, and second sight as part of a "Secret Commonwealth" coexisting alongside the human one. The work reflects Kirk's attempt to reconcile folklore with theology and natural philosophy, suggesting that these "subterranean people" were intermediate beings between men and angels, neither wholly spiritual nor corporeal. His tone is speculative yet respectful, recording local testimony with precision and wonder. Kirk's text was not published during his lifetime; the manuscript circulated privately until 1815, when it was printed by Sir Walter Scott, who recognised its importance to Scottish literary and supernatural tradition.

The circumstances of Kirk's death in 1692 deepened his mythic reputation. Local legend holds that he was taken by the fairies of Doon Hill, his spirit imprisoned in the Otherworld as punishment for revealing their secrets. According to the tale, Kirk appeared to his cousin, Graham of Duchray, and instructed him to throw a knife over his apparition during his posthumous appearance at his child's baptism, which would have released him. Graham hesitated, and the opportunity was lost, leaving Kirk forever bound to the fairy realm. His grave stands in the kirkyard of Aberfoyle, but many still refer to Doon Hill as The Fairy Minister's Hill, believing that his soul lingers there.

Kirk's *Secret Commonwealth* has since become a cornerstone of Scottish folklore studies, bridging theology, anthropology, and early psychology. It preserves one of the clearest windows into seventeenth-century Highland belief, offering scholars a firsthand account of how pre-modern Scots understood the interplay between visible and invisible worlds. His work has influenced writers and thinkers from Sir Walter Scott and Andrew Lang to contemporary folklorists and poets who continue to revisit the tension between faith and folklore, reason and mystery.

Selected Bibliography

- Kirk, Robert. The Psalms of David in Meeter: Translated according to the Original Texts. Edinburgh: 1684.
- Kirk, Robert. The Secret Commonwealth of Elves, Fauns and Fairies. Written c.1691. First published by Sir Walter Scott, Edinburgh: 1815.

About the Editor

Clive Gilson was born in 1962 into a household steeped in sport and rhythm. His father was a senior amateur and lower-league professional footballer, while his mother, equally formidable, was an award-winning ballroom dancer. Their spirited household didn't just hum with ambition, it danced to it.

After earning a degree in History from Leeds University, Clive took an unexpected turn into the then-nascent world of information technology in the late 1980s. Yet, the call of story and stage never left him. Alongside a thriving tech career, he freelanced as a journalist and book reviewer, earning one small by-line in the national press, and also spent over a decade performing in village halls and professional theatres across the south of England.

A true inheritor of his family's sporting zeal, Clive later pivoted into live sports broadcasting. In the 1990s, he became a trusted rugby 'stato' for the BBC, ITV, EuroSport, and TVNZ, bringing insight and analysis to major tournaments including the Heineken Cup, Six Nations, World Sevens, and Rugby World Cups.

As a writer, Clive has made his mark across genres. His debut novel, *Songs of Bliss*, was published in 2017, followed by *A Solitude of Stars* in 2019. Since then, he has released three acclaimed short story collections, *The Mechanic's Curse*, *The Insomniac Booth*, and, in 2025, *Melodies in Black Ink*.

He is also an award-winning poet and the author of a biography detailing the life of a former professional footballer, namely his father. Since 2018, Clive has served as Managing Editor of the Firesides Tales Project, a global storytelling initiative that has published over 30 collections of folktales, fairy tales, myths, and legends from around the world.

Today, Clive continues to write fiction rich in folklore, memory, and quiet transformation, combining his deep love of narrative with a lifelong fascination with the human spirit.

For more about his work, visit clivegilson.com, where stories are always waiting to be found.

ORIGINAL FICTION BY CLIVE GILSON

- *Songs of Bliss*
- *Out of the Walled Garden*
- *The Mechanic's Curse*
- *The Insomniac Booth*
- *A Solitude of Stars (Cry Havoc, part 1)*
- *A Symphony Of Sorrows (Cry Havoc, part 2)*
- *Melodies In Black Ink*
- *Acts Of Faith*

AS EDITOR – *FIRESIDE TALES* – Western Europe

- *Tales From the Land of Dragons* – Welsh Folk & Fairy Tales
- *Tales From the Land of The Brave* – Scottish Folk & Fairy Tales
- *Tales From the Land of Saints And Scholars* – Irish Folk & Fairy Tales
- *Tales From the Land of Hope And Glory* – English Folk & Fairy Tales
- *Tales from Gallia* – French Folk & Fairy Tales

AS EDITOR – *FIRESIDE TALES* – Northern Europe

- *Tales From Lands of Snow and Ice* – Scandinavian Folk & Fairy Tales
- *Tales From the Viking Isles* – Icelandic Folk & Fairy Tales
- *Tales From the Forest Lands* – Finnish Folk & Fairy Tales
- *Tales From the Old Norse* – Scandinavian Folk & Fairy Tales
- *Tales from Germania* – German Folk & Fairy Tales

AS EDITOR – *FIRESIDE TALES* – Southern Europe

- *Tales From the Land of Rabbits* – Spanish & Portuguese Folk & Fairy Tales
- *Tales Told by Bulls and Wolves* – Italian Folk & Fairy Tales
- *Tales of Fire and Bronze* – Greek Folk & Fairy Tales

AS EDITOR – *FIRESIDE TALES* – Eastern Europe

- *Tales From The Samodivi* – Balkan Folk & Fairy Tales
- *Tales From the Land of the Strigoi* – Romanian Folk & Fairy Tales

- *Tales Told by the Wind Mother*– Hungarian Folk & Fairy Tales

AS EDITOR – *FIRESIDE TALES* – *North America*

- *Okaraxta* - Tales from The Great Plains
- *Tibik-Kìzis* – Tales from The Great Lakes & Canada
- *Jóhonaa'éí* –Tales from America's Southwest
- *Qugaaĝix̂* - First Nation Tales from Alaska & The Arctic
- *Karahkwa* - First Nation Tales from America's Eastern States
- *Pot-Likker* - Folklore, Fairy Tales, and Settler Stories from America

AS EDITOR – *FIRESIDE TALES* – *Africa*

- *Arokin Tales* – Folklore & Fairy Tales from West Africa
- *Hadithi Tales* – Folklore & Fairy Tales from East Africa
- *Inkathaso Tales* – Folklore & Fairy Tales from Southern Africa
- *Tarubadur Tales* – Folklore & Fairy Tales from North Africa
- *Elephant And Frog* – Folklore from Central Africa

AS EDITOR – *FIRESIDE TALES* – *Middle East*

- *Tales From The Meddahs* – Turkish Folk & Fairy Tales
- *Tales From The Hakawati* – Arabic Folk & Fairy Tales
- *Tales Told By Balebos & Gusan* – Jewish & Armenian Folk & Fairy Tales

AS EDITOR – *FIRESIDE TALES* – *Asia & The Far East*

- *Tales Told By The Kathaakaar* – Folk & Fairy Tales from India
- *Tales Of The Gùshì Yuan* – Chinese Folk & Fairy Tales

AS EDITOR – *FIRESIDE TALES* – *Animal Tales*

- *Dog Tails* – Folk & Fairy Tales featuring our canine chums
- *Cat Tails* – Folk & Fairy Tales featuring our feline friends
- *Horse Tails* – Folk & Fairy Tales featuring our equine friends
- *Pig Tails* – Folk & Fairy Tales featuring our porcine friends

AS EDITOR – *FIRESIDE TALES* – *South & Central America*

- *Tales From The Caribbean* – Folk & Fairy Tales from Caribbean islands
- *Tales From Central America* – Central American Folk & Fairy Tales
- *Tales Told From South America* – South American Folk & Fairy Tales

Reviews

I have edited Clive Gilson's books for over a decade now – he's prolific and can turn his hand to many genres. poetry, short fiction, contemporary novels, folklore, and science fiction – and the common theme is that none of them ever fails to take my breath away. There's something in each story that is either memorably poignant, hauntingly unnerving, or sidesplittingly funny - *Lorna Howarth, The Write Factor*

*Ragged A**** Ruffian* reviewed on Amazon in the United Kingdom on 27 January 2021 - A truly heartwarming, interesting, story with a wonderful narrative. Unquestionably a splendid read

A Solitude of Stars: With deft turns of phrase and an imagination that would make Philip K. Dick jealous, Gilson foresees a dystopian future, the seeds of which are definitely being sown right now. The story is a chilling glimpse of what may come to pass, warmed by a thread of love that raises the narrative beyond despair. I found the stories disturbing and breath-taking in equal measure. The Apparat and Dirigiste tribes are ranging across our solar system seeking peace by waging war, raising the question; is humanity actually capable of peace? A riveting read. - *Rob Swan, The Write Factor*

Songs of Bliss gripped me from the start - I had to read right to the end. Loved the humour. Impressed by the surprising empathy that I felt for rather - on the face of it - unlikeable characters. Look forward to seeing it in print. - *Maighdean-Mhara, commenting on Authonomy*

I just wanted to thank you once more for your help acquiring this beautiful collection. It's found a new home at the top of my library. I've already stumbled onto some wonderful stories in a couple of the collections, and I can't wait to get more. Have a wonderful holiday and a great new year... - *Richer Daniel Laporte, California, December 2021*

Melodies In Black Ink: A collection of darkly captivating short tales, each inspired by the melodies that move us, the lyrics that linger, and the stories hidden between the notes.

Gilson (editor of the international Fireside Stories series) offers a dark, poignant collection of genre-crossing stories, all inspired by songs, that explore the fragile intersections of love, loss, resilience, and the shadows we carry. Ranging from children with superpowers to accounts of blossoming love, abusive relationships, unexpected pregnancies, and the isolating rhythm of a machine-driven society, Gilson's stories capture raw textures of the human experience in a key suggested by their musical inspirations, which include lushly brooding tracks from Kate Bush, This Mortal Coil, Angel Olsen, The Cure, and Youssou N'Dour (the sublime "7 Seconds," a duet with Neneh Cherry.) Gilson has a gift for moment-to-moment storytelling that grips and then lingers, like Gorilla Glue stuck to one's fingertips, resisting even the harshest solvents of reason.

Life goes wrong in unpredictable yet resonant ways throughout these 26 compact tales, and Gilson's vivid portrayals of scenery and emotion make it easy to lose oneself in these narratives, drowning in a wave of feeling that refuses to let go. From the Scottish Highlands to space travel to the blood-soaked earth of Danish-Viking battlefields—told from the perspective of Ulfhednar and his sacred wolf, Ulric— these stories span wide imaginative terrain. Despite some big ideas and SF elements, characterization is compelling. "The Jakey and the Nae Chancer" introduces Elliot and Fiona, who have perfected the art of detachment, the latter of whom "was almost certain that her heart was too delicate to risk breaking again." One of the most heart-wrenching stories, "Be Well," is inspired by a devastating loss. It's a piece that does more than tug at the heart, it reaches in and seizes hold with unrelenting intensity.

Adding a unique dimension, each story concludes with a toast to the song and artist that inspired it, an invitation to experience these briskly potent stories on another sensory level, with a soundtrack tying words to melody, emotion to rhythm. Melodies in Black Ink is not light reading—but it is deeply moving, with haunting emotional rewards.

Searing, surprising stories of urgent feeling, inspired by beloved songs.

Tales From The Land Of The Brave

The US Review of Books
Professional Reviews for the People

Melodies in Black Ink: This work is not just another set of tales linked together by a myriad of characters who sometimes appear in more than one narrative. In fact, this is much more than just another short story collection. It is also a reflective, musical journey. Accompanying each story is an explanation of the song that inspired the writing. Most impressive is the wide expanse of musical genres, artists, and songs included in this book. From Wardruna to Metric to Blue Oyster Cult to Dot Allison, the book's audience will experience a musical journey unlike any other. The incorporation of the notes discussing each inspirational song provides an informative background. It also provides historical context, along with the author's personal anecdotes, about each song.

What makes this book even more realistic is its honest, vulnerable, and sometimes gritty portrayal of the characters and their existences. One story in which all of these themes and characteristics culminate is "Going Underground." It is a story in which even the main character's name, Daniel Grimes, reflects the character's harsh, gritty environment and existence, as well as the difficult decisions Daniel must make. Daniel embodies rebellion against the status quo after having lived a life in which he originally "played by the rules. All it got him were ration credits and a little coin, enough to rent a bedsit and eat slop." "Going Underground" is a daring story with a dystopian tone. Deepening that dystopian tone is the fact that the author cleverly disguises the story's time period, and the tale can be read as either occurring in the past, the present, or the very near future.

Music lovers will appreciate this book because of the role music plays in each and every story. The stories, too, are a testament to not only the power of music but also of the necessity of interdisciplinary studies and the humanities. The stories are a novel type of ekphrastic writing in that, rather than responding to visual art, the stories are responses to music. The fluid, poetic writing in each story mirrors the magic and lyricism inherent in the songs the author utilizes. These stories are powerful, emotional, and moving. Most of all, they are beautifully and unquestionably human.

RECOMMENDED by the US Review

Book review by Nicole Yurcaba